*This is a remarkable story written with insight and verve. It is a story which had me at the edge of my seat wondering how it would resolve itself! The author quintessentially understands the world views of his various characters and how these play themselves out when faced with a potentially cataclysmic event—called the breach—which is set to destroy the world. Cusiter is ruthlessly honest in the dialog allowing his characters to be genuinely consistent and yet be challenged by the other. There is no easy solution offered but the reader is drawn inexorably to the value of self-sacrifice as a model for living.*

*This is Mac Cusiter's first published book and an oeuvre well worth the read. It has originality and is daring in its desire to explore the role of a person's faith commitment under stress. I look forward with great anticipation to many more books flowing from this author's imagination and pen.*

**Dr. Frank Stootman – Computational Astrophysicist**

# THE BREACH

## BY

## Mac Cusiter

# The Breach

Designed by Acorn Book Services

Publication Managed by Acorn Book Services
www.acornbookservices.com
acornbookservices@gmail.com
304-995-1295

Cover Design: Mac Cusiter
Cover design from image © Alexeyrich | Dreamstime.com

Gurumbi Publishing
ISBN: 978-0-9941582-0-8

Printed in the United States of America

*To my beloved wife Val
for her perennial encouragement and love*

*The author would also like to thank Lauren Carr
for her invaluable help and advice
and the Acorn Book Service editorial team
for their meticulous care
and attention to detail*

# THE BREACH

# PROLOGUE

**Statement by the Executive Committee of the Division of Particles and Fields of the American Physical Society on the Safety of Collisions at the Large Hadron Collider:**

Soon, the Large Hadron Collider at the European Council for Nuclear Research will collide protons at energies never before achieved in the laboratory. This has raised concerns in some quarters that new particles created in these collisions might cause serious damage to our planet. In fact, this question has been addressed in the report entitled "Review of the Safety of LHC Collisions" issued recently by the LHC Safety Assessment Group. This report explains why there is nothing to fear about particles created at the LHC. Actually, collisions just like those the LHC will make have been produced by cosmic rays bombarding the earth throughout its existence. It would take about 100,000 LHC experiments to match the number of cosmic ray events that have already occurred. We can rest assured that our planet will not be affected by the four experiments about to be conducted in Geneva.

According to the well-established properties of gravity described by Einstein's relativity, it is impossible for microscopic black holes to be produced at the LHC. There are, however, some speculative theories that predict the production of such particles at the LHC. All these theories predict that these particles will disintegrate immediately. Black holes, therefore, will have no time to start accreting matter and to cause macroscopic effects.

**Scientists Not So Sure "Doomsday Machine" Won't Destroy World**

Still worried that the Large Hadron Collider will create a black hole that will destroy the Earth when it's finally switched on this summer?

Well, you may have a point.

Three physicists have reexamined the math surrounding the creation of microscopic black holes in the Switzerland-based LHC, the world's largest particle collider, and determined that they won't simply evaporate in a millisecond as had previously been predicted. Rather, Roberto Casadio of the University of Bologna in Italy and Sergio Fabi and Benjamin Harms of the University of Alabama say mini black holes could exist for much longer—perhaps for even more than a second, a relative eternity in particle colliders, where most objects decay much faster. Under such long-term conditions, it will become a race between how fast a black hole can decay—and how fast it can gobble up matter to grow bigger and prevent itself from decaying.

Paul Wagenseil
Published January 28, 2009
FoxNews.com

# CHAPTER 1

Daniel Van Dekker stared silently through the windscreen into the darkness of the Rue du Lac, each passing streetlight illuminating the dark lines of worry deeply etched into his face—worry bordering on panic. He needed a miracle, and deep within his heart he despaired of finding one. He was a man with the weight of the world on his shoulders. Although the Atlantian idiom was universally applied metaphorically, in Dekker's case, it was true.

Dekker glanced at Hans, the man driving him back to his hotel. His face wore a similar expression, although he had done his part, and done it well. Dekker gave an almost inaudible moan; now it was up to him, and he had absolutely no idea how to proceed. Even the comfort of Jasmin's arms would not suffice to lessen the burden he bore, yet he would welcome it, and soon, for the hotel was coming into view further down the street.

He needed a miracle.

"Viel Glück, mein Freund. Ich werde beten Sie einen Weg finden," Hans said. (Good luck, my friend. I pray you find a way.)

"Me too."

The driver grunted and brought the car into the kerb next to the hotel. On the darkened pavement, a man stood watching him. The car pulled away into the night. The man walked towards Dekker, as if he were about to shake his hand. Perhaps this was the miracle he'd been waiting for he thought. The man came closer in the silence.

"Professor Van Dekker?" The stranger approached him, his right hand extended.

"Yes."

The hand whipped into his coat. Now it was holding a silenced Glock pistol.

Dekker stared uncomprehendingly at his assassin. No, this could not be happening—not to him, the singularly and tragically most important person in the human race. If anyone was to survive, it had to be him, or the entire world would follow him into the grave. *There's some ghastly mistake.* He needed to explain.

While his tongue attempted to form the words, the gun flashed in the darkness.

Dekker threw himself sideways in a hopeless attempt to dodge the bullet, which must already have entered his body. So great was his anguish that he didn't feel it.

The gun flashed again, his assassin's face calm, unperturbed—the unfeeling face of a man whose business was death.

The pavement was rushing up towards Dekker's face far too fast. His head crashed against it; his sight went out. His last despairing thought, before the blackness took his mind away altogether, was that God had chosen to abandon the human race after all, and Dekker didn't blame Him.

# CHAPTER 2

In 1965, many years before this deplorable incident, Australia acquired its first experimental nuclear reactor. Located near the foothills to the southwest of Camden in New South Wales, it was originally designed to research technology associated with the nuclear power industry. When the debate in Australia moved against the use of nuclear power in 1980 and forced the facility to change direction, it morphed itself into a centre for nuclear research to the benefit of science and industry. From this turbulent childhood, it grew into an institution of world-recognized excellence. Thirty years in all it had stood, and it took just twenty days to destroy.

Those who so enthusiastically orchestrated its demise were concerned about the political fallout from the reactor continuing to operate. Had they known that the fallout of their decision on the twenty-fifth of August would ultimately make a nuclear explosion on the Camden plains a happy day, the Australian Institute for Nuclear Research (AINR) would have still been making its excellent contribution to science.

But they didn't.

Joseph McTierney had a round, podgy face and a stomach to match. He was a numbers man. It was his first term as Federal Minister for the Environment, his second year in parliament, his third attempt at marriage.

His fourth child lay cradled in his arms. His current spouse had named her Patience, presumably to remind him of the virtue missing in his life. Sycophantic to his political masters, McTierney was the epitome of the village bully. These traits, coupled with a personality entirely dedicated to his own preservation, had served him well.

The new father looked down at the small and unwelcome product of his loins and reflected on the lesson she taught him by simply being there: large problems come from very small beginnings.

McTierney was also the federal member for Camden, and he didn't even live there. He had hated the land from the moment he had fallen into a trough of sheep dip on his father's property at Bringelly. Now, it appeared that the spirit of the land he had cursed in his heart had ironically risen up against him. That an experimental nuclear power station should be planted in his electoral backyard was purely the cynicism of the gods.

For some reason known only to fate, a particularly cold night in September of 1994 had devastated the sheep stations on the Southern Highlands. The properties around Camden had been hit worst of all. Sudden cold spells were not at all uncommon, but what made this occasion unique was a comment made in the local paper by an outspoken station owner at Cawdor not far from the AINR establishment.

"It's that bloody nuclear reactor what's affected the sheep so's they can't tolerate the cold. Weakened them, that's what it's done, with all that radiation and heat and nuclear stuff."

The paper suggested a meeting "for concerned parties" in the Camden town hall, and out of that had risen the Property Owners against Radiation and Nuclear Energy. "PORNE" was born. They organized, rallied, spoke to talkback radio, and demanded that the government compensate them for their stock losses, fund their medical bills, give them health check-ups, radiation-proof their homes, and widen roads so they could make their escape when the reactor blew. Images of the residents of Camden roasting in a nuclear blast fire were drawn by a local artist and sold in every store in town. At least he wasn't complaining.

Mrs. Margaret Warburton, whose property was within sight of the nuclear power station, was one of the first interviewed on television. She made a statement to a nation of shocked viewers, "Since they started that wretched thing, I've seen flashes of light in my head—you know, like the astronauts did. Day and night. It's all that radiation. Fair drives me demented, not to think of what it's doing to my brain."

She would have told them she saw aliens riding her cows, too, but they didn't ask.

As federal member for Camden, McTierney knew he should have taken action sooner, before the whole thing had gained momentum. Mindful of elections coming up during the next year, he finally organized teams of experts to inspect the properties—as a caring representative of his constituents.

Lots of men and women in white coats arrived with black boxes that measured everything, found nothing.

PORNE read the reports and pronounced them "a tissue of politically motivated lies." The levels of alpha, beta, and gamma radiation had been measured, but what about neutrons? What about neutrinos? Antimatter? Electromagnetic fields from the generators? What about the thermal output affecting native wildlife? Chemical isotopes poisoning the ground water that hadn't surfaced yet? Unfettered by the knowledge of anything that happened inside a nuclear power station, their creative imaginations ran freely. There was money to be had here, and they could smell its approach.

The Australian public, who didn't know very much about nuclear power stations either, but who knew a great deal about political cover-ups, was happy to follow in the path of outraged indignation.

On the fifth of August in 1995, the Minister for Environment, motivated even more by his deep concern for the political fallout in his electorate, tabled questions in Federal Parliament:

"Since Australia no longer looks to nuclear power to solve its energy needs, why is a nuclear reactor still operating in my electorate, endangering human life? Is it true that the Australian Institute for Nuclear Research can, and occasionally does, connect their fifty-megawatt experimental nuclear reactor to the national power grid? Does this not make a mockery of Australian nuclear free energy commitments?"

Dr. Daniel Van Dekker, Research Director for the AINR, was a man who tolerated fools badly. Those who didn't know him well described him as taciturn, direct, truthful, bad tempered, and naïve.

His friends would have described him as a caring man at heart, even if he didn't have a sense of humour, and they would have said that his naiveté sprung from his one-eyed passion for physics. He expected all the rest of the world to love it as much as he did and couldn't understand anyone thinking that research into the mother of all sciences was not fundamentally important to the understanding of everything else.

Both those who knew him well and those who didn't would have agreed that he was brilliant in his field, even though he often arrived at his office wearing different coloured socks.

Dr. Daniel Van Dekker had followed the rise of public opinion against the Institute firstly with indifference, then disbelief, and finally alarm.

A physicist of international renown, he had come to the institute some four years ago and was responsible for the growth in its academic reputation. Industry had benefited from the structure testing services that they offered. Australia's standing in the community of atomic particle physics research was commanding a new international respect. Indeed, many nuclear power stations across the world were running more safely because of the techniques he had pioneered.

He stared around the panelled room at the blank, unfriendly faces of the parliamentary select committee he had been summoned to appear before and wondered what he had done to warrant such an interruption to his valuable research. Still, it would be over and done with in a couple of hours.

The inquiry dragged on for four humiliating days.

Ironically, it was the last five minutes of questions from the head of the select committee that heralded the death of the institute.

"Once again, Dr. Dekker, did any amount of radioactive material from any part of the plant ever enter the environment outside the containment building, in liquid, solid, or gaseous form?"

"No".

"Has there ever been an incident in which you lost full or partial control of the reactor in either start-up or shutdown, or in which a control alarm was triggered during either of these processes or at any other time?"

"No."

"Has there ever been an incident in which any employee, visitor, contracted technician, or other member of staff suffered from any exposure to radioactive material or radiation?"

"No."

"Do you believe that security at the nuclear power station is sufficient to guard against the threat of international terrorism?"

"Yes, of course it is. What use would anything we have be to a terrorist? We do research. We do not manufacture weapons grade plutonium."

"Are you confident that your security is such that nobody could enter, damage, or take control of the facility in such a way as to cause any damage to the general public or the environment?"

"I am completely confident that our security measures are adequate. I would remind the committee that the amount of nuclear material in the reactor's core could fit inside the average filing cabinet. You are dealing with a research reactor that is very small compared to those facilities designed to deliver thousands of megawatts of electrical power. There is no nuclear fuel on site which could be used to make atomic bombs. We are, in essence, an educational and research institute, not a nuclear power station. We only connect to the grid when we wish to offload excess energy in some useful form rather than raise the temperature of the local environment."

"Thank you for your cooperation, Dr. Dekker."

This excerpt made the evening news.

The following day the morning crew from a Sydney television station who were notorious for their pranks entered the institute posing as teachers for the year twelve high school group visiting that morning. Unchallenged, they walked into the containment building and deposited a small box with an electronic timer on top in one of the corridors. The box contained some pieces of wood wrapped up in red paper with "C4 high explosive" labels on them. On the wall near the box, they placed a small camera that relayed pictures back to the television station. It was a full twenty minutes before the box was noticed, and the pictures of all hell breaking loose were enjoyed by a wide television audience. The next day, the show made the international news service and went worldwide by the end of the week.

One week later, on the twenty-fifth of August, the prime minister signed off on a document that shut down AINR and gave instructions to decommission the reactor. Joe McTierney lay back in his leather office chair with a glass of eighteen-year old single malt and an equally expensive cigar and, for the first time, smiled at his secretary. Fate, he felt sure, had seen fit to restore his fortunes.

Fate, however, had done no such thing.

In contrast, Daniel Van Dekker was frenetically busy. Within hours of the fateful decision he had filed an injunction in the high court, given an erudite interview on Channel 2 news about the loss to Australia of such an internationally high profile establishment, and contacted some very influential friends.

AINR was not going into obscurity without a fight. It was one thing to decommission a nuclear reactor, even a small research one, and quite another to carry out the task. It was not just a matter of walking in with the demolition crew and flattening the place. You don't just empty the core coolant as if you were draining a swimming pool.

The process was likely to take years, even if it were driven hard. Dekker knew just what to do to make it particularly difficult, horribly expensive, and politically unpleasant. There were nasty radioactive materials to handle, nasty radioactive waste materials to store and transport, and nasty radioactive pieces of plant to decontaminate. Specialist technicians in this area were very rare and very expensive.

The locals might not like a nuclear reactor in their backyard, but they were going to like the process of removing it even less. By the time he was finished, they would wish they had never begun—indeed, they would.

Dekker scheduled a meeting with his staff. Plan A, he thought, and if that failed, he would orchestrate a Plan B.

On the eighth of September, 1995, Joe McTierney felt the first rumblings of trouble. In his office sat Paul Nicols, Scientific Advisor to the Prime Minister's department; Alan Tebbut, Deputy Prime Minister;

and Dr. Robert Cann, Professor of Physics from the University of Sydney. The topic of conversation was the ministerial directive to decommission the AINR reactor.

Cann was speaking. "The process is straightforward but specialized. It has to be done carefully. It would be essential to involve Dr. Van Dekker in a consultative role."

"Dekker has been making quite a fuss about the closure," Paul Nicols said. "He is undercutting our scientific credibility on the world stage. The PM doesn't like it. I would rather proceed without him"

"That's all very well in theory, Paul, but, without Dekker's help, the process will take longer and cost much more. There also could be safety issues if we dismantle structures we are unfamiliar with. There have been a lot of mods done on the reactor since it was first built."

"Listen, the pair of you," interrupted McTierney. "It's just a stalling game. Down at AINR, it's business as usual. Nothing's being done, and Dekker thinks it will go into the 'too hard' basket if he stalls long enough. He needs to be booted out of the place straight away—he and all his staff. Then we might get a bit of cooperation out of them."

"And who's going to do the booting? You, Joe?" replied Tebutt, raising his eyebrows slightly. "I'd like to wager you haven't a chance of getting Dekker to walk out of his beloved AINR."

"These academic types are such pushovers. No trouble—"

"I think that course of action would be most unadvised." Cann turned to Paul Nicols. "It would be much better to secure the assistance of Dr. Van Dekker. Why not promise to fund some other form of atomic physics research—set up some other institute in place of AINR? He is a reasonable man and no fool. He would respond well to that sort of approach."

"He'll respond well to my sort of approach, let me tell you," said McTierney. "And it's much cheaper. The bastard will do as he's told, or I'll find a way to send him back to Holland with his clever little tail between his clever little legs."

McTierney left the building with his plan of action confirmed. No one had ever resisted his bullying, at least not for long. This was going to be his hour of glory.

The intercom beeped. Dekker reached out and lifted the receiver. It was Bill Trent, head of AINR security.

"Daniel, J. T., and his minder have just driven into the car park."

"Thanks." Daniel touched several keys and spoke into the handset. "Attention all personnel. Minister Joe McTierney has just arrived." He put down the receiver.

Not unexpectedly, McTierney and his personal assistant walked unannounced and uninvited into the office of Daniel Van Dekker. The good gentleman was seated at his desk studying some papers. There was no evidence of impending departure at all. The people in the offices they had passed were going about their business as usual.

McTierney smiled to himself. Soon the fur would be flying, or there would be blood on the floor. Without an introduction, he selected his most belligerent tone and began. "What the hell are you doing here?"

"At the present," Dekker replied, "we are completing work on a neutron-scattering experiment involving some interesting new materials—"

"So I noticed," McTierney interrupted. "What I didn't notice were any signs that the decommissioning process had been commenced."

"It hasn't."

"And I suppose you're going to give me a reason?" McTierney sneered.

"Decommissioning a reactor is a complex process. In the meantime, we have several unfinished projects that will need to be completed, as well as some work for the faculty of Mechanical Engineering at Sydney University."

"And how long do you propose to take on these projects?"

Dekker answered, "They should be completed in a couple of years."

"I beg your pardon?"

"Then we can get down to planning the decommissioning process."

"And how long do you envisage that taking?"

"Ten years, at least," Dekker replied, never raising his voice.

McTierney exploded in a string of expletives.

Dekker seemed almost puzzled as though he didn't understand the language—which, in part, was true.

McTierney concluded his tirade. "I'm telling you, this is unacceptable. You have been given a ministerial ultimatum to close this establishment. Failure to comply will result in prosecution."

"I don't think so. The decommissioning will take twelve years. Get used to the idea or do it yourself." Dekker had not raised his voice or shown the slightest agitation.

"I damn well will do it myself."

"Then you would be an even bigger fool than I think you are, if that were possible."

McTierney looked as though he was going to explode. For a full five seconds, he couldn't speak. His face turned a very unappealing shade of red and it seemed as though he couldn't breathe properly. His voice, when he finally found it, was modulated with a sputtering rage that would have usually sent his adversaries running from the room.

"You will complete the process … in … two … months … or … get … out … now."

Dekker answered in a totally calm voice. The sound of it made McTierney want to smash his head against a filing cabinet. "I will not. If you think you can decommission a reactor in two months, you must be barking mad. Does insanity run in your family, or is it just you?"

"Get out!" Tierney screamed at him.

"I beg your pardon?" Dekker replied with a bewildered look. "You can't mean that."

A fresh and even longer tirade of foul expletives poured out of McTierney. "You heard me, take yourself and your staff off the premises. They're surplus to requirements. If I have any say in the matter, you'll be deported within the month."

"You can't be serious! You actually want us to leave now—this instant? All of us? Walk out?"

For the first time, McTierney began to smile inwardly. He was in command. He read the carefully crafted expression on Dekker's face as fear. He had seen that response a hundred times before and knew how to follow through. "Now. Or I'll have every person on this site carted off under police arrest for disregarding a ministerial directive in the public interest and disregarding public safety. By the time I've finished with them, they won't be able to get a job sweeping streets. When you chose to get in my way, you chose the wrong man."

Incredulity in his eyes, Dekker stared at him. "Let me understand. You are ordering me and my staff to down tools and walk out, right this instant, or you will place us all under arrest?"

"You're really very slow for a doctor, aren't you? Five minutes, and I phone."

"Very well." Dekker said.

"What?"

"If that's what you're ordering me to do, I will have to comply."

He touched some keys on his computer keyboard and picked up the handset from the intercom. "This is a directive to all staff, effective immediately. In compliance with the orders and authority of Joe McTierney, you are to leave what you are doing and exit the premises. Now. Please do not take anything with you. This applies to all staff. Leave your security passes with Bill Trent on the way out. When everyone has left the premises, Bill will lock all doors and hand Mr. McTierney the security cards in the parking lot." He turned to McTierney. "Happy? Fast enough for you? You'd better come outside to the car park so that security doesn't lock you in."

"Don't think you've heard the last from me." McTierney said.

"I'm sure I haven't." Dekker reached into his pocket and extracted a small, silver voice recorder. "Just let me check I've made a good recording of this conversation."

He touched some controls on the small device. McTierney heard his own sputtering voice. " … take yourself and your staff off the premises. They are surplus … "

"Yes," said Dekker. "It seems to have worked satisfactorily. I wouldn't like us to forget what your instructions were." He shut down the machine. "Well, I'll be off then."

Dekker walked straight in front of McTierney out into the corridor, joining the throng of people heading for the exit. Strangely, none of them seemed very shocked or distressed.

Half an hour later, McTierney was standing in the empty car park holding a bag of security cards. A gentle breeze ruffled the gums around the perimeter. Cows grazed in the paddocks. A fly buzzed around his head.

All was very peaceful.

Since the elation of his spectacular success, McTierney had experienced a slowly growing sense of disquiet. He was holding all the keys. Why did he feel as though Dekker was playing him like a fool—and why did he feel that somehow, despite the fact that he had decimated the man, that Dekker was still in control?

He was holding the keys to a nuclear reactor facility and he hadn't the faintest idea what to do with them. He shrugged. It was up to somebody else. He had done his job par excellence.

He dialed Alan Tebbut, the deputy prime minister, to report his success. "They've left. I've got the keys. Get your boys over here and trash the place."

"I beg your pardon?" Tebbut gasped. "Are you saying all the staff, including Dekker, has left? Gone?"

"Told you I could get them out. Not a soul remaining. Now get your bright boys down here and start cleaning up the mess."

Tebbut was not quite as thrilled as McTierney thought he would be. He continued slowly, considering the implications of his words. "You say the whole staff just downed tools and left? What state is the reactor in? Was it operating? Had it been shut down? What processes were running?"

"How the hell should I know?" McTierney snapped at him.

"Well you had better pray the thing is stable. Otherwise, your name will go down in history as the first person to precipitate a nuclear disaster in Australia." He rang off.

Half an hour later, Nicols arrived by chopper with Tebutt and Cann. They were not happy. By the time they had completed a tour of the silent facility, their unhappiness had reached truly alarming proportions.

Camden boasts some of the best restaurants in Australia. Dekker and a small group of AINR scientists were enjoying a superb Indian cuisine.

Harold Brown was speaking. "It won't stop them, you know. We might have won the first round, but we will ultimately lose the game."

Dekker replied. "True, but we may be able to bargain some consolation prizes on the way through. What are you going to do, Harry?"

"I've applied for a research post in Edinburgh, and I think I have a chance. I'll stay and help clean up this mess, though."

Julie Oates looked up from her favourite dish of Chicken Vindaloo. "It won't be long before we hear from them. I left the neutron-scattering window open wide. It alarms within about four hours, so it should be alarming now."

"And the reactor is running on standby," said Frank. "It will alarm in about twenty-four hours. Let's see if they know how to shut down the core."

"But the thing will shut down safely, won't it?" Harry said through a mouthful of Lamb Rogan Josh.

"Of course it will," Frank said. "But they don't know that. There will be little red lights all over the control console. They won't have the faintest idea what to do with them."

"You filed the operations manuals correctly, didn't you, Harry?" Dekker asked. "I wouldn't like to think we left them without any help whatsoever."

"Absolutely. Filed where you would expect them to be: Diffraction-Neutron generator- procedures–operating instructions. There are a lot of online manuals as well. I believe they are password protected, though."

"And who has the passwords?" said Julie with a little laugh.

"I think they're on the machine in my room," said Dekker. "And I have the password for that. A rather long one, in fact. No, I don't think we will hear from McTierney anymore. He is just a trumped-up hatchet man who has overstepped the mark. I imagine he is feeling the temperature of the water rising around him right now. No, we will hear from Tebutt, I expect, and the deal will finally be negotiated with him."

They did hear from Tebutt, and a very worried deputy prime minister he was. He was apologetic about the way in which the staff had been evicted. He was apologetic about the language McTierney had used. He was apologetic about the inconvenience and the threats and the demeaning insults and just about everything else, but would Dr. Van Dekker and the staff please return to make sure that the reactor complex was safe and arrange an orderly shut down of all projects and the reactor in particular?

Dekker delivered part two of the package.

"I've arranged to visit Holland in a week for discussions with some of my colleagues over there. In the meantime, I will ask my staff to return and secure the reactor. There was never any danger to the general public, of course. When I return, I will present a list of suggestions to the prime minister that may serve to compensate for the loss of one of the best research facilities in the world. I feel this would expedite the process greatly."

Even so, it took a full two years to decommission the reactor. Most of the radioactive material was removed from site, and the remainder was stored at the bottom of deep wells filled with water. Its presence in the Camden region was regrettable, but the risk of contamination during transportation—not to mention the cost—made it necessary to keep it there. They also had not taken the trouble to remove the large cooling tower, which had been erected during the beginning of the project to support a full-fledged nuclear power station on the site in case the experimental reactor had been up-scaled when Australia embraced nuclear power. It then stood as an empty icon of a discarded dream, and the local residents wished it to hell every time they saw it. Perhaps they could use it for storing fodder for the winter.

# CHAPTER 3

In March 1998, six months after the decommissioning had been completed, Daniel Van Dekker walked up the stairs from Science Road into the Physics building of the University of Sydney. He glanced at the notice board to his left and took the stairs to the first floor. He walked along the corridor and knocked on the door that bore the name of Professor S. Cole and, next to it, the name of Dr. E. Caruthers.

A laminated card was pinned to the door underneath the brass nameplate. It read: "If you are in desperate trouble, please go to room 185."

He was in trouble.

Out of curiosity more than anything else, he wandered down the corridor to the nominated room, glanced at the sign on the door, and wandered back to where he came from. He knocked.

The door was opened by a smiling young woman with a pleasant, attractive face who ushered him into a chair. "Professor sends her apologies for keeping you waiting and asked me to make you a cup of tea or something."

"And you would be?" Dr. Van Dekker asked.

"Elizabeth Caruthers. I work with the professor. Sort of a research assistant, really. Would you like the tea or something now?"

"I'm fine, thanks."

"You'll pardon me for asking," she said in a hesitant voice, "but you're the Dr. Van Dekker who was in charge of AINR, weren't you?"

"Too true, I'm afraid."

"I was so sorry to hear about all the awful rubbish that closed you down. Sometimes it makes me a bit ashamed to be an academic in Australia." She paused awkwardly, then, as if she had come to some personal decision, went on. "It's none of my business, of course, but I imagine you've come for some sort of assistance?"

"I saw the sign."

"That's really for students." She paused again, looking a little uncomfortable. "I've been following the history of the AINR closure, you know. I'm really very sorry. Australia lost a lot of very good physicists."

Once again there was a small, embarrassed silence.

"I err … I was wondering," she began, "have you ever met Professor Sarah Cole before?"

"No, not personally. I've heard about her work in superconductors, though. Not many people haven't. I've come for some advice in that area, in fact."

Elizabeth checked about her to make sure the lady in question had not materialized through the door. Then she went on, speaking quietly. "Please don't think me indiscrete or anything, but Sarah is a very unusual person. She hates people who gawk at her. It puts her on the left foot straight away, if you get my meaning."

"I'm not sure I do," Dr. Van Dekker said. "I'm not in the habit of gawking at people."

"No, of course you aren't, but when you see her you'll know what I mean. She really doesn't like people making personal comments about her at all. If you stick to business, you'll find she's really very nice."

At that very instant the door to an office on the left opened and a flustered young man walked out.

An irritated voice followed him. "If you don't want me to throw your next pathetic effort into the same rubbish bin, put some thought into it first. If you can't do that, then don't waste my time."

The student left looking as though his world had just collapsed around him.

Most everyone has experienced a bad moment when they feel certain the next one is going to be bad squared. Dekker was having one now.

The voice continued. "Elizabeth, please send Van Dekker in now."

Dekker entered the room. In the first second, he understood Elizabeth's comment.

Professor Sarah Cole was jaw-droppingly beautiful. In fact, she was the most beautiful creature Dekker had ever set his eyes on in his life. She appeared to be in her early twenties, but that wasn't possible. Her face was flawless, and from what he could gauge from the unhelpfully shapeless lab coat she was wearing, her figure was flawless, too. Her long hair was tied into a simple ponytail behind her head, yet even so it rippled down her back like a shimmering golden waterfall. A pair of large, speaking blue eyes stared steadily at him, and Dekker had the uncomfortable feeling that they could see right inside his head. Her voice was soft and compelling and slightly lower than usual for a woman.

Yet, strangely enough, he felt none of the common male reactions that come from being in the presence of such a beautiful creature.

Some time ago, Dekker had met a man who could play a piece of music perfectly on the piano after he had heard it played once by someone else. But that was all he could do. He couldn't even tie his shoes. Instead of feeling inspired at hearing him play so beautifully, Dekker had experienced an unsettling xenophobia, and for months afterwards his conscience goaded him for his attitude.

Despite the man's extraordinary gift with music, Dekker had felt he was in the presence of an alien who physically resembled a human but in reality was something different and, in being different, being less.

Glancing at Sarah Cole, the same feeling came upon him with a vengeance, only now he was the one who felt merely human and totally inferior. "I'm losing my mind", he said to himself. *Xenophobia – what next? I'm cracking up. What happens now?* He felt around his collar and glanced in every other direction around the room except hers.

The alien spoke. "Good morning, Dr. Van Dekker. To what do I owe this visit?"

"Good morning, Professor. I fear I may be in breach of your instructions on the door, although I did attempt to carry them out."

"You visited room one hundred eighty-five?"

"The toilet," Dr. Dekker said. "I can assure you, I have spent many hours of contemplation in similar venues without successfully arriving at a solution to my present dilemma. I remembered the paper you delivered in Geneva on high-temperature superconductors. The mathematical solution you proposed was erudite and brilliant. It's your unparalleled expertise in this field that brought me here. I need your assistance as one physicist to another. I've read every paper you've written. They have convinced me that there is no one living who knows more about superconductors than yourself."

Sarah Cole smiled. "You've been speaking to my colleague, haven't you? Or, rather, she's been speaking to you? Yes, she has, I think, which means she favours you. Sit down, Dr. Dekker, and talk to me. You may dispense with the flattery. It will not assist your request."

Dekker did. Being meticulously careful to only glance at her from time to time, he recounted the events leading up to his visit. "You see, in payment for the decommissioning, I demanded that they set up some sort of institute or other to continue research into atomic physics and recover some of the brilliant people who were working with me. They will endeavour to keep costs to a minimum, and we may have to attract additional funding from elsewhere as well. I had thought of attempting some fusion experiments—you know, fusing hydrogen atoms into helium. People have been attempting that for a long time because of its promise to provide enormous reserves of energy without the use of nuclear power. I thought we might generate a few shekels from other sponsors."

"Those people tried and failed," she noted. "Why should you be any different? They will want you to fail, you know."

"I'm aware of that. I said fusion experiments because of their fundraising potential. In actual fact, I don't seriously expect to succeed in such an endeavour. It's really not the primary aim, it just has to appear so."

"Then what is your primary aim?"

"To conduct high-energy collision experiments," replied Dr. Dekker. "See if we can find any evidence for the Higgs Boson and particles like that."

"I feel your sponsors are extremely unlikely to agree to the billion or so dollars required to construct a sufficiently large accelerator. One is already in operation at Geneva and, to the best of my knowledge, even it isn't powerful enough to do the sort of work you are proposing."

"I don't need a huge accelerator. All I need is a magnetic field at least one order of magnitude greater than anyone else has managed to obtain. My idea is to fire tiny bursts of extremely high-energy negative ions and positively-charged ions into a very intense magnetic field, causing them to spiral tightly in opposite directions. There would have to be quite a number of very high-energy collisions. I would be looking for the generation of neutrons as evidence. Not many but, if we could observe just a few, we could examine any other particles being generated along with them in the collisions, they might tell us something useful. The length of the field need only be a few metres."

She asked, "How would you energise your particles in the first place?"

"By using very short bursts of microwave energy," he answered. "No existing hardware could generate the power we would need on a continuous basis, but if the generators were pulsed on for say one or two milliseconds and then off for about a second or so I think we could develop energy bursts of around a gigawatt—a thousand megawatts. That is a lot of energy to be concentrated in a very small space. The ionized particles would be travelling at almost the speed of light before they entered the field, and then they would spiral in opposite directions, the negative ions one way, the positive the other. The extremely high-energy collisions may cause fusion, or perhaps other interesting particles would be released."

Professor Cole was silent. Dekker stared resolutely out the window.

Finally, she spoke. "Do you think it wise, Dr. Dekker, to play with such high-energy collisions? I know physicists would love to find evidence for the Higgs Boson. They would like to be able to recreate the conditions they believe occurred soon after the Big Bang. Sometimes

I think such desires amount to arrogance. Perhaps there should be other boundary conditions that define where scientists should and should not tread other than just what they are able to do. You have been doing useful work in neutron scattering. These interactions you propose are thousands and thousands of times more energetic. Do you feel it warranted to pursue such research?"

"I do. Science has always shown the courage to probe the unknown, even when such ventures were fraught with danger. Look at the discovery of radioactivity itself—the isolation of radium, the first fission experiments ..."

"Which led to the atom bomb."

"And to nuclear power," he countered. "The problem lies with people who use our discoveries for evil purposes, not with the discoveries themselves. Besides, I think the likelihood of success is small in this case, but we may discover other interesting things on the way."

"I personally hope the likelihood of success will be zero. What sort of current were you thinking of?"

"One hundred and fifty thousand amps."

"As you know," she said, "I've been working on superconductors, which operate at relatively high temperatures but with much less current than that. We are close to perfecting one that could run at only negative fifty degrees celsius and carry power without loss from state to state. It isn't really too much of a problem to construct one capable of carrying higher current. The theory—my theory, in fact—will still apply. However, the operating temperature will have to be much lower, within one degree of absolute zero, around negative two hundred seventy-two degrees celsius. Does this pose a problem for your shaky funding?"

"I think it could be arranged. We would need a liquid helium plant, but such things are not worth millions. Do you really think it could be done?"

"As I said, the theory still applies. Such superconductors are not going to be cheap. Their physical size cannot be too large, or you will not be able to make your magnet core small enough to generate a super large field. What field strength do you propose, Dr. Dekker?"

"Around ninety to one hundred tesla."

Sarah Cole smiled. "That's more than ten times the field used in the accelerator in Geneva."

"They don't have your superconductors. Besides, the path on the accelerator is twenty-seven kilometres long. Mine will be just three meters."

"They will be expensive to produce," she said. "I don't want to waste my time."

"I have a property in the Hague. If they don't fund me, I will transfer the title into your name. I'll put it in writing if you wish."

Sarah scrutinised Dekker without speaking. He glanced into her face, hoping that she would not think he was gawking. Try as he would, he couldn't turn away. There was something indefinably different about her, something that rather frightened him. He had heard of people who claimed they could read another's thoughts, and in her case he was almost prepared to believe it. The pause lengthened into a period of uncomfortable silence.

At last, Sarah spoke. "Why are you doing this, Daniel? And don't try to patronize me with rubbish."

Dekker sighed heavily. "They shut down AINR because of a lot of nonsense from a bunch of neurotic farmers. Australia lost some of its best minds, and it didn't even notice. All that mattered was political expediency. We became a laughing stock in the scientific community. I feel responsible. I should have fought harder. I should have seen it coming and done something sooner. I should have developed some sort of rapport with the Camden farming community. I want to undo some of the damage I failed to prevent. That's the simple truth."

"Yes," she replied. " I believe you. Very well. I will design your superconductors for you. It is up to you to get them manufactured."

"I am profoundly grateful. When do you think the prototype design will be ready to go to the manufacturing and testing stage?"

"There will be no prototype. What I design will work the first time. I told you, the theory is intact. All I have to do is adjust the operating parameters and make a few other alterations to cope with your intense magnetic field. You can dispense with a testing phase—or not, if you don't trust me sufficiently. I would need twenty-four hours to check the design."

"I beg your pardon?" Dr. Dekker responded. "With respect, I would never expect you to ..."

"I'll email the design parameters to you. You'll have to organise manufacture, but I suggest you use the Kilraen Group's facilities in Switzerland. They're doing some other work for me already. May I have your address?"

Dekker thanked her. He left in a mood of incredulity and disbelief. Surely there was more to it than the good Professor Cole had intimated. Still, the proof of the pudding would be in the eating, and Dekker only half-expected to hear from her again within a month. No doubt his scepticism was completely valid, but there were certain other things he did not know about Sarah Cole, and if he had known them he might have been even less anxious to make her acquaintance, let alone to ask for her help.

The next morning, Dekker logged on to his service provider and opened his email. There was a message from Professor S. Cole with an attachment. He opened it and printed it out. It was a scan of a number of hand-written pages.

There were scribbles here and there around the edges; some sections were crossed out and started again. But there was not doubt about it. There was the final design: a superconductor that would, she claimed, carry a current of two hundred thousand amps at a temperature of negative two hundred and seventy one point five degrees celsius.

Dekker stared at the pages, his hand not completely steady.

So it was true, the woman was indeed the genius others had claimed. Not only had she designed the superconductors, but she had also wired through the specifications to Kilraen Superconductors, Geneva, suggesting Dekker contact their head engineer Hans Leeman to arrange final details.

Underneath, Sarah had written: "I like the Hague. Hope your funding is cut. Keep me informed. Regards, SC."

Dekker folded the paper and placed it in his desk drawer, his mind's eye once again seeing Professor Cole sitting at her desk the instant he had walked through her door.

A genius—his colleagues had been right—a brilliant mind contained within a heavenly body. The combination had unsettled him to no end.

Geniuses were meant to be plain: gifted in some areas, but deficient in others. It was only fair to the rest of the human race. Sarah Cole appeared to be exceptionally endowed with every possible attribute.

For an insane second, Dekker wondered if he had entertained an angel unawares, but he dismissed the thought as preposterous. If mutations in the human DNA could produce someone who could give you a ten-figure prime number without being able to add two and two, a totally dysfunctional pianist, an imbecile who could calculate every date in the Julian calendar, then it was possible to produce a genius with an exquisite body. It was just less probable, that was all. Why that particular coded combination should have had such a disquieting effect on him was a mystery.

# CHAPTER 4

Alan Tebbut was an unhappy man.

He and Paul Nicols were dining at Centrepoint Tower in the heart of Sydney CBD. The slowly revolving restaurant gave a magnificent view of the harbour and the city lights. Tebutt wasn't looking. The excellent lobster and the bottle of vintage New Zealand Semillon Blanc passed his tastebuds unappreciated. In two days, he had to report to the prime minister, and he was dreading the occasion.

"The proposal is worth about ten million dollars," he said. "And he wants an affiliation with some university or other worked into the bargain. We don't have that sort of money."

"Then don't agree to it." Nicols's taste buds were definitely capable of enjoying the excellence of the meal and the wine. He glanced appreciatively at the slowly moving panorama in front of him.

Tebutt continued. "I have little choice. We made promises as part of the decommissioning deal. If we don't come through with our part, Dekker will go to print somewhere. He's quite capable of making us look bad in the eyes of the general public, and we could well do without one more scandal at the present moment. It's been quite a year for scandal. Any more would be dangerous. Furthermore, there's a lot of pressure on the PM from overseas. I'm in a nasty position."

"What does Dekker want you to set up, exactly?"

"He's interested in doing some nuclear fusion experiments. If they're successful, then we will lead the world in the development of fusion energy—cheap, without the need to use nuclear fuel with all its disposal problems. He's persuaded someone from Sydney University to design some special superconductors for him—hanged if I understand what that has to do with it. The whole proposal was agreed to before we knew the cost. Now he's worked that out to the last cent. The bill is enormous. He wants to use one of the buildings on the AINR site and have another one built the size of an aircraft hangar. He wants support staff and students and colleagues. In other words, he wants AINR recreated without the nuclear reactor."

"Why, Alan", laughed Nicols. "Your problem is simple. I have the solution for you."

"I'll bet you haven't—unless it's paying to have him assassinated."

"Nothing like that," Nicols laughed. "I've been having discussions with a couple of the chiefs of Global Power Consortium—you know, the international energy company. Owns reactors and power companies all over Europe and in the States. They offered to buy our power utilities, but that laid an egg in the house. Now they want us to agree to set up some nuclear reactors in the Northern Territory near the uranium mines and feed the output to the national grid through Alice Springs. The greens are coming round to nuclear power over carbon-burning fossil fuels, and if the government signs with Kyoto I think it will become too expensive to use anything else. That's why GPC is interested. It's all in the future, but at the present they're looking for ways to ingratiate themselves with the PM. This fusion power research thing might interest them. If Dekker pulls if off, it will be a real feather in our cap, and if he doesn't, then he will have so much egg on his face he will never be able to scrape it off. He'll be persona non gratia with a multinational corporation, as well as with Canberra. Exit Dr. Van Dekker. Either way, you win."

"You think they would consider funding the lot?" Tebbut asked.

"Ten million is a fart in a stiff breeze to them, though it might be expedient to cough up some of the dough just to show them you're genuinely interested. Make them think you're doing them a favour by letting them make a small contribution to something that could make them deliriously wealthy."

"You may be right," Tebbut said. "Following on from your genius, how about we actually set him up to fail? We give him the plant he wants so he's got no excuse. We allow him all the engineering staff to get his experiment up to the failure stage, but we don't allow him to import dangerous expertise from overseas. He has to pick students from Australian universities on post-doctoral fellowships to work with him—and we limit these to say, no more than two. Very politically correct. That way, Dekker will be seen as the one to blame if anything goes wrong. Make it his show—lock, stock, and barrel. He deserves it."

Nicols said, "But if he succeeds, he will get all the glory, don't forget."

"There'll be enough glory to go round. If he does, the patent rights will belong to us. We'll make sure that's part of the deal. Fusion energy is green energy. The patent rights should be worth billions."

"What about the university affiliation? Would Sydney or New South Wales be interested?" Nicols asked.

"I don't know," Tebbut answered. "I think we should ask the University of Southern Sydney if they would like to take it on because the facility is sort of in their geographic area."

"But USS doesn't even teach physics. They closed the physics department a couple of years back. Too many of their students failed the course. Ruined their reputation. It's mostly computing and accounting and business courses on their campus. Why would they consider taking on Dekker?"

"Because we offer them money. We give them a generous allowance to take on the administrative load of the new department and dangle the glory carrot that would be theirs should Dekker succeed. The place is run by accountants. The vice chancellor used to be a kindergarten teacher. She's politically ambitious. I'll get my staff to draft her one of those modern business proposals, you know, one full of graphs, tables, and analyses, carefully written in corporatese, full of political innuendo. I'll bet you another lobster dinner at this place she goes for it."

"You're on—and that includes the wine."

# CHAPTER 5

Dekker pushed back the portfolio on his desk and lay back in his favourite chair. His wife had long since gone to bed. A tiny smile wrinkled his lips. So that was the deal. He had little choice but to accept, although he could see what was written large between the lines. Two students, he thought. Just two students. He had to choose them with great care.

And he did.

His first choice was a new PhD student from the University of New South Wales who had completed a thesis on sub-atomic particle physics. Dekker had read the thesis carefully and decided that Mark Francis Chambers was an exceptionally bright young man, a conclusion also borne out by an outstanding academic record. He was twenty-four years old, had taken out the university medal at the end of his honours degree, earned the Dean's merit list every undergraduate year, and never scored less than a high distinction.

Had he met the man, Dekker would have seen someone of neat appearance, medium height, blue eyes and brown hair already thinning over his forehead, a somewhat shy and quietly spoken individual who thought a great deal and said much less. He had lived by himself since his parents had died in a car accident when he was still an undergraduate. He wasn't gay. He didn't have a girl.

On Sundays, he went to church. Mark Chambers was a Christian. To his Christian friends, he was a cool guy with a carefully thought-out worldview. To his other mates, he was a cool guy but don't get him started on religion.

Candice Leblanc was a post-doctoral electrical engineering student from Sydney University whose transcript read rather like Mark Chambers's without the university medal. Her doctoral thesis was entitled "High Power Microwave Generation Control and Transmission Systems." It would never make the bestseller list, but after reading it—some of which was in French—Dekker had concluded that the woman had skills that would be extremely useful to the team, and so he made his second and last choice.

Candice was slightly shorter than Mark Chambers, vivacious and pretty. She had brown eyes that sparkled and hair to match, cut into a pleasant bob that kissed her shoulders when she bounced, which she did most of the time. Soft, full lips that often smiled added to the friendliness of her face. She was lithe in build and endowed with shapely breasts that she tastefully revealed to the world in different degrees depending on the temperature, the company, or how she felt at the time. Rounded thighs and shapely legs clad in flawless olive skin completed the picture.

Candice was a young woman who loved to live life, not to just let it pass by unnoticed. Those who lived in her neighbourhood at Mt. Annan would often see her running in the soft dawn light with weights on her hands and ankles, singing softly to herself in French.

Mark had responded to the offer in the *Sydney Morning Herald* to join the team because he had a deep love of physics; also, the prospect of successfully initiating fusion and contributing to the world's energy needs excited him.

Candice had responded to the offer because it sounded like fun.

The Back Alley Café, which was rather ironically located in the main street of Camden, made excellent coffee. In this informal public venue, Dekker first met with his two prospective colleagues.

It was January 1999 and hot. A sultry breeze blew idly down the street tossing wrapping papers and adding to the lazy feeling of the afternoon. The tables in the street were unoccupied. At that time of day, the few patrons enjoyed the air-conditioning inside.

Dekker was the first to arrive. After just a short while he noticed a red-faced young man in a suit and tie enter the café with a train ticket still in his hand. Dekker beckoned him over to his table. "Mark Chambers? Daniel Van Dekker. Glad you could make it."

"The gratitude is all mine, Professor Van Dekker. It is an honour to meet with you. I cannot tell you how very much—"

"Please excuse, are you Professeur Van Dekker?" The young woman who had followed Mark Chambers through the door made her way over to the table. She held out her hand. Her eyes sparkled. "But of course you are. I recognize you from your face in the papers with all that scandal last year."

"And you would be Candice Leblanc?" Dr. Van Dekker shook her hand.

"Candi, if you please, Professeur. It is hot, yes?" With what Candi was wearing, though, it was unlikely she was feeling the heat. She wore a low-cut blouse of some wispy material with flowers all over it, a miniskirt with a different set of matching flowers, and a pair of yellow thongs. Clearly, Candi did not regard this as an occasion worthy of formality.

Wiping the sweat off his forehead, Mark glanced at his would-be colleague and wished he had followed her approach, if not quite to the same extent.

"This is Mark Chambers. Mark, Candi. Would you both like a coffee or something cool?"

"Coffee, please. Black, strong." Candi smiled at Mark. "It is a pleasure to meet with you both. The project sounds like such a lot of fun. We will all do great things together, yes?"

"I hope so," Mark said. "It is a pleasure to meet you, Candi. Oh, a chocolate frappachino, Professor—thank you."

"You will have to stop calling me that, Mark. My name to both of you is Daniel. Can we stick to first names from now on please? It does make things a bit easier. Now stay there and get to know one another while I order the drinks."

"Have you travelled far?" Mark said, attempting to open conversation.

"No. I'm living at Mount Annan—only about fifteen minutes away. It took much longer to get to uni. And you?"

"I live at Heathcote, so it took the best part of an hour. I might move, though, if this job looks like going on for a while."

Candi smiled at him. "I hope it will. If we succeed! Fame, glory! I like the sound of that. It's nice to meet you at last. I read about you on the Internet. You are so very clever. The university medal and all. You must love your physics as much as you love your girl, yes?"

"Yes …" Mark said. "I mean, I'm not attached at present. I've heard about you, too. You just finished up at Sydney, didn't you? Why did you come to Australia?"

"C'est la vie, n'est ce pas?" Candi replied. "My friends in Paris—I studied at the Sorbonne—they say 'why do you want to come to this land of kangaroos and primitive farming people?' Les gens stupides! Candi aime vivre, Mark, et elle n'aime pas rester à la maison et devenir un légume. Pardon, Candi loves to live, Mark. I don't want to become the vegetable."

"You've done brilliantly since you came. Your PhD in electrical engineering received special international recognition. Microwave power generation. You've published several papers that have been well reviewed as well."

"Oui, you check Candi out," she said. "I play with microwaves. Candi check you out, too. You're a particle physicist. I don't know much about particle physics. I was very surprised Daniel wanted me when he could have had another real physicist like you."

"But I need you both," Dekker said, returning to the table. "Now let's talk about the project, make sure that you are both happy. Forget what you've read in the application blurb. That's for the benefit of our sponsors. We are going to conduct some unique collision experiments at high energies. I've managed to get some very special magnets that can deliver a field of about one hundred fifty tesla."

Mark and Candi were astounded. Both, apparently, had heard of magnetic fields, but never of one like that.

"But that field strength is at least ten times any I've ever heard of. No one has achieved anything like that before," said Mark, inadvertently wiping the sweat off his forehead with the back of his hand and looking stunned at the same time.

Candi laid her hand on Dekker's arm, excitement in her eyes and her voice.

"How are we generating this super new field?"

"We have been privileged to have a very special superconductor designed for us," Dekker explained. "It carries around ten times more current than has previously been possible, hence ten times the field strength. We have to cool the material down to almost absolute zero to get it to work, however."

"So, we have these new field magnets," she said. "What are we going to do with them? I have never been near a field of that magnitude. Does it do bad things to girls?"

"Not that I know of, but you will probably have to walk slowly. There is a lot of paramagnetic material in girls, you know. Guys too. If you walk too fast near a field like that, you will begin to feel very hot."

"So we use the field to concentrate high-speed ions in some circular track like they have in Geneva?" enquired Mark.

"No," Dekker answered. "We don't have the funds for anything of that order of magnitude. We can't make our magnet so large. We generate a stream of hydrogen ions and electrons at very high energies using a magnetic double-layer accelerator and feed them almost at right angles into our super strong field."

"So the particles spin in opposite directions?" Mark asked.

"Correct," Dekker replied. "Now, let's consider a tube of about three metres in length with this intense magnetic field running along its length. If we fire the particles in at almost ninety degrees, they will not only spiral, but they will also drift along the tube."

Candi said, "Getting closer and closer together until some of them must bang into each other."

"That's right, Candi." Dekker continued. "As you know, neutrons decay by themselves to hydrogen ions, protons, and electrons, giving off energy. What if we have enough energy in those collisions to reverse this process?"

"Then we will produce spinning neutrons," she said. "But what of it?"

"Neutrons have no charge. At this stage, they will be travelling around in a tiny circle at almost the speed of light. Perhaps they will stick together. The attractive force due to their mass at that tiny distance would be very large."

"And perhaps they make a tiny black hole, or a not-so-tiny one?" she asked. "This is not a good experiment. I read a novel last year about a black hole that hit the earth and—"

"No, Candi." Dekker smiled at her. "Any black holes formed would be so small they would evaporate almost instantly, so it's not a problem. We simply use this method to produce a stream of spiralling neutrons. That's the first step. If we are successful, we will be the first scientists in the world to make neutrons from hydrogen ions. There should be a few papers there at least. Now comes the clever part. If we build another one of these neutron generators in which the protons—and therefore the neutrons produced—are spiralling in the opposite direction, and allow the two streams to collide, neutrons colliding with neutrons. These collisions should be much more effective than collisions of charged ions. It's my hope they will result in other particles being observed, such as the Higgs Boson. Now if we observe that, we will go into the history books."

"But we would need to start with ions travelling at almost the speed of light—ions with the enormous energies, or there will not be any neutrons produced at all." Candi waved her arms around like a charged particle in a magnetic field. "Eventually, the hydrogen ions will recombine with the electrons and produce the hydrogen atoms that won't deflect in the field. How are you going to accelerate your ions?"

Dekker replied with a smile. "I'm glad you asked. We will excite the particles with a little dose of microwave energy prepared by the expertise of Doctor Candice Leblanc."

"And what sort of little dose were you thinking of?"

"About two gigawatts," Dekker answered calmly.

There was as short pause. Candi's already-large eyes opened to a degree that surprised Mark a great deal.

She said several words in French that he was glad he couldn't translate, and then she went on. "You're not serious. Such energy. It does very bad things to girls, and to boys, too. Besides, there is not the microwave amplifier—klystron—that would deliver this power. At least none that we could fit inside a building. And another thing—"

"I don't want you to produce that sort of energy continuously," Dekker explained. "Just tiny bursts of it. One little millisecond burst every second. Let the klystrons cool down, the power supply recharge, allow the system recover between bursts. You think you could do that?"

Candi didn't answer at first. Concern had taken the place of excitement on her face. Finally, she spoke. "It might be possible. We would need some very expensive klystrons, and the mother of all power supplies. I will think about the ways, yes, and we will see what is possible, what is not. This is not easy. Candi will be very busy—and very well-cooked if anything goes wrong—we all would be. Three roasts we will be, and others beside if they are anywhere near. What funds have I got to play with?"

"Whatever you need. Let me know." Dekker smiled reassuringly at her. "Now Mark, you have a homework assignment, too. I want you to work on the power supply and construction of the 'new field magnets,' as Candi calls them. I will work on the magnetic double-layer accelerator, and the design to get the microwave energy into the hydrogen gas in a way that doesn't flash fry us all. I would like to be able to offer you an office on site, but as yet the place is still being constructed. Nobody works during January in this country, so it will be at least June '99 before we see any substantial construction, and we will be lucky to have the first experiment working before this time next year. We can use a building on the old AINR site from about March onwards, but in the meantime we will talk by email and meet here each week to discuss the project together. Now I take it you're both on board? Good. I have quite a bit of paperwork for you to complete, and when we've done perhaps we can have dinner. This café also serves meals. Suit everyone?"

They left the Back Alley Café around eight o'clock in the evening. It was much cooler outside because of a storm that had unleashed its fury earlier in the afternoon. Three excited people, each looking forward to what the coming year would bring, in total blissful ignorance of what it actually would.

Dekker headed for his car, Candi toward hers.

After a few paces she stopped, turned around, and called to Mark, who was walking back in the other direction. "How are you getting home?"

Mark stopped, turned round, and walked back some of the way towards her, not wishing to shout his business into the vacant street. "I thought I'd see if there was a train. Either that, or get a taxi."

"It's a long wait for a train, and the taxis are very rare at this time," she said. "Why don't you spend the night at my place? Go home tomorrow. This is a good idea."

"Are you sure it's not inconvenient?"

"Why would I offer if it was?" she replied. "Come on! Don't let Candi's driving scare you!"

It was only a short drive out to Mt. Annan, shorter than Mark would have believed possible, and he wondered if Candi thought the little circles with numbers in them were speed suggestions rather than speed limits. At least there wasn't much traffic. Candi chatted all the way there, which Mark was glad of because it was late and he was tired. When he was tired, his ability to make light conversation decided it was time for bed and left him. He sat there enjoying the sound of Candi's voice. Her excitable French accent and occasional clumsy phrase were rather appealing.

Candi stopped the car in front of a modern brick house with a well-tended garden in the front—at least it appeared well-tended from the light of the streetlamp across the other side of the road.

They walked up a paved path to the front door. Candi let herself in, turned on the light, and expertly threw her ring of keys into a shallow bowl on a small period table in the hall. It was exquisitely carved, inlaid with marble on the top, the craftsmanship of the marquetry on its sides extraordinary in its beauty and design.

He followed her down the hall into the lounge room, where Mark noticed the same pattern of furnishings extended there. The room was not overburdened with furniture, but each item was of impeccable quality, each piece carefully chosen to fit in with overall theme of French Renaissance. Only two small paintings hung on the walls, reproductions of a Monet and a Lautrec, reproductions painted by another artist, not some cheap photographic print.

This woman had taste and elegance.

Two bottles of vintage French Beaujolais lay side by side in an otherwise empty wine rack. Mark's eyes travelled over to the kitchen. Gleaming pots and pans hung from a rack suspended from the ceiling. A large round specimen of Port Salut, as yet un-sampled, rested in the centre of the granite bench. Several other observations convinced Mark that Candi's taste in food was as epicurean as her taste in furniture was exquisite.

"What made you rent here?" he asked her.

"I'm not renting. My parents are—how you say—well off, and they wanted to invest in some Australian property. I bought this house for them. Nice, isn't it? Better value at Mt. Annan than on the north side of Sydney. For the price of a run-down unit I could have all this, and it doesn't take long to get to work, especially now! I chose the furniture. Do you like it?"

"It's certainly very convenient with our new jobs. I think you have impeccable taste. Thank you for this, Candi. I am really looking forward to going to bed."

Candi turned round to face him, lifted her arm, stroked his cheek with her hand, and smiled into his face. "So impatient. I will freshen up a little first. There is another shower next to the laundry. You can do the same."

"I'm afraid I don't have any pyjamas"

"Neither do I," she laughed. "Saves a lot of time. The bedroom is in there."

"Where do you want me to sleep?"

Candi stopped in the doorway, a rather puzzled expression on her attractive face. Mark repeated his question, assuming she hadn't understood.

"You are making the joke," she said. "Australian men are so different. In the bedroom, of course, but first we enjoy ourselves, yes?"

It took Mark a good thirty seconds to realise what Candi meant. It had been such a casual suggestion, as if sleeping with a woman you had just met belonged to the same category as sharing a bowl of chips with her. No other woman within the circle of his existing friends had ever offered herself for an evening's casual enjoyment, and he found himself at a loss as to how to answer her, how to refuse without seeming ungrateful or impolite. The longer he left it, the worse it was going to get. He took a deep breath and went into the bedroom.

Candi was already down to her underwear. She looked up, annoyed. "Mark, I am not ready yet. It will be much nicer after we are fresh and clean. Please have the shower first!"

"Err … Candi, I think there's a misunderstanding. Thank you for your very kind offer, but I don't want to sleep with you at all."

Candi paused in her undress, her eyes turned toward him, incomprehension written all over her face. "I thought you said you didn't have a girl. Am I wrong?"

"No, I don't. It's just that … "

"Oh!" Candi's face turned pink. She snapped the catch on her bra back on and walked over to Mark, whose face began to reflect a growing state of apprehension. "I am so sorry! How terribly insensitive and inappropriate! I apologise! I didn't know you were gay."

"Gay?" Mark replied, "I'm not gay, and I don't have a girlfriend. I'm not in love with you, Candi, and anyway, casual sex like that just isn't the right thing to do!"

The embarrassed expression on Candi's face evaporated, only to be replaced by one of annoyance. Her eyes seemed to glow brighter, and her eyebrows lifted slightly. There was an edge to her voice when she spoke. "Love? You think I am in love when I offer you to share my bed with you? You overstep yourself, Mark. To finish the evening with some pleasure, that was … what do you mean this is the wrong thing to do?"

"I don't believe in sex outside of marriage."

"Get out of my bedroom this instant!" Candi's hand shot out and propelled Mark backwards through the door, while the other grabbed hold of the handle and slammed it shut in his face.

Mark returned to the lounge room feeling very uncomfortable and about as happy as a fish in a snow storm. Now he bitterly regretted accepting Candi's offer of a place to stay. But how could he have known?

He could hear the sounds of water running from the hot water service in the laundry and the distant sounds of French shouting coming from the en-suite in the bedroom. What was coming next?

Half an hour later Candi emerged wearing an attractive low-cut top and a pair of black designer jeans that extended less than a third the way along her thighs. Her hair curled down to bounce on her shoulders in a most attractive manner. All in all, she looked like a young woman about to go to a party, not to bed. "Come on, Mark, I'm taking you home to Heathcote."

"That is very kind of you, but it's a long way out of your way."

"I have phoned a couple of friends. We're going to party in the city. I feel like a party after this evening with you. Come on!"

Mark followed her back down the hall and out the front door into the car.

Candi seemed neither angry nor happy. Disinterested would have been a more accurate description. It was as though his words had placed him in a category of people she kept at arm's length, polite and distant, publicly accepted, privately rejected, socially tolerated, personally despised. Somehow she managed to communicate her attitude by the way she looked at him, which on consideration was no mean feat.

Mark got into the passenger's seat, privately wishing that he was already through his own front door. They set off. In contrast to her mood during the inward journey, Candi was quiet for the most part. Five minutes from Heathcote, she spoke. "You are one of those religious people, aren't you?"

"I'm a Christian, yes."

"A scientist who believes in God! So rare. Such a disappointment. I should tell you, Mark, before we are colleagues, I hate anything to do with religion. If you want us to get along, keep your religious opinions to yourself. You are just like the rest of them, bound up by a whole lot of useless, archaic rules that make you so socially—what it the word, when you are sitting on the toilet and you can't do your business?"

"Constipated."

"Constipated," she said. "You can't even enjoy an evening using what you say your God has given you! He makes the beautiful bodies but you can't use them for the pleasure they are made to enjoy! No, that is the teaching of the celibate priest who want others to share in his misery. Perverts!"

All this time, Candi's voice had been getting louder, her driving, faster.

Mark sat silent in the passenger seat, praying for safety. He didn't dare tell Candi what he was doing. There was no point in making matters worse. A few minutes more and the car screeched to a halt outside his home. Mark thanked Candi for the ride and got out, grateful to be alive. The car screeched away and Mark headed up the path to the front door, rather saddened by the turn of events. There were going to be difficult days ahead, he could see. In his heart he also knew there was a part of him that would have enjoyed the evening as Candi had planned it, and it troubled him. A vision of himself rolling around on the bed with her naked body rose up unhelpfully from somewhere in his mind, and it troubled him even more. Some of the enjoyable anticipation had evaporated from the future.

Candi squeezed her car into the last available parking space in Kent Street, got out, and hurried down towards the wharves.

Sally and June were meeting her outside a large restaurant come nightclub called James Squires. There was a brewery attached to the premises as well, offering a large range of different and thoroughly excellent beers and ales.

The evening would begin there and end wherever.

Despite the lateness of the hour, there were still lots of customers about, mostly young people, and the sound of loud music was coming from the discos in the clubs lining the city side of the long foreshore promenade.

Here and there, couples were entwined together in a prelude to some later public mating and, as Candi glanced at them, she felt her resentment towards Mark's prudish attitude rising in her heart. He had not even been all that attractive and he was almost certainly no great lover, yet she had been willing to give him the benefit of her expertise. And he had rejected her, rejected her for such a pathetic, narrow-minded, prudish, holier than thou reason. She felt her fists involuntarily clenching at the recollection of it.

Why should she be so annoyed? Because he had made her feel cheap, that was why. What right did he have to pass judgement on her personal lifestyle? Was not her body her own to do what she wanted with? Thank goodness she was mature enough to move on and make something of the evening, not just sit at home and brood. At last, there was Sally with her boyfriend Kane, and June with … some real hunk of a guy!

All thought of Mark forgotten, Candi ran up to them, waving her arms and shouting. "Sally, cherie! June, Kane! And who is your friend?"

The girls gave each other a pat-on-the-shoulder sort of hug that signified social acceptance but little else, and Sally performed the eagerly awaited introduction. June smiled the sort of smile that said, in language loud and clear to every female on the planet, "He's mine, get your eyes off."

"Candi, this is Roger Gaunt. He plays football for Wests. Roger, Candi Leblanc."

"But of course!" Candi said. "I have seen your picture in the paper! It is so good to meet you in person!"

Roger, dispensing with any form of social greeting apart from a grunt, ran his eyes over her from head to toe.

Candi, completely aware of his gaze, turned her body slightly to maximise the attributes he obviously found appealing, all the while staring straight into his face with her eyes large and a most beguiling smile on her lips.

June, observing this disturbing turn of events, moved in to apply countermeasures—not quickly enough, because by then Candi had linked her lithe arm around one of Roger's tree trunks, and Roger, damn and blast him, didn't seem to mind at all.

"Where shall we go?" Candi asked. "Do you like to dance? Do you know where there is a good place?"

"Yeah, babe," Roger said. "June and I were just going there. Up on George Street. You okay with that?"

"But of course! We will all go, yes?" Candi replied.

Sally and Kane voiced their approval, and June murmured some expletive that could have been understood for "yes," her eyes simmering at Candi as though she would have liked to have thrown her off the pier wrapped in heavy chains. The latter ignored her completely.

By the time they reached the first-floor disco on George Street, Candi and Roger were chatting to one another like old friends, which meant that Roger was talking incessantly about football and Candi was making encouraging sounds in reply. Kane and Sally followed on behind, while June tried to make a threesome with the others in front. However, the large crowds of people on the footpath, not all of them completely in charge of their limbs, made the task increasingly difficult, and it wasn't too long before she was definitely the third wheel in the party.

The final coup de grace came during the disco itself. Candi could really dance. Whether it was because of the previous events of the evening or simply the presence of competition or purely the joy of movement, she poured all her considerable store of energy into it. Her physical fitness, her ability to move every part of her body seductively, becoming one with the music itself, her hair bouncing delightfully around her face, she gyrated before Roger's approving gaze. It wasn't too long before the others had retired, exhausted, for drinks, leaving the two of them on the dance floor.

Closer and closer they danced until Candi felt Roger's arms around her, his kiss on her neck. "You want to go somewhere?"

Australian men lacked the language and the romantic finesse of those in her country, but the message, however blatantly direct, was the same. She returned his embrace, secure in the knowledge that the evening was going to end just exactly the way she had intended it to.

# CHAPTER 6

I t was the last day of April 1999. The summer had been stiflingly hot. Outside the window of the warehouse on the AINR site, the grass in the paddocks had turned from green to brown to dust. Only the reddish-brown earth remained. Here and there, a cow wandered, chewing fodder that had been dumped earlier that morning.

The building of the new facility was taking place slowly. Cranes lifted the special carbon fibre girders into place and men hammered sheeting and poured concrete. It was hot inside as well; the air-conditioning had never worked well when the building was a warehouse. Now that it housed personnel, it was completely inadequate.

Dekker scratched his forehead and re-read the page in front of him. Page fifty-eight of sixty-four of the application for research funding at Southern Sydney University. He had received the package the week before. The cover letter stated that if he wanted any funds from the university he had to complete the thick application that was attached and return it within seven (7) days in order to be received by the vice chancellor's department before the university's academic committee met.

Dekker had phoned the vice chancellor. "Why do I have to fill out this form? I already have my funding. They are building the premises as we speak."

The vice chancellor's secretary answered, "The material sent to you should have been sent three months ago. It was an oversight."

"But seeing as the funding has already been allocated," Dekker replied, "why do I have to fill out this form?"

"If you don't fill out the proposal," she said, "we cannot assess it at this year's academic committee meeting. Then you will have to wait until next year for your funding to be approved, and late applications are always regarded unfavourably. I suggest you fill the proposal form out and fax it back to us immediately."

"Or I will not get the funding that has already been given to me?"

"Yes."

Dekker had put the phone down and silently prayed that the person he had been speaking to would receive appropriate medical attention before she picked up the phone again.

Several more phone calls unfortunately had much the same effect. The funding should not have been approved. It had not been approved, may not be approved, would not be approved unless the academic committee approved it. The long and short of it was that he had to fill out the application, and he had tried, really he had. Questions one through one hundred fourteen had been exasperating. Questions one hundred fifteen to one hundred seventeen were the crowning glory of a fruitless exercise:

115. Outline and justify the measures you propose to ensure continued quality outcomes of your research. (Two pages of lines are provided for your answer.)
116. Describe and justify the mechanisms you propose to monitor quality assurance processes relating to your research product. (One page of lines is provided for your answer.)
117. Describe, justify, and assess the customer focus systems you are proposing to implement in connection with your project. Show how these operate synergistically with those approved by the university. (Three pages of lines are provided for your answer.)

Dekker thought seriously and then wrote:

115. Make sure I'm still alive.
116. Keep your department as far away as possible.
117. I don't want customers. Tell them to keep out.

He faxed the whole lot off two hours before the deadline, glanced out at the workmen labouring on the site, and decided to go home. It was moments like these when he really needed his wife, Jasmin, to calm him down.

Later on that same evening, Mark parked his recently acquired second-hand Toyota outside Bill and Mary's home in Engadine. Sounds of laughter came through the open windows, for most of the Bible study group was already there.

He was late, as usual, and this was not about to improve.

The week before, he had taken up his lease on a property in River Road Elderslie, an older house but comfortable, and at a reasonable rent. It was much further from Engadine to Elderslie than from Engadine to Heathcote where he had been staying, but the commute from there to the new experimental site on Burragorang Road in Camden had become impossible.

It seemed to Mark that no matter how early he left, there were always a few hundred commuters who decided to leave earlier, just to make the journey longer and the driving more difficult. He could cope with bumper-to-bumper traffic when it was crawling at a few k's, but not when it was doing one-hundred-and-ten down the freeway. Rain or shine, they travelled at the same ridiculous speed, barely a car's length in front and behind. If he opened up a gap in front, some idiot would zip into it, and if he tried to travel slower, some idiot would put his hand on the horn.

Mark clicked the doors locked on his vehicle, walked up the path, and knocked at the front door.

Bill answered it for him. "Late as usual, Mark!"

"Thanks. Been a busy day. The project is taking its toll on my sanity. I'm tired."

Bill invited him inside. "Have you eaten?"

"Not for a while," Mark confessed.

"Mary will fix you up something. Mary, can you get Mark a sandwich?"

His wife duly commissioned to provide sustenance, Bill accompanied the new arrival back to the lounge room where the group had already gathered.

There was John and his girlfriend, Katey; Alan; Cassie—without her boyfriend that night and looking a bit sad—;Sharon; Mick; David; and Angela with Ross, her husband of six months.

Mark sat down with them and opened up his Bible. "It's Luke, isn't it?"

"Chapter one, verse one. Do you have the study guide?"

"Thanks, Katey," Mark replied, "I got it in the mail last week. Good choice, John."

At this point, Mary arrived with two large sandwiches and a glass of soft drink to match. She set them on the small table near his chair with a smile. "No one minds if you eat, Mark. Go on, you seem so tired." He thanked her and began his assault on the first chicken and ham sandwich.

Bill addressed the group. "Before we start our time of study, is there anything anyone would like to share with us so we can pray during the week? Mark, how is the project going? Spare us the details, we won't understand them."

"The project is going well, but I'm having a bit of a problem with my one and only colleague."

"Van Dekker?"

"No, he's a perfect gentleman most of the time, and about the only thing that gets him annoyed is the university administration. They're enough to make any sane man annoyed. No, it's Candi, the girl who's working with me."

Sharon, whose mouth was often poorly connected to any other organ blurted out, "You're falling in love with her, is that it?"

"Not exactly." Mark paused to take a sip of his soft drink. "Professionally, we deal well together but, personally, we're poles apart. She hates Christians, probably because of some bad experiences she had with the church when she was a child, but maybe not. I find her hard to cope with."

Angela asked, "Does she keep giving you a hard time because of your faith?"

Angela was a sweet, young woman. Mark had always intended to ask her to go out with him, but somehow he never got round to it. The next thing he knew, she became engaged to Ross and, finally, married him.

Without realizing it, Mark sighed. He wondered just how much to share with his group of friends and how much to keep to himself. Answering the question, he thought, should be enough. "Not exactly. The whole topic of religion is completely verboten and, if I mention anything remotely to do with my faith, she turns into a little ball of French fury. Most of the time, she's really nice, in fact, nice and distant. On an intellectual level we gel pretty well. But, on any other, we're polite and impersonal. I try not to be, but you can't get close to someone who has put up walls, can you?"

"Do you want to get close to her?" Sharon asked. "I mean, she's an unbeliever. You have to be careful. Is she pretty?"

"She's very pretty, Sharon. She's full of life and energy, and she's clever, clever at her job and clever at reading me. I can't read her, though." Mark shook his head. "No, I don't want the sort of closeness you're hinting at. I want to be her friend, to win the right to talk to her about what matters in life. It makes me sad to see someone with so much to offer walking in the wrong direction."

"I think you should get out of there before you end up compromised."

Mark regretted bringing the subject up at all. He glanced at Sharon, completely unaware that his expression told her unequivocally there was no chance of his being compromised with her at any rate. He tried to respond in a manner he knew his Lord would approve of. "There's no possibility of leaving right now, Sharon. Before you ask why, I am under contract to see a project through. As a Christian, I have to fulfil what I have promised to do."

"What would you like us to pray for, Mark?" Bill cut into the next question that was forming on Sharon's lips.

"That I will live in such a way that helps Daniel and Candi see that God is real." He felt like adding, for Sharon's benefit, "You can pray that I will have the strength to master the overwhelming desire I have to sleep with her." But he didn't. Foolish remarks like that were broadcast news to Sharon.

They duly prayed, Mark finished his sandwiches, the Bible study went into full swing, and the clock ticked round to ten before Mary announced that supper was on and she would kick them all out in half an hour because she and Bill wanted to go to bed.

During supper, Bill took Mark aside from the others. "I apologise for Sharon's careless remarks, but I wanted to ask you bloke to bloke if you were having any other problems with this woman. Some young women are a bit uninhibited when it comes to men—always trying to get another guy into bed just so they can say they have the power."

"She's a pretty girl, Bill," Mark said. "Any man can get caught up with fantasies if he lets himself wander in that direction. No, Candi isn't trashy at all. I have no doubt her views on sex are quite different from yours and mine, but she doesn't try to snare me into her bed. Just the reverse, if you want to know. She isn't cheap like that. Pleasure is her reason for living, but not cheap pleasure. I was in her home once. You should have seen her choice of furniture, there wasn't much, but there was only the absolute best. Same with the food she eats. She would rather go without than have a poorly prepared sandwich. Yesterday, it was gourmet homemade bread from stone-milled flour, fresh avocado butter, the best ham off the bone, freshly cracked pepper, and sea salt. She washed it down with a bottle of Swiss water. She doesn't drink much, but she buys only good French wine. That sort of thing. I think she sees pleasure as the ultimate purpose in life, and she's smart enough to realise that doesn't mean throwing your life away on drugs and sex and booze. She's very self-disciplined. She begins her physical exercises at four thirty in the morning. She told me she runs around Mt. Annan until five thirty, goes home and cooks some gourmet breakfast—I think it was eggs Hollandaise yesterday—and drives to work after a shower and all the other stuff girls go through. Arrives at work groomed, coordinated and fresh as a daisy. At least the security guards appreciate it."

With a slight grin, Bill said, "I think she's more important to you than you realise, perhaps."

Mark eyed him squarely in the face. "You may be right, but I don't think so. I think you're reading my commitment to the experiment we're doing as feelings for Candi. I hope you're wrong because, let me tell you again, she wants nothing to do with Christians. Just pray for me like I asked, can you? Oh, and one other thing. I didn't get round to telling everyone because I was tired and the Candi business took up so much time, but this is probably the last Wednesday evening I will be able to make it here."

Some explanation followed, and Mark left quietly, not wanting there to be another long discussion at that time of night. Reviewing Bill's comments in his mind, he drove home carefully. Was he attracted to Candi? Not in that way. Did he like her? Yes, he did. Who wouldn't? Did she like him? No, she didn't. He just wanted her to see life from another point of view, that was all. Or at least he thought that was all.

By the end of August 1999, the main building complex had been completed: a large laboratory surrounded by a dozen rooms that were to be used for various maintenance and construction purposes. Three of these were offices, one for each of them. Mark found the short journey to Elderslie a blessing with the long hours he worked.

Dekker still commuted to Carlingford. For days on end, he would stay all night in his office and go home on the weekends. Jasmin was not happy.

The large amounts of electrical power needed for the experiment required the use of a specialised three phase switchboard. Numerous requests to the university emphasising the urgency of this installation had fallen on deaf ears, and their relationship with the purchasing department had reached an all-time low when Dekker, in complete frustration, had paid them a visit to tell them what he thought of the unacceptable delay. They replied by explaining that the equipment had to be approved by several departments, it was expensive, and a large deposit had to be paid. Dekker had complied with every request. Eight weeks had rolled past, and now the need to have the power connected was becoming critically important if they were to complete the first stage and be ready for the tests scheduled to begin in May the following year.

It was a Tuesday. Mark and Candi watched in disbelief while two electricians wired up the enormous switchboard that fed three-phase power at many amps to the outlets positioned strategically around the lab. The circuit breakers had to be specially brought in for the job, and they were not small.

The two men working on the job weren't small either. Karl looked like a typical Scandinavian, and Jem could have come from anywhere. Despite their different ethnic backgrounds, both workers obviously shared a common love of beer.

Candi was watching with what seemed casual interest when she suddenly called out to Jem, who was wiring up a breaker on top of a ladder. "You have reversed the phase connections on breaker two. If you do that, all the circuits on that phase will have reversed phase outlets. That will cause a serious problem with our experiments."

Jem peered down to see who dared question his ability to wire a switchboard and, realising the criticism had come from a young woman, contorted his face into the most patronising expression he was capable of. "Look, sweetie, who's got the licence, you or me?"

The edge to Candi's voice when she replied should have given the man cause for pause. It didn't. "You've reversed the phases on breaker two. My experiment uses two outlets. If they are not in phase, I will damage the power supply to my klystrons."

Jem leered down at her from his height on top of the ladder. No doubt, from that angle he had an excellent view of Candi's well-developed attributes and, adding lewdness to stupidity, he decided to comment on them. "Your klystrons look just fine to me. Why don't you go put them away somewhere and do what you're good at?"

With several French expletives and one mighty kick, Candi sent the bottom of the ladder sliding outwards across the floor, leaving Jem holding on to some wiring with one hand and a metal bracket with the other. His legs were kicking madly in thin air, which looked very funny indeed, though the language he was using would have made a sailor blush.

From his observation post on the other ladder, Karl watched these proceedings with a rather stunned expression on his face.

Oblivious to the racket coming from up on high, Candi walked into her office.

Attracted by the noise, Dekker came out of his to see the end of the show.

Karl had climbed down his ladder by then and was helping Mark lift the other one back up toward his stranded companion, who was informing the whole world that the cables were giving way and he was going to fall. Rescue arrived in time and Jem scrabbled for the ladder, grabbed hold, and climbed down to the floor.

The charade was not over yet. The man was still shaking with sputtering rage. "Where's the bitch?" He screamed, and seeing Candi's form through the glass in her office door, strode off toward it, intent to do murder.

Mark got to the door before him. The door opened, and Candi stood facing the angry man with her colleague in between.

Mark spoke quietly. "That's enough. You are not injured, but if you don't correct your mistake, some other people will be."

"Get out of my way!"

Mark didn't move a muscle.

Jem came closer until his face was almost touching the other man. "I said, get out of the—way!"

"Back off." Mark didn't moved an inch. His voice was calm and soft.

At that point, Karl reached the door and shouted at his mate, "Leave it, Jem. She was right. You've connected breaker two round the other way. I said leave it! Just an honest mistake, no need for everyone to get hot and bothered."

The deciding factor arrived in the form of Dekker. He walked up to Jem the Furious and spoke with a voice that would have commanded the attention of a dead cow. "Your carelessness could have cost the life of one of my staff. You deserve to be reported for negligence, as well as for sexual harassment. Get out of my sight before I phone your supervisor. Not fast enough. Start searching for another job!" He took a mobile phone out of his pocket and dialled some numbers.

With another string of expletives, Jem stormed out of the building, followed by his mate.

Mark turned round towards Candi. Her face was very white, and her eyes stared at him in a way he hadn't seen before.

Dekker was the first to break the silence. "Do you think I'm running a circus here? You could have injured the man. What were you thinking?"

Candi burst into tears. She went over to her desk and, without sitting down, scribbled a note on a piece of paper, no doubt with the express purpose of flinging it into Dekker's face on the way out. She turned round to find him laughing. Her face taking on an incredulous expression, she crumpled the paper into her fist.

Dekker continued, still chuckling to himself. "It's a pity you didn't leave him up there a bit longer. Did you see the way he was kicking his legs, and that beer belly wobbling all over the place? Serves him right. Next time just call me, would you? You put yourself in danger. I can't afford to have either of you injured. Please don't do that again."

With that, he went out the door to leave Mark and Candi alone. A fresh burst of tears followed his absence.

Mark, not knowing quite what to do, went over to her and put an arm around her shoulders. "What was the note all about?"

To answer, Candi moved away, straightened out the paper in her hand, and held it out to him. In large, angry letters it read, "I quit."

"Throw it away. You don't want to quit. It's not like you at all to let something like this get to you. Dekker was concerned about you, that's all. None of us expected you to kick the ladder out from under the idiot. I think he's the type of man who can't control his temper as well as some of us can."

She saw the smile on his face and returned it rather tearfully. "I have learned something about you today. You are a brave man, Mark. He looked as though he wanted to kill you, and you answer him so calm, so softly. You don't move away. He sees you are not afraid of him, and he stopped. I was afraid of him."

She came over to his side, wrapped her arms around him and gave him a hug, something she had never done before. "Thank you, Mark," she said.

Alone, Karl returned a half an hour later, fixed the incorrect wiring, finished the job, and left.

# CHAPTER 7

On the first of March 2000, Roger Gaunt took the unprecedented step of moving out of his luxurious apartment in Seven Hills and moving into Candi's slightly smaller and far less ostentatious home in Mt. Annan. Not that there hadn't been full and frank discussions on the subject beforehand. Roger had wanted her to move in with him, to which she replied that he had absolutely no taste in furniture and that Seven Hills made her daily commute too long. Roger had countered by saying that if she really wanted to be with him she could make sacrifices, and Candi had responded with exactly the same sentence. Roger said it was either his place or she could say good-bye to the times they spent in heaven together in the bedroom. Candi had declared that the only place she was going to heaven with him night after night was in her bed at Mt. Annan.

Roger argued his mates would think he was barking mad, and Candi had replied that they could all think what they liked. Did he want to go to heaven with her every night, or not? This last argument, crafted entirely around Roger's own desires, won the debate.

Roger, being a connoisseur of the female sex, had long since learned that this girl could take him to heaven far better and for far longer than any other woman he had ever had, and the list of comparisons wasn't small. He liked the way she made no other demands on his life; she was content to enjoy him the same way as he was content to enjoy her—with none of that messy and unnecessary commitment nonsense.

The one and only concession she had granted was allowing him to put his huge TV and VHS player against the wall in their bedroom so he could watch his replays from the convenience of their bed. She wasn't having the wretched thing in any other room in the house. It was big and ugly and thoroughly out of place.

They had celebrated their new living arrangements by dining in Camden's finest and most expensive restaurant, for Roger was not lacking in cash.

After spending quite a long time in heaven that evening on the pre-requisite bed, Candi lay with her head on the pillow next to him with her arm draped partly around his chest. It wouldn't go all the way round.

Roger began the conversation with a compliment, which was surprising. Being a man of few words, he rarely had many to spare in the praise of anyone other than himself. "Babe, you were really hot tonight. How'd ya get so good? Must have had a lot of practice."

"Like the great lover Roger Gaunt has had a lot of practice."

"Yeah, well, you live, you learn," he said with a lift of one of his shoulders. "You don't mind?"

"But no, of course I don't mind," she said, "as long as you never bring another woman into this bed, that's all."

"Make sure you're always the one who's in it, then."

She drew her arm more tightly around him. "Parfait. It is good, this life, isn't it?"

"Sure, babe, feeling good is good. Look babe, I'm really sleepy and I've got a big game coming up."

"Are you sure you don't mind coming to live in my house?" she asked.

"No, babe, you're paying for it," he yawned. "Doesn't take me long to get over to Parramatta in the Alfa. This makes it worth it."

"Bonne nuit, Roger."

"What was that?"

"Goodnight."

"You too, babe." He was asleep in less than five minutes.

Some light from the streetlamp across the road had managed to creep over the top of the curtains and was making soft moving patterns on the ceiling. Candi lay on her back and stared at them for a good half an hour, feeling less and less like sleeping at all. Men were all the same: make them happy, and they fall asleep. She wished their time in heaven would have the same effect on her. At least Roger didn't snore.

Now she felt hot, and the more she thought about it, the hotter she felt until she could stand it no more. She threw off the sheet and slipped out of bed.

After taking the bathrobe hanging on the bedroom door and draping it about her naked body, she headed for the kitchen. The refrigerator beckoned, but the wine rack called the louder.

Within a few minutes, Candi was sipping a large, crystal wine glass of Beaujolais. Perhaps it would make her sleepy.

It was quiet, so quiet.

The refrigerator gave a little shudder and stopped its regular humming. Outside, a solitary cat yowled to its mate. Perhaps it was the silence, perhaps the lateness of the hour, or perhaps it was simply her being the only conscious person in the house, but a sensation of utter loneliness seemed by slow stages to creep upon her—bringing with it the very feelings she had always sought to remove from her life—the yawning, mocking pointlessness.

One day, she would grow old. Men like Roger would opt for younger models, her body would refuse to comply with the demands she gave it, and she would be alone.

Some undefinable yet crucial element was missing from her life. In the quietness, she began to mourn its absence and wish with all her heart that she could give a name to the unwelcome void that had opened in her soul.

Another glass of wine followed on from the first.

She had felt hot before, now she felt cold. It was time to go back to bed and snuggle against Roger, who was always warm. She chastised herself for becoming so irrationally morbid. She had a fantastic lover in her bed, an exciting job, and generous parents. She was sexy and smart, a young, powerful woman.

Passing into the bedroom, she shed the bathrobe, lifted the sheet, and pressed her back against Roger's. His warmth flooded into her, yet the undefinable chill that had enveloped her heart was not so easily dispersed.

As the first light of dawn touched the sky, her thoughts had become sufficiently tired and muddled to allow her to sleep. Not for long, though.

The alarm rang, Roger woke up, and after several unsuccessful attempts to interest her in satisfying his physical desires, he got up and drove off to training—leaving Candi in the kitchen with an instant coffee and a bad headache.

She hated days that began like this. A long shower and a couple of tablets had dulled the headache, but now she was late for work.

Dekker was expecting her to go through some klystron orders with him first thing that morning, and he wasn't going to be pleased.

Such was life.

She gulped the last dregs of instant coffee, which she hated, stuffed the remains of a croissant and ham into her mouth, and headed for the front door. Forcing herself to drive within the speed limit, she arrived at work as Mark was walking out the door.

"Morning, Candi."

"Where are you off to, Mark?"

"The new field magnets have been finished. They're arriving in a few minutes. I thought I'd go outside and wait, just to make sure that the delivery goes okay. Yours came earlier—it's in the lab. Dekker is waiting for you."

"Thanks."

Dekker looked up from the paperwork flooding his desk, instantly confirming to Candi his anticipated state of mind. Being a married man who had such old-fashioned ideas about fidelity and propriety seriously reduced the number of weapons in Candi's arsenal of feminine wiles.

Very sensibly, she began with a simple apology. "I'm late. Sorry. Couldn't sleep for some reason. Not your problem. Are those crates out there our klystrons?"

Dekker regarded her for a second before replying. He was an observant man, and he correctly opted for a walking-on-eggshells approach. No doubt there were good reasons why she hadn't slept, but he really didn't want to find out what they were. Wisely circumventing the explosion that would have occurred had he chosen direct shock tactics, he motioned her to a chair and picked up a sheaf of paper. Careful to keep his voice calm and quiet, he said, "The university has sent us fifty Klystron SuperSonic active speaker arrays, one per crate, rated at five kilowatts each. Total cost, quarter of a million dollars. Steal at just five grand apiece."

Candi shot out of the chair and snatched the paper from Dekker's hand. "They've arrived? In those crates out there? Is this what you're telling me?"

"Go see for yourself," he said. "I saw the lorry arrive, but seeing as you weren't here to check the order, I let them unload them in your project space."

"What?"

"I leave you the joyous task of talking to the purchasing department. Welcome to the third degree of hell."

Candi's face clouded over with pure fury. "Give me the phone!"

"Why don't you connect them all up?" Dekker replied. "Speak into the microphone, and the purchasing department will hear you from here. Tell the rest of Camden while you're at it. Very instructive for them."

He thought she was going to throw the phone at him, and prepared to initiate defensive measures.

Candi, barely controlling herself in the presence of her kindly supervisor, managed to dial the number. It took all of ten minutes on hold to get the purchasing officer to pick up at the other end. After that, the conversation began in an impressively direct manner.

"Leblanc here," Candi said. "What imbecile cannot tell the difference between vacuum tubes and the amplifiers for rock bands?"

"I am being very sorry, but could you be telling me the order number on the requisition that you are referring to?" His accent was so thick and heavy Candi had a great deal of trouble understanding him at all.

She snatched up the paper Dekker had been holding, turned it the right way up and quoted a number on the top.

"But I am begging your pardon," the thick voice replied, "that is the number of the delivery docket form. So your delivery has been arriving this morning, and you are wanting to clear it through payment?"

"No! You have sent the wrong material!"

"Then can you be telling me as I have been asking before several times the number of the order you claim has been sent to the wrong address?"

Candi turned to Dekker. "Daniel, have you got the order number there?"

"They haven't sent me one yet," he answered. "I put the request on a A-Ninety form, which covers all equipment coming from the grant I'm not supposed to have received yet and someone else wrote out the order."

"We don't have the order number. You do." Candi barked into the phone.

"Then how is it that you be knowing you have the wrong equipment? You should refer to the person who wrote out the order. Who was it?"

Candi replied, barely in control of her temper. "I have no idea who it was—hold on. Grant number USS one nine eight sixty-five a a z sixteen slash three."

"Please hold." Ten minutes later, the man picked up the phone again. "Hello, that grant has not been approved yet. It is waiting on the clarification of some details on your ARF form."

"ARF? What is this ARF?" she asked. "Are you a complete imbecile?"

"Academic Research Funding form. Yours has not been approved."

"Then why have you dumped enough sound gear for a U2 concert on the floor of my lab?"

"It is because you have been ordering it," he answered in a matter of fact manner. "I am now telling you that if you are using this department's funds for conducting your own rocking concerts, you will be facing prosecution."

Candi, resorting to her native language, screamed several no doubt descriptive phrases down the phone at a level that would have rivalled the output from a Klystron SuperSonic at full power. The phone cord came out of the wall as the instrument flew across the room.

At that point, Dekker, watching Candi's flaming face, thought he had better intervene. Her punishment was becoming greater than she could bear. He had waited too long, though, because without uttering a single word the woman marched out of the office as though she were going to commit murder. If Dekker had known her better, he would have raced after her with tranquiliser darts, but he didn't. He turned back to his computer and began to compose a letter to the manager of accounts on the subject of incompetent staff.

A short time later, Patty Greenwood picked up the phone in the customer service section of the purchasing department and answered the friendly female voice on the other end of it. "Hello, that's nice of you, I hope you're having a nice day, too. No, that would be Mr. Muthy. He's not in right now. No, I don't know exactly where he is, but he usually goes out into the courtyard for a smoke about now. He should be back in his office in about ten minutes. Well, it was nice talking to you, too."

Several hours later, with nothing but disconcerting silence from Candi, Dekker left his office in search of more information.

A palette of three Klystron SuperSonics had vanished. But why had only one palette disappeared? He walked to the entrance of the lab to see if there was a truck in the process of loading the rest, only to find the loading bay empty of all but a single forklift in the corner of the yard.

Dekker went to find Mark at the other end of the lab supervising the small crew of engineers in positioning the new fields onto their hydraulic runners. "Have you seen Candi?"

"Err, not recently," Mark said. "She was here this morning. I saw her come in."

"Well she's gone off somewhere leaving me with a whole pile of high-power speaker systems cluttering up the lab."

"Is that what those things are? Who ordered th—"

"Don't start," Dekker warned. "If you see the woman, tell her to come and see me."

While passing Candi's office on the way back, he peered through the glass panel in the door, and there she was, working at her desk as though nothing in the world had happened, calm and composed. Dekker flung the door open and strode in. "When did you get back here?"

"But, Daniel, I've been here all morning working on the klystron amplifier designs."

"Like hell you have. What's going on?"

"Going on?" she replied innocently. "I don't understand."

"What have you done about the rubbish out in the lab?"

"The speakers?" she asked. "I'm sure someone will realise they have made the mistake and take them away. There is no need for you to worry or stress yourself."

"Am I going mad, or is everyone else?" Dekker muttered loudly.

"Daniel, you need to have the lunch. Would you like to go out with Candi? There is a nice café in Camden..."

In place of an answer, Dekker strode out of the room into his own office and slammed the door.

The sky had darkened, and it wasn't long before Dekker heard the soothing patter on the galvanised steel roof of the laboratory followed by the refreshing aroma of rain.

He enjoyed the sound of rain on the roof. He had an alarm clock by his bed that played him to sleep with a small library of similar sounds: rain on a roof, rain falling in a stream, or a gentle sea washing on the shore. He would listen to them as he drifted off to sleep—absorbing the ambience secure in the knowledge that he wasn't going to get wet.

The soothing sound became softer and softer over the next hour, but it had done its work—leaving Dekker more or less relaxed as the afternoon drew toward its close.

The phone rang.

"Is that Professor Van Dekker? Bates of main campus security here. We are making some routine enquiries about an incident. Is it true that you were sent a whole lot of speaker systems by mistake this morning?"

"Yes," Dekker said, "and it was by mistake, let me tell you. We didn't order them."

"I think that's pretty clear, Professor. Can you give us any idea how three of them ended up restricting the movements of an officer on our campus?"

"Just what nonsense is this?"

The security officer explained, "It appears that the senior purchasing officer, a Mr. Muthy, was chased around the courtyard of the administration building by a security officer driving a forklift loaded with three of your speaker units."

"I beg your pardon?"

"Apparently this went on for some time until the driver of the forklift managed to herd him into a corner and wall him in with them," the security office continued. "He couldn't get out, and it was several hours before he was able to attract the attention of other staff. Unfortunately, it rained during the afternoon, and Mr. Muthy was in a rather bedraggled and agitated condition when they found him. It seems the gentleman is somewhat claustrophobic, and the combined effect of being squashed in a corner and rained on precipitated a nervous breakdown. He rushed at the security officer who was supervising the removal of the crates and tried to strangle him. Very unfortunate. Mr. Muthy had to be sedated and taken to hospital."

"Do you have a description of the person responsible?"

"Unfortunately, no," the security officer answered. "Mr. Muthy didn't see his face because it was hidden behind all the crates and he was too occupied with trying to avoid pursuit. The gentleman is rather overweight. The customer service staff are not being all that cooperative in the investigation. Do you have any forklifts missing?"

"No," Dekker said. "My staff have been here all morning. I noticed a palette of three units had been removed several hours ago and assumed the purchasing department was in the process of retrieving them after we had alerted them to their error."

"Well, thank you, Professor. I believe someone is going to take the rest of the units back to the store for reprocessing."

"As long as they don't come back here. Give Mr. Muthy my regards." Dekker rang off.

He thought for awhile before going back to Candi's office. "I think I will take you up on that offer for coffee. Oh, by the way, you don't happen to have a forklift licence, do you?"

Candi smiled at him with wide, innocent eyes. "We all had them at power engineering. So much heavy equipment to move around, and Professor Williams was always having the trouble with the forklift operators. He made us do the course. Do you have something you want me to move?"

"No. Are you going to drive me to Camden?"

"Daniel, of course I am!" she said. "Come on! Would Mark like to come too?"

Half an hour later, the three were sitting at the Back Alley Café.

Dekker looked across at Candi and smiled. Candi opened her big, brown eyes wide and smiled back. It was a moment of complete understanding.

# Chapter 8

The actual klystrons arrived by special courier two weeks later. Candi checked every crate.

Even without the klystrons, the two weeks had been filled with activity.

Near the entrance of the lab, on the left-hand side of their offices, an impressive, high-voltage power supply and some very large high-voltage capacitors had been enclosed in a wire cage that extended a long way towards the roof. On one side of the cage, the microwave generators and switching unit would be located, and the output waveguide would be loaded on the opposite side. The waveguide would eventually transport the huge pulses of energy into Dekker's double-layer magnetic field apparatus, which was being built closer to the collision tube, now surrounded by Mark's huge, new field magnets sitting on their hydraulic trolley.

On the far right side of their offices, further down the lab, was the high-current power supply that would feed the magnets themselves. It hadn't been coupled up yet.

On the other side of the lab, opposite their offices, was the cryostat and pumping units to cool the magnet down to one Kelvin, or negative two hundred and seventy two degrees centigrade.

The team of engineers, mechanics, and fitters had worked well together, and Dekker wished they could remain employed for the duration of the project because they would surely be needed to build the mirror image of the apparatus if the first experiments were successful.

Once the klystrons had arrived, Candi supervised the construction of the pulse unit. There was a lot of metalwork involved, a lot of calculations to do, and a lot to assemble.

Candi was meticulous; each component was triple checked for size, finish, welding, and anything else that would have affected its performance.

Mark, observing this process from a distance, found himself admiring her genius with a twinge of jealousy. She was building something entirely new; he was simply assembling components that were the product of someone else's genius, and not of his own.

Little by little, the pulse unit neared completion. The output from the whole array was fed into a complex set of waveguides, culminating in the long waveguide that would transmit power into Dekker's accelerator. The latter was slowly taking shape, but its construction was a much simpler affair, based around some clever arrangement of magnetic fields provided by some run-of-the-mill superconductors.

The tricky bit was the coupling of the microwave energy in such a way that the ions in the accelerator would surf down the microwaves in the tube without spreading the energy unhelpfully throughout the lab, flash frying whatever or whoever was in the vicinity. Dekker relied on Candi's genius to keep that from happening. The two would spend long hours together scribbling on the white board in his office. A growing sense of unease replaced Candi's usually vivacious confidence.

A very private person, Dekker was almost obsessive when it came to the project. He rarely discussed anything else. It never even occurred to him to spend time getting to know his colleagues personally. The project was both the beginning and end of their common world.

When he was not part of that world, he was part of his wife's. In Jasmin's lovely company, Dekker was completely content. He wished he could spend more time with the woman he adored, especially when he was forced to remain at work until the small hours of the night.

On those occasions, Dekker would take the evening meal Jasmin had prepared for him out of the fridge and stare at it for a second or two before ringing her. "Jasmin, my darling, my dinner was delicious."

"You haven't started it, have you?"

"How did you know?" he would ask.

"Because you always ring me as soon as you look at it," she would say with a smile in her voice. "It's all right, Daniel. I know you hate being apart from me in the evening. The project is important."

"It's not because I'm trying to be a great physicist."

"It's because you're burdened by what happened to AINR. I know, Daniel. I understand."

"Bless you, Jasmin," he would say. "I'm sorry … I feel I have to re-dress the balance, and I'm not sure we will succeed, even with this. You know I love you very much?"

"Of course I do. When you come home tomorrow night I'll have something special for you to look forward to."

"Bless you, my darling."

Sometimes their conversation would continue for the best part of an hour. Dekker would put the phone down with regret and go to heat up his dinner. Then he would go back to work and eventually retire to an inflatable mattress in the back of his office, feeling bereft of her presence until he went to sleep.

Candi's world extended only to the moment in which she lived. Provided she was able to maintain denial of any life outside this tiny margin, she was completely content.

Roger provided her pleasure at night, the project provided her pleasure during the day.

In this context, Dekker was important because it was his project. She enjoyed the mental challenge he presented to her, and she relished supervising her team of engineers—obedient servants to her personal creation. Within these constraints she was grateful, hardworking, friendly and distant. Dekker's world and hers had intersected, and she was content to live within the boundaries of the intersection, not be-yond them.

On the other hand, Mark troubled her, because he refused to inter-sect at all with her moment-by-moment life. Indeed, just by his presence, he seemed to threaten its existence, shaking its boundaries with notions of accountability, severing it from its isolation, and placing it in the terrifying stream of time that yawned from eternity to eternity. Fear of facing any sort of eternity, anything to do with purpose or reason for existence, anything hinting of divine retribution made her passionately angry for reasons she had never had the slightest desire to explore.

So Mark remained on the periphery of her vision. She treated him with collegiate respect and friendliness devoid of personal connection. There could never be a peaceful intersection of her world and his. The result would be a supernova in which her world would be destroyed.

Why did she feel her defences inadequate against such an unspoken threat?

She had tried—unwittingly, at first—to destroy his archaic prudery, and then to deliberately mock his narrow-minded attitudes in general, all without success. In fact, the less he seemed to respond, the more she found herself compelled to push against his boundaries—not for any other motive than the sheer relief of seeing them fall. Somehow she managed to convince herself that if they did it would prove his entire worldview was founded on nothing more than fear and thin air.

Trouble with the construction engineers began with the last component in the great Candi construction, the waveguide that would transmit all the power to the accelerator. They had done their best to comply with her detailed specifications and had delivered the item on time, only to have it rejected. The inner surfaces were not polished to her satisfaction, and the whole construction was two millimetres short of the specified length.

That was not acceptable.

There was a weld halfway along that Candi could still feel when she ran her fingers over its surface. She had demanded that the engineers show her images of the inside of the tube, taken every centimetre by a special camera worth a lot of money.

The engineers had argued that her standards were simply beyond their engineering capabilities—beyond any engineering capabilities on the planet. Candi had told them to do better and lost her temper.

Dekker would not take part on any side of the argument, so the only other potential ally was Mark. To seek shelter or solace from him went against every notion of self-protection Candi possessed.

The situation was taken out of her hands one morning as she was sitting on part of the klystron cage, watching a team of furious engineers retreating on the tide of her wrath, the latest rejected waveguide carried between them.

Most unexpectedly, Mark came out of nowhere and sat down beside her. He was way too close.

Candi stood up and turned round to face him. Now she was looking down at him, and somehow this superior position made her lower her defences enough to begin the conversation. "How's the magnet going?"

"It will be okay when I connect the bus bars up," he said. "They need cooling as well, and the Freon pumps haven't arrived yet. How's the klystron project?"

"Don't you have eyes in your head?"

Mark smiled to himself. Even if he had been as blind as a bat, he could have scarcely missed the recent slanging match with the engineers conducted at full volume, even if he didn't understand some of the French phrases that had crept in towards the bitter end of it. It wasn't her temper that had alarmed him. It was the way the optimistic creature normally living in her skin was slowly yet surely being replaced by an angry one whose degree of annoyance appeared to be deepening by the day.

Perhaps he could help, though from the expression on Candi's face he doubted it. "What's getting to you?" he asked.

"What do you think is getting to me? What do you think I'm trying to do here? Keep these fools of engineers amused? Why can't they follow simple directions?"

"I think you may be exceeding the limits of their ability," he replied. "One of them told me you rejected that waveguide because it was a millimetre too short. Is that right?"

Candi exploded. "I write down it has to be a certain length. They make one that is shorter. I tell them. They complain. Why do they do that?"

Mark tried not to seem patronising. "The whole thing is metres long. I guess all they have to do is to wait until a warmer day and get you to measure it again. It will expand more than that with every degree rise in temperature."

"You're so clever—and so stupid!" she yelled. "The guide is made from INVAR alloy that doesn't expand with temperature. Why don't you go back, play with your magnets, and leave me alone?"

"You're worried about the power transfer, aren't you?"

If he had said anything else, Candi would have walked away—no doubt with a few extra comments just to make sure Mark would never think to venture into her personal world again. At least she would have been in control. But now, her control had evaporated, and leaving was no longer an option. She stared at Mark like a hamster owner whose pet had just soiled his best carpet. "Imbecile! Do you know what happens if I make the small mistake? If the waveguide is not perfect?"

She grabbed Mark by the arm, dragged him to his feet, and pulled him along towards the control panel next to the cage. "You see this? This button? I press this and you die, Dekker dies!"

Her hands were gripping him by the shoulders, shaking him backward and forward. "If there is the tiniest flaw, the slightest imperfection, I turn you into a vegetable, and you cannot even pee when you want to. There are people to carry you, feed you, and despise you for the rest of your life. Are you listening? Yet you look at Candi and tell her she is stupid for making trouble!"

Her distress should have prompted a soothing reply. Yet, Mark often sensed Candi cared less about him as a person than she did about the colour of her handbag. Also, he didn't like been shaken by a shouting female. For those reasons, he replied in a manner more angry than calculated to calm. "What about the one who pushes the button? You left yourself off the list of casualties. I take it this horrible fate includes you. The real problem is you're frightened of doing these things to yourself. Why not admit it?"

He was rather sorry he had spoken, because the arms that were shaking him pushed him backward with such force he almost landed on the floor.

When he had recovered his balance, Candi was standing a short distance away. Everything about her, from the defiant lift of her chin, to the tears trickling silently down her face, from her arms rigid down her sides to her hands clenching and unclenching into fists said "keep away or you die."

It wasn't as though Mark was completely insensitive to body language—as though he couldn't read the message Candi was sending to all the world around. Yet for some reason, he found himself deliberately re-entering the danger zone until he was close by her side. He wrapped his arms around her, holding her until her head was on his shoulder and rubbing her back with his hand.

Her body felt like a tree trunk—hard and unbending. All of a sudden, it softened and he felt Candi's arms around him—holding him tightly against her. Now she was crying in earnest, the sound muffled by his dampening shoulder.

"Candi, that was very callous of me," he said. "It's all right to be afraid. I'm glad you care enough to make sure the waveguide is perfect before you power the monster up. Why don't you tell the engineers what you've just told me? I'm sure they would appreciate someone who cares about those around her."

He kept holding her and rubbing her back.

Dekker had come up behind, drawn by the unfamiliar sounds. Seeing that matters were apparently under control, he gave Mark a nod and went back into his office.

Repeating his words, Mark spoke gently into the mass of hair on his shoulder. "Candi, its all right to be afraid. I'm sorry for my careless words. I never expected you to care about me at all, and I suppose I rather wished you did. I apologise."

It was a long time before Candi said anything. Little by little, the crying stopped, although she didn't try to get out of his arms. Mark kept rubbing her back, wondering what was coming next. Eventually, he felt her arms release him, so he stepped away a little.

Candi looked up into his face, and for the second time since they had met, he had the feeling that she was seeing him as a human being—not just another cog in the team.

"You apologise?" she asked. "I am the one who was shouting, and yet you apologise. You were right, Mark, and Candi is ashamed to tell you. I only think of the girl behind the button, no one else. I say to myself, get this wrong, and this is what will happen. I turn myself into a useless nothing, alive and not alive. I see pictures of people forcing tubes into me because I cannot pee or even use my bowels, of being left alone and silent in bed all day. No one comes to see me. I am alone and forgotten. I am not loved any more. I can feel no pleasure. Pain in the heart is all that is left. No one cares about me for the rest of my life. I want so badly to die, but I cannot even end my existence. For me this is the hell, Mark, and I am terrified of it. Now you see me for what I am. Why are you still standing there? This is how I think. Don't you despise me?"

He never knew what prompted him to do it, but reaching out, he folded his arms around her shoulders again, drawing her into them. When she was close enough, he lowered his head and buried a kiss in her neck, trying to make her understand that he understood and had not rejected her. He felt her arms tighten around his shoulders again. Then she stepped back—looking intensely into his face with an expression that was difficult to fathom. It could have been surprise or gratitude or a complete lack of understanding, or a mixture of all three.

After what seemed a long time, Candi reached out her hand and touched his cheek softly. "Thank you, Mark."

With those words, she turned and went into her office, quietly closed the door. For just a moment in time, the world of Mark Chambers had shaken the world of Candice Leblanc.

Supernova or not, she had been powerless to prevent it.

# CHAPTER 9

Dekker left the lab that afternoon with mixed feelings.

Candi was showing signs of stress. Mark was steady, but considering he had fewer problems to solve, that was not too surprising. What was shocking had been the way he had stepped into Candi's personal space, and even more amazing was that she had allowed him to come there.

The last thing Dekker wanted was a couple of colleagues in love. Romance affected performance and vigilance. It turned the brightest people into irrational bunglers.

He smiled to himself because he had experienced exactly the same phenomenon when he had fallen in love with Jasmin during the final year of his doctorate. Everything had turned upside down, and his supervisor had almost torn his hair out trying to return him to rationality.

Had it been worth the long hours spent recovering his scattered research in the mornings after evenings spent with her? Yes, it had. Even if his thesis had been rejected, it was worth it.

Why should he be anxious about the behaviour of his colleagues when he had followed the same path?

Upon thought, Dekker concluded this was different. He could perhaps identify with Mark, but not with Candi. No, she was as different from Jasmin as night was from day.

That was it—Dekker was concerned Mark would end up being destroyed. If that happened, the project would not go well, and a great deal hung on its success. If he had actually been able to see inside the mind of that worthy young man he would not have worried.

He couldn't, so he did.

It had been a long and wearisome drive because the main roads department had been doing work on the freeway. In peak hours, it turned the highway into a long two-car wide parking lot. To make matters worse, some vehicle, not taking too well to the stop-and-go conditions, had decided it was simply not going to go at all—reducing the parking lot to one car in width.

Dekker observed that such situations served as true windows to the human condition—selfish, ruthless, careless. One driver had taken matters into his own hands and cleverly decided to drive up the shoulder on the left, a flanking manoeuvrer that had worked well until he came upon another broken-down car blocking his path.

No one likes to have another vehicle making progress when they are making none, so being the kind and thoughtful people they were, they all bunched up to prevent the interloper from getting back into the stream. After a while his patience had run out, and he had barged his way back in. Unfortunately, he cut across the path of a particularly huge four-wheel drive whose driver was either not paying attention or simply intent on keeping him out. Accident number two—followed by an entertaining punch-up, which blocked the one remaining lane until other drivers got out and threatened the antagonists back into their vehicles to negotiate.

Dekker drove into his garage a good hour later than he had intended to and got out of the car to find Jasmin by his side, her arms wrapped around him and her soft voice in his ear.

"I was worried," she murmured. "Can you phone me next time?"

"I'm so sorry, darling. It's been a very bad drive. No excuse. Is dinner ruined? If it is, can I make up for it by taking you out? There is a nice restaurant in Pennant Hills, not far. Would you like that?"

She kissed him, her arms still round his shoulders, and he kissed her back, speaking softly against her cheek. "It is so good to be back. Coming home to you is the best thing I've done all day."

"The project is not going well?"

"Well enough. There was an altercation with Candi and the engineers today. The woman is losing her self-confidence. I would never have thought it possible."

"She's a lot of trouble, that one," Jasmin said. "Unpredictable, bad temper, and selfish to a fault."

"She's also very clever and completely essential to the project," he said. "Something interesting happened today. She got upset and allowed Mark to comfort her. Most unexpected."

"She doesn't get along with him, does she?"

"Our Mark is a Christian like you, Jasmin, and Candi can't stand them. He doesn't think much of her sexual ethics, either, and I have the distinct impression that he knows more about them than I ever want to. He's a caring man, Mark—it goes along with his Christianity. I think his faith could have sponsored the incident that ended up with him calming her down. I don't want him to get seduced by a woman like her. Did I mention that she's got an attractive manner about her?"

"You might have said it once or twice. Do you find her attractive?"

Dekker smiled at her and tightened his embrace. "Not in the least, my love. She's typical of the young things who live by their feelings, who live for what gives them the most … enjoyment, kick, that sort of thing. Not my style at all. I think people like her are rather shallow. Right at the beginning, I asked her why she wanted to join our little team, and she said it was because she thought it would be fun. My only concern is that when it's no longer fun, she'll up and leave—and she would be hard to replace. What have you been conjuring up for dinner?"

Jasmin smiled at him, ran her hands through his hair, pulled his head close, and gave him a long, passionate kiss. "It's a salad with curried cold chicken."

"I love your cold curries! What's for desert?"

"A glass of Marlborough Sauvignon Blanc, some Edam, and me."

"Perfect!" He lifted her up into his arms and carried her, laughing, into the dining room.

On the end of the table was a pile of mail. Dekker surveyed it quickly while Jasmin went into the kitchen to bring in their meal.

Quietly, he opened a packet, examined the contents, and placed a small item in his pocket.

The meal proceeded with enjoyable conversation and laughter. Two candles burned on the table as they always did for the evening meal. While Jasmin was fetching the Edam and wine, he rose from the table and turned off the lights. Then there was only candlelight. It sparkled in Jasmin's deep brown eyes across the table while she poured the yellow liquid, made richer in the flickering yellow light.

Dekker raised his glass towards her. "To you, my dark-eyed beauty. Long and many be the years my eyes behold you."

She smiled at him and reached out to clink her glass against his. "Long and many be the years you hold me in your arms, Daniel my love. Are you ready for the rest of your dessert?"

"Indeed, but what's this? Your anniversary ring is missing from your hand. It usually sparkles in the candlelight."

Jasmin's face clouded. It had been over a month since she had worn her ring, and each day she had prayed Daniel would not notice. She had come back from shopping in the city and discovered its absence, cried for an hour or so, and tried to think of ways in which she could hide her naked finger from the man who had knelt down beside her in a very expensive restaurant and placed the beautiful anniversary ring on it. Fortunately, her husband seemed not to notice at all, for which she was extremely grateful.

On this particular night, she had been too careless. What an awful time for the truth to finally emerge. She felt tears welling up in her eyes and was about to confess all … but what was this? Daniel was by her side kneeling, and in his hand was the ring she had lost.

"My love, in memory of so many years spent in the joy of your companionship. So lucky am I that I get the chance to give this to you twice."

She felt, rather than saw, for her vision had gone very blurry, the ring slip back into its home on her finger, and she threw her arms around the man who put it there. "Daniel, you found it! How did you know?"

"No, my love. I knew you had lost it, I've known for weeks, so I wrote the jeweller in Utrecht where I bought the first one. He remembered it and sent this copy. It arrived this afternoon, at just the perfect time for me to give it back to you."

"Oh, Daniel!"

He felt her body, warm and eager against him, her arms around his neck, and her lips kissing him all over his face. Picking her up carefully in his arms, he carried her tenderly to the place where they would celebrate their joyful dessert.

Candi arrived home in a subdued mood. She noticed Rogers's Alfa in the driveway, and parked her Corolla in the street. She had told him countless times to park in the garage so she could occupy the drive. Not once had he taken any notice.

She let herself in with her own key, not bothering to knock. Hearing no sounds from the bedroom, she walked straight through to the kitchen.

Roger was finishing off a large pizza. "Hi, babe. You're bloody late. What kept you?"

"And hello to you too, Roger."

Roger grunted in reply, glanced at his watch, and, taking the last piece of pizza in his hand, headed off for the bedroom. "There's a broadcast of the semi-finals from New Zealand on in a few minutes. After that, wanna go to heaven?"

"What have you brought me to eat?"

"Pizza, but you missed it. Doesn't take long to get another one in Narellan. Have to go. Get a shower before we start, will you? You're a bit off." Without another word, he left the room.

Candi felt hungry. Surveying the contents of the pantry, she decided there was enough to make a soufflé, and set to work while sounds of the match filtered down the hall. At least Roger hadn't depleted the contents of the refrigerator. If it wasn't prepared food, he never touched it. A couple of eggs found their way into the mixture, and soon the whole concoction was baking in the oven.

Candi sat down to read the mail. The only letter addressed to her was an electricity bill. She threw it on top of the pile belonging to other creditors and opened a bottle of wine, a Hunter Valley Shiraz, which she had taken a particular liking to. The soufflé would take a little more time in the oven, so what better opportunity to enjoy the excellence of the vine? Going over to the refrigerator, Candi produced a small jar of olives, a triple cream Brie, some biscuits, and a tub of paté. Those would serve as an appetiser. Ten minutes and another glass of red later, the souf-flé was perfect.

She toyed with the idea of seeing if Roger would like a helping, but then decided not to ask him and sat down to enjoy her meal at the kitchen table by herself.

There was no point in heading toward the bedroom while the semi-final was still in progress, so she went over to the bench, picked up the novel she had been reading, and returned to the table—wishing the sounds from the bedroom would come to an end.

The novel was rather engrossing, so she didn't even notice when Roger turned the television off. Minutes later, he appeared in the door-way. "You want it babe, or don't you? Gotta get up early tomorrow, so if you want to go to heaven it's gotta be now. You had a shower yet?"

"No, I've just finished dinner all by myself. I will go and have a shower now."

"Can't wait that long, babe. Come on, get your gear off." With that romantic remark, he picked her up bodily over his shoulder and carried her head down along the hall. She might be a bit on the nose, but then a guy had to compromise.

Halfway to the bedroom, the load over his shoulder reached out her arms and ran her hands over his back and down his thighs in a most tantalising manner. "Roger, why don't we begin our trip to heaven in the shower, the two of us? It is nice when our bodies are all wet. Candi can show you how it works."

Roger, whose body was always willing to try something new, carried her directly into the bathroom.

Mark arrived at his home in River Road, threw his bag into the study, a pan on the stove, and a steak in the pan. A couple of potatoes landed in the microwave—suitably scored to avoid explosion—and some beans found their way into hot water on the stove. In less than ten minutes, he had a meal on the table, and he sat down to eat it feeling rather tired.

He was not the sort of man who was easily given to feeling lonely, but that evening he found himself wishing there was someone else around his table sharing his meal with him. He thought of Candi and wondered if she was alone, too.

His thoughts then turned to Dekker and the wife he never spoke to anyone about. Were they happy? He could hardly imagine Dekker with a wife, and smiled to himself. What would she see in him? A man whose only thought was for his physics, who saw all of life in relation to it. How can you look at a woman in terms of only mass, length, and time? "My dear, the airflow around your surfaces may be laminar, but your rotational inertia is just a trifle high." She would have be a very special woman, and he would really like to meet her.

If Dekker could get married, then there was hope for geeks like him. But how would he ever meet the right woman?

Mark missed the people in his old Bible study group, and Angela in particular. He didn't hear much from her since her marriage to Ross, but then, that was perfectly right and completely understandable.

He wouldn't have missed them so much if he had been in any way successful at joining a group in his new church at Camden, St. Luke's. He had tried, really, he had tried. He found, in a remarkably short time, that the only people deemed acceptable were those whose families had lived in Camden for the last hundred years, or who had at least grown up as toddlers crawling around the pews and going through the Sunday School.

There were few people his age, and all of them were married. The single people went to a service in the evening. They were all younger, mostly teenagers who kept very much to themselves and treated an outsider as though he were completely invisible.

The attractive young women were paired up with the young men. Those not so fortunate gathered together in groups and giggled softly through the service while pointing to various individuals in the pews in front of them.

The young preacher was full of enthusiasm, which was encouraging, but each time he shook Mark's hand he couldn't remember his name. The conversation often went the same way.

First there was the wringing handshake, the big smile, and then he would say, 'It's so nice to see you, err …"

"Mark."

"It's so nice to see you Mark. Have you been before?"

"Yes, last week."

"Oh, that's right, you're working with Sally in the council, aren't you?"

"No, I'm working with the university on a physics project."

"Oh, one of those clever academic people. Physics was never my forte, I'm afraid. Oh Madeline, could you go and see if ... I'm sorry, have to go and see John. Why don't you fill out a membership card? There's one on the table over there."

He'd filled out three, and no one had made the slightest effort to contact him.

Abandoning his attempts to be accepted among the young, he had gone along to the family service in the mornings. No one made any effort to welcome him, but then, no one made the slightest attempt to reject him either. The preaching was good, the singing uplifting on the whole, and he enjoyed chatting to people over the cup of instant coffee afterward, even if they could never remember his name. He often thought of introducing himself by a new one each week, just to see if they would ever become confused, but he decided they wouldn't notice.

Then he had met Andrew.

On this particular morning, most of the crowd had dispersed early because there had been some misunderstanding as to who was bringing morning tea, with the result being that there wasn't any. The enthusiastic fellowship that erupted after each service might have been the result of the great preaching and the uplifting singing, but it was short lived without food.

One other arrangement had gone haywire as well. The task of transporting the man in the wheelchair from his present place in the foyer to his home had been left, as is often the case, to that greatest of all procrastinators, someone else.

The crowd dwindled until just the two of them remained. Andrew was an older man, Mark judged, somewhere in his late fifties, and his hair—or what was left of it—was completely grey and a little tufty around the ears. He had bushy, eyebrows above light brown eyes, an angular nose, and a large mouth curled up at the edges in a small but perpetual smile. He wore a blue woollen jumper that told all the world he valued nostalgia over appearance, a pair of neat black trousers, which, in contrast to the jumper, were immaculately tailored, and shoes to match. His arms were strong and muscular, no doubt toned from manoeuvring the wheelchair, which was one of those types with the wheels angled in slightly at the top and equipped with stainless steel grips around the edge so that each could be turned by hand.

*"There's nothing fragile about him,"* Mark thought to himself. *"I bet he could go really fast in that thing."*

As if he had read Mark's thoughts, the stranger put down the brochure he had been flicking through, and with one spin of the wheels brought the chair from the other side of the foyer to the periphery of Mark's personal space. The smile on his face broadened into a greeting. "You're Mark Chambers, aren't you?"

It surprised Mark to no end that someone to whom he had never been introduced would actually know his name.

The surprise must have shown in his face, because the older man laughed and held out a large hand. "Andrew Callan. Heard you speaking to our young rector a few of Sundays ago. Have a good memory for names."

"That's rather unusual around here." He reached out and took the proffered hand, and found his own in a vice-like grip. "Pleased to meet you, Andrew. I was wondering how you were getting home. Do you wheel yourself?"

"To Tahmoor? No. Bit too far. Usually one of the ladies takes me, the same one who was meant to be bringing morning tea. I'm not above asking for a lift if you have a car big enough to put the chair in the back. It folds up pretty well."

So Mark found himself heading out towards Tahmoor with Andrew's chair in the back and enjoying the first real conversation he had had with anyone from the church since he had begun to attend.

They were not yet halfway to their destination when Mark learned about the car accident that had taken the life of Andrew's beloved Suzie and left him alone in the world. All of a sudden the pain he had felt when his own parents had died the same way surfaced in his heart as it hadn't done for many years. Staring ahead at the road, Mark concentrated on his driving and hoped his passenger would not notice the tears in the corners of his eyes. He could imagine Andrew would be naturally nervous at being in a car, especially driven by a stranger whose vision of the road had become a little blurry.

The older man sighed. "I miss her, you know. Selfish in a way, she's having a wonderful time in heaven with her Lord, and, well, I feel a little jealous at times. She knitted this jumper for my birthday just before it happened. I'm always wearing it—you can probably tell, can't you? One of the reasons I don't like summer is I have to take it off. You must think me rather strange."

There was quite a pause before Mark trusted his voice enough to reply. "I really don't. My parents died in a car accident when I was eighteen."

He couldn't say much more, yet those few words marked the beginning of a close friendship that the two men had both, unknown to each other, desired for years. Half an hour later, they arrived at Andrew's pleasant-looking home, set well back from the road among a small forest of liquid amber trees, and the sun, streaming through their bare branches, cast warm shadows on the sandy brickwork of the high gabled house.

"You will stay for a cup of coffee—or something."

It wasn't a question; Mark would not have refused if it had been. He lifted the chair out of the back, managed to unfold it, and wheeled it around to the passenger door, surprised to find it already open and Andrew standing on the ground supporting himself with one arm on the roof of the car.

"I can stand up, you see," Andrew said. "Not for long. I can even walk a tiny bit, but it's very tiring. Thank God I can, otherwise I would have to have someone living with me all the time."

"I'm sorry." Mark could think of nothing more to say.

"I manage, let me tell you. The garden gets the rough end of it, but inside I keep house quite well. We have to go round the side up the ramp. Come on, Mark. There's no need to push me."

An hour later, the two men emerged on the back veranda, Andrew carrying a couple of beers in his lap and Mark a large plate of turkey and camembert sandwiches liberally spread with cranberry sauce. Andrew transferred himself from the wheelchair to a chaise lounge, and Mark sat on another comfortable chair beside the slatted table, and so began the most pleasant afternoon he could remember for ages.

He learned how Andrew and Suzie had both been chemical engineers. They had begun going out together during their honours year at the University of New South Wales, and they had married as soon as Andrew had become research engineer at a large chemical company.

Andrew asked a lot of very intelligent questions about the project Mark was involved in. He had an uncanny knack of filling in the details that Mark, in an effort to be discreet, had carefully left out. "So, you're doing research with super-energy collisions. Doesn't that make you a little nervous?"

"Not really," Mark answered. "There's pretty well zero chance we will see anything anyway. No one else has—and they have been using much larger accelerators than we're building up the road."

"I think I would be a little fearful if I were in your shoes," Andrew said cautiously. "Those sort of energies are not commonplace, even in particle physics, if my reading isn't all that out of date."

Mark steered the conversation in another direction by introducing the subject of Candi and her dealings with certain electricians and purchasing staff, which managed to make Andrew laugh. They talked on and on until the sun had almost set, the bare branches of the liquid ambers this time casting long, dark shadows across the veranda. Eventually, the two men parted as newfound friends. Mark offered to potter around doing odd jobs in the garden. Andrew promised to give him a call during the week to see how the project was going.

Returning from his reverie, Mark collected the utensils from his solitary meal and filed them in the dishwasher. He kicked off his shoes and lay down on the settee, lifted his Bible from its usual resting place on the coffee table at his arm, and opened it to the second letter Peter wrote to the church—the passage set down for that day in his reading guide. He read:

*Do not fear what they fear; do not be frightened. But in your hearts set apart Christ as Lord. Always be prepared to give an answer to everyone who asks you to give the reason for the hope that you have. But do this with gentleness and respect, keeping a clear conscience, so that those who speak maliciously against your good behaviour in Christ may be ashamed of their slander."*

Did he fear? Not really. He could usually argue his Christian position pretty well, if anyone asked him. No, that was not the problem. It was the gentleness and respect that had been somewhat lacking, and there had been times when he had defended his faith with more desperation than necessary.

He turned on the television and put a *Doctor Who* DVD on the player.

For no apparent reason, the words of the first verse he had read kept coming back to him, the ones for which he could see no immediate application. "Do not fear what they fear, do not be frightened. But in your hearts set apart Christ as Lord."

He had many faults, no doubt, but being frightened wasn't one of them. He had done a lot of stupid things in his pre-Christian days, some of which would have surprised Candi to no end, but he had never been frightened, as he could recall, of anything. Not to say he was above fear, it was simply that he had never ever been in any sort of terrifying situation. God had been gracious.

He put the thought aside and concentrated on the movie. He liked *Doctor Who.*

Over the next three weeks, Mark managed to dedicate part of every Saturday to helping Andrew with chores around the garden—or, rather, he had done the chores with Andrew watching and making encouraging remarks.

Paths had been cleared of their burden of fallen leaves, weeds had been collected from various garden beds and placed in the compost bins round the back, and several over-exuberant shrubs had been cut back to proper proportions to wait for the spring.

Usually, lunch was sandwiches on the back veranda. On the last occasion, Andrew heated up the curry he had made a couple of days before and Mark cooked rice and pappadams for an evening meal eaten in the dining room because it was cold and had begun to rain outside.

Andrew finished the last pappadam and pushed his plate across the table. "So this Candi is a bit of a wild child, is she? Do you find her attractive?"

"She's clever and very pretty and we've become better friends of late," Mark answered, shaking his head slightly. "If you mean something more than that, no, certainly not on her part. Candi would never be interested in a Christian. She hates them usually. I think I'm the only one she would ever call a friend."

"Rather sad, that. You must feel a bit on the outer at work, then."

"I do at times, but the pace of the project keeps me very occupied. It's not at all dull, let me tell you."

"I can imagine," Andrew smiled. "It's going well?"

"We're still in the construction phase. No measurements as yet. The next hurdle is Candi's high-power microwave generators. We're almost up to the testing phase."

"I'll pray for your safety. Still not thrilled about those energies you're working with. Do you trust this woman's ability? She's holding quite a few lives in her hands it would seem."

"You're right, Andrew, but as a matter of fact, I do." Mark gathered up the plates and headed for the kitchen.

# CHAPTER 10

The very next week saw the completion of the perfect waveguide. Candi had taken Mark's advice and tried a fresh approach with the engineers who responded to the truly horrible picture she had painted for them should they not be able to come up with the goods.

On Wednesday morning, the team of engineers came into the lab with a large metal cage containing what looked for all the world like a huge cooking pot. It was so large that Candi could have taken a somewhat vertical bath in it without offending any standard of propriety—apart from getting in and out.

Sizing the ceramic utensil up against her, Mark wondered if she had something of the sort in mind. He ventured, in as diplomatic manner as possible, to ask her what it was.

"It's to test the generator," she answered his question. "I fill the pot with water and connect the waveguide up to the cage. I measure the water temperature, then give it a pulse. If I'm still alive, I measure the new temperature. I can get a pretty good estimate of the power delivered, and if there isn't any leakage, I will know all is well."

The first test occurred the following day.

Candi came in very early to make sure all was exactly as it should be. She waited until Mark and Dekker arrived and asked them to come into her office.

"I am going to test the generator this morning. Daniel, could you ask all the engineering staff and the machine fitters to leave the building and go right outside the grounds?"

"I can do that," Dekker replied. "No point in having them around."

Candi waved her arms at them. "I want you both outside the grounds, too."

Mark looked up from the piece of paper he had been studying. "I beg your pardon? You want us out of here as well? Perhaps we ought to stay in case anything happens to you."

"If something bad happens to me, it will happen to you too, silly," she said. "I'm not planning to have anything bad happen to me, if you really want to know."

Dekker's brow wrinkled with concern. "Candi, are you sure you wouldn't like us to trigger this by remote control? I think we could do that fairly easily."

"Thanks, Daniel, but I'm not sure we could," she replied. "We could arrange to fire a pulse by remote control, but then we would have to have some way of reading the leakage field monitors, and we simply can't do that very easily. Besides, even if we could, we would have to keep coming back and resetting the power controls. No, this way is best."

"This is a pretty brave thing you're doing, Candi," Mark said. "But we're all responsible for this project. How about you let me do the test and you wait out on the road?"

"Thank you, Mark, but no, I have to do this. You remember what you said, what I said? I ... I want to prove something to myself. I need to prove something to myself. Do you understand? Besides, I have faith in my design. If I have made the mistake, I am not going to let you be hurt by it. I thought about that and I figured out that I don't want to live with the knowledge that I hurt someone because I was careless."

"I'm not happy about this, Candi," Dekker said. "I should be the one—"

"Daniel, please let me do this one thing. I must. I can't explain in English, maybe not explain at all. Please?"

Muttering something, Dekker went over to the cupboard and pulled out two UHF radios. He handed one to Candi. "Channel twelve. Keep your hand on the key while you are doing the test. If the slightest thing goes wrong, tell us and abort. Promise?"

"Promise."

"Come on, Mark. Let's get everyone out."

Fifteen minutes later, a crowd was gathered on the road a good three hundred metres from the building.

Dekker pressed the transmit key on the radio. "Candi, are you receiving me?"

There was a pause and a click, and then Candi's voice came over the instrument. "Loud and clear, Daniel. I'm beginning the sequence now. Power supply is entering standby mode … I'm disengaging safety interlocks on the klystrons … the leakage detectors are operational … the pulse unit is armed … here goes!"

There was an awful sound in the radio, and Dekker, normally so completely unflappable, almost jumped out of his skin. He pressed the transmit button. "Candi! Candi! Are you all right?"

There was a long pause. Dekker looked as though he was going to run headlong into the lab and damn the consequences. Beads of sweat broke out on his forehead. He tried again. "Candi! Are you all right?"

The radio crackled and Candi's laugh sounded loudly through the speaker. There was an audible sigh of relief from the crowd.

"Sorry," she laughed. "Got so excited I dropped the radio. Didn't feel a thing. Water temperature went up five degrees. No leakage worth speaking about."

"What power was the pulse?" Dekker asked.

"Five hundred megawatts."

"Why didn't you start small?"

"Candi believes in herself."

"We're coming in!"

Dekker strode off toward the lab with Mark following. By the time they arrived, Candi had pulsed the water on maximum power, two and a half gigawatts. She might have believed in herself, but she didn't want company while the test was going on.

Mark had no idea how many millisecond pulses had gone into the cage, but by the time they arrived the water in the pot was steaming.

Dekker ran straight up to her and gave her a great bear hug in his excitement. "Dr. Leblanc! You have just made the most powerful microwave generator this world has ever known! Congratulations! Superb job!"

Candi was glowing from head to toe, and not because she had absorbed any leakage. "Well, Mark, what do you say? Candi did the right thing after all?"

"Candi did the very brave thing after all," Mark said. "Thank you, Candi. That took a great deal of unselfish courage."

"I am the best, no?"

Both Dekker and Mark replied together, laughing. "You are the best, yes!"

"We are having a celebration tonight!" said Dekker, still laughing. "Do you realise all we have to do is move the accelerator into position? We are within hours of our first experiment! I am so very proud of each of you!"

Candi was laughing happily. She wrapped her arms around the others, squeezing them together. Mark was a little surprised that Dekker didn't seem to mind. Perhaps he was just as excited as she was.

Spirits were running high all that afternoon as the three of them supervised the engineers moving the accelerator into its final place. The output end was moved up to the stainless steel injection port, and the two were bolted together. Last of all, the waveguide was lined up with meticulous care and attached to the feed on the top of the unit.

By half past five, the whole incredible apparatus was ready for the first experiment, and the vacuum pumps had already begun their work of removing every last trace of air from the accelerator and collision tube. It would take all night.

Mark had yet to test his power supply and the magnets, but whether it was overconfidence or his trust in the magnet design, he never doubted for a moment that they would work.

True to his word, Dekker took them to dinner at the Back Alley Café. Somehow, he must have managed to pass on some detailed instructions to the manager and staff, because they were met at the door by Annette and escorted past the other diners, up the stairs at the back, and into a large single room.

Candi took one look at the beautiful table with its lighted candles and tasteful vases of flowers and clapped her hands. Bottles of champagne rested in their ice buckets, and each setting boasted an array of several knives, forks and spoons. Clearly the meal they were going to partake of this evening was not one they had ever seen on a menu in the Café below.

Mark wondered just how Dekker had managed to organise it.

Annette showed them to their places with all the care and bearing of a head waitress in one of Sydney's five-star signature restaurants. "Is everything all right, Professor Dekker?"

"Everything is perfect, Annette. You've gone to a great deal of trouble. Thank you."

The meal was superb, so good in fact that Candi wondered if they had imported another chef especially to create it. There was an entrée of pork wrapped in prosciutto sitting on asparagus spears in a little pool of delicious sauce. The main course was duck served on Parish mash and an equally delicious sauce, and caramelised vegetables with rosemary marinade. For dessert, they filled up the corners with homemade sticky date pudding and Irish coffee.

One bottle of champagne stood empty, the other only half full. Mark had not even finished his glass; Dekker was on his second, so all the rest had been enjoyed by Candi. It seemed to have had no effect on her at all. Certainly it did nothing to kerb her excitement or dull the laughter in her eyes.

How attractive she looked when she was happy! She grabbed her handbag and pulled a newspaper clipping out of it. "See!" She said excitedly, "I am famous! I have my picture in the paper!"

Dekker took the proffered scrap of paper, glanced at it, and passed it on to Mark.

The article was headed "Gaunt Voted Best Player" and showed Candi with her arms around a young man in a football jersey who would have made Arnold Schwarzenegger seem positively puny.

"This is the guy who plays for Wests," Mark asked. "How do you know him?"

"I met him the night I dropped you back to your home at Heathcote, remember, Mark?"

"Faintly."

"He's my partner now," she explained. "We live together. He is handsome, yes, and very good at football. Very good at lots of things."

"I take it that physics and microwave generators are not two of them."

Candi laughed. "No! But he knows how to make Candi very happy, and he knows how to make love. He is very good at that!"

"No doubt because he's had a lot of practice," Mark thought to himself.

Some of his thought must have reached his face, because Candi, reading his expression of disapproval far better than he would have wished, opened her eyes wide, tilted her head slightly to the side, and laughed in a rather provoking manner. "But of course you do not think I should be making love at all, do you? You must have the wedding bells first. Don't you ever want to make love to a woman, Mark, just because she is beautiful and willing without any thoughts for tomorrow? If you were really honest with yourself, not castrated by all that religious morality that tells you to feel guilty if you even look at a girl, you know you would. What does your heart say? Is all your testosterone used up in making love to your physics? You should wake up, Mark, and smell the roses, not just measure their petals. Candi is right. You would like to, yes?"

Dekker put his mug of Irish coffee down on the table, somewhat incredulous at the unexpected turn of conversation. He could see a simmering fire growing in Candi's face, and a quiet but immovable expression settling into Mark's. This was not good, but how to prevent the oncoming storm? He opened his mouth to speak, but Mark got there first.

"I'm sure I'm no different in that respect from any other man, your Roger included, but I choose not to give free reign to my desires. I believe the God who made us knows best how we ought to live, whereas you make it up as you go. If it makes you feel good then—"

"Then why not do what gives you pleasure as long as no one else is hurt?" Candi asked sharply. "Or is your God offended by enjoyment? Let me tell you, Mark, it's all lies and hypocrisy. Do you know I used to go to church every Sunday with my parents? Then they split up and I went with my mother. Even as a teenager I go. I never once hear anything that tells me how to live, just the endless stream of things I get punished for. Twice a year I am made to go to confession. The priest is a dirty old man who smells of communion wine. He wheezes. He asks me, a young girl, personal questions about my body. He asks me if I have the sex, and I tell him, yes, every night, and I make up stories about what I do and how I do it to make him wheeze faster. I try to make him have the heart attack. When I was eighteen I moved away to university and I've never gone near a church again. How can you be part of that?"

"I'm not part of that—it's ugly and hypocritical. I agree with you, but it has nothing to do with the truth of Christianity."

Candi was simmering to the point of explosion. "Nothing to do with Christianity? This was the church! If the church has nothing to do with Christianity, tell me, what does? What absolute nonsense are you speaking?"

"I'm afraid not all churches believe the same things or behave the same way."

"No? But why? Because there is no truth there, that's why!" she sputtered. "You say I make it up as I go, but that's exactly what you Christians do. Make it up as you go. Make a profit on the way, make people pay for their sins, feel bad every time they laugh! I enjoy using my body for what it was made to do, Mark. How can the way I am made be a sin? I do not choose the way I'm made!"

Dekker made another attempt to rescue the evening. He had been brought up a Catholic himself, and Jasmin was still a practicing one. He could imagine Candi might be telling the truth, but not all Catholic churches were like the one she described. As far as God was concerned, Dekker didn't really have an opinion. He looked at the world around him, and its beauty and complexity spoke to him of a God, but its horror and suffering made him hope there wasn't one. Clearly the time had come for him to intervene if the evening he had planned for celebration wasn't going to turn into a disaster.

"A toast," he said, pouring some fresh champagne into Candi's glass. "To our first experiment. May it make us all famous!"

Candi, rising to the occasion instantly, linked her arms with Dekker and Mark and gave them each a quick kiss on the cheek.

"May it make us rich!" she said, and all three laughed as they drank.

The rest of the evening passed enjoyably with both Mark and Candi taking great care to avoid certain subjects.

Mark was a little on the subdued side. He couldn't help admiring Candi. She had been so annoyed with him, and she probably still was inside, yet she had the ability to put her feelings aside for the sake of the party. He watched her smiling at Daniel, laughing as he told her a story about the way he had once locked himself out of his house, her arm resting on his, delighting in his every word and encouraging him to talk about his own life, something he never usually mentioned. Daniel was laughing and enjoying himself as he should have been. So much life, she had, and the evening would have been so much less joyful and light hearted if Candi hadn't been there.

Roger was a lucky man, and he had better not cheat on her! Mark wondered if he was jealous. He sat pondering the words she had spoken. Was he attracted to her? Yes and no. Her worldview, no, but her joy and her excitable passion for life, yes, anybody would be.

She was teasing him, her eyes shining. "Do you know Mark was wearing this same shirt when you first saw him? He's only got three. This one, a blue one with stripes, and a silly one with tropical fruit all over it that should be turned into a cleaning rag. Am I right?"

"I stand amazed, Candi!" he replied. "I didn't know you took so much notice. I'm genuinely impressed. Now that I know you're aware of my appearance, I promise to dress better."

"And you've only one pair of socks. They're brown."

"Wrong," he countered. "I've got eight pairs of socks, and they're all the same. Bought them on sale years ago."

It wasn't exactly an evening of deep conversation, but it deepened the friendship, which, in the months to come, would become so very important to all of them. As the evening drew to a close, Candi got out of her chair, pulled Dekker's out from the table a little, and sat on his lap, her arms around his neck.

"Thank you, Daniel. It has been a lovely evening, and it is all due to your kindness. Let me tell you, I have never worked for a man who is kind and thoughtful like you. I want you to know it means a lot to me, and I'm glad I said yes to coming and joining you."

Dekker, a little taken aback, patted her on the shoulder. "It's been quite an education for me too." He looked across at Mark. "I'll share this with you. When I was told I could only choose two colleagues for the project, I was very worried because I knew the government actually wanted us to fail. I cannot tell you the long hours I poured over all the applications that came through, and, even when I picked the both of you, I wasn't sure I had got it right. Well, I made the right choice, the perfect choice. I'm proud to be working with you both."

Candi kissed him on the neck and then, surprisingly, got up and went over to Mark, who, not wanting Candi to sit on his lap, had gotten up from his chair. She reached out her hand and touched his face, looking at him with kind eyes. "Daniel did make the right choice, Mark. If I had to choose a colleague and a friend to work with, it would be you every time."

He looked at her in astonishment, realised his mouth was open, shut it, and stammered a reply. "I … well … thank you, Candi. I .. I'm glad we're friends, very glad indeed."

It sounded rather lame, but Candi smiled back at him, looped her arm around his, dragged him towards Dekker, and looped her other arm around the man.

"Tomorrow we will be famous! Tomorrow all three of us will have our picture in the paper!"

They laughed, and Candi received two simultaneous kisses, one on each cheek.

Ironically, every word she had spoken turned out to be true.

It was the tenth of May, 2000.

# CHAPTER 11

I t was Thursday. It was early—not yet half past eight.

Candi arrived in the car park just as Mark was getting out of his vehicle, and together they went into the laboratory. Dekker was waiting in the doorway.

There was an air of intense anticipation when the three greeted one another. None of the other engineers were scheduled on that day, so they were completely alone. The cryostat pumps hummed gently in the background and the fluorescent lights on the ceiling above buzzed in harmony.

"Right," said Dekker. "This is it. From now on, standard procedure. You two, all metal objects out of pockets. Belts, wallet, credit cards. We can put them here in this box near the door and collect them when we come out. I'll see you over near the control panels."

Mark took off his belt and replaced it with a piece of webbing he had taken out of his pocket. A small pile of belongings accumulated in the box. Candi removed her top and handed it to Mark.

He turned around and stared at the girl attired in nothing above the waist except for a lacy black bra before slowly turning back, still holding her top in his hand—a movement completely unheard of in Candi's repertoire of male responses to her shapely form, and one that she was not sure she liked.

It might have been the excitement, it might have been a reaction to what she regarded as his narrow-minded attitudes, it might have been simply a desire to be admired rather than turned away from, but she decided to tease a little.

Holding the garment, Mark wondered what was causing the delay. "What are you doing?"

"Underwire bra. Do you like it?" The bra joined the others in the box. "May I have my top? Come on, Mark. I'm over here. Haven't you seen a girl's breasts before?"

Still discretely looking in the opposite direction, Mark reached out his arm with the garment. "Take it, please."

Candi took it from his hand and replaced her top. When Mark turned back to her, she was laughing at him. "Look!" She jumped up and down on her toes. "I'm a bouncy castle. Isn't the physics of soft tissue oscillations remarkable? Are you all right, Mark? You're blushing."

"Ah ... yes, I guess I am."

"You've probably committed a sin," she said. "Would you like me to hear your confession?"

"For goodness sake, let's go. Daniel will be wondering what happened to us."

"Watch those naughty thoughts or you won't be able to concentrate." Candi took him by the arm and skipped into the lab, pulling him along with her and laughing out loud. It was an infectious laugh, and by the time they had reached Dekker, who was near the accelerator, Mark was smiling, too.

Dekker looked around at the massive amount of assembled equipment and silently, slowly nodded his head. His young collaborators had nearly performed miracles. He waited near the wall at the hydrogen flow valves to conduct operations.

"How is the vacuum?" he asked. "Mark, can you check, please? Candi, can you bring the klystron power supply on line?"

Mark crossed the floor and read some displays. "Vacuum is good. Cryostat temperature is two degrees kelvin—within operating range. Newfield superconductor cores are at the same temperature."

Candi went over to her operating console and threw some switches. "Microwave leakage monitors operational." More switches. "Klystron high-voltage supply has entered standby mode. Pulse unit is armed."

"Vacuum on accelerator tube is good," Dekker replied. "Releasing safety interlocks on hydrogen injection. Mark, can you begin building the new field magnets up now?"

Mark switched on the bus cooling unit and watched the little green light blinking to indicate normal operation. This was his moment, and he felt his pulse quicken when he activated the current build-up sequence. "Beginning field creation now. Current passing five hundred amps, nine hundred, one thousand …"

"Not too fast," Dekker cautioned. "There's a lot of energy stored in that field. Tell me when we get to one hundred and fifty thousand amps. Monitor the field and the leakage field at the ends."

"Field current passing one hundred and ten thousand amps," Mark said. "Bus cooling is running okay. Bus temperature is rising to forty-six degrees celsius. One hundred and twenty thousand amps, one hundred and thirty … forty, fifty. Field current steady at one hundred and fifty seven thousand amps. Core field, one hundred and fifty two tesla. Leakage field, three point two tesla at four metres, nine point five tesla at two metres. Engaging superconducting shunt."

There was a thump as the mechanical switch closed the current path with a section of superconductor.

"Disconnecting source current. Successful. Field still holding at one hundred and fifty two tesla." Mark could not keep the excitement out of his voice.

Dekker said, "Okay. Mark, check radiation detectors."

"Checked."

"Activate ion trap and detectors."

Mark looked over toward the odd-looking device at the end of the collision tube designed to separate the charged ions from the neutrons they hoped to create. "Activated."

"I'm going to send five microliters of hydrogen into the accelerator," Dekker said, excitement modulating his voice. "Candi, can you give me a ten megawatt pulse? Go!"

The accelerator made a strange noise. *Pock!*

"What was that?" Mark sounded alarmed.

"That was the sound five microliters of hydrogen gas make when you fry them with a ten megawatt pulse of microwave energy. Leakage field was hardly measurable," Candi replied.

"Mark, did we register any ions coming down the end of the collision tube?" Dekker asked with an anxious tone.

"You bet we did. A large packet. Lots of nasty x-rays on the shields. All monitors show safe levels."

"Candi, next time give me a one hundred megawatt pulse," Dekker said. "Now!"

*Pock!* Louder than before.

Mark called out. "Ionised packet received by trap."

"This time five hundred megawatts. Now!"

*Pock!* Much louder than before. There was a bright flash from the accelerator cage, and the ion trap recorded a very energetic packet indeed.

"Mark, have we recorded any neutrons?" Dekker asked.

"None. Sorry."

"Candi," Dekker said, "give me a one gigawatt pulse."

"Are you sure?"

"Just do it."

*POCK!* Beep!

"What beeped?" Dekker called out to Mark.

"I don't know…wait! Yes I do! We've got neutrons! Lots of them! The beep was from the neutron detector!"

They all cheered.

Dekker continued. "Candi, everything still okay there?"

"Everything. Supply is fine. Klystron temperature is within limits. Leakage field is OK."

"Crank it up to two gigawatts," Dekker instructed.

*POCK!* Beep! A really bright flash from the accelerator cage.

"More neutrons!!" Mark yelled. "This time there were hardly any other ions! Unbelievable! We've done it!"

"Excellent!" said Dekker, the excitement modulating his voice. "Now let's see if we can generate a stream of packets. I'm going to send a continuous flow of hydrogen into the accelerator. Can you give me a stream of two gigawatt pulses?"

"Here they come!" Candi called out.

*POCK!* Beep! *POCK!* Beep! *POCK!* Beep!

"This is incredible!" Mark exclaimed. "We're converting all the ions into neutrons—really energetic neutrons! There's no charged particles hitting the traps at all! Amazing!"

*POCK!* Beep! *POCK!* Beep! *POCK!* Beep! *POCK! POCK! POCK!*

"We've stopped producing neutrons." Mark said.

"Hold the stream!" Dekker said. "Candi, can you check that we're still delivering two gigawatt pulses?"

"Testing." *POCK!* "Yes, we are."

"No ions recorded, either." Mark sounded worried.

Dekker called out. "Candi, Mark, check again. It's not possible. Something's wrong. Candi, are you positive we're sending that amount of energy into the accelerator?"

"Of course, I am," she said. "Why don't you watch it? What do you think makes that flash?"

"Mark, check the ion detector magnets. We have to be producing ions. Check the new field magnets. Move slowly."

Mark went over towards the magnet assembly. He could feel a strange warmth through his body as he slowly approached. He checked the magnetometers. "The new field strength is steady at one hundred and fifty two tesla. Ion trap magnets are operational. Detectors are powered up. Fire off another burst, Candi."

"No!" Dekker yelled. "Mark, stand back from the collision tube first. Don't move quickly. Wait! Okay, now Candi, do it."

*POCK!*

Mark rubbed his hand over his forehead and stared at the instrumentation panel in front of him. "No ions at all. No neutrons and no ions. Nothing is reaching the end of the tube."

"That's totally impossible," Dekker almost shouted. "Check the temperature and vacuum on the tube."

"Tube temperature is two Kelvin," Mark said. "Vacuum is good. Everything is within limits. "

"Shut everything down," Dekker said. "Candi, begin the discharge cycle on the capacitors. Mark, begin draining energy from the new fields. Either we've damaged a detector or we've got a blockage somewhere.

Candi, when the energy has drained from the capacitors, engage safety interlocks and check the klystrons. Perhaps they weren't delivering all the power they were supposed to be. Check for physical damage."

Mark engaged the high-current supply, removed the shunt, and set the supply to slowly decrease the current. Candi engaged the safety interlocks on the klystrons and switched in the dummy loads to drain the power supply.

Dekker turned off the hydrogen injection valves, set them to safety so the vacuum would be maintained, and called the others over. "We can't do much more until the supply gets down and the magnetic field current reaches zero. Mark, download the flash cards from the neutron detector. My goodness, those energies are high! Well, we did it once, and we can do it again!"

"What do you think went wrong?" Candi asked. "I'm sure we were still outputting microwave energy."

"It certainly looked like it, Candi," Dekker agreed, "so where was all that energy going? Into the collision tube, by all accounts. If it was being lost through the end of the accelerator we would have seen it punch a hole in the metal. I suppose we should check in case there is a hole."

Dekker threw a few more switches on the accelerator panel. "Voltage is almost at zero. Come on. Examine it carefully for anything that looks as though it might have melted. Move slowly when we get near the end of the new fields."

They moved toward the end of the accelerator searching for something that would explain where several two gigawatt pulses of energy had ended up. As far as they could see, there was nothing. They moved from there to the injection port on the collision tube, but there was still nothing.

"Vacuum is still holding," Mark said. "I'm almost certain we won't find anything. If we had punched a hole in the end cap, we would be losing vacuum."

"The obvious answer is the ion traps," Dekker said. "We must have burnt them out with the very high energies. I know you understand this, but if we are pouring two gigawatt pulses of energy into one end of the collision tube, it has to be coming out the other. Energy doesn't disappear into the void. Let's check them."

They did.

As they moved to the end of the collision tube. they began to feel the heating from the enormous magnetic field, even though it was decaying.

"Look," Candi said. "Your magnets are making me sweat. What am I supposed to be looking for? Remember, I'm not the physicist here."

"Any signs of melting, anything broken inside the glass tubes of the detectors, a loose connection, whatever could be stopping us from getting a reading. If there were no neutrons, there must be ions. There can't be nothing!"

They spent a good half an hour checking the ion trap detectors. Mark and Dekker could swear there was absolutely nothing wrong with all they had seen.

"You know what this means?" Dekker groaned. "There must have been an imperfection in the field, right inside the magnets. The plasma in the tube has deflected into the glass and melted it, and the vacuum has collapsed the whole lot. The next pulse of energy would have gone straight into the lining of the new fields. My guess is you won't be able to even get them to slide off the tube. It's the worst kind of accident we could have had. I'll have to talk pretty hard and fast to get funding for another set. Damn and blast!"

"Daniel, I don't think that's the case." Mark checked the vacuum gauges as he spoke.

"What else could it be? I'm too old to believe in energy-eating fairies."

"Well for starters, the vacuum is still holding," Mark said. "I know that could be because the glass envelope has melted itself sealed, but I was watching the vacuum gauges. They never hiccuped the whole time like I would have expected them to. Another thing … why are the new fields still operating if we fried some of their coils? The sheath inside isn't so robust. One of Candi's gigawatt pulses would have gone through it like a knife in butter."

Candi wiped the sweat off her forehead and made a face. "Mark's right. The magnets are still holding. That's why I'm sweating like the pig."

Dekker smiled at her. "You're jigging. Stand completely still and you'll cool off."

"I can't stand still, never could. Haven't you noticed?"

"Mark, there's nothing else for it," Dekker sighed. "Tomorrow, we'll have to disassemble the neutron detector and slide the new fields off the tube. It should be obvious what has happened then. If we still can't see some damage, I'll give up. It will be there though, alas."

"I've an idea,"Candi said. "Why don't we go and have the lunch? There's nothing much we can do here."

"Good thinking, Candi. Mark, would you go out and get our security guards to keep an eye on things while we're gone? I don't want people wandering around in here while the field is coming down."

"I'll go and see Jack. I think it's his shift."

"You'll find him watching porn in the security office," she said.

"Thanks, Candi. Meet you in the car park."

Jack was pretty unresponsive to Mark's requests, and it took some time to drag him away from the "important business" he was conducting on his desk computer. Mark didn't ask him what it was. Eventually, he agreed to go over and secure the main lab while they were away at their conference, which was Jack-talk that meant "if you're going to have lunch, then I am too." Mark went out into the car park to find Dekker standing by the door of his Mercedes and Candi on the phone. The men sat down in the car leaving Candi to her phone conversation outside.

Dekker leaned closer to Mark and spoke softly. "From Roger, the god. Seems he's had a bad match or something. Word to the wise, say nothing."

"Thanks," Mark replied. "What a strange day!"

"Bizarre. I still think we've damaged the new fields, or at least we will when we try to slide them off the tube. Have to be careful of broken glass, the vacuum is still on. Perhaps we should turn off the pumps before we try."

"I have no idea what's going on, Daniel, but I think the new fields are okay. Perhaps the glass has fused to the inside, but it doesn't explain something."

"Which would be?" Dekker asked.

"We sent lots of pulses down after the fault occurred, enough to punch right through to the outside case of the magnets, let alone damage a coil. We would know if that happened."

"I take your point. The only other explanation is that somehow the accelerator is absorbing all the energy itself—either that or Candi's machine is not coming up with the goods."

"Word to the wise," Mark said, "don't mention that."

"No fear," Dekker chuckled. "Don't want another explosion. It's hard not to worry, but it's all speculation until we get the new fields off the tube. If there's no apparent damage there, we'll have to talk to Candi about her generator. Maybe it hasn't changed power but instead shifted frequency or something."

"Here she comes," Mark said. "Hope the Back Alley isn't crowded. I don't feel like crowds right now. What do you fancy for lunch, Candi?"

"A large bottle of Beaujolais and a croissant. Don't ask. Is it my fault that Roger-the-Invincible gets sent off?"

Mark tried to hide his enjoyment engendered by this news. "I think we might have to go somewhere else for a meal like that. Any other choice?"

"I can do without the croissant," she said.

"Then it's the pub at the roundabout."

"No! No, I don't want to go there," Candi said. "The café is parfait. I'll choose something else. You think my generator is not working, don't you?"

Both Dekker and Mark answered simultaneously with a good deal more passion than strictly necessary. "No!"

Candi gave a little grunt and lapsed into silence, staring out the window at the fields, rich green with late autumn rains. Suddenly her face brightened, and she leaned forward to thump Dekker on the shoulder. "But we did it! We have made a name for ourselves! Just think, without the great big billion-dollar accelerator, we did it! Chambers, Dekker and Leblanc! I can see the papers already! We are being so morbid! If we can do it once, we can do it again. Why are you so worried? There is the simple explanation, all we have to do is find it. All that energy! It will be obvious when we see where it has gone. You can't hide the elephant in the bedroom!"

Dekker laughed. "Candi, you are good for us. You're right. We should be celebrating, not feeling miserable. There's a good restaurant in the old Camden Bank building. That's where we're going—and Candi can have her Beaujolais with her croissant if she wants to. My shout."

That's where they ended. It was a good meal. Generous to a fault, Dekker paid for it all for a second time within twenty-four hours.

They returned to the lab to find Jack conspicuous by his absence, the front door unlocked, and the magnetic field still around one tesla and falling.

Dekker went into his office and began to make enquiries about the cost of repairing the new fields, but he quickly wished he hadn't.

Mark made a copy of the data he had downloaded from the flash cards containing the neutron detector data.

Candi painted her toenails bright red.

There was really not much to do but wait until the field reached zero.

Dekker left first. He was a realist at heart and knew he had to face the strong possibility of some heavy financial losses. There was no point in staying, and he knew Jasmin would be waiting.

Around five thirty, Candi went over to Mark. "The capacitors are completely at zero. I have to go now. Roger will want some company tonight. He has had a bad day, did I mention that?"

"We haven't actually had a perfect day here, either. Perhaps you should give him a call and tell him you'll be late. We still haven't solved the problem."

"I wouldn't do that to him. Besides, we comfort one another. It is good after a bad day."

"You comfort one another?"

"We make love, of course," she laughed. "We are good lovers. You should get yourself a girl, Mark. You need someone to make love to. There's a big part of your life missing. After today, I need something to make me feel better. We were so close to it, we were doing it, making history, and then it vanishes! Poof!"

"Don't you mean pock?" Mark asked.

"Very funny. You should go home. I have a friend, Abby. She's a bit religious like you. I ask her if she's busy tonight. If she's free you could take her out. Maybe take her other places if things go well."

"Thanks, Candi. No, you go home and, well, have a nice evening. I want to shift the new fields off the tube so we can make sure that it is still intact. I might even stay here the night and think about a few things. It will be a better day tomorrow."

"Okay, bonne nuit!" She bounced out of the door.

Mark watched her retreating figure until she was out of sight. Pictures of what they would be doing while he shifted the magnets flitted through his mind. With some effort, he banished them and went back into the workshop to get a spanner.

# CHAPTER 12

It was after nine o'clock before the field had drained, the bus bars were disconnected, and all the other things removed to allow the new field magnets to be slid to the left to expose the collision tube.

Double checking all had been detached, Mark activated the hydraulic pumps and began the process, slowly, very slowly, half-expecting to hear the shattering of glass as it detached from where it was probably welded to the inside of the magnet's core.

Nothing of that nature happened. The whole magnet assembly slid slowly, quietly back to reveal a collision tube that appeared to be—at first inspection at least—perfectly intact and undamaged.

When the magnet assembly had reached the end of its travel, he switched off the hydraulic pumps and moved over to inspect the collision tube more closely.

It was totally unimpaired.

No cracks, no blockages, no places where the tube had melted and imploded—nothing.

He made his way carefully from the neutron detector along the length of the tube to the injection end. Nothing.

He examined the injection port from the accelerator. It was, as they had thought earlier, completely undamaged.

Mark breathed a sigh of relief. The new fields were undamaged. Daniel would be pleased.

*"It must be the accelerator,"* he thought to himself. He moved up and down the device—repeating the same inspection they had carried out that morning. Nothing appeared to be damaged in the slightest degree.

*"Has to be the microwave generator. Candi will not be happy when I tell her,"* he thought. Still, he had seen the vivid flash the last time she had sent a pulse and had judged it to be just as bright as each of the others.

He walked down the length of the collision tube again with his face very close to it, checking for anything that might have been causing a problem. Perhaps there was a tiny piece of melted silica inside? No.

Just as he was about to turn away, something caught his eye. It was hardly visible, probably a reflection of light on the surface of the tube.

Somehow it didn't look right.

Mark put his face very close to the tube and cupped his hands around it.

"That's not possible," he said to himself. "It must be some odd reflection."

He went back into his office and emerged with a torch.

Going over to the main switchboard next to the door, he turned off all the lights. With the aid of the torch, he made his way back to the collision tube. He switched off the light and stood rigid, staring.

It was not a reflection because there was no light in the lab to reflect.

He moved his head carefully over and then under, then round the other side of the tube. In the centre of the collision tube there was a tiny razor-thin line of light. It began abruptly about ten centimetres from the neutron detector end. It was so thin and so faint, Mark could hardly see it, even in the darkened laboratory.

There was no doubt about it.

It was longer than he first thought, slowly growing in length as his eyes adapted to the dark. He could see about thirty centimetres of it now. It was brightest at its point of origin, gradually became fainter towards the injection end, and then disappeared entirely.

He gently touched the outside of the tube. It felt neither hot nor cold. Using his torch, he carried a portable magnetometer over to the tube and ran its detector along its length. There was no magnetic field, no heat, no electrostatic charge, just a tiny razor-thin line of light that began abruptly and diminished into nothing.

Mark's entire understanding of physics told him what he was seeing could not exist—must not exist. You did not get energy from nothing. Mark felt sweat forming on his forehead, and his hands holding the magnetometer were not completely steady.

What he was seeing must not be real, could not be real.

There was always an explanation for the unusual, even the bizarre, he told himself. If he had turned around and seen a zebra in the laboratory, he would have been amazed, yet his mind would have quickly adjusted to its existence and formulated a number of reasonable hypotheses as to how it had arrived there. A truck conveying animals to the Western Plains Zoo had been involved in an accident and zebras were wandering the land; the university had sent them one by mistake. Whatever, there was an explanation that fell within his understanding of the physical universe.

If he had gazed across the tube and seen the Archangel Gabriel standing there, he would have been frightened, but, once again, his Christian understanding of the unseen heavenly realm that broke into the physical from time to time would have accommodated what he saw.

There was no zebra, and the laboratory was not filled with heavenly glory. There was just an almost imperceptible razor line of pale light, and it filled him not with amazement but incomprehension, not with excitement but foreboding bordering on panic, as though he had taken all the batteries out of his torch then found to his horror he could still turn it on.

Something totally alien and horrible had entered the world—indeed, he had summoned it somehow—and its diminutive presence was entirely sufficient to shake the very foundations of his understanding of physical reality, and they were deep indeed.

Whatever it was, it was self-sustaining. There was no energy being supplied, yet a razor-thin line of atoms inside the tube were being ionized.

He shone the torch over to the vacuum plant. The vacuum in the entire apparatus was perfect. He returned to the tube, willing himself to see nothing, but the razor-thin line of pale light was still there.

Putting the magnetometer down, he went over to the switchboard and turned on all the lights. Taking a spanner, he physically unbolted Candi's precious waveguide from the accelerator and watched it crash to the floor. He took a heavy-braided, copper lead, attached one end to earth, and threw the other over the high-voltage bus lines that supplied the klystrons. There was no spark, no voltage. He turned off the lights and went over to the tube again.

Still there, that pale, thin, obscene anomaly. Energy was being supplied to atoms in the tube, energy that he was not supplying. Energy coming from—where?

The knot tightened in his stomach. He felt physically ill. He went back into his office and rang Daniel Van Dekker.

It was exactly ten p.m.

Jasmin Van Dekker was usually content to let evenings with her husband evolve in their own manner, but this was an exception. For some reason, she had been feeling romantic all day and could hardly wait until Daniel came home. Determined to excite the same desire in her husband, she met him at the door wearing a low-cut, black dress with her hair loose and falling down all over her shoulders.

She kissed him softly on the lips, sensing by his response that his day had been a less-than-ideal prelude to an evening of love and intimacy. Even so, she was determined to have the upper hand.

She set him down in front of his favourite curry and a bottle of Traminer Riesling, and managed—quite successfully—to look inviting and delicious. After dinner, they retired to the sofa and cuddled, reminiscing about happy times.

By mutual desire, they headed for the bedroom.

The phone rang. Out of habit, Dekker made the mistake of picking it up.

"Daniel, this is Mark. I'm so sorry to trouble you at this hour, but there's something going on here that you should see."

Dekker groaned. "Listen, Mark, it will be there tomorrow. I can't come now. We'll talk about it in the morning."

From the bedroom, Jasmin called out. "Are you coming, Daniel? I'm waiting."

"I know it's inconvenient," Mark said. "I'm sorry. I can't talk about it on the phone. Something has gone really wrong—really, really wrong. I've found out why nothing was going down the tube. We may have started something we shouldn't have. Please—"

"Daniel, what are you doing? Are you on the phone?" There was a note in Jasmin's voice that Dekker recognized.

"I'm coming, love, just a second." Then into the phone, Dekker said, "Mark, I cannot come. Go home."

"But you *must*," Mark said. "Can't you understand? I wouldn't call if it wasn't serious. Please!"

The tone in Mark's voice troubled Dekker even more than the words. It wasn't excitement and it wasn't impatience—it was fear. Whatever else Mark had exhibited during the planning and building phase, it was never fear.

"I told you, I'm otherwise engaged," Dekker said. "If you force me to come down there and I find it could have waited until tomorrow, you can consider yourself off the project. Is that clear? Now, can it wait?"

"No."

"Damn! You had better be right, Chambers." Dekker hung up. The third and last summons came from the bedroom. Dekker headed down the hall, but somehow the mood had evaporated.

Jasmin was lying seductively naked on the bed. She raised her arms above her head and smiled at him. "You took your time."

They made love, but his heart wasn't in it. As Jasmin began to sense his diverted attention, hers wasn't either. Half an hour later, Dekker got up from the bed and went toward the bathroom.

"Where are you going?" she asked.

"I have to go to the laboratory. That phone call was from Mark. He says there's something wrong."

"Surely it can wait until the morning?"

"Apparently not," he said.

"Good night, then." Jasmin rolled over and tucked the sheets around herself.

She was troubled. Daniel adored her and was always delighted to make love to her. This, she knew. Nor was she unaware of her powers of persuasion, yet something had arisen unexpectedly to overpower them. She turned out the light but did not go to sleep for a long while.

It was quarter to midnight when Dekker arrived at the lab. He was in a foul mood.

He entered to find the lights on, Candi's precious waveguide on the floor, and Mark scribbling numbers on the whiteboard in his office.

Dekker's mood did not improve. He barked angrily at Mark. "This better be good, or you are really out of a job."

Mark didn't even reply. He took a torch in his hand.

"Please follow me." He went to the switchboard and threw a breaker to plunge the entire building into darkness. Using the torch, he led Dekker to the collision tube. He turned off the torch.

"What am I supposed … Just what in the name of everything holy is that?"

"That's what I wanted you to see," Mark said. "There's no power of any sort being supplied to the tube. What you are seeing is self-sustaining. Those atoms are being ionized by some energy source that we are not providing. I'm worried sick."

Dekker stared. He moved his head around the tube just as Mark had done. He shone the torch towards the accelerator, confirming that it was dead. Still and silent, he stared at the pale razor-thin anomaly in the pitch darkness. His thoughts following the same path that Mark's had a couple of hours earlier.

All feelings of anger evaporated from Dekker's mind. "I apologize for my attitude on the phone. You were very right to call me. Take this torch and turn on all the lights. I am heading toward my office. I know the way."

When he reached his desk, Dekker picked up the phone and dialled. "Security? Jack, is that you? I want a twenty-four hour security mounted on this building. I want someone guarding the door at all times. No one with the exception of Mark Chambers, Candice Leblanc and me is to have access. None of the other engineering staff are to come in. I'm going to phone them in the morning, but in case I don't manage to … what? You are going off duty now? That's unacceptable. Overtime? All right, I'll ring the University and clear it with them. In the meantime, wake up Fred and Simon and get them to take it in shifts. Patrol the place. No one gets in or out apart from us. Is that clear? "

Apparently, it was. Five minutes later there was a knock at the door.

Dekker went out. "Jack, thanks for this. No, you can't come in. Nobody includes you."

The security guard argued. "I have to click this thing against the check discs on your doors before I finish my shift or I won't get paid my overtime."

"There's a possibility of dangerous radiation," Dekker said. "I cannot allow you inside the building."

"But you're here."

"In order to prevent the danger from occurring. Please, do as I say. Have you contacted the others?"

"Yes," Jack said, "but they want clearance from our boss on campus first. They're worried they won't get paid. Have you contacted campus security for approval?"

"Stay here." Dekker strode into his office, picked up the phone, and dialled.

A recorded voice answered him. "This is campus security for the University of Southern Sydney. Please leave your message after the tone. If there is an emergency, please ring customer service after hours on this number."

Dekker listened to the number and then dialled it. "This is customer service after hours. Please leave your message after the tone and our friendly staff will take action as soon as possible. Thank you."

Dekker slammed down the phone. He went over to the door where Jack waited. apprehensively, looking around as if he expected to see the deadly hand of radiation reaching out to grab him.

"I cannot contact your office," Dekker said. "I will do so in the morning. Now unless you want to be responsible for putting people's lives in danger, get out of my lab and guard the premises."

There was a certain tone in Dekker's voice that warned Jack all further discussion would be very much louder and very much more unpleasant. He retreated through the door to go back to his office to fill in an overtime claim form.

Dekker phoned Jasmin. "Darling, I'm so sorry to wake you."

"I wasn't asleep. What's the matter?"

"And I'm sorry about this evening," Dekker continued. "Mark was right to call me. I will be here all night. I'm sorry, Jasmin."

"Daniel, what's gone wrong? Have they cut your funding? Has there been an accident? Is everyone all right?"

"Jasmin, can I ask you to do something for me when you get up—before you go to work?"

"Of course."

"Could you go to St. Benedict's and say a prayer for us there?" Dekker asked.

"What do you want me to pray for?"

"Wisdom, I think. We are going to have great need of it."

It was an anxious Jasmin who replied. "Daniel, are you safe? You've never wanted to pray about anything before. You're scaring me. Can't you tell me what's wrong?"

"There's no need to be scared, my darling. I'm not sure I want to say anything further, not because I don't trust you, but because I don't know what to say. Oh, and one more thing—pray quietly, please."

The long hours of the night passed with much discussion. They would write on the whiteboard, rub out what they had written, drink coffee, write more, and then drink more coffee. Dawn shone through the window onto two figures: Dekker lying back in his chair with his eyes closed, thinking hard. Mark was asleep with his head slumped onto his desk. They were awakened by a shriek from the doorway to the lab, followed by a string of expletives in French.

"Candi has arrived," said Dekker, "and noticed her waveguide on the floor."

Candi burst into the room. "What insanity has been going on in here? It took me weeks to …" She noticed the state of the two figures in the room and checked the tirade pouring from her lips. "You look dreadful. What on earth is the matter?"

Mark slowly raised his head from its resting place on the desk and tried to focus on her.

"Good morning, Candi," he mumbled. "Did you have any trouble getting in here?"

"There was a security guard asleep in a chair near the door—Simon, I think. Seemed a pity to wake him. I just walked in. Why?"

"We have discovered why there are no ions getting to the end of the tube," Dekker said. "Come and see for yourself."

They went out into the lab toward the collision tube.

Dekker pointed at a spot around ten centimetres from the neutron detector end. "There. Notice anything?"

"A silica glass tube about two centimetres in diameter filled with nothing. What am I supposed to notice?"

"There's too much light around. You can't see it unless you know what you're looking for," Mark said, shaking his head from side to side in an attempt to regain his senses. He irrationally hoped that when they came to look in the morning there would be nothing to see.

Dekker went over to the hydrogen injection valve and opened it slightly to allow a tiny stream of the gas into the dead accelerator cavity, and so into the collision tube. A brilliant razor-sharp line of red light appeared in the tube. It grew in intensity until it abruptly stopped about ten centimetres from the end. The brilliant red changed into a white, and then into a bluish-white razor of light, so intense it was impossible to look at without pain.

Candi jumped back from the tube and covered her eyes. Dekker shut off the gas. The line slowly faded until it was invisible again.

Candi spoke in a soft, shocked, almost reverent sort of voice. "What in le nom de Dieu was that? How did you supply energy to the tube? Where are the ionised hydrogen atoms going to? Why did the light stop before the end?"

Dekker came over from the injection valve and gripped her arm. "We don't know. Mark discovered this last night. We've been here all night trying to figure out what the hell is happening. Mark disconnected the waveguide to make absolutely sure there was no energy coming from the klystrons. He knew there wasn't, but in the face of something that defies every theory in physics to date, he had to be sure. The hydrogen gas atoms are being accelerated towards a point in the centre of the tube about ten centimetres from the end. The acceleration is so great that they give off light. When they reach the point where the light stops, they vanish. We don't know where they go."

Candi was silent. Her hand reached out and unconsciously folded itself around Dekker's arm. "Like a black hole? It drags matter into it..." Candi's eyes widened, and there was fear in them.

"No, it isn't a black hole," Mark said, shaking his head. "If it was large enough to be stable, it would have accumulated enough mass to drift downward under gravity toward the silica walls of the tube. When it hit them, it would have gone straight through, then through the floor and so on, gathering mass as it went. By now, there would have been a big hole where the lab is and a lot of x-rays around. No, it's not a black hole."

"That's the trouble. We don't know what it is. It shouldn't exist—we shouldn't have made it exist, but we did." Dekker shook his head from side to side. "And it's self-sustaining. I don't like this situation one little bit."

Candi replied, the fear spreading to her voice. "What are we going to do about it? How do we stop it?"

"We don't know. We have to learn a lot more about what's going on here before we can suggest a way to stop it." Mark continued. "That's the job for today. We must secure the place at all costs. We can't have people coming in here and playing around. This thing is self-sustaining. I don't have to tell you that it's very dangerous. Look what happened when we fed a tiny amount of hydrogen into the tube. Right now, it's sitting in a vacuum, but I shudder to think of what would happen if the glass envelope broke. Daniel is going to contact the chancellor this morning. He's already contacted all the other staff and told them not to come in. The university will want to know something about what's going on before they agree to the security measures we want, and, at present, we don't know what to tell them."

Candi stared at the empty collision tube, her face reflecting the growing fear in her heart. "What happens if we can't shut it down? If we have made something that is ... not reversible? I am beginning to be very afraid. I should never have ... mon Dieu, we are in trouble, aren't we?"

"We may be in a lot of trouble, Candi, but let's not panic so soon," Dekker said. "We're looking at an unexplained phenomenon that could be very, very dangerous as Mark said. If we're going to make sensible decisions, we need more information. Panicking will not get us anywhere."

Dekker sounded far more calm than he felt. He patted Candi's hand, which was gripping his arm, not just to encourage her but also so she wouldn't discover he wasn't entirely steady himself. "Must not panic the troops," he told himself.

His face grey and haggard, Mark sat in a chair by the control panel. He had slept hardly at all, and it was clouding his reason in a most unhelpful way. He tried to think what should be done next and came up with a large, unhelpful zero.

Candi set the direction for the day's activities. "We have to be more quantitative. We need to know what sort of energies are involved, what sort of energy is being given off by this ... what to name it ... breach in the laws of the universe. Voilà! That is what I will call it, the breach. Daniel, do you have that Luxmeter handy? I will take measurements. Can you let some hydrogen into the tube? I'll measure the brightness accurately."

"I'll get it," Mark said. "Daniel can play with the hydrogen valve. I'm not sure I want to."

Candi made her measurements and recorded the rate of gas injection.

A short time later, she came out of her office looking much unhappier than she had when she went in. "The energy output is around one thousand watts for every gram of hydrogen we let into the tube, which is quite enough energy to melt the glass envelope." She shook her head, trying to shake off the conclusion she had reached. "This is very dangerous, very frightening. I do not like this result. If we were to open the injection valve to its fullest extent, we would be delivering around ten grams of hydrogen per second. This would output over twelve thousand Joules of energy. The glass envelope would be vaporised. I don't want to think about what would happen next."

Mark stood ashen faced.

Dekker picked up a spanner and headed for the hydrogen feed. "I'm disconnecting the hydrogen feed altogether. Then I'll seal off the injection port so nothing can get into the tube. If the discharge ceases after a few days, we can pour in some more hydrogen to see if the breach has closed itself off. If we get no discharge, then we bring the tube back to atmospheric pressure. If all is well and there's no discharge, we can finally relax. I'm not going to attempt further experiments with collision energies of that order of magnitude. We will have to rethink where we go from here."

"We had better get together on the report then," Mark said, "and hope that the university does the sensible thing. If that glass were to..." Visibly distressed, he sat down on the side of Dekker's desk.

Candi watched him. The sight of Mark afraid added one more destabilising element to her already-shaken world. She thought of going over to him, but she stopped herself because she had no idea what she could possibly say. Instead, she sat on another chair not far from Dekker and stared steadily at the floor feeling guilty about her part in the whole business. Her conscience was giving her a bad time, which was so unfair! Hitherto, she had been able to ignore it, but at the moment it was hammering for attention. She deliberately thought about shoes.

"We need help," Dekker said. "I need help. I know some pretty learned colleagues at Berkeley and some others working with CERN on the accelerator in Geneva. I think we should get them out here as soon as possible. This is a case for corporate wisdom if ever there were one. We've reached a turning point in atomic physics."

"It may be a turning point for the world if they can't find a way to shut the ghastly thing down." Mark spoke through his hands. "If only we had known that this possibility existed! How could we have known?"

"It's an odd thing," Dekker replied grimly. "Professor Cole said something to me I wish I'd taken more notice of. She said there should be another boundary condition to science. We shouldn't just do something because we can do it—we need to think about what we should do. She warned me about such high energies. I wish to God I'd listened and thrown the whole project in the waste paper bin. I swear I did not envisage this! I dread the thought of telling her what's happened."

Possibly inspired from her contemplations on the cost of fashionable footwear, Candi came back to the discussion. "If they are going to do some experiments, these clever scientists, they are going to need some equipment to experiment with. There's no point in getting them all the way out here just so they can look at that little thin line and say 'goodness gracious! How awful!' How will we fund them?"

"It's a good point, Candi," Dekker said. "I will add it to the report recommendations. We already have increased security, a worldwide call for help, and now additional funding so we can do urgent research. I'll try to spin it so that the university will think they are going to get glory and honour out of this, which will be true if all goes well."

"They'll get something else if it doesn't." Mark said.

Candi exploded. "For goodness sake, we haven't died yet! Why not at least try to exercise a little optimism? I don't think well when I'm terrified—do you? Do either of you? We're going to find a way. Someone will. There are a lot of clever people around. One of them will have the answer. Someone always does."

"All right, point taken." Dekker dragged his laptop within reach. "Mark is simply a realist, and right now I wish I wasn't one of them, too. Come on you two, let's draft the wording. We don't want to panic the place, either, or we'll be knee deep in reporters and other fools by morning."

Mark put his hands over his face again and visibly shuddered. The thought of reporters with cameras and big bulky gear hovering around the collision tube made him feel violently ill. Then there would be politicians trying to turn the whole thing into some political advantage. Welcome to hell itself. His thoughts seemed to yawn over the brink of despair.

Candi brought him back. "Mark, Mark! Daniel wants us to work out the wording. You're better at this than me. My English has problems sometimes, and I can't think of clever words. If we get it finished we can email it to … who do we email it to? The chancellor, I suppose. Someone who has power to act immediately."

Mark grunted a reply, and, by dint of enormous effort, began to address himself to the task. It took them longer to compile than they thought it would because they had to carefully choose each word so that they made the situation serious enough to precipitate action, yet not so serious as to incite panic.

Candi tried to get them to use simpler language and not so much physics. Dekker typed the draft on his laptop as they composed it.

After an hour, Dekker phoned Fred, the security guard on duty, and asked him to fetch some sandwiches from Camden. You would have thought he had been asked to give six litres of blood. An hour passed before the sandwiches arrived back, even if the change didn't. The trio kept working while they ate.

It had grown completely dark by the time Dekker typed the last few words into the document.

While the others were concentrating on the task, Mark took his torch and went out into the darkened lab. He stopped at the tube and stared at the thin hairline of light. He cupped his hands around it and reflected how thin the glass that held them back from destruction was.

As a young man, he had walked centimetres from the cliff edge at Nowra and stared down to the sea rocks three hundred metres below without any sense of fear. He had often pulled a live power cord from its socket with his hands only millimetres of plastic from a voltage that could have taken his life, and he had felt no sense of danger at all.

He stared at his hands and felt more frightened then he had ever been. The light from the ionised gas streaming into the breach shone through his curled fingers, coldly illuminating them. The significance of the change from the previous evening suddenly and shockingly dawned on him.

"My God," he choked out loudly. "I can see my hands! I can see my hands!!"

The sound of feet running behind him caused Mark to swing round.

"Stop!" Mark screamed. "You might hit the tube!! Here, let me shine the torch for you."

"What's the matter?" asked Dekker breathlessly.

"I can see my hands! There's enough light for me to see my hands. Last night I could hardly see the light at all, and now I can see my hands!"

"It certainly seems brighter." Dekker muttered staring unwillingly at the razor-thin line of light.

"It's the wrong colour." Candi said.

"What do you mean?" Mark asked, dragging his eyes away to face her.

"Hydrogen discharge is orange red at low energies. This is white. Moment. Shine the light." She went back to the office and then returned with a CD in her hand. She held the recorded surface up to the thin line of light. It broke up into many coloured lines from red through green to blue. "This is not hydrogen. It's the spectrum of some metal."

There was silence.

At last, Dekker replied, "We've been fools. I've disconnected the hydrogen feed line. How could it be hydrogen? The only metal around is the stainless steel of the injection manifold at the start of the tube."

"Dear God," Mark said, his voice trembling with emotion, "It's pulling atoms off the injection manifold from three-and-a-half metres away!!"

There was more silence.

Dekker found his voice first. It wasn't steady, either. "We can't stop it."

"The breach is widening," Mark said. "The experiments we did today have widened it. The more it's used, the wider it gets, and the more power it has to attract atoms. It sucks them in as if it were a black hole. We're really in dreadful trouble." He sounded as if he had difficulty breathing.

The pallor of Candi's face was not apparent in the light coming from the breach. Inside, she felt as if her world was being invaded by aliens—or one alien in particular. Making one last try at optimism, she said, "There's a lot of metal in that injection port. It will take a long time to eat through it. Perhaps we can put some more metal there just in case."

"Unless its pulling atoms off one tiny area," Mark countered, "in which case we may not have as long as we thought."

Once again, Candi was stunned into silence. Her eyes were wide and frightened. Her last attempt at optimism lay dead on the floor. Even from where she stood, the light from the breach reflected in her eyes, and she could see her hands holding the CD. Truly, life had taken a most unexpected turn. Her every effort was directed into fitting the breach into the category in which she placed everything else: a problem for the moment, and nothing more.

Her phone rang loudly. Candi almost jumped out of her skin. She pulled it out of a little pouch around her waist and answered it.

"Babe, it's Roger here. Are you sleeping with that bloody geek?"

She snapped the phone shut and returned it to her pocket. "Life just keeps on getting better," she muttered to herself. She turned around and went back towards her darkened office, feeling as though she were about to throw up.

# CHAPTER 13

In the morning, Dekker emailed the final report and phoned the chancellor. Things did not go as well as he had expected them to go.

"I'm afraid you cannot contact the chancellor, Dr. Van Dekker. She is attending a conference on access and equity for women in engineering courses."

"The university doesn't run any engineering courses," Dekker pointed out. "Who are you?"

"I am the personal assistant to the chancellor. I notice you have sent a report of your work directly to her. Be advised, Dr. Van Dekker, that you should process such information through the proper channels. Next person in your reporting line should be the dean of your faculty, and then, if necessary, the chairman of academic committees, then, if necessary, the vice chancellor, then..."

"I am sorry to interrupt you, but this is an extremely serious matter that ..."

"And then, should the matter require a decision involving university policy, it will be referred to the chancellor for consideration. Failure to observe such protocols could result in serious consequences. I notice that your funding has not yet been approved. There were outstanding quality assurance matters unsatisfactorily addressed in your application. The matter has been referred to ..."

"For God's sake, woman," Dekker said, "I have an extremely danger-ous situation down here requiring immediate assistance. The ..."

"Then the matter should be taken up with occupational health and safety. In the future, do not expect this office to be your point of contact with the university. I am transferring you now."

Dekker threw his coffee mug at the wall.

"This is occupational health and safety. How can we help you?"

"This is Dr. Van Dekker. I have a serious situation here requiring immediate action. In the interests of public safety, I need an increased security presence on this campus so ..."

"We cannot authorize security matters, Dr. Van Dekker," the voice on the other end of the phone line said. "Only the vice chancellor's department can do that. I note your premises have not been inspected by our department, and all experimentation must be delayed until they are."

Dekker said, "We have been conducting experiments that have resulted in a potentially serious situation ..."

"Any such experiments are unauthorized by this university. Conducting unauthorized research will lead to your funding being re-viewed unfavourably. I will send some officers to your campus to review the situation and report back. In the meantime, please provide me with your report on the procedures you have put in place to create a safe work place environment and explain how these procedures have been unable to prevent the occurrence of a dangerous situation. I trust there will be no danger to my officers who will visit your campus?"

"There will be because if they turn up inside this building, I'll shoot them."

"Dr. Van Dekker, I must inform you that this department takes occupational health and safety very seriously, much more seriously than you do, apparently. The officers will arrive sometime next week, and should you carry out any threat against them, you will find your-self in custody of the police." And with that, she hung up.

Dekker rang campus security. Their collective synergies were out of phase from the start. "This is Dr. Daniel Van Dekker here—"

"Mason, head of section. On what authority did you issue instructions to the staff deployed on your premises to increase their hours and so involve them in overtime?"

"There is a situation here requiring their operations to be intensified," Dekker said. "That's what I am ringing about."

"You should be aware that they will not be paid overtime because the activities you asked them to engage in were not authorized by this office," Mason said. "Accordingly, I will withdraw them from duty for the same number of hours as they worked in excess. This will not affect your budget. In the future, any changes to security arrangements must he cleared through the vice chancellor's office, and then this office will attempt to implement them."

Dekker hung up.

Not only would he have no security, but he would also have official visitors: nosey, ignorant visitors with notepads and no brains. He picked up the pieces of his coffee mug from the floor and threw them individually into the bin with a good deal more force than was necessary.

This university, he concluded, was an asylum run by the inmates, and being attached to it was turning into a curse.

However, if he had been in the office of Millicent Veronica Smythe-Harris, personal assistant to the chancellor, he would have been surprised.

"Margaret, I am so sorry to interrupt you …" the personal assistant was saying to the chancellor.

"Millie, the conference is going wonderfully well! Is everything all right back there?"

"You have been emailed a report from Dr. Daniel Van Dekker," she reported. "He was on the phone with me this morning and urgently wanted to speak with you. I told him this was inappropriate, but I think you should read his report. It doesn't make any sense to me, but the matter may have some political fallout for the university. I'll have it couriered over to you straight away."

"Thanks, Millie. I'll have a squiz at it between lectures."

Dekker's report didn't make any sense to Chancellor Margaret Marriott, either. To her, it sounded like a lot of doomsday hype wrapped up in gobbledygook. But Margaret Marriott was not stupid. She latched on to one item in the report with interest. Energy. This project had been funded by Global Power Consortium. When they came on board, they had agreed to fund other projects at the university as well. She had every reason to keep them happy. Energy was their business. This screwed-up physics project was producing unwanted energy. They were experts in energy.

She phoned Karl Kashinsky, her contact with GPC. She asked if he would be interested in reading Dekker's report. As it turned out, his answer was "yes." She emailed it to him, went back to the next stimulating lecture, and forgot all about it.

Jack ambled into Dekker's office that afternoon to inform him that he and the other guys had been ordered off duty.

"So university security has removed all security from this campus?" Dekker exploded.

"I don't know nothing about what the security unit is doing. The boss said something about not being needed since you've told all the other engineering guys and fitters not to come back until further notice. All I know is that we've been reassigned to their other campus out at Richmond. Damn inconvenient. It's all to do with that overtime business. We still haven't been paid—got time in lieu, which none of us wanted." Jack slouched off, obviously in a very bad mood. Not only was the Camden campus closer to his home, but it was also probably the only place he could sit in his office and watch videos for most of the day. It had been quiet, peaceful, and entertaining. Ah, well, all good things must come to an end.

Dekker drove himself to the hardware store in Camden to buy very large locks and lots of heavy duty chain. He needn't have bothered. The very next day a small army of security guards arrived at campus. This lot was very different. They were efficient, they were armed, and they were on duty twenty-four-seven. You didn't get past them without showing a special pass that they had issued.

"I thought university security was not going to send anyone to this campus." Dekker said to the head guard after he had been briefed on the new security arrangements.

"I don't know anything about university security," he replied. "All I know is that we were hired to guard this place. We're a private firm specialized in high-level security."

The real reason that the university would accede so generously to his request never crossed Dekker's mind at all. He was a rational man with a generous heart, and, at some level, expected his fellow human beings to be the same. The university had responded appropriately to his first request. He expected to hear they had also favourably considered the others in the near future.

Because he and Mark were the only two particle physicists on the project, they spent many hours conferring with one another, and with a Professor Hans Zimmerman in Switzerland, who shared their deep concern. The latter gentleman had even gone to the extent of requesting that the University of Southern Sydney take him on for a sabbatical to work with Daniel. However, the only reply he had received was to the effect that the project conducted by Drs. Dekker, Leblanc and Chambers was under review and was likely to be closed down because of occupational health and safety concerns, so there was no possibility of them taking on an additional member of staff, no matter who he was.

This rather insulting reply troubled Dekker even more.

All three men agreed on the extreme danger of interfering with the "anomaly" unless it was first contained in a more substantial manner. Its delicate existence at the far end of a three-metre long glass tube, protected by absolutely nothing else, made each of them feel physically ill. They had done their best to keep people away, but the situation was precarious, to say the least.

Mark had done several calculations based on the carefully measured intensity of the discharge and concluded for the time being there was enough steel in the injection port to contain the breach for roughly eighteen months, by which point they would be surely much further along the path to shutting it down.

That particular morning, Dekker and Mark stood side by side outside the barricades they had erected around the breach. They were staring at the thin white line, which had grown bright enough to be seen in the light of day. Each of them, including Candi, would make regular pilgrimages to this place, partly because the breach, by its very alien nature, seemed to have power to draw them in, unwilling and fearful, and partly from the hope of arriving and finding it had shut itself down since their last visit.

"It's a particle problem," Mark said, staring fixedly at the breach, "and it will require a particle solution. Some sort of new quantum bridge is involved, and that's where we should direct our thinking. There's a lot of dark matter in the universe. How did it get there? Perhaps we've discovered one of the mechanisms. Let's hope it's not irreversible."

"Hans is inclined to agree with you, Mark," Dekker said. "The trouble is, we can't do any more experiments with the wretched thing in the form it's in now. It's too vulnerable in that glass tube. Every time I see it I get the shakes, if you really want to know."

Mark tore his gaze away and turned toward Dekker. "You and me both. I've been praying for wisdom, Daniel, but as the days go by I seem to be getting less and less of it, and not more and more."

"It's because you're exhausted. No one performs well when they're exhausted."

"And you're not exhausted?"

A tiny smile crossed Dekker's face. "At least I have Jasmin. Even though I trust her with my life, I haven't told her what the problem is—but she knows it's pretty serious. She's a remarkable woman, Mark. I would like you to meet her one day. When I get home, there's dinner on the table, everything laid out just the way I like it, as though all is right with the world. She knows I can't tell her the details and she doesn't press me, she just listens to what I can say. Somehow she makes me feel as though it will be all right, although I don't rightly know how. I come home dispirited, and I leave the next morning full of hope. That's her doing. I wish you had someone like that."

"I wish I did, Daniel," Mark said. "You know, it's the fear. I feel if I leave this place, even for five minutes, something terrible will happen, but when I'm here I keep staring at the wretched thing and it terrifies me. I can hardly think straight. I've never been frightened of anything this much before, and I don't know how to handle it. I even find it hard to pray sometimes."

Dekker turned towards Mark, his eyes registering surprise. "Surely your faith is a great help in times like this?"

"Oh, yes, it is," Mark said. "I know that if I die I'll go to heaven, not because I've been anything special, but because Jesus died and rose again for me. That's not the problem. It's this: I know I wasn't the only one who made this happen, but I was one of them. I feel as though I've actually put the world in peril and I owe it to everyone to fix the mess I've made. But I don't think I'm going to come up with the goods. That's the problem, if you really want to know."

Dekker silently nodded. He didn't answer because he didn't have an answer. In his low moments, he, too, felt a horrible, gut-wrenching guilt. "Do you think there could ever be forgiveness for us, Mark? Do you think God can pardon a sin like this?"

"Have you asked Him to forgive you, Daniel?"

"No, I don't really know how to. I suppose I should go to Mass or something."

"Just ask Him," Mark said. "You don't need anything else. When you go home tonight, find a quiet moment and ask God for forgiveness. God's Word says 'If we confess our sin, He is faithful and just and will forgive us for all our unrighteousness.'"

"Is it possible to be forgiven and not feel forgiven?"

Mark sighed deeply, his own guilt weighing heavily on his heart despite the many times he had begged for wisdom and forgiveness himself. "Yes, Daniel, I'm afraid it is. Sometimes it's hard to take God at His word. I know He's forgiven me, but I'm having trouble forgiving myself."

"You know," Dekker said, "I've never really been a religious man, but this type of thing sorts out your beliefs, doesn't it? Kind of brings into focus the important aspects of life you're always going to think about tomorrow—manana—but you never get around to thinking about them because there are so many seemingly more important matters to deal with. Do you know Jasmin prays for me before I go to work? She puts her arms around me and says something like 'Dear Lord, give him strength and wisdom and let him know where its coming from.' It's been her faith, and not mine, that's brought my thinking around, Mark. I've never told anyone this before."

"You need to tell her. She'll be so incredibly encouraged if you do. Ask her to pray with you."

"I might do that. You won't tell Candi any of this?"

"Candi?!" Mark fought back a grin. "Mention that she needs forgiveness, and you put your life at risk. Besides, I don't want her angry with me. I can do without one more problem right now."

"Is there anyone in your church you can talk to, Mark?"

"There's Andrew, " Mark said, "but I can't tell him what the problem really is, and I don't want him to guess. He's a good guesser, too. I've asked him to pray for me, the wisdom thing, like Jasmin prays for you. I guess it's helping, but sometimes I feel a bit low."

Dekker reached out his arm and gave his young colleague a hug around the shoulder. It was the best he could do to show him that he knew exactly how he felt.

Dekker's arms fell down by his sides and he sighed deeply. "I'll have to tell Professor Cole about this sometime. I've been putting it off. I know what she's going to say, and I don't want to hear it. I think you'd better add courage to the things you pray for me."

Mark smiled as he turned away from a last look at the breach. "She's a very unusual person, you said."

Dekker actually laughed. "Unusual? Unique. Venus the genius. She unsettled the life out of me, can't tell you why."

"And you have to tell her?"

Dekker sighed deeply again. "I think I owe it to her. You see, she was right when she told me those energies were a bad idea. I wish with every fibre of my being I'd taken notice. Not your problem. Perhaps I'll leave it for a day or so."

Both men went back to their offices in silence.

Candi spent the week since that last dreadful evening slowly taking her microwave generator apart as if that would somehow atone for her having built it in the first place.

In fact, it had had the reverse effect.

In the exercise, she was destroying the creativity that had given her so much pleasure over the previous months, and which had, in the end, enabled her to triumph over her fear. That fear had gone, and another one not so easily exorcised had taken its place.

She spoke to no one about it: not Roger, because he was sceptical of all he did not understand, nor Mark, because she was not a physicist, nor Dekker for the same reason.

By the end of the week, she had stretched her optimism to the maximum and almost succeeded in persuading herself that it was but a temporary problem—something they would look back on and laugh about—nothing more than a new and different moment in the disconnected particulars of life—unpleasant and insignificant in the whole meaningless scheme of things.

The fear, ebbing and flowing through her consciousness, was constantly working to undo that process, and by the end of the week it was still far from complete.

She often thought about simply buying an air ticket to Paris and leaving greater minds than hers to work on the problem. After all, what use was she? Sooner or later she would hear that all was well, if she hadn't already forgotten the whole sorry business in the whirl of enjoyment she would wrap around her life as soon as she arrived home.

Somehow she could not leave. It worried her because she could not understand her own reasons for staying.

The breach, it seemed, had the ability to draw more than metal atoms into its power. She would walk past it many times a day, just to see if by some hand of fate that obscene hairline of light had gone away. But it was always there, and it always sent a shuddering chill rippling up her spine. In her darkest thoughts lay the notion that if she did not deal with the breach, it would find her, no matter where she was. Each time it seemed a little brighter, but it was hard to tell when the imagination was required to work overtime just to come to terms with its existence at all.

She was staring at it from the other side of the barricades she had helped to make, designed to give even the most cynically curious cause for pause. "Extreme Danger," "Passing this point puts your life at risk," and "Stop. Lethal Radiation. GO BACK."

She turned to admire the one she had designed for the benefit of any French visitors: "Sortez-vous, idiots, ou vous allez mourir!! " But she had drawn flowers all round the edge to soften the effect.

Mark spent his days—and most of his nights—working in his office. His whiteboard resembled an explosion in a pen factory. There were papers in ankle-deep piles all over the floor. He said little and looked grey with weariness. The more he worked, the more depressed he became because no line of thinking produced anything other than a blank wall. He had no experiment, no way of obtaining more data that would not add greatly to the already perilous situation, so it was all theoretical hypothesis and guesswork. He hoped that somehow a simple method of reversing the process would fall out of the sky, and then he would be able to go to the others and say "it's simple, all we have to do is …" and that would be that.

As the days went past, he despaired of ever finding a simple solution. Such optimistic thoughts were merely a pipe dream sponsored by fear.

One afternoon, Candi, who was peering through the small glass panel in his office door, found him sitting at his desk, staring at nothing, and trying unsuccessfully to pick up a pen with his right hand. She opened the door as loudly as possible, and, setting her face into a delighted smile that she didn't actually feel, bounced across the chaos towards him. "Mark! Chéri, Mark! I'm going to take you for coffee."

He gave no response.

Forcing the light-hearted mask to remain on her face, she went over to him and grabbed the hand still methodically trying to find the pen that had, by then, sought refuge on the floor. "Mark. I'm taking you for coffee. Come back to me! Mark, you cannot keep doing this to yourself! In a month you will be having the nervous breakdown, and then where will we be? You have to keep sharp, or you will make the wrong call, and Candi will be sucked into the breach. I do not like this idea. When did you last have the good sleep? Come on, Mark. I'm taking you out of here."

Pulling him by the arm, she managed to extricate him from the flood of papers on the floor, through the door, and out into the lab. He seemed to come to just past the warning signs, and turned to her in surprise. "Candi! I was somewhere else. How did we get here? It's really bad, isn't it?"

"I'm not taking you for coffee. I'm taking you home, and whether you like it or not, I'm putting you to bed."

She bundled him into her car and drove straight to Elderslie. It was only a short journey, but, before she stopped outside his home in River Road, he had fallen asleep, his head propped against the passenger window. Candi got out of the car, went round and opened his door. His head, suddenly deprived of its resting place, almost fell out onto her shoulder.

"What? Oh, thank you, Candi. Where are we?"

"Home. Where are your keys? Come on, Mark. Walk."

He was still groggy when they reached the front door. Candi opened it, and they went inside. She guided him into the bedroom, flopped him down on the bed fully clothed, pulled the pillow over, and shoved it under his head. He was already asleep. Undoing the laces on his shoes, she drew them off and put them at the foot of the bed. Then she loosened his trouser belt, covered him with a single blanket, walked out of the house, and shut the door behind her.

Walking back to the car, she was struck by a single and rather foreign thought. Here was a man who actually needed her, needed her to care for him in a way that had nothing whatsoever to do with desire. No one, in the long and varied history of men in Candi's life, had ever needed her like that.

She shut the car door and started the engine, still turning the idea over in her mind. Commitment was still the dreaded enemy of freedom, yet at the same time she could not deny that there was something rather nice about being needed as a friend without being wanted as a woman.

She decided she rather liked it.

On the other hand, Dekker spent the time more wisely, but no more productively, widening his network of colleagues. They were all talking to each other through emails that were flowing back and forth with growing rapidity. The university had fortunately forgotten to bar his phone to overseas calls, and, by the end of the month, they were going to be somewhat distressed at the size of the phone bill. As the net widened, so, too, did the concern.

The eminent theoretical physicist Stephen Eagles had become involved, and on his own initiative he had established a think tank at the Massachusetts Institute of Technology.

Many of his learned colleagues had urged Dekker to make the situation public, if not in Australia, then in Great Britain or the United States, but the latter had thought the better of this course of action.

"It will only incite panic," Dekker told them, "The political situation here is unstable, and the university is a positive threat to any reasonable discussion. They have no apparent appreciation of the gravity of the situation. I counsel the utmost caution at this point. If any of you gentlemen can think of a way to improve our position, I would be most grateful, but the best solution all round would be to find a way to close the breach. If we could agree on that, I would go public, in the UK first, I think, and then I would bring pressure to bear on the Australian government from the top down, and not through these idiots we've had the misfortune to be dealing with so far. The minister for the environment is a gangster."

They had reluctantly agreed and gone back to rework the problem. If only they had been able to collect more data. It was an intensely frustrating exercise to be faced with an impending catastrophe without recourse to a single experiment.

# CHAPTER 14

It was eight o'clock.

Candi had taken Mark home earlier that evening and had not returned, leaving Dekker alone in the laboratory. Summoning up his courage, he picked up the phone and dialled the number Sarah Cole had left on the bottom of her email. After several rings, the lady herself picked up. Daniel identified himself and began the tale, finding he had to clear his throat after almost every word. However, the story took surprisingly little time to tell and ended with a silence so long he wondered if the line had gone dead.

Eventually, Sarah spoke. "So, Daniel, your foolish high-energy experiments have imperilled the world."

"I fear so. I had no idea ..."

"Did I not tell you there are areas where science should not tread?" She replied, her voice tinged with anger. "Where the risks of disaster are too great? What sort of myopic optimism led you to believe that your adding to the weight of scientific knowledge in this would benefit a morally inept human race?"

She was angry, and Dekker knew it. He struggled to frame a reply. "I admit that I was totally wrong. I should have listened to you. I curse myself for not doing so, but I cannot understand the connection you make between a scientific experiment, even one like this that went awry, and the morality of the human race."

"You cannot, or you will not? You suppose all who learn of this "breach" will unite with one voice to shut it down?"

"Of course they will! Any other action is unthinkable! Insanity!" Beads of sweat began to form on Dekker's forehead. "Surely you don't believe..."

Sarah Cole interrupted him. "These eminent scientists, the ones you've contacted, are no doubt all on their way to study the breach first hand—clutching the pleading requests they've received from the University of Southern Sydney in their hands.?"

The question left Dekker somewhat short for breath. At last, he managed to stammer a response. "No, for some reason nobody has received any such request. I am at a loss as to why not."

"Yet you tell me the university has responded with high-level security on the site." It was more of a statement than a question. "Tell me, Daniel, doesn't it strike you as somehow inconsistent with your theory of universal benevolence?"

Dekker wiped his forehead with the back of his hand. What right had this woman to dress him down in such a fashion? Had she not agreed to design the blasted superconductors in the first place? He tried to keep his escalating rage out of his voice. "I suppose you have some better idea, based, no doubt, upon your pessimistic stance on the depraved nature of the human race?"

"They were sent by someone else," she snapped. "Why can't you see that? Human nature is flawed, Daniel, and you of all people should believe it. I admit I'm responsible to a large degree. I did design your superconductors in a moment of weakness. I regret doing it as much as you regret not taking my advice. Now I will have to try and make amends. There is nothing else to say now, but we'll see each other again before this sorry business has run its course. Goodbye."

Dekker put down the phone and wiped his forehead again with a handkerchief. Sarah Cole had made him feel the same way he had when he was a little boy and his father had applied the wooden spoon of education to his seat of learning. He hated it then, and he hated it every bit as much now.

Elizabeth Caruthers laid another slice of mushroom on the pizza she had been preparing with Sarah Cole when the phone had rung.

Sounds of various items hitting the floor in the lounge room brought the pizza preparation to a sudden and premature end. She wiped her hands on the nearest tea towel and headed towards the source of the disturbance. A reasonably large book on general relativity executed a curved trajectory into the wall. It was followed by a cushion, a smaller book Elizabeth had been reading, and a stuffed rabbit that usually presided over the room from its throne on top of the television.

"What on Earth is the matter?!" Elizabeth asked.

Sarah turned round to face her with fire in her eyes. "I've done it again! Allowed myself to pander to another stupid man! Damn him! Damn me!"

Elizabeth advanced on the angry woman. Tactfully, she removed a small china ornament from her hand. Pushing her towards the sofa, she sat down and pulled Sarah down next to her. "Now," she said while carefully stowing the remaining cushion out of reach, "what miserable male has caused the beautiful and gentle Sarah Cole to fly off into a demented rage?"

Sarah grimaced and then smiled at her friend. "I've just had a most distressing call from Daniel Van Dekker. You remember, the man you schooled before he came in to see me. You're partly to blame, you know. If you hadn't schooled him, he'd have ogled me like all the rest of them and I would have booted him out. None of this would have happened."

"And just what has happened?" Ignoring the jibe, Elizabeth raised her eyebrows.

"Van Dekker's experiment went wrong. They've created a potentially hazardous situation, and they're too bloody naïve to see what's happening. This is serious, Elizabeth. I'll have to go on an unexpected lecture tour of Great Britain. Need to see Ross Baker."

Elizabeth smiled and uttered a little chuckle. "The man who thinks you're an angel? Shame he wasn't here tonight."

"There's no need to bring that nonsense up. I wish he had been. Would save me all the trouble of going to see him."

"He's some sort of spy, isn't he?"

Sarah actually laughed. "No, he isn't. If you promise to keep a secret, I'll tell you. He's head of MI6. Dekker and his team are in danger of being sucked into something very nasty. Ross is the only person I know who could assist them—or who could at least find out what's going on. Believe me, they're going to need help. Bother! I've got so much other work to do!"

Elizabeth read the lines of worry on Sarah's beautiful face. "It's really bad, isn't it? I've never seen you so upset."

"I'm responsible, Elizabeth. I should never have cooperated with Dekker. Yes, it's very nasty. No need to worry you at this stage." Sarah smiled. "Are the pizzas ready to cook? I'm feeling in the need of food. Oh, and there's a bottle of Chardonnay in the 'fridge. I'll fetch the glasses."

The very next day, Sarah Cole left for Heathrow on the evening flight, leaving a very worried Elizabeth Caruthers behind her.

# CHAPTER 15

Sarah Cole was uncannily precise in her analysis of the situation. There was no follow-up because the matter, unknown to Dekker, had been passed on to the research division of Global Power Consortium.

At that very time, a group of men were sitting around a large table in a very well-appointed conference room within a stone's throw from Lake Geneva. Lights from the city reflected in its dark waters through windows running the entire length of the room. It was doubtful if any of those present were watching them.

At the head of the table sat Louis Hakim, General Manager of Global Power Consortium. On his right was George Jenner, chief executive officer; and on his left, Peter North, manager of their engineering division. The remaining places around the table were occupied with various other managers and financial directors.

One of the latter, a Francis Bennett, was speaking. "I hear you, Director, but it seems to me that the whole project is fraught with uncertainties. It's a potential political problem, and, if your engineering division is correct, a considerable risk to public safety."

"That's true, Bennett," Hakim replied. "Yet I am reliably informed there may be a unique opportunity afforded to us as well. The dangers, as far as I can make out, are the opinions of three scientists, only two of whom have much training in the relevant disciplines. The third is a woman, a power engineer. Not an insignificant one, either. In the years to come, I would consider her becoming a member of our technical staff. As much as it pains me to do so, I will ask our CEO to explain the situation to you all again. Would you mind, George?"

The man addressed rose from his chair. "I will deal with the issues one at a time.

"Firstly, and most properly, there is the issue of safety, which so concerns the three scientists who have inadvertently created this anomaly, or whatever they might choose to call it. Their concerns are completely understandable. They have produced a quantum bridge of some kind, a place in space and time that draws matter into itself and gives off energy in the process. They do not understand how it works. This in itself makes them afraid, because two of them are accomplished physicists and they cannot account for it at all.

"The quantum bridge is at present contained in a rather precarious manner inside a fragile glass tube. The consequences of that insubstantial vessel breaking would be enough to worry the life out of any reasonable human being. I have read the report and feel that even if we do not decide to go ahead with this proposition, we should at least take some steps to render the situation more stable.

"On the other hand, it may be possible to increase the safety aspect and take advantage of this new technology. Remember when we first discovered nuclear power. There were those who, quite rightly, were concerned that we had unleashed a monster, but we have tamed that monster, gentlemen, and now it serves the human race in peace and deters the threat of war. I believe we have come to another such turning point.

"Imagine it: as matter streams through one of these quantum bridges, becoming undetectable, energy—pure, uncontaminated energy—flows out into our energy-hungry world. There is no pollution, there is no waste, and there is no problem of unpleasant radiation."

Another of the dark suited managers said, "But there may be a problem of containment. What happens if we need to shut such a plant down? If there's a population shift, some government doesn't pay its electricity bill, or the plant becomes damaged through neglect or hostile activity. What do we do then?"

"A good point, Collins, and one I have considered," George said. "There are many clever people in the world of science, and I do not doubt that it will be only a short time before a solution to that problem is found. What matters now is that we have an operational quantum bridge available to us and that we can explore the possibility of using it as a source of energy. It is a unique opportunity. If we do not seize it, someone will find out how to shut the thing down, and they will be loathe to repeat the experiments that brought about its existence. No, gentlemen, I believe that if we are going to harness this new technology towards the world's energy needs, we must act immediately. In the process, we will contribute to the safety of the surrounding area by securing the bridge within a much more stable environment."

"I have read the report by Dekker and company," Collins said. "They believe that throwing material into the quantum bridge actually widens it. Perhaps the situation is not as controllable as we think."

Jenner glanced down at the sheaf of papers in front of him. "There is very little evidence to support this conclusion, Collins, for the simple reason that Dekker and his co-workers are not prepared to take the risk of doing experiments while the bridge is confined in such an unsatisfactory manner. They are right. This lends weight to our proposition. As we investigate the power-producing ability of the bridge, we can test these claims. Remember nuclear power, gentlemen. A runaway process of nuclear fission was tamed and controlled. On the face of it, I do not think this is nearly as dangerous as the latter."

Hakim had been listening to this discussion, leaning back in his chair with his eyes half-shut.

Anyone who was not at all familiar with the man might have made the mistake of thinking he had lost interest in the proceedings.

Peter North, who was glancing at the figure to the right of him, was not such a man. He knew Hakim well enough to read the eyes half-closed and the fingertips pressed together as a cobra ready to strike.

Apart from that, Louis Hakim was somewhat of a mystery. His face was neither Middle Eastern nor Caucasian, and his eyes gave no additional clue as to his heritage. If North had learned the truth, he would not have been surprised that Hakim had been born in Iran to an Irish father wanted in Britain for his activities with the IRA, and an Egyptian mother who performed in a Cairo nightclub as a belly dancer. Hakim had never known his mother, for she had left long before he could remember very much at all, but he spent long enough with his father to entertain the theory that he had probably strangled her.

Hakim had certainly come to know his father was no stranger to violence. There had been money enough to meet his needs, and he had made wise use of it. His father disappeared before he was twenty, and the young Hakim had never felt even the tiniest twinge of regret. He learned to be clever with money, good at organising people, and cunning and ruthless all by himself.

Little by little, Hakim had become powerful and wealthy. He learned swiftly that the only purpose in acquiring these things lay in enhancing his ability to acquire more of them.

Through his half-closed eyes, Hakim saw North staring at him, and smiled. The time had come to end this charade.

Louis Hakim sat up, placed his hands squarely on the table, and announced, "We have gone through this before, gentlemen. I will call a halt to George's efforts to make you see sense and say one thing more. We run a nuclear power industry. We produce a lot of waste. This waste is becoming a problem for us. It is costly to remove, even when we dump it in the backyards of third-world countries. The time will come when this may not be an option, either because their governments will object, or the cost will escalate unacceptably. What will we do with the waste then? Chemical processing? That is even more expensive, and the products are still radioactive for thousands of years. I am anxious to hear your response."

There was none.

"On the other hand," Hakim said, "if we are able to establish these quantum bridge plants around the world, we can feed our unwanted waste into them and harvest a great deal of energy in the process. If you can't see the financial benefits of such a scheme, then I suggest you start looking for another organisation to work for."

There was no hiding the veiled threat.

On cue, Franz Berkmeyer, head financial adviser, stood up and drew the assembled company's attention to a folder in front of them.

"Gentlemen, I have prepared figures based on the assumption that we will be able to harvest energy from these plants using nuclear waste. The cost recovery on the waste, as you see, rises to twelve point five billion dollars by the end of the decade. Assuming we will be able to generate only one tenth of the energy produced in a reactor through burning this fuel, we will generate over fifty billion dollars worth of power without spending a single dollar on uranium enrichment. Within the next twenty years, this will multiply the profit base of our company by an estimated two hundred and fifty-seven percent. In short, it would become our chief source of income. There is a lot at stake here, gentlemen. Of course, there's risk involved. The quantum bridge may collapse when we attempt to feed the waste into it. It may collapse anyway, and we may be unable to create another one. I have added a statistical analysis of these factors at the end of the report. My recommendation is that we agree to seed funding up to twenty million dollars—and remember, we'll be sending it to Australia, where our dollar buys more—and set up an experimental 'quantum energy device,' for want of a better term."

There was not a great deal of discussion after that. The worthy gentlemen around the table may not have understood a great deal about quantum bridges, but they understood a great deal about money. Within the hour, the meeting had come to a close, leaving Louis Hakim and George Jenner alone.

The former turned to the latter. "George, I am taking you at your word on this project. I trust you have not misled me concerning the risks involved."

"I believe I have given you the correct advice, Louis."

"I hoped you would say no less, because the consequences of making a mistake, of underestimating the factors involved—especially the risks—would take a toll on your health, George. I would not like to see that happen."

George did not reply, but a cold shudder ran down his spine.

"There are matters to attend to, George. I am sending you and North to Australia on the morning flight out of Zurich to take care of them. I don't want any trouble from the Minister for the Environment or the university. Try to do it the nice way first. Then, if you have any problems, we will enlist other measures. I have your word you will not disappoint me?"

"Of course, Louis. I'm on my way."

"Thank you, George. I knew I could depend on you. I wish to be informed of your strategy. I look forward with great interest to our next correspondence. You should go and enjoy yourself. Use the company card. The evening is late, but I am sure you will find suitable diversion still available. My secretary can always assist in those more delicate matters."

George assured him that he need take no further trouble and hurried from the room. There was a lot of careful planning to be done before he faced Dekker and company.

So it was not so many days later, the Minister for the Environment, Mr. Joseph McTierney, received a generous invitation to lunch at Star City casino. McTierney enjoyed visits to the casino for a variety of reasons, especially when he was using other people's money. The table he was seated at was littered with the remains of a very expensive meal, supplemented by an excellent whiskey, all supplied by George Jenner, the CEO of GPC.

Jenner was speaking. "You say that there are holding ponds of radioactive material near this site in your electorate?"

"Unfortunately, yes." McTierney let him know how he felt about AINR in general and Daniel Van Dekker in particular. "They were left when the experimental reactor was decommissioned. I fought against it, but the cost—er, environmental risk—to have them shifted was just too great. I wish them to hell. While they are there, we are all at risk of contamination by groundwater seepage."

"Then you would have no objection in seeing them removed from the site at no cost to yourself or your electorate as part of our proposal?" Jenner asked.

"I would heartily endorse such a move."

"Then I think we have some common ground. You say that there is a cooling tower on the site as well?"

"The cooling tower is huge," McTierney said. "It was built while there was a possibility that Australia would embrace nuclear power. The idea was that the experimental reactor be up-scaled into a fully-fledged nuclear power station. Thankfully, that never happened. I mean, nuclear power is of course completely safe, but my constituents would never agree to having it in their backyard. You know what I mean."

"I understand you perfectly, Joseph," Jenner said. "I take it you would then express your endorsement of the pilot phase to the prime minister? All that needs be done is to communicate our discussions to the chancellor of the university."

"Do you foresee any problems in that direction?"

"None whatsoever," Jenner said. "In fact, the university is very much in favour of the project. They have been quick to point out that the intellectual property used to create the quantum energy device is theirs, and that its use will cost us money. The chancellor is politically ambitious. She has plans to expand Southern Sydney campus on a grand scale. I have no doubt as to where she sees much of the finance for that exercise coming from. It's Dekker himself who will want to give us grief—him and the two devotees who work with him. We will have to tread carefully there. I've had some discussions with our GM, and we are working on a little plan."

# CHAPTER 16

I t was a Friday afternoon when the email from the chancellor reached Dekker's inbox. He read it several times in complete disbelief, printed it out, and read it again.

He was not a man given to dissolving his sorrows in alcohol but, if there had been a bottle of whiskey in the vicinity, he would have made use of it. He felt ill—so ill that he dragged the wastepaper bin to the side of his chair in case he actually vomited. His hands were visibly shaking.

Never in all his life had he been forced to face a situation like this. Life had descended into a bizarre parody of reality, a black comedy, a nightmare.

He could hear Sarah Cole rebuking his myopic optimism concerning the human race, and reluctantly acquiesced to her opinion. He re-read the printed words and, with the other hand, reached for the wastepaper bin, summoning every last ounce of self-control to prevent himself from being sick. It would not do if his colleagues next door heard him vomiting. He had to be calm. But how could he be calm? Was he going mad?

Candi, who was actively engaged in the process of returning the breach to its rightful place as someone else's problem and resuming her happy existential existence, was painting her fingernails and deeply engrossed in the latest copy of Harper's Bazaar when Dekker called her into his office. She screwed the little brush back into the bottle and waved her hands in the air to help her fingers dry. It gave her time to think.

Daniel had sounded very odd on the phone—perhaps he was ill. Her sense of being needed came to the forefront.

Picking up the half-drunk mug of coffee from her desk, she headed for his office. When she arrived, Mark was already there. One glance at Dekker confirmed her conclusion. The poor man was ill. Mark was standing near the wall looking dreadfully apprehensive. Thank goodness they had a clear-headed woman on the scene.

Dekker picked up a printed sheet from his desk and made his first attempt at reading it. His voice seemed to choke, and his hand involuntarily reached for the wastepaper bin. He tried again, but his voice constricted in his throat.

The apprehension flooding over Mark had reached Candi's heart and, with it, the reality of the present came flooding unwillingly back.

"I have heard from the chancellor," said Dekker, swallowing hard. "It seems that she passed our email on to some organisation called Global Power Consortium, a multinational that runs power grids and reactors across Europe and the States. They ... they see the breach as a source of free energy. They want to exploit it."

No one spoke.

Mark looked as though someone had pithed his brain like a frog. His face was totally blank, and his eyes were staring as though they were fixed on some non-existent object.

Candi dropped the coffee mug she had been holding. Coffee splashed all over her new shoes. She didn't even notice. "Pardon? Exploit? This I do not understand. Explain, please?"

Mark said nothing, his eyes still staring at the unseen. His heart was racing madly, but even he was not aware of it.

Candi went on. "Are you saying they don't want to close the breach? Is this what you are saying?"

"Wait," Dekker said. "There's more. They seem to think that they will get more energy out of the breach if they feed heavy nuclei into it. They want to feed the radioactive waste from the holding ponds into the breach and harvest the energy it produces."

Candi swore in French. Her eyes were huge and filled with horror.

Mark thought his world was ending. He felt sick, and his head swam. He struggled to come to terms with the words he was hearing.

He could not.

No one in his right mind could propose such a course of action. It was like taking a hydrogen bomb they were trying desperately to defuse and throwing it into a furnace.

The scene before his eyes went blurry. He knew he would have to kill someone. He didn't know who, or how or when, but for the sake of the human race some madman would have to die. Would he make a good assassin? He was losing his mind.

He opened his mouth, but nothing came out. Seeing nothing, he stared wildly about the room.

Candi marched over toward him. With the palm of her hand, she pushed hard against his chest, forcing him back onto the wall. His hands flew up above his head to prevent himself from falling. He was about to cry out, but Candi, the palm of her hand still against his chest, reached up and covered his mouth with her lips. She held them there against protest, pressing hard against his own until she felt his body come to terms with what she was doing. His arms fell and touched her shoulders. With the palm of her hand, she pushed herself back from him. The wild, staring incoherence had left his face, replaced by incredulity and incomprehension.

His right hand went up to his lips, moist from Candi's embrace. "Why?"

"Distraction," she said. "You were blowing up. You were losing your mind. Any second and you would have run out of this room and done something insanely stupid."

"I think I need more distraction."

"It only works once. If I do it again, it does something else."

"You're telling me," Mark said.

The short interlude had given Dekker time to collect his scattered wits. "Both of you, listen, please. This is what they are proposing. All I can do is hope they're doing this because they don't understand the situation. The chancellor is not a scientist. GPC may not be in possession of an accurate picture. There is a meeting between us, them, and the chancellor scheduled for next week. Thursday, yes, Thursday. We must prepare our case well."

"Don't let Mark speak," Candi suggested. "He will give them a lot of physics with passion but they won't understand any of it. They don't need to be informed—they need to be persuaded. Let me speak—I know just how to handle men. If they won't listen, I start to cry and, if that doesn't work, I stand up on the table and scream at them and, if that doesn't work—"

"I'm afraid you can only be there as observers and can only speak if called upon to do so," Dekker said.

Mark muttered something under his breath and collapsed into a chair. He put his hands over his face.

Candi exploded. A book on Dekker's table sailed into the wall, and his wastepaper basket collided with the door. Several other items became airborne, while Candi, screaming at the top of her voice in her native language, made contact with them. She was almost weeping with rage.

Mark watched apprehensively from the safety of his chair. Dekker actually smiled because he thought she looked rather funny when she was furious.

After a while, she sat down, picked up a biro, and viciously snapped it in half. "That was the chancellor. If ever I get my hands on … sorry. I lose control." She flung the pieces in the direction of the wastepaper bin lying next to the door. "So we are to be with the rope in the mouth—gagged? We cannot say anything? I feel like I am going to vomit."

"I've felt like that for a while," Dekker said. "Try not to. You need not doubt that I will put our case as persuasively as I know how. We will work on every word together. Firstly, we have to make sure they understand the consequences of such action. Talking with the chancellor is a complete waste of time. No, we address our case to the GPC engineers. Mark, what are you doing?"

"I'm praying."

"Oh, for goodness sake, not now!" said Candi, oblivious to the irony.

There was an uncomfortable silence while Mark crouched in his chair with his head in his hands. Candi sat silent for a whole minute, wondering why her life had degenerated into a farce. "Is he saying anything?"

"Who?"

"The thing you're praying to."

"I'm praying for wisdom, I'm praying that God will show us mercy. I'm asking for help."

"You should not put your faith to such a test," Candi said with an icy edge to her voice. "No God will save us. We have to save ourselves."

"And if we can't save ourselves, Candi? Only a foolish man scorns the help of God. My faith is not under test any more or less than your unbelief."

"If Mark wants to pray, I think we should encourage him," Dekker said, unexpectedly supporting Mark. "We would be arrogant indeed to claim we know enough to reject the existence of God. The breach is a good example of our lack of knowledge. It was our lack of understanding that created it in the first place, and our lack of knowledge that prevents us from closing it. I'm not above asking for help from the Almighty."

"You are both going mad." Tossing her head, Candi rose to her feet. "I'm going home. On Monday, I'll be fresh and relaxed. I'm too angry to be of any use now. Enjoy your praying. I'll see you next week."

With that, she left.

Candi drove home to the accompaniment of pop music, French foul language, and occasional tears. The combination made her drive fast and furiously—her hand thumping the horn as though every other driver on the road was the enemy. She reached her little house at Mt. Annan in record time, parked the car in the garage, and went in.

Roger came out of the bedroom where he had been watching, as usual, to rugby match replays. He was stark naked. He moved into her path, and with the expertise of long practice, undid her belt and slipped her jeans and panties to the floor. With his hands around her waist, he pressed her thighs against his. "Want it, Babe?"

She pushed him off. "Roger, I've had a bad day. I haven't come home panting to have sex in the hall. In five minutes you'll be back watching rubbish and I'll be washing off in the shower. You want us to go to heaven, then do it properly."

She stepped out of the little pile of clothes on the floor and headed for the bathroom.

"Sure, Babe, if that's what you want. You know how much I want to make you happy."

He went back into the bedroom, turned off the player, and read the time display. It was half an hour to the final. Their stay in heaven—or at least their first visit—would have to be less than thirty minutes.

One hour later, Candi was wrapped in a bathrobe and sitting in the kitchen. Sounds of the rugby final mixed with Roger's uncouth comments floated out of the bedroom. She shut the kitchen door to keep them out and went back to the piece of cold pizza she was eating with the remainder of a bottle of Hunter Valley Shiraz. An hour later, a second empty bottle stood beside the first. The wine had taken some of the fury out of her mood, but that same indefinable, creeping anxiety had risen like a ghost out of the darkness to haunt her. She shuddered, picked up the phone, and rang Mark's mobile number.

"Mark, this is Candi. I'm sorry for what I said. I didn't mean to hurt you. I was angry. If you want to pray to your God, it's fine by me. You can pray for me, too, if you want to."

"What do you want me to pray for, Candi?" he asked her.

"For faith in something real. My world is just a house of cards, Mark. I am a little bit drunk, so I tell you. One card away and the whole comes—poof!—sliding down flat. My bottom card is slipping, Mark. The house is shaking. I don't think about life. It's too hard. If it is good to feel, then it is good to do. Can your God make me feel good? I don't feel very good now. Do you want me to come over?"

"I'm still at work," he replied.

"Do you feel good at work, Mark? Is that why you're there?"

"No, I don't feel good, Candi. Sometimes you can't. I'm here because we have a problem, and I have to help solve it or we are in serious trouble. Sometimes you can run away from the things you don't like, or things you don't want to accept, and sometimes you can't. Sometimes they come and find you. This is one of those times. The breach will find us unless we shut it down. I know it will."

"I don't have your faith, Mark. When I was a little girl, they took it away from me. Does faith ever come back, Mark?"

"Faith isn't some irrational feeling that drifts into your life like a whiff of perfume that you like and decide to accept," he said. "Christian faith is believing something reasonable, something you can respond to holistically. I don't have to turn my mind off to believe in God and be a Christian."

There was a long pause.

"I'm lonely, Mark. Is life another word for loneliness? Are you lonely? You can have me, and then we wouldn't be lonely tonight. Would you like that?"

Another pause.

"What would Roger say?" he finally responded.

"Roger would say 'are you sleeping with that geek?' And I would say, 'yes I am.' Roger has a very limited vocabulary."

"Does he love you, Candi?"

"Love me? What is love, Mark?" she asked. "He loves the way I can make him feel. We go to heaven together, and that is very nice. That is really very nice. That is real. Will you take me to heaven, Mark?"

"No, but I know how you can get there."

"You are too religious, Mark. A girl offers you her body, and you don't even seem to notice. I'll just have to be lonely then, Mark. I think you're lonely, too, and that's why you make love to your physics. I'm feeling sleepy now. Sleep is good for loneliness. You have missed your opportunity, Mark. Goodnight."

When the second replay had ended, Roger came back into the kitchen to find Candi asleep with her head on the table and her hand on a piece of pizza. He took her hand and lifted it tenderly to release the trapped food and lowered her hand gently down again. Supplementing his prize with a glass of milk, he turned off the kitchen light and went into the bedroom to eat.

No sense in waking her up when he wanted a good night's sleep. She might have wanted to talk about problems the way girls always did when he wanted them to shut up. There was a match tomorrow, and he needed all his energy for the game.

# CHAPTER 17

The fifty-story office block in Fischer Road Crow's Nest rose in a graceful curve towards the skyline, its sail-like structure dominated only by a huge lightning rod that pierced the sky from its base on a curved platform extending out from the fortieth floor.

The boardroom was on floor forty-seven. Its windows framed a magnificent view of the harbour, the bridge, and the Opera House. Sail crafts and ferries criss-crossed the blue waters leaving little white trails in their wake.

Seated around the conference table were George Jenner, CEO of Global Power Consortium; Margaret Marriott, chancellor; Peter North, head of GPC's engineering division; Graham Clissold, business manager to the University of Southern Sydney; Daniel Van Dekker; Mark Chambers; and Candice Leblanc, in that order.

Dekker had expected GPC to open the discussion. He was disappointed.

Acting as chairperson, Margaret introduced each participant in turn and handed the floor to her business manager.

A graphic bearing the crest of the university sprung to life on the screen at the end of the table, and Clissold stood to speak:

"Ladies and gentlemen, welcome, and thank you for coming. I would first like to express my gratitude to the general manager of Global Power Consortium for allowing us to use their magnificent company venue for this meeting. We are indebted to their generosity. We are here to pool our collective synergies and knowledge to manage the extraordinary discovery made by Dr. Dekker and his team of scientists, Doctors Chambers and Leblanc. Let me encourage you all not to be afraid to dip your toes in the water and shorten the launch curves on this wonderful new opportunity to leverage the utility of GPC's enterprise-wide processes. Firstly, we need to take a temperature check and—"

"Would you mind speaking English for the benefit of us poor physicists who never thought it worthwhile to learn whatever perverse dialect you appear to be using?" Dekker interrupted.

Margaret gave him a look of intense displeasure.

Clissold beamed in his direction. "Of course, my dear Dr. Dekker. Make sure we don't get lost in the noise, that we're singing from the same hymn book, eh? Let's cut to the chase and hit the ground running. Now, our strengths. I've listed these on the first slide."

He reached for a small pod-like thing and squeezed it. A slide flashed up on the screen.

"Strengths. One. We have the knowledge to create a quantum energy device.

"Two. We will own the intellectual property rights and can demand royalties from any other enterprise that wants to swing for the fence.

"Three. Initial calculations suggest vast amounts of energy could be harvested at no cost to our natural resources and with no carbon footprint.

"Four. We have the technical knowledge and expertise to design the first power plant.

"Five. We have the funds through GPC to engage in the necessary capital works."

Mark interrupted him. "Even the thought of turning this accident into a power plant is insanity. The only question we have to—"

"I'm sorry," interrupted Clissold. "I believe you are present at this meeting in the capacity of a technical witness to be called upon if required. We can't have people raising the red flag at this point, or we will never keep ahead of the game."

"But—!"

"Please!" Clissold interjected, "we'll take your input soon. Let me finish, and then we can put it to bed."

Dekker spoke, "My colleague is anxious for the research division of GPC to be aware of certain dangers associated with this proposed project of yours. I trust you will give him leave to articulate those dangers before this meeting is over."

Clissold replied. "We will certainly be calling on Dr. Chambers later on in this discussion. Now, to continue, these are our strengths. These," he squeezed the small pod again, "are our opportunities." Another slide flashed up.

"Opportunities. One. This technology is world marketable, especially in countries that do not choose to embrace nuclear power.

"Two. We could patent the technology before our competitors get a handle on it.

"Three. Our pioneering posture will enable us to set aggressive but achievable goals in the world power market."

There was silence.

Mark and Candi were too stunned to speak.

Margaret was beaming. This was the beginning of her path into the dizzy echelons of political power.

George Jenner and Peter North watched the proceedings with faces set to convey the impression of mild interest. On the inside, Jenner was congratulating himself. The ducks were being lined up.

Clissold looked around the table, obviously pleased at the effect his presentation was having so far. He mistook the stunned expression of horror on the faces of the scientists for speechless admiration of his business acumen.

He continued. "But now, we must—in all fairness—consider our weaknesses."

Another slide.

"Weaknesses. One. We may not be able to duplicate the success in creating more QEDs.

"Two. We have not actually measured the power output achievable from this technology.

"Three. The cost of safely converting the experimental setup into a fully operational power station has not been estimated, and could be large."

Candi found her voice in time to respond to the last point. "The cost could be larger than you think, you imbecile! It may cost you the planet and everything on it, including your tiny brain."

Clissold laughed. "That is very amusing, Dr. Leblanc."

Margaret gave a little laugh.

The GPC men continued to express bland interest. Clissold, indifferent to Candi's venomous glare sent in his direction, went on. "Now we come to the threats. This is a matter for some discussion." He squeezed the pod. The next slide appeared.

"Threats. One. The use of this technology could have serious environmental consequences."

"Now, Dr. Dekker," Clissold said, "this is where we would like to hear from you and the other scientists who have expressed this concern."

Dekker got to his feet. He produced a party balloon out of his pocket. He inflated it and tied the end in a knot.

"Ladies and gentlemen," he said. "The inside of this balloon represents the physical world, the dimension in which we live, which we are all familiar with, and which we observe and measure. Outside this balloon is another dimension. We know little about it. It may be occupied by the shadow particles that physicists have theorized are coupled to the particles we can see. The rubber of the balloon represents the boundary between these two dimensions. It is not 'out there somewhere,' but instead wrapped around each particle of each atom. It is close and parallel with our physical, observable world. Until now, this boundary had never been penetrated. What happens if I take a pin and make a very small hole in the rubber of the balloon? The air inside is drawn out into the space outside the balloon because the pressure out there is less than the pressure inside. The air rushes out, tearing the fabric of the balloon and making the hole bigger. This in turn causes the balloon to deflate faster, tearing an even larger hole. In a very short period of time, the whole boundary collapses."

He took a pin from his coat and punctured the balloon. There was a loud bang.

Dekker continued. "This is what you will do if you feed material into the breach. It will become wider, and in becoming wider it will suck more and more matter into the other dimension. This in turn will widen the breach even further and cause a runaway scenario. In a short time, the breach will widen to the point where it will suck in everything around it, including the power plant you are contemplating. After that, it will continue to suck in the world around it, all the while giving off more and more energy. The substance of the earth will be vaporized as it disappears into nothing. Eventually, the planet will cease to exist. I cannot believe you would seriously consider jeopardizing the safety of the entire planetary ecosystem—even the planet itself—in order to make cheap electricity for a short period of time. We do need to act quickly, not to widen the breach, but to close it. I have repeatedly requested that the university bring the very best minds to bear on this impending disaster. I can excuse their inaction only on the grounds that they do not understand. I trust that will not be the case with you two gentlemen."

He nodded towards Jenner and North and sat down.

Margaret and Clissold clapped.

Jenner spoke quietly, "Thank you for your input, Dr. Dekker. May I ask, was it you who discovered this breach, as you call it, or your colleague Dr. Chambers?

The question took Dekker by surprise. "It was Dr. Chambers who made the discovery. He was—"

Jenner interrupted him. "Thank you, Dr. Dekker. Who proposed the scenario you just so skilfully illustrated?"

"We all took part."

"But as I understand it, Dr. Leblanc is not a physicist, but a power engineer. The input of Dr. Chambers would have played an important part in the development of this Armageddon scenario, would it have not?"

Dekker looked puzzled. "Yes, of course it would have."

"Dr. Chambers, is it true that you are a Christian?"

Mark started in his seat. "Yes, that's true, but what I believe has nothing whatsoever to do with the situation here. This is—"

Once again, Jenner interrupted him. "We are here principally to discuss the claims that you have made concerning this discovery, and as they are mostly your claims, I think what you believe has every-thing to do with the conclusions you have reached. Is it true that the Bible speaks about the end of the world in some gigantic cataclysmic Armageddon?"

"Christians hold on the basis of Biblical authority that history is moving from a God-created beginning to a God-determined end," Mark said. "I am not prepared to believe that the end of the age as it is de-scribed in the Bible begins with this scenario. Indeed, I sincerely trust that it will not."

"And you personally believe that?" Jenner challenged.

"Yes, I do."

A smirk came to Jenner's lips. "I submit that your conclusions are also a matter of personal belief rather than scientific conclusions, Dr. Chambers. Although you state that you do not believe this to be a world-ending event, Dr. Dekker has described it in just those terms. I believe that your personal disposition toward a religious scenario has prejudiced your impartiality as a scientist and led you towards this highly fanciful 'end-of-the-age' hypothesis."

Mark stared at him. He realised that his mouth was open and made the conscious effort to shut it. Jenner's approach was unexpected and unreasonable. "We have based our conclusions on sound physical ob-servations that have been carefully checked," Mark argued. "Should you wish, we can step you through them. Other eminent physicists—several of whom have no religious views—are in agreement with our conclu-sions. How can you even begin to consider these views as simply a matter of my personal opinion?"

"Because that is precisely what they are," Jenner said. "Have any other physicists visited the plant? No. In fact, has any other scientist, apart from yourselves, even seen the breach?"

"Because we were not given permission from the university to—"

"I'm sure that the chancellor would not have been averse to such consultation," Jenner interrupted him to say. "Would you have been, Margaret?"

"Of course not," Margaret replied with the self-confident smile of someone who suffered from convenient amnesia. All three scientists were on their feet.

"That's not true!" Candi shouted.

"We have a letter—several ..." Dekker said, his voice trembling with emotion.

Mark added, "The university expressly forbade us to—"

"The university," Margaret replied, drawing herself up straight in her chair and staring at the three of them with ill favour, "was following your directive that no one else should be permitted on the premises because of safety issues."

"Precisely my point," Jenner said. "This report in front of us is the sincere belief of three scientists who have scared themselves into a prejudiced scenario fuelled by personal religious belief. It must be regarded in such light. I would be happy to have the engineers associated with GPC make a thorough assessment of the issues at hand and report back. I will give my personal guarantee that nothing will be done to jeopardise any public safety. We will call on the assistance of other physicists if and when the need becomes clear. I would hate Australia to suffer the embarrassment of hearing about this Armageddon scenario only to be shown that it was clearly a figment of the imagination. Should this become public knowledge, it would reflect poorly on the university, indeed, as well as on every Australian scientist.

Margaret gave a gasp of horror. "You don't intend to make this disastrous business public, I hope! The university would be forced to disown the project if that happened!"

"If the university were to endorse our approach to the problem," Jenner said. "I see no need for the public to be informed at all."

Dekker rose to his feet and with an almost superhuman effort mastered the rage that threatened to overpower him at any moment. "I would counsel the chancellor to ignore the implied threat in Mr. Jenner's words. We have made measurements. We have reached conclusions based on those measurements. The conclusions we presented to you are the results of research, not of conjecture. This is a matter of truth, not of faith."

"But everything is a matter of faith, Dr. Dekker," Jenner said. "I do not believe in absolute truth. No one in our modern world does. Truth is always influenced by personal beliefs, so it must be assessed in the context of the beliefs of the person delivering it. I have no doubt that when you spoke to us about the dangers here you sincerely believed you were speaking the truth. It is up to these persons around this table, and in particular the chancellor, to assess whether the things you believe are true for you are also true for them. I have given the chancellor the absolute assurance that we will do nothing to endanger the public or yourselves, for that matter. I repeat: should our engineers believe the situation to be dangerous, we will put all the resources of our company toward closing the quantum bridge. I can do no more. I am simply requesting that the university allow other minds to assess and verify the conclusions reached by these three scientists—or, rather these two scientists and one engineer—that my company believes are prejudiced by religious views, even though they may be sincerely felt."

The pencil Dekker had been toying with suddenly snapped and scattered along the table. Mark and Candi glanced across at him with concern. The volcano was about to erupt.

"And your engineers wouldn't be biased in favour of company profits?" Dekker asked. "Just how stupid do you think we are?"

Jenner smiled at him. "Have you actually performed measurements that show the quantum bridge would become unstable over time if we were to feed other nuclei into it? You speak about evidence and observation. Have you performed the experiment? What experiments have you done to justify your conclusion that this so-called breach will continue to widen and not simply settle down to a manageable size?"

Dekker said, "We have gone no further than to feed hydrogen atoms into the breach, and our observations have shown it to have become larger. We are unable to shut it down. Isn't that enough?"

"With respect, Dr. Dekker, no, it isn't enough," Jenner replied in the same calm voice. "We have no desire to shut down the quantum bridge. Your country needs power. It will continue to need power. The continual use of coal to provide that power is contributing to global warming, which will have disastrous consequences. There is no religion involved in that conclusion. You speak of protecting the planet, which is just what we want to do. If you want to put God into the picture, may we not equally regard this discovery as a gift from the hand of the Almighty? A gift that will save the planet from the consequences of using carbon-based fuels?"

"If you want to pursue this madness, why not try shutting it down first? Then, if you're sure you can close any breach made, you can safely open them again."

At that, Clissold jumped up from his chair and began waving his arms. "But that would take time. We would lose our marketing advantage. As I pointed out in the first slide …"

With several loud expletives, Dekker launched himself across the table at Clissold. The man dropped the little pod he was holding and tried to make a bolt for the door. Dekker, sliding off the table, grabbed him around the shoulders and shook him violently.

"Are you completely insane?" Dekker shouted into his face. "This is not a marketing exercise! Do you have a brain at all? I'm talking about the safety of the world, not about making money!"

Margaret jumped up to her feet, scattering her chair behind her. She looked genuinely shocked. "Dr. Dekker! This is uncalled for!"

Dekker dropped the little man's shaking form on the ground and turned round to face Margaret. "And you!" he shouted. "What you know about science could be written on half a postage stamp! You're an opportunist, pontificating cretin who assesses everything in terms of its personal political advantage. Don't you realise the seriousness of these issues?"

Margaret drew herself up to her full height and maximum contempt. "Obviously you, for one, do not, Mr. Dekker. Your research project is, as of this moment, cancelled. Your employment with this university is terminated."

For answer, Dekker, his face livid with rage, advanced on Margaret. He picked up the sheaf of notes lying next to her on the table and hurled it across the room.

Margaret almost fell backward over her fallen chair, picked it up, and pointed its legs towards him. "Security!" she shouted. "Security! Help!"

Out of nowhere, security guards burst in through the doors. They grabbed Dekker and escorted him outside. Mark and Candi were left standing on their feet, speechless.

Margaret appeared as though she was going to faint. Jenner ran to her side and escorted her back to the table, sat her down on a chair, and gathered her notes together. North made his first contribution to the proceedings by pouring her a glass of water.

Margaret gathered the remains of her natural superiority, and addressed the meeting. "Please sit down, Dr. Chambers, Dr. Leblanc. We will continue without Dr. Dekker's input, seeing as how he cannot control his temper. Now, Mr. Jenner, you were saying?"

"I was saying that the conclusions reached by Dr. Chambers have been coloured by religious beliefs. I believe this has to be taken into account when we assess the threats that Mr. Clissold was talking about. I have asked him to include these factors in his assessment. Are you all right, Clissold?"

Mr. Clissold was scrabbling about on the floor searching for his little pod. He rose victorious with the item clutched in his hand, his tie skew-whiff, and his hair dishevelled. He straightened his tie and squeezed the pod.

"I have attempted to assess the 'Chambers Scenario' risk by allocating it a value of one hundred percent and multiplying it by a factor. This factor is based on the number of apocalyptic scenarios proposed by various religious groups at particular dates, and the number of those which actually took place as prophesied. As you can see, the factor reduces the risk to zero. I have added a number of other factors," he said as he squeezed another slide onto the screen, "but as you can see, the risk factor only increases by a small margin."

Mark stood to his feet. He was cold and could feel his palms sweating. He was shaking. "This is not an inquiry. This is a mockery. I will have no further part in it. If you will not listen to reason, then we must find others who will."

He placed his chair slowly and deliberately against the table and walked out of the room followed by a silent Candi. The door shut quietly.

Jenner turned to North and spoke quietly, "That went well."

North made no reply. He had watched the proceedings as one would watch a stage play and had felt increasingly disconnected as a member of the audience.

Inwardly, he was appalled at the contemptuous, callous manner in which Jenner had dismissed Chambers. He had come to the meeting genuinely believing that the quantum bridge experiment may have been a godsend to the energy-hungry human race, but his confidence had been shaken. He took one look at Jenner, smirking quietly to himself and estimated that the cost of voicing his feelings would do nothing to further his lucrative career. Perhaps it was best to keep them to himself for the time being.

With the three scientists out of the way, Margaret Marriott's feeling of superiority and control began to rise. "On behalf of the university, I do apologize for the behaviour of my former staff, Mr. Jenner," she said. "They will receive letters of dismissal by this afternoon."

"I am not offended in the least," Jenner said. "Chambers and Leblanc are familiar with the experiment and would be crucial to the safe transition into a working power plant. It is possible that you do not understand there are real risks. If you have removed them from your staff, I will enlist them in mine."

"But the presentation by our business manager has shown those risks to be negligible—"

Jenner said, "The presentation by your business manager was useful to this company for an entirely different purpose. Thank you for your time, Margaret, Mr. Clissold. Peter and I have other business to attend to. Refreshments should arrive shortly. With your consent, we will take our leave."

With that, the two men left the room.

Outside the door, it was Peter North who spoke. "Dekker and company will not take this humiliation lying down. They will attempt to make trouble in other directions."

A self-confident smile creased the corners of Jenner's mouth. "Indeed they will. However, I have plans for all of them. We need Leblanc and Chambers, at least initially. I think I can persuade them to stay and join us, at least in the short term. Dekker is another matter. I think he deserves a sabbatical overseas. Let him consult with his colleagues. Remember the meeting we had in Geneva. There just might come a time when we will want to know how to close the quantum bridge. I suggest we encourage them to think about some way to do it—as long as they can't try anything we don't want them to. If they cause trouble, they can always be removed from the equation by other means."

North didn't reply. There was a tone in Jenner's voice that filled him with dread. Other means? What other means? It was best not to ask.

Jenner had not missed the expression on North's face however. "Something troubling you, Peter? I was about to put you in charge of operations down here at the plant. Perhaps I will send Slater instead, at least initially. You already have a lot on your plate."

North made no reply.

Meanwhile, the hungry occupants of the boardroom were consuming an excellent morning tea.

Margaret spoke. "Graham, that was wonderful. I think you handled the awkward business with Dekker very capably. As far as I can tell, George and that North man were delighted with the outcome. I want you to prepare a business plan for the expansion program we've talked about, assuming we will now obtain the funds. I'll send an email to all staff to lift morale. I think it's been slipping a little ever since those forced redundancies in the nursing department."

Clissold spoke through the cake that he had stuffed into his mouth. "Margaret, that's a wonderful idea. I'll get a handle on it right away."

# CHAPTER 18

Candi had taken Mark's arm as they walked silently out of the building because he seemed unaware and unresponsive to the things around him.

In truth, Mark was in shock—stunned at the path events had taken. He blamed himself for not being able to give a better answer. Somehow, he had allowed himself to be manipulated. It had happened all so fast ... and then Dekker had lost his temper, and with it any remaining chance they had of bringing sweet reason back into the argument.

What a way to play into the hands of the opposition!

He never expected the chancellor to rise above her level of manipulative political ambition, but he had expected the others to understand. They did understand, and their understanding rendered their actions inexcusable. His input had been understood and callously rejected. There was nothing he could do.

In the silence of his own heart, he began to pray. "Dear God, we are in desperate need here. I cannot stop these people. I have no plan, no idea, and no power. Help us, or we're finished." He gradually began to return to the world. He became aware of sounds and of the words being spoken to him.

Candi's words. They were filled with concern. "Mark, listen to me. Please, chéri, I am going to drive you home. We will have a coffee at the Back Alley, yes? Mark, please speak to me—you're frightening Candi!"

Mark slowly turned his head toward her. He found he could speak. "Candi? I'm sorry. I was somewhere else. Where are we going?"

"I'm taking you for coffee and lunch at the Back Alley. I'm going to drive. You came on the train. I'm going to take you back. We're going to talk about what to do—how to fight these cretins, these imbeciles! Yes, we will fight. We will not sit back and let them do this, treat us like the merde. This is the beginning, not the end. Mark, are you hearing me?"

As a reply, Mark squeezed the hand that had wrapped itself around his arm. He felt sick again, and his legs seemed to be somehow disconnected from the rest of him.

Sensing his body beginning to sway, Candi held onto him more tightly, concern rising in her heart. "Here, the car. Now, I open the door—that's the way." She pushed him into the front passenger seat and shut the door.

Minutes later, they were wending their way south on the M5 motorway. Neither spoke. Candi wondered what she would do if he was still in shock by the time they reached Camden.

When the car turned onto the main street, Mark spoke at last, "Thank you, Candi. I'm feeling a bit better. I think it was shock. I've never felt so utterly beaten and helpless before. I've been very bad company. I'm sorry."

"No, no, you must not be sorry," she said. "I worry, that's all. I don't know what to do. I might have to say a prayer or something." She smiled at him. "See, you are changing my thinking already."

They went into the café and sat at their usual table. Annette the waitress came over. "The usual? Are you eating here as well? What's the matter with Mark?"

"He's had a very bad morning," Candi explained. "The usual drinks, then we'll eat. Croissant and ham for me, and that chicken thing you make for him. Thanks, Annette."

They ate and drank in silence, the food assisting in the recovery process.

After a long time, Candi broke the silence. "Are you back on Earth now?"

"More or less."

"We must make plans," Candi said. "I have an idea. We contact Channel Seven News and tell them the story. Soon everyone knows, and GPC are on the back foot, yes?"

"It wouldn't work. You remember that idiot minister for the environment?"

"Mc. something?"

"McTierney," Mark said. "Don't you remember that fiasco? Daniel went to the media, and before long AINR was shut down. What would we say? We have accidentally created a rift in the fabric of space that threatens to destroy the world, and we can't close it? How do you think they'd react? The most likely scenario is that GPC would become the heroes who wanted to turn the disaster into something useful. There would be mass panic, some tourist company would want to sell tickets to see the breach in action, and we'd be thrown in jail for creating a lethal environmental hazard and disregarding public safety. Our reputations wouldn't be worth ten cents from then on."

"I see what you mean," she said. "Then if the media is out, what do we do? After this morning, the University will kick us out without a reference, Dekker will be deported—I will be deported! You will get a job serving hamburgers. I do not like the ending to this story."

"Somehow we have to work out how to shut it down," Mark replied, finishing off his coffee. "If we can't do that it doesn't matter what they do. In the long run, something awful is bound to happen. How long will that frail glass tube remain intact? All we need is some-one to fall against it, or the vacuum pumps to shut down and the breach will melt the glass. Then the barrier is down, and the breach starts eating the world. The energy will destroy the buildings. The heat will mean nothing can get near it. Talk about doomsday—we're just two millimetres of glass away from it now."

"I like you better when you're too stunned to speak. You know how to frighten a girl, don't you?"

Mark covered Candi's hand with his own and gave it a squeeze. "I'm sorry. I know I should stop being such a harbinger of doom. It can't end this way, it just can't. I don't believe this is the way God brings about the end."

Candi looked straight at him, her face a question. "God has told you this? You hear his voice in your head, or are you giving me the bullshit to make me feel better?"

"The world doesn't end this way. Not according to the Bible. It ends when God wants it to end, and some things that haven't happened have to happen first. I've no idea when the world is going to end, mind you, but I don't think it's now. That means we—somebody—is going to find a solution. How that will be possible from the inside of a hamburger shop, I have no idea at all."

A voice from the table to their left spoke. "But you won't be working in a hamburger shop."

They turned round. Both spoke together. "Dekker!"

"How long have you been there?" Candi asked.

"I came in while you were both off in some other world." Dekker joined them at their table. "I hoped I'd find you here. Mark goes off the planet regularly, but you were keeping him company this time, Candi. I came in, ordered some food from Annette. Neither of you noticed me."

"They let you out, then?" Candi spoke. "I'm surprised GPC didn't hand you over to the local police for assaulting the little cretin. Served him right!"

"I'm fine, Candi," Dekker sighed. "I shouldn't have lost my temper. As it turns out, it made no difference. I've had a little chat with Jenner. He found me confined in building security. More importantly, he is going to offer you both a job."

"I would rather work for the devil incarnate," said Candi with great emphasis. "I will tell him what he can do with his job. He can stick it right up where the sun never shines." Several impassioned French words followed.

Dekker held up his hand. "Wait. He wants to offer you the jobs of consulting physicist and consulting engineer in the construction of his wonderful new quantum energy plant. You will both accept, or I will belt you both over the head with this bread roll until you need medical attention."

Candi was not at all amused. "But why? Why do you want us to work for that piece of—"

Mark interrupted her. "Because then we would be able to ensure the breach doesn't reach the outside world, and because—if we ever do work out a way to shut it down—we'll have half a chance of still doing it."

"Exactly, Dekker said. "Think about it. What happens if their engineers, who know and care nothing about what we've been doing, accidentally break the tube, or shut down the pumps while they're reconfiguring the power, or let too much gas through while they're experimenting to see if the breach does what we've told them it does? Disaster. It'll be too late when there's a brilliant ball of energy crackling where the lab once was. 'I told you so' is a very poor response while the world burns. You must take the job. Jenner will try to persuade you with this sort of argument. Listen to him and be prepared to grovel a little. Convince him you'll cooperate fully."

Candi looked far from convinced. "And what will happen to you? Has he offered you a job, too?"

"I'm afraid Mr. Jenner has other plans for me. He is a very clever man, Mr. Jenner. He doesn't trust me to not cause him trouble. We can't go to the media, but I could still give him a run for his money, which is something he doesn't want. No, I have agreed to deport myself out of his way—with his help, of course."

"What?" both Candi and Mark exclaimed.

"He wants to get me out of the way. Under the auspices of the university, the company will offer me a sabbatical in Europe somewhere—Holland, probably. If I don't take it, I am fairly sure something unpleasant will happen to me. It may happen anyway, but they would rather throw the dead cat into someone else's backyard, to use language like our dear Mr. Clissold uses. No, I intend to accept their offer with gratitude."

"But that means we are on our own here," Mark said. "And we need your help to work out how to close the breach. How can you help us when you are on the other side of the world?"

"But I can only help you from there. I'm not going to Holland where they expect me to go. I'm going to work with Professor Kilraen at the University of Glasgow. We have been friends for a long time."

"Kilraen," Candi said. "I have heard this name. There's a large company in Europe called the Kilraen Group. Any connection?"

"There is," Dekker said. "Professor Kilraen's wife is quite an entrepreneur. In fact, she's probably one of the wealthiest women in the world. A strange creature. I met her once. Incredibly beautiful, very brilliant, very accomplished, and very ruthless, but she loves her husband. Once Professor Kilraen has heard our tale, he'll help us. I think his wife will help us too for his sake. There are many brilliant physicists on the continent. I want to work with them on the problem. With Kilraen's help, I can travel around and contact them in a rather inconspicuous fashion."

"How come?" asked Mark.

"The Kilraen Group has its own fleet of aircrafts," Dekker explained. "They own an ancient castle on the Isle of Skye with their own airfield next to it. I want to make this place a base of operations and move around in their jets as an inconspicuous passenger. If I can swing Kilraen's cooperation, and perhaps even his wife's approval, I'll have a multibillion dollar organization on my side. We'll have to find a way of keeping in touch with one another. This is something that GPC will not want, so it must be done carefully. I expect them to be capable of anything, so your lives may even be in danger once the plant has become operational—if it ever does. They won't need you after that. If they think you're working with me, they may decide to remove you even earlier. That's our first problem."

Candi looked frightened. Turning to Dekker, she asked in a low voice, "Do you think they would—murder us?"

"I put nothing beyond them," he answered. "It wouldn't look like murder. There would be some sort of accident, I suppose. Very unfortunate. Two brilliant scientists killed in the course of duty. No doubt they'd set up a trust at the university for students who wanted to study computing or business management or something. Margaret Marriot would be publicly sad and privately grateful."

"When do you leave?" asked Mark.

"I will be in Glasgow by the end of the week," Dekker said. "I will not stay there, however. You won't know where I am. GPC will not know where I am, otherwise it would be dangerous for all of us. We don't have long to set things up. I'll work on a solution to our communications problem, and Mark, you'll keep working along with some others on the problem of the breach. Candi, you'll help him by doing your best to keep him from burning himself out, which is probably the most important thing you can do. He's likely to get himself exhausted, then he won't be able to think. I'm relying on you to take care of him. Is that okay?"

"Mais bien sûr. I promise."

"I also want you to play an active part in the construction of this new energy plant. If we're going to shut it down, we need to know exactly how it's controlled in the first place." Dekker paused. "My dear friends, this may be the last time we will meet in the Back Alley Café. I will look back on these hours as some of the most pleasant I can remember."

He grasped Candi's hand with his left and Mark's with his right, gave each a long squeeze, and lapsed into an embarrassed silence. More coffee arrived.

For the first time, Mark searched the other faces in the café with suspicion. Were any of them working for GPC? He doubted it, but then who could tell? The time of care-free, friendly discussion had come to an end.

Dekker left the café first. He wasn't at all looking forward to telling his wife the news, because he loved her dearly and knew Glasgow would not have even rated as a place she would want to stay. But move she must, he thought. She wouldn't be at all safe at home.

Candi and Mark stayed in the café. They discussed ways of communicating with Dekker without much success.

At around six o'clock, Candi glanced at her watch. "I'll have to go, Mark. Roger is expecting me." She paused, looking a little uncomfortable. "Mark, the other night—I had too much to drink. I was feeling very lonely. You were the gentleman. You could have taken advantage, but you didn't. You're a good man, Mark. I wish I had what you have—your faith and all that. You're different. You've never tried to make a pass at me, never even made one dirty remark. The other men I know would have. They talk to my boobs and try to put their hands on me. You treat me like a friend. I'm glad you're my friend, Mark. I don't know the words to say how much."

Mark looked up at her. Her eyes were wet with unshed tears. He reached out and touched her hand, and for a moment neither of them spoke except with their eyes.

"Thank you, Candi," Mark said at last. "I'm glad. We're going to need one another in the weeks to come. Your friendship is incredibly important to me. I want you to know that."

Candi smiled at him, leaned over, and planted a soft kiss on his cheek. They got up from the table and went out the door together. Candi drove Mark home to his house in Elderslie and then continued on to Mt. Annan.

Roger was in the kitchen heating up noodles in the microwave. He turned round when she entered the room and grunted. "Flamin' microwave seems to be slow tonight. Why don't you have a look at it? You're supposed to know everything about this kind of stuff, aren't you?"

"And 'hello darling' to you, too."

"Okay, I'm sorry," he said. "The selectors have put me in the box for the next match. I'm pissed off at them. Took it out on you, sorry."

Candi hugged him. "But soon you will be on again, yes?"

"Probably. Want some noodles?"

"No, I ate earlier with Mark."

"Getting pally with the geek, aren't we?" Roger replied.

"He's just a friend, Roger. Are you jealous?"

"Hell, no. What's he got? You can't go to bed with a brain!"

"You do," she retorted. "You think I'm stupid?"

"Nuh, you're okay. You know how to do it. Never had such fantastic sex 'til I met you."

"Roger, can I ask you a question?"

Roger looked at Candi apprehensively. When a woman said that you knew something unpleasant was coming. He hated times like this. Heaving his thighs into Candi was something he understood and enjoyed. Talking to her about serious matters was something he didn't.

"Sure, fire away." He answered, rather dreading what was to come.

"Are we friends, Roger? Do you like me?"

"Babe, I've told you I love you lots of times."

"Yes, but do you like me?" she asked, her eyes large and pleading. "Am I your friend as well as your lover? We never talk about anything. We just get into bed and enjoy one another. Do you think that's enough in a relationship?"

"Sure, Babe. You know it is. Told me the same thing lotsa times. Gotta go. Game's on in five minutes." He reached out and stroked her hair, letting his fingers run down her neck and over her breast. With that assurance of his continuing intimacy, Roger left the room.

Candi poured herself out a glass of milk and shut herself in the study.

Jasmin read the look on Dekker's face as soon as he stepped out of the car.

Without a word, she kissed him tenderly on the lips. Wrapping her arms around one of his, she led him into the lounge rather than the dining room. With welcoming words, she sat beside him on the settee and kissed him on the cheek.

"Daniel, my love," she said in a soft voice, "the time has come for you to unburden your heart to me. For months all I have heard are dark hints and veiled descriptions of some great impending disaster. I've seen you come home night after night so distressed I'm frightened you'll die from a heart attack. Each day is a little worse than the last, and now this evening I see something in your face which frightens me even more. I'm your wife, Daniel. The time has come for you to share the burden you carry. It's become too large for you to bear alone. Something has happened today to take all the hope out of your eyes. There was never much there, but now what little remained has gone forever, hasn't it?"

He sighed, the long, slow sigh of a man teetering on the brink of despair. "How can you read me like this? I can't read you! How do you have the strength to love a man who is such a burden on your life?"

"I'm a woman, Daniel, have you not noticed? God gives me strength when I need it. Have you not seen it working? There is nothing worse than knowing a horror is coming but not knowing when or how, or what to do to protect yourself when it does come. This has been my burden, and I have borne it faithfully. Now it's time for you to tell me, Daniel, the nature of this demon I am already terrified of so that we may stand together as you fight against it."

He opened his arm. She slid in against his shoulder and he drew her close.

"Jasmin, I have lived the life of a fool. I've ignored the God whose hand I can see plainly in your life. As my days have grown darker, so the light of the faith and strength God has given you has shone all the brighter. I have many questions, beloved, but I do not doubt any more that your faith is solid and its object is real and living. You are right. Forgive me. I thought I could face the menace alone, but I cannot. You've been drawn into a horror of my own making. The demon you fear was summoned by my own foolish hand. I feared once I had told you the truth you wouldn't love me as much. I couldn't live with that."

"Love you less, Daniel?" she replied, smiling into his face. "Do you think you have to earn the love I give you? There is another name for love that has to be earned."

He couldn't speak. Jasmin wrapped her arms around him, felt his chest heaving with great breaths while he regained his composure. After some time he pressed her arms against him and began.

The evening sky darkened into night, and his shirt was damp from Jasmin's silently shed tears before he had finished.

Without raising her head from his chest, she finally spoke, but not to him. "God in heaven, we call on you for mercy. We ask forgiveness for what we have done in ignorance. Send us help. Give Daniel and the other scientists wisdom. We have no power in ourselves. You liken yourself to a good Shepherd. Your sheep are in peril, good Lord. Come quickly to our rescue."

Hers was not the only "Amen."

Jasmin raised herself from his chest, wiped the unshed tears from his eyes, and snuggled her head into his neck. The effect was to make Dekker, who had almost never cried in the whole of his life, burst into uncontrollable sobbing. Rocking backward and forward, he held her while trying to tell her he was sorry—to find words to express the inexpressible, overwhelming love he felt for her and the deep, deep gratitude he felt toward God for His magnificent wife.

An hour later, they were in the kitchen. Dekker sat on a stool while Jasmin collected the cold remains of the dinner she had long ago prepared. He watched her with the same heartfelt gratitude to God moving through his heart. Never had he thought he could love her more deeply, yet that evening had proven him wrong. "I would lay down my life for you" he thought to himself, "and still bless the day I found you."

She placed his dinner in front of him and sat on the opposite side of the bench. He took her hands in his. "I think I would like to give thanks to God this evening," he said.

# CHAPTER 19

Mark had remained wide awake in his unit that evening. Unconsciously scribbling patterns on the back of an exercise book, his mind slid deeper into misery at the thought of working with the madmen from Global Power Consortium with only Candi for support. Pictures of the woman swearing at them in French and throwing things flashed before his mind. It wouldn't be long before someone collected a flying spanner on a sensitive part of their anatomy and she would be turfed out, leaving him alone—one man against a world gone stark-raving mad.

The phone rang, jerking him back to the present world. He stared at the weird patterns covering the back of the exercise book and wondered what they meant. He picked up the phone.

"Mark, is that you? It's Andrew here. Wondered if you could possibly come round and help me.

"What's the problem?" Mark asked.

"Well … I feel somewhat embarrassed to tell you," Andrew said. "I was putting my dinner on the table and my leg just went under me. I grabbed the bookcase and ended up on the floor with the damn thing on top of me. I've managed to tease the phone over to ring you, but I can't move at all."

An hour later, Andrew was sitting up at the table and finishing off the fresh meal Mark had prepared for him. The bookcase was back in its original position, even if there were still a lot of books lying all over the floor.

Andrew was looking a good deal better than he had when Mark had arrived. He wiped the last traces of gravy from his face, lay back in his chair, and gripped his rescuer by the hand. "Thank you, and thank you. I didn't feel like food, but I needed it. Stupid thing to do."

"That's really okay. I needed to talk to you and I didn't realise that, either. Perhaps this is God's doing after all."

"Well, next time I wish you'd just pick up the phone. Must be something serious. It's gone wrong, hasn't it?"

"Wrong?" Mark groaned. "It's turned into a nightmare. I'm sorry to do this, Andrew, but—before I go on—you have to give me your word that you'll say nothing of this to another living being. No one else can know. If anyone else finds out, there will be the most dreadful consequences."

His eyes never leaving Mark's face, Andrew nodded his head slowly. "You have my word. Now what have you done?"

"We've created a monster and we don't know what to do with it. The breach, Candi calls it, and that's as good a name as any because I really don't know what it is." He groaned again and ran his hands over his face. "This is in essence what has happened."

Mark was very thankful that Andrew sat silently while letting him tell the whole ghastly tale. It was finished in a surprisingly short time. Even after the telling, Andrew was silent, which surprised Mark even more because he had expected his friend to throw up his arms in horror and rave on about what a fool he had been. He was more than grateful, if a little apprehensive, for the continuing silence.

Eventually, the older man asked, "Who's in charge of this world, Mark?"

"God is, of course."

"Do you think for a moment God is unaware of what you've done?"

"Of course He isn't!"

"Then you will find a way to shut this … breach thing down."

"That might be a trifle difficult when an insane power company is doing their best to widen the blasted thing!" Mark said grimly.

"Nonetheless, they may have a part to play in the solution," Andrew said. "It doesn't strike me as too safe, this world-eating monster confined inside a thin glass tube."

"Safe! It scares the sense out of me every time I look at it. I have nightmares about it, if you want to know, and none of them end well."

"Listen, Mark. You must hold on. You say there are clever men working on the solution. You're a clever man. Don't give up. God has put you there for a purpose."

"I'm there because I helped create the wretched thing, that's all," Mark said. "I feel responsible, so horribly responsible, Andrew, and I just can't leave the mess I've made. I think it would find me even if I tried."

"Of course you're responsible. Be responsible for shutting the bloody thing down."

"Do you think I can, Andrew? Do you have that much faith in me?"

A smile began to crease the older man's face. "I have a lot more faith in the God who gave you a clever mind. You'll do yourself no end of harm if you burn yourself out with worry and fear so you can't think straight at all. Work with these fools and make sure the thing is contained more securely. Perhaps it will disappear when they feed their rubbish into it and they'll lose a packet. Would serve the blighters right!"

They talked on into the night, and no matter what he said, Mark could not shake Andrew's faith in the God who made him. It wasn't fairyland faith either, for this man was trained as an engineer and was not unable to appreciate the danger.

Eventually, Andrew glanced at the clock on the wall above them. Both of its hands were pointing to the ceiling. He stifled a yawn, reached out, and grabbed his friend by the arm.

"Mark, it will not be easy," Andrew said. "There may be great cost involved in the solution. I'm not such a fool to think that a monster of this magnitude is easily defeated, but I believe it will be. I'm no prophet, nor the son of one, but I also believe you are the man God will use to provide the solution. It's late, too late for someone as exhausted as yourself to drive home. There's a bed made up down the corridor, please use it. Before we retire, we should pray."

They prayed earnestly for the next half an hour, and then Andrew, with a little help because he was still not very steady on his feet, pointed Mark to a room down the hall and disappeared into his own room.

Mark opened the door and found, to his embarrassment he was looking into a woman's bedroom. Andrew lived alone. Whose could it be? Someone who rented a room? Live-in help which Andrew, completely out of character, had never mentioned?

His eyes wandered over the top of the dressing table, adorned with the usual woman's toiletries: a hair brush, a dryer, a bottle of perfume, and various other face-painting items, but the thing that caught his attention was the photograph of a young woman.

She was wearing an evening dress tastefully cut in the front displaying a perfect décolletage, black hair rolling down her shoulders in waves, huge, deep brown eyes under long black eyebrows, a soft, shapely nose, perfectly symmetrical cheekbones, large heart-shaped lips and a long, graceful neck.

Was this a picture of Andrew's wife when she was young? If so, she was a stunningly attractive woman.

Mark sighed to himself. He wished there was a woman in his own life, someone who understood and loved him.

The only woman in his life was Candi, and he was sure that she would never fall in love with him. But could he ever fall in love with her? He thought of her pretty face sparkling with life and of her appealing figure. Any man would be attracted to that, and many had been, including the jerk she was living with.

His mind flashed back to their first evening when she had offered to sleep with him, and how guilty he had felt knowing that part of him wanted to say yes, and still wanted to say yes.

Why was he fantasising like this? He was exhausted, that was why. Temptation was always most powerful when you were frustrated, alone, and tired, and he was all three.

He got undressed and slipped into the welcome sheets, thanking God for the wise counsel of his friend. In a short time, he was sound asleep.

It was late in the morning when he awoke, and after dressing quickly, he made his way into the kitchen where he could hear the sounds of Andrew messing around with breakfast.

"Morning, Andrew."

"Sleep well, Mark?"

"Brilliantly."

Mark came over to the bench were Andrew was seated next to his wheelchair, flicked the switch on the electric jug with his left hand, poured some cereal into a bowl with his right, and with the carelessness of early-morning drowsiness, said the first thing that came into his head. "Andrew, I didn't know you had a live-in housekeeper, and such an attractive one at that."

Even as he said the words he realised he had made a serious mistake.

Andrew's early-morning smile disappeared from his face as though someone had flicked a switch. He turned away toward the coffee machine and spoke so softly that Mark could hardly catch the words. "I don't."

Mark stared at the change in Andrew's face and poured another bowl of cereal on the bench at the same time. He had unwittingly trodden on a painful page of Andrew's life, but how could he have known? Was she his mistress? No, he wouldn't believe it. But then …

"Anna was my daughter," Andrew said. "She was killed along with Suzie in the accident."

Mark sat down on the stool next to him. He stared at Andrew and cursed himself and his careless tongue.

The picture of Anna in all her beauty rose up before his eyes. He had slept in her room, so full of her presence that she could have been still living in it. Somehow, her spirit had seemed to rise up along with her picture. He felt her longing to assuage her father's grief, to fill his life with the joy of her own. An overwhelming anger filled his heart. How could God condemn His children to live with such grief? Why?

"I'm so terribly sorry …" Mark stuttered the words.

Andrew went over to the pantry and spent a long while searching for something on the shelves. Finally, he came back with a small pot of jam identical to the one already on the bench and sat down. There were tears in his eyes.

"I couldn't bear to put her things away," he explained. "Somehow, when I went in there to freshen up the bed, I'd look at them and imagine she was only on a holiday. I don't go into her room very often."

Mark had to get out because the pain was too close and too real. Memories of the terrible day his parents died came bursting in with such force they almost obscured his vision of Andrew on the other side of the bench. "I think I should go. I don't feel like breakfast. There's a lot to do in the lab." Mark rose from his seat.

"Sit down." The tone in Andrew's voice brooked no argument. "We need to talk more than you need to work. Finish the breakfast you don't want. I'll be on the veranda."

Wishing he was miles away, Mark slowly scraped the cereal off the bench into another bowl and returned it to the packet. Picking up a jug with the greatest reluctance, he added some milk to the remaining cereal and somehow managed to finish eating the mixture without tasting any of it. He threw another capsule into the coffee machine and made himself a strong black cup, drank it slowly. He carried the dishes over to the sink to give his courage more time to build then made his way out onto the veranda.

Staring out into the garden, Andrew was the first to break the silence. "There's anger in your face, Mark. Tell me why."

The directness of the approach did nothing to lessen the feelings Mark had tried to hide. "She is ... was so beautiful! To have lost her as well as your beloved Suzie, and you haven't escaped injury yourself! Last night you reminded me that God is in charge of all. You gave me hope that I might succeed. This morning, I learn He thinks nothing of destroying your loved ones and filling your life with endless grief! Only one look at her picture and I longed to hear her speak, to see her laugh. I can't imagine how terrible it is for you, how hard it is to live with such grief. How can I understand the love of God in all that?"

Andrew wheeled his chair over to the veranda railing, stood up, leaned against it, and waved his arm in the direction of the garden. "It's just like it was when Suzie was alive. You know, I'd go out onto this veranda and sit with my back to it all because I couldn't bear to see it overrun with weeds and falling apart. It reminded me of her death every time. Each morning was so hard to live through. Then you came and undid the damage. You became the hands and feet and encouraging voice of God to me, Mark, when I needed to feel them. When God wants to express His love, He uses human hands and hearts."

"I helped because I wanted to," Mark said. "It's been such a blessing to work in your garden."

Andrew turned from the garden to face Mark. "Of course it has, but you weren't the only one blessed. Last night you swore me to secrecy. This morning, I'm going to request the same favour." His eyes never left Mark's face. "Do I have your word that you will repeat nothing of what I am going to tell you to anyone?"

"Yes, yes, of course."

"You won't like what you hear." Andrew grimaced slightly. "I was a chemical engineer, a good one, but in the last ten years of my life I took up another occupation. I worked for an organisation designed to protect Australian citizens from corrupt and evil men. I was very successful. I can't go into details, but one day some men I hadn't finished dealing with decided to take me out of the game altogether. They almost succeeded. When I woke up in hospital after the so-called car accident and learned Suzie and Anna were dead, I wished with all my heart they had succeeded. I spent a long time screaming at God and everyone else."

Andrew paused.

Mark's voice reflected the horror he was feeling. "They were … murdered?"

"Yes," Andrew said. "Because of me. Because I stood against evil men. Add that to my grief."

Mark stared at him, saying nothing.

"There's a cost for standing against evil, Mark," Andrew continued. "There always is. If we are unwilling to pay, then evil triumphs, and the price of redemption becomes higher. The price of our cosmic rebellion and indifference towards God cost Christ His life, which he willingly gave. Such is the example of sacrifice. It is because of Him that I will see Anna and Suzie again, and we will spend eternity in each other's company. Up until yesterday, I never knew why God would want to keep me here when I would have been so much happier in Heaven."

"I'm not sure I understand," Mark faltered. "You know why you were spared, despite the suffering you've gone through?"

"Now I do. I have one more task to complete."

"A task? What task? Who for?"

Andrew's face broke into a rather enigmatic smile. "I'm here because of you, Mark, yes, I'm sure of it. There was never any doubt about me needing you, but now I understand something else. Very comforting. Makes sense of it all. Such a relief. I'm here because of you and this breach thing."

"I'm not sure I understand …"

"No, I don't suppose you do," Andrew replied. "Let me ask you a question, Mark. It may help you decide whether to remain angry with God, the God who redeemed you at the cost of His Son. What else would you like God to do to show you He loves you?"

Mark was silent for so long that Andrew thought to repeat the question. Finally he spoke, but very quietly. "Nothing. It's enough."

"Don't forget we live forever, Mark. This chapter of our lives may be very hard to endure, but we have an eternity to look forward to because of Christ. Sometimes we may be called upon to make the ultimate sacrifice, to give up our lives so that evil cannot triumph, but when we do, we have in reality lost nothing of our eternal existence. We've even added to its joy."

Mark stood up, walked over to Andrew's side, and threw his arms around his shoulders. "You're like a father to me." He couldn't say any more.

After a while, Andrew released Mark from the bear hug he was giving him, sat down in his chair, and wheeled it in the direction of the kitchen again. "I need another coffee."

"Me too."

The morning was well spent before Mark drove out of the tree-lined drive at Tahmoor and turned onto the main road. It had been a morning neither man would forget.

Andrew watched him go until his car was out of sight, then turned and wheeled himself into the study. After a moment's thought, he removed a key from his pocket, inserted it into the side of the phone on his desk, turned it, picked up the receiver, and dialled.

"Andrew Callan. Director Brian Hill, please. Yes, this is a secure line. Yes, he may be in a meeting. Get him out of it. Give him my name."

The same enigmatic smile crossed his face as he waited, listening to the tuneless muzak pouring out of the earpiece. The muzak stopped. A man's voice took its place.

"Brian here. Is that really you, Andrew? After all these years. The little red light on the receiver at this end tells me this isn't a social call. What have you been up to, you old dog? I thought you had well and truly retired. Not that we wanted you to, as I recall."

"Nice to hear your voice, Brian. There's some matters we should discuss. We need to arrange a meeting as soon as possible. Perhaps you could send one of your taxis to pick me up. I promise to make it worth your while."

After a little more conversation, Andrew replaced the receiver, extracted the key, and returned it to his pocket. By then, the enigmatic smile had broadened into a definite grin.

# CHAPTER 20

The day before he was due to depart, Dekker made a surprise visit to the campus. Mark and Candi were there. They had heard from Jenner about their jobs. Both had said yes. They had heard from the university, dismissing them from their post-doctoral studies. Neither of them had bothered to reply. Dekker came into the room and glanced around.

"Has anyone visited the premises?"

"No, not while we've been here, but we haven't been here all the time." Candi said.

"Shall we take a stroll among the gum trees?" Dekker motioned toward the door.

When they were quite a distance from the building, he went on. "From now, you cannot be too careful. I've been shadowed by someone ever since I left you in the café the other day. He stays outside our home in a car. I set the police on him yesterday, but today some other car is back.

"Now to more pressing matters. Yesterday, a correspondence student by the name of Ling Mai enrolled in accounting at the University of Southern Sydney. She paid her fees for a whole year. She will be a very good student. Occasionally, she will receive correspondence from her sister overseas—pictures, mostly. Occasionally, she will email her sister and send her pictures of the places she has visited around Sydney."

Mark furrowed his brow and Candi looked cross. What were they supposed to make of this nonsense?

Dekker smiled. "I see you don't get it. Before I go, you will memorise her student ID and password. The security on student accounts at Southern Sydney is as slack as all hell. Provided a student pays their fees and submits their assignments, the university is not interested. There's no monitoring of student email. I don't think they would know how. Jasmin lectured in mathematics at the National University in Canberra several years ago. She has some grateful students. Ling Mai would do anything for her. Jasmin will do all the assignments. Ling Mai will do very well."

"I don't see what you're driving at," Mark said. "So she does well. How does this help us? If we start sending you stuff on her account, someone will notice it. They may not monitor student mail now, but I can tell you if GPC wanted them to, they would."

"Quite so," Dekker agreed. "No, we will not send anything to arouse the slightest suspicion at the university level. If Jenner and his crew knew we were using a student account, things would be very different—so they must never find out." He handed each of them a compact flash card. "Keep these safe and secret. Each of them contains a small program that will run on your laptop. You mustn't store it there—always run it from the flash card. When you shut down, it will leave no trace on the hard drive. This program encodes a message into a picture—with two hundred fifty-six-bit encryption, no less, so even if someone found out what you were doing, it would take some time before they could crack your encryption phrase and read the message. You can encode simple diagrams the same way as well. If anything more complicated has to be sent, we will arrange the details by text encoded into the pictures. Choose pictures of tourist sites around Sydney. Take them yourselves. Pictures have header files containing data about the camera and when the picture was taken—all that stuff. Don't let people see you taking them. When you want to send a message, go somewhere public away from the plant and encode it into a picture. I believe the Back Alley has a WiFi hot spot. That would be a good place, but there may be others as well. Keep the pictures on the flash cards, too. Nothing that would give any clue as to what you are doing is to remain on your laptops. Log on to Ling Mai's account and write a chatty letter from Ling Mai to her sister Sun Kyung. Her address will be on the email she will send you—from me. Attach the picture file. Watch out for tails. If someone is shadowing you, Mark, SMS Candi with the word 'Coffee?' and vice versa. Be cryptic. They'll be monitoring your computers and your phone. Rely on this. Use it to your advantage, if you can."

"How will we know when you've sent us a message?" Candi asked.

"Good question, Candi," Dekker said. "Ling Mai will let you know. She will ring you from a public phone box. When you answer, she will say 'wrong number, very, very sorry.' Those exact words. You will know it's time to log on. Whatever you do, don't get caught with these flash cards. Now, here are the details of the account and the password. I will test you both to see if you remember. Don't write them down anywhere."

Half an hour later, Dekker left. Another tail picked him up at the gate and followed him down the road.

Candi held onto Mark's arm. "I'm very afraid, Mark. These people, they value life like small change. Dekker is being followed. That means we will be followed. I'm not brave, Mark. I can get my way with most men, but people like these do horrible things to women."

"They can't touch us, Candi, at least not yet. Remember that they haven't set up their power station. They're probably monitoring our emails and scanning our files. Let's make sure they get the wrong message. We'll have to be careful about what we store on our laptops. Do you have a computer at home?"

Candi shook her head. "No, I use my laptop, and Roger hasn't even got one."

"Okay, same with me. The problem is what to do with these cards. If we're caught with them, we're really in trouble. Let's check out the WiFi spot at the Back Alley, and if it works properly then we have our public place. Anyone watching us would think we are just catching up on work."

Candi waved the flash card in her hand. "What about these?"

"I think we should find a place to hide them on the premises. Maybe we could stick them under the table or something."

Candi shook her head again. "No, they move the tables around, and I've seen them upside down and stacked at the end of the room while someone cleans the floor."

"What about the toilets? Perhaps we could find a nook in there. The cards are not all that large."

Candi brightened at the thought. "Good idea. We might need some little waterproof cases to put them in."

"I can organise that," Mark said. "Saw some in the supermarket that would be ideal."

"Then we could duck into the toilet, come back with the card, stick it in our laptop and do our business while the whole world watches us." Candi said, warming even more to Mark's idea.

"Then visit the toilet just before we leave. Do you think we're being over cautious? Sounds like some spy movie, doesn't it?"

Candi looked into his face, suddenly serious. "I'm still frightened, Mark. Daniel is worried, can't you tell? If he's worried, then I think the danger is real."

They had begun to walk back toward the main building, but Candi stopped, reached out for Mark's arm, and held it. He turned round. "Mark, this is awkward for me. I don't want to give you the wrong idea. When we are in the public café, there may be people watching us closely when we need to talk to one another very privately."

"Yes, that may be the case."

"There is a way we could do it, but we have to give them the wrong message about us."

"I'm not following you." Mark said.

"We pretend to be lovers. I can whisper in your ear and get very close. We have to put on an act. I'm good at that, but you're hopeless."

"Hopeless?"

"If I get really close and kiss you," she said, "you'll turn red all over and the game will be up."

"How do you know that?"

"I saw your face when I kissed you the last time. A tomato blushing," Candi said laughing.

"That was pretty intense. I didn't expect it. I've never been ..."

"No, I didn't think so. That's why it worked."

"You think we should practice?"

There was a smile on Mark's face that Candi misread completely. "If I kiss you I don't want you to think I have any of those feelings toward you, because I don't, and I really don't want you to have any of those feelings toward me."

"I thought you didn't mind who you made love to you, as long as he made you feel fantastic. As I recall, you once offered to share your bed with me." Mark was still smiling.

Candi, on the other hand, was moving rapidly into defensive mode. "That was before I find out that you attach making love to other things I don't want to give you—to give anyone. To make love to Candi, you must think like Candi. No commitment, no strings, just enjoy the pleasure and the passion for its own sake. Your religion destroys all that."

"It's all right, Candi. I promise I won't misunderstand your intentions," Mark laughed softly. "But there's more to love than the kind that begins and ends in the bedroom, and your heart's crying out for it, I know it is. I just wish you would hear what it's saying to you. "

Candi scowled at him. He was so arrogant, so ignorant, standing there smiling patronisingly at her—a man who had never once felt the ecstasy of sleeping with a woman. She felt a fierce anger suddenly boiling up inside her. "This is the angel dust again, isn't it? The empty words. Since you see so deeply into Candi's heart, Candi tell you something she knows about yours. I may be the forbidden fruit, but you still want to touch it, don't you? Don't you?!"

She suddenly grabbed him around the neck and kissed him passionately on the lips, drawing her body seductively up against his until she was standing on her toes. She felt the intake of his breath, his body becoming rigid. Then she pushed herself away, angry with him and angry with what she had done. "See, you are the blushing tomato again."

"Yes, I am," Mark said sharply. "Of course I am. What are you trying to prove? That I'm a man? Well, Candi, here comes the truth. Guess what? I am a man, and I have every sort of desire toward a beautiful women that any man has. The only difference is that I don't give those desires free reign in my life. You don't want me to feel sexually attracted toward you? Then don't provoke what you don't want to receive."

He turned on his heel and walked away.

Candi felt as though she had been slapped in the face, and to make matters worse, she knew she deserved it. How would any other man she knew have reacted to her words, her actions? She didn't have to guess. Why was it that when Mark behaved so decently toward her she became so incredibly angry? Why was it that the more he refused to respond to her powers of seduction, the more she wanted to seduce him? He was enslaved by a stupid religion whose killjoy moral code belonged with a bygone age. Why did she suddenly feel so guilty? Mark was quite a way ahead now. Suddenly she began to run after him—not quite knowing why she did so.

"Mark! Mark! Wait, please!"

He stopped and turned round again, frowning. What was coming next? Candi ran up to him, looking very serious, with no trace of her former anger in her eyes. "Mark … I'm sorry. I'm sorry, Mark."

Her own words sounded lame in her ears. Surely this was the time for the sorrowful angel strategy: the tears, the large eyes staring soulfully into his face, so effective in twisting men to her will. Yet she couldn't bring herself to use it. Such a response was so fake, so foreign to any sort of friendship, and deep in her heart she knew this man was her friend, perhaps even more of a friend than her lover. How strange that sounded.

He was looking at her, neither sad nor angry, his eyes serious, his face devoid of any other expression. He spoke quietly. "That's okay, Candi. Friends?"

"Friends, Mark."

They went back to the laboratory together.

Candi hoped Mark would not turn round and see the tears that seemed, for some annoying and inexplicable reason, to be welling up in her eyes. Watching for the right moment, she raised her hand and quickly wiped them away.

Mark was none the wiser, thank goodness.

The following day, Mark went to the supermarket and bought two plastic containers that just fitted the small flash cards. He showed them to Candi, and they decided to pay a visit to the Back Alley for coffee and reconnaissance. It was a most opportune time. The café had just that morning replaced all the tiles in the toilets. A whispered conversation followed, after which Mark stepped out and bought several items from the hardware store, plus a cake slide and a tube of toothpaste from the supermarket before returning to join Candi, who had been chatting to Annette.

He excused himself and went straight into the toilet, carrying his recent purchases under his shirt.

"Is Mark okay?" Annette asked. "He went to the toilet when he came in before."

"He's been feeling a little unwell. I think it was something he cooked last night. Better not have the banana bread. Just a croissant and ham for both of us."

Mark had not returned when Annette brought the food to the table. "He's been a while. Do you want Robert to go and check on him?"

"No thanks, Annette, but you're so thoughtful. Look, he's coming back now."

Mark had been very busy. With the aid of the cake slice, he had removed a freshly planted tile from the wall and, using the knife, cut a neat rectangular indentation in the plaster board behind it. He had to wait until the toilet was empty because this made quite a bit of noise. He inserted the small plastic case into the hole and stuck it there with fast setting adhesive, and then he put the tile back with industrial Velcro to cover the little pocket he had made in the wall. He took some white toothpaste from the tube and smeared it into the joint to look like grout. Now it was impossible to tell he had tampered with the tile at all. The operation had taken less than ten minutes. He had carefully cleaned up the evidence on the floor with paper and flushed it down the toilet. Exiting the cubicle, he had washed the final traces off his hands and returned to join Candi at the table.

"Are you sure he should be eating this?" Annette asked while gesturing toward the food.

"Mark, is your tummy up to a croissant and ham?"

"Of course it is. What happened to the banana bread?" Mark asked before reading the meaning behind Candi's arched eyebrows and wide eyes. "Oh, I see, yes, good idea, Candi. Better not tempt fate."

Slightly confused by the mixed messages, Annette left them.

She whispered in his ear. "How did it go?"

"All right." Mark explained the procedure to his partner in crime.

"Where's the stuff?" she asked.

"In my shirt."

"What use is it there?"

"You'll have to retrieve it," he said. "Thought I'd leave that to your seductive imagination."

"You're hopeless. What am I supposed to do? Put my hands inside?" Candi said. "That's what guys do to girls. Look, I'll lean over to give you a nice little kiss and you take them out and put them in my handbag. It's on my lap. Careful!"

"You're distracting me," he whispered. "I've dropped the cake slice on the floor."

"You're hopeless. Put your arms around me." Candi fished the other items out of his shirt and stowed them in her handbag.

Mark shook with suppressed laughter.

"Why are you laughing?"

"You're tickling me," he chuckled.

"Hopeless!" She picked up the cake slice from the floor and stowed it in her handbag as though it were a completely normal thing to do. Then she headed for the toilet.

Annette watched her disappearance with some concern. When Candi had still not returned twenty minutes later, Annette came over to their table again. "What's the matter with Candi?"

"I think she has the same tummy bug. Must be going around."

"You shouldn't kiss people when they have tummy bugs. You've probably given it to her."

Mark felt as though this wasn't the appropriate time to talk about incubation periods or anything technical like that and instead simply nodded his agreement.

"Would you like me to see if she's okay in there?" Annette offered.

"No thanks," Mark replied. "Candi wouldn't like anyone to make a fuss. She'll be out soon, I hope."

It was another ten minutes before Candi, her hair suitably tousled, came back into the room.

Annette rushed over when she sat down. "Are you all right? I asked Mark if you wanted help, but he said no."

"Thanks Annette. I think I have the same tummy bug—threw up in there."

"Mark ate your croissant as well as his own," Annette said, frowning. "I don't suppose you should eat anything, should you?"

"I've got a very empty tummy," Candi said. "I think I need food to dilute the bug. Can you bring me a chicken sandwich on rye with mayonnaise and one of those nice black forest cakes from the window?"

Annette murmured something about how she didn't think it was a good idea, but, true to her training, she went off to fetch the food, thinking it might be useful to bring a bucket in from the yard to have on the ready.

"What the blazes happened to you?" said Mark with concern on his face.

Candi pressed her lips into Mark's ear and whispered, "I broke the bloody tile!" She turned her head so that Mark could reply in a similar fashion. When no message was forthcoming, she whispered, "What are you doing now?"

"Getting your hair out of my mouth," he said. "Can't you move it off your ear?"

'You're meant to nuzzle in. For goodness sake, don't you know anything about women?"

She lifted her hair, deliberately exposing her right ear, and almost pushed it into his face. "Go ahead, Max. This looks like a fourth-rate movie. Ninety-nine is ready. Speak!"

Mark tried, but every time he put his mouth near Candi's ear, she would collapse in a fit of uncontrollable laughter until both of them were lying back in their chairs laughing their heads off.

Mark, exercising stoic self-control, eventually managed to get his head into the appropriate location and laughed into her ear. "What did you do?"

Another rearrangement of heads took place.

Annette was watching with an expression of amused fascination on her face.

"I took another one off near the floor," Candi said. "Almost got caught by some old biddy coming in. Put the broken one there and used the other one." She chuckled. "Told her I was searching for my contact lens. I held the broken one in place with my foot and shoved the other one up my top. I was worried she might want to help me look."

"We'd better have a rapid return to health tomorrow," Mark said. "I think Annette's worried we might be infecting the customers with a nasty stomach virus."

Candi started laughing again. "You're tickling my ear, and Annette thinks we're gone mad."

"How do you think we go as secret agents?" They were both laughing again.

"Hopeless!"

The sandwich and cake arrived. Mark ordered mud cake and more coffee. Returning to her place behind the counter, Annette checked that the bucket was still under the counter and went out into the yard to fetch a mop.

The next day, they practiced going to the toilet and retrieving the cards. The operation took about five minutes. Replacing the toothpaste and cleaning round the tile was the longest part of it. By Thursday, they had reduced this to three minutes, provided the toilet was clear.

Only just in time. The next day they were watched.

The two men entered the café and took a table on the other side of the room. Candi fetched a mirror from her handbag and made up her face. She leaned over toward Mark and whispered from behind her compact. "Those men on the far table are watching us. I've never seen them before. Don't look. Get your laptop out and let's practice."

Mark retrieved his laptop from its case on the floor and stuck the compact flash card in its slot while lifting it onto the table. He booted the machine and watched with satisfaction when it found the local WiFi network. He logged on to the university student email server.

All was going well.

Candi finished making up her face, took out a brush, and began to do her hair. It gave her an opportunity to survey the surveillance. One of the men was concentrating on stirring his coffee, and the other pretended to be admiring the view behind her. The fact that neither were apparently taking any notice of Candi preening herself was suspicious indeed. Two other young men on the other side of the café certainly had noticed.

She drew herself up straight, thrust out her chest a little, and flipped her hair across the side of her face. The two young men were obviously taking interest, but the others, apparently, had no interest in her at all.

"Proof of ill intent," she thought to herself.

In a slow and deliberate movement, she turned toward Mark, wrapped her arms around his shoulders, and drew him close. When his left ear was touching her lips, she murmured. "There is no doubt about it. How's the connection going?"

Mark spoke softly. "Okay. We're in to the mail server. Nothing has come through. I'll shut down. Do you want to put your card back?"

"Okay." She stood up and went towards the toilet, deliberately passing close to the two men who had suddenly become interested in reading the menu. A short time later, she was back.

Mark had shut down the machine and returned it to its case. The flash card was in his pocket. "Another coffee? Then we had better get back to work."

"Thanks, Mark," Candi said. "Latte, please."

Mark waved at Annette and placed the order, and then he headed for the men's room. One of the young men on the other table had got up and was moving deliberately toward the vacant chair by Candi's side. She gave him a look that would have set lava solid in a second. He changed direction and moved toward the counter.

In five minutes, Mark returned. They drank their coffees in silence, paid Annette, and walked out of the café.

"It's begun, Mark. I'm feeling sick inside."

"It'll be all right, Candi. Remember, they need us. I think they were just making sure we weren't trying to meet with someone on their forbidden list."

"I think we should leave our laptops on our desks tonight, then we can see if someone has played with them while we are away."

"Do you have a piece of software that will do that?"

"No." Candi said. "It's called a strand of hair. You can borrow one if you'd like."

"Thanks," Mark said. "I will."

They got into Candi's Toyota and headed for the lab. Mark noticed another car had pulled away from the kerb and was travelling along behind them. It tailed them all the way to the entrance before turning round and going back towards Camden.

# CHAPTER 21

Apart from the security guards, Mark and Candi had been left more or less alone since Dekker had been dismissed from the project.

Peter North had come with papers they had to sign. "You understand, this is commercially sensitive material we are dealing with," he said, "and signing this document binds you to maintain confidentiality. Should it become evident you have breached this condition, you will be subject to instant dismissal. The company will treat such behaviour with the utmost seriousness. It would be very foolish for either of you to communicate with Dekker or anyone else concerning what is going on here. Do you understand?"

There was no mistaking the threat.

The company, he said, was busy planning the infrastructure necessary for the first phase of the project. He seemed strangely reluctant to look at the breach. They provided him with diagrams of the experimental arrangement, the collision tube dimensions, and the pumping systems. He was not at all interested in the new field magnets or Candi's microwave creation. Taking the signed paperwork with him, he left the premises as soon as he could.

A pattern developed that was to remain the same for quite a few weeks while North and many others worked on their plans.

Mark would come in early and leave late, filling more exercise books with notes and wearing out more pens on his whiteboard.

Candi would come in late and leave early. Roger was not scheduled to play for a couple of weeks, so they had been able to spend more time together, which she appreciated. She usually arrived about midday, brought Mark lunch, and sat with him to make sure he ate it.

Careful to avoid controversial subjects, they talked. Sometimes they went for a walk together under the gum trees to give Mark some fresh air. Neither of them realised how these times together were deepening the relationship between them. Neither thought of them in those terms, yet both of them looked forward to the interlude.

For Mark, the pleasant hour spent in Candi's delightful, sunny company was a relief from the endless circle of unprofitable theorising, and he always felt cheered at the end of it.

For Candi, it was an opportunity to make good on her promise to Dekker, and, contrary to her own dread of commitment, she found she was enjoying it. Mark depended on her, and taking care of him brought an unexpected warmth to her heart. He never ate properly, and he worked too hard. Her usual range of distracting devices was greatly reduced, but never once did she make the slightest attempt to flirt with him, and never once did she steer the conversation toward religion.

On Tuesday, Candi received the first "wrong number" call, so they went to the café for lunch that day. Only Candi took her laptop. She visited the ladies room and retrieved the card, came back to the table, and apologised to Mark for having to do some work during lunch. A chatty letter came through from Sun Kyung about her holiday in Scotland, and attached was a picture of Edinburgh castle. Candi decrypted it. The message read:

> *Operation successful so far.*
> *Cooperation from Professor and Lady K. secured.*
> *Moving all the time.*
> *Hope you R OK :)*

Candi as Ling Mai wrote a reply telling Sun Kyung about her trip to the Rocks at Sydney and attached an encoded picture of Sydney Harbour Bridge. The message read:

*Message received.*
*Shadowed constantly.*
*No progress on shutting down.*
*Luv C, M :)*

Mark drank his coffee and watched the screen in an apparently disinterested way.

Candi shut down her laptop and palmed the flash card into her pocket. "Could you order me a turkey bagel and salad? I'm off to the bathroom again. Won't be a minute."

In a short time, the card was tucked away in its safe little niche behind the tile. Candi returned, passing close to the two men who were sitting at the table on the other side of the café. Going back to Mark, she bent over him from behind. Her hair, which had steadily grown longer since they had first met, fell down all over his face.

He felt her lips touch his ear.

"They're recording our conversation," she whispered, kissed him on the cheek and sat down.

"I wonder what our employers are up to," Mark said in a slightly-louder-than-normal voice. "I'm getting tired of the inaction. For the salary we're earning, I would have thought we might be called upon to do a little more. I'm really getting sick of doing crosswords and playing solitaire."

"Just enjoy it, Mark," she said. "I sit out in the sun. Frank—you know Frank, he's the really tall security guard—he's found me a banana lounge. I think he likes watching me lie on it and sun myself."

They finished their meal with carefully crafted light conversation designed to hint at their eagerness to begin work.

It wasn't long before their contrived wish became true. The following Monday, a team of engineers arrived in train with Peter North.

He introduced one of them. "This is Tony Slater, chief engineer. You will report to him. He is responsible for the transition phase from experiment to pilot power station. Your input will be important to ensure the safety of this process. I will return to our Australian office, and Slater will report to me."

Tony Slater was around thirty-five. He was thin with olive skin and short black hair that he wore gelled to the top of his head. He smelled strongly of aftershave. He wore a black suit and a bright red tie that had pictures of naked women outlined in silver on it. Candi took an instant dislike to him.

Peter spoke to the assembled throng of staff. "Doctors Leblanc and Chambers are now going to demonstrate the breach. Please do as they say without question."

Dreading what he was about to do, Mark led them past the barriers to the collision tube.

They stood round talking and laughing with one another. "This is the end-of-the-world breach, is it?" one of them said. "I must say, it looks just like a piece of deadly glass tubing!" The others laughed.

With the bright light of the morning sun streaming through the high windows of the lab, the razor-thin line of pale light was not easily seen. Mark went over to the injection port and turned the valve, allowing hydrogen gas to enter the tube. The razor-thin line of light flashed brilliant red and then grew to a dazzling bluish-white.

There was absolute silence. Candi scanned the group. With the exception of Slater, all the others seemed shocked to the core. North looked alarmed, and Candi detected more than an element of fear in his staring eyes.

Slater spoke, his voice a thinly veiled sneer. "Turn it up. Is that all this thing is capable of? What we have here is a light bulb, not an energy source for a power station. Is this a joke?"

"If I double the flow of hydrogen into the port, the glass will melt and the vacuum in the tube will implode the glass walls onto the breach. When that happens, you'll have all the energy you're after, because before you can get out of the building the breach will be feeding on you." Mark said, his voice tinged with anger.

Slater uttered a scornful, cynical laugh. "Do it," he said. "Let's see the proof of the pudding. I don't believe it."

It was North who replied. "Mr. Slater, you will now and in the future pay complete attention to Dr. Chambers. We do not want to jeopardise the project at this early stage, let alone put ourselves at risk. If Dr. Chambers considers a procedure dangerous, you will modify it until he is satisfied that it is not dangerous. He has complete authority to do so. I trust I am making this company policy clear."

Slater swore under his breath. "At least let me get an engineer in here to measure the actual output from the thing," he replied. "Because if we can't get good estimates of likely energy output now, there's no point in wasting the company's money constructing a useless power plant with no energy to run it."

"You may do that, Mr. Slater. Make sure Dr. Chambers is present at every stage," North said with a grimace.

The group went about setting up their offices and generally familiarising themselves with the laboratory. Some made careful measurements of the building using laser equipment, while others checked out the cryogenic plant and vacuum pumps.

No one went near the breach.

The next day, a consulting engineer arrived along with some very nice photometric measuring equipment. "This is Michael Willis," Slater said to Mark and Candi. "He's here to make energy measurements on the—discharge. Can we give him something to measure?"

The four of them went toward the tube.

Michael Willis was a young man. He was athletic in form and walked at a fast pace. He gave the very impression of an efficient and effective consultant who would get in, do the job, get out, and move on with the next one. He placed the adjustable table he was holding close to the tube, and, adjusting it to the right height, lifted the instrument on top of it. "Just what am I going to measure?"

"Some gas will be ionised at the end of this tube," Slater answered. "I want to know how much energy is radiated."

"No problem."

Michael Willis took the cover off his instruments, lifted a probe out of its cushioned place in the lid, turned round to admire Candi, and dropped the probe on top of the glass. The tube vibrated madly with a hollow, ringing sound. There was a flash of bright orange light from inside.

Candi screamed, choked, and vomited all over the floor. Mark made a gasping sound, and Slater swore profusely.

"What the devil's going on here?" Michael Willis turned round to face the horrified group, incomprehension all over his face. "It's only a piece of glass. If it breaks, get another one. It won't shatter the budget." He turned from one face to another, reading the fear on some and the abject terror on two others. "Just what the hell's going on?"

Candi was shaking, rooted to the spot. Mark, his face ashen grey, went over to her and gripped her arm hard. "It's all right," he said quietly. "The tube hasn't fractured."

Then to Willis, Mark said, "Please take more care in future, would you?"

Extremely puzzled, Willis grunted and returned to setting up his equipment. Who were these people? What was the matter with them? What were they terrified of, because it was bloody clear they were terrified of something.

After he had finished, Willis turned back to Mark. "Everything is ready. You say this is a hydrogen discharge I'm supposed to be measuring? I've placed sensors close to this precious piece of glass, but not touching it. This means the readings will be less precise. Are you sure you don't want me to place the sensors directly on the surface? We will get better …"

"No, thank you. Please stand by." Mark went to the valve and set it for the usual ten milligrams per second flow.

Willis stared at the discharge in disbelief. He mechanically turned to his instruments and began measuring the radiation. After several minutes, he held up his hand. "You can stop now, I have sufficient readings. What's going on here? Why does the ionisation stop before the end of the tube? Where is the accelerating voltage being applied in order to create this ionisation in the first place? I don't understand what's happening."

Slater answered him. "Please use my office to complete your calculations and prepare your report. When you leave this building, you will forget anything you may have seen here. Is that clear?"

"No, it's not," Willis replied, "If you think you can bloody well shove me around, you have another think coming. There's something very strange going on. You've confirmed it. Answer me. What's causing the ionisation? I see no high-voltage supplies. Where's the energy coming from?"

"Your report in half an hour." Slater said. "Please state the margin of uncertainty in your measurements as well. When you have finished, call me."

An hour later Michael Willis left, an angry man.

It was Wednesday morning. Mark was working in his office when Candi arrived with the morning paper in her hand.

She came in, shut the door, and leaned against it. Her pretty face wrinkled up. Tears streamed down. Although she made no sound, her body shook with sobs. Unable to speak, she ran over to Mark and clung to him.

Mark wrapped his arms round her tightly. From the depths of his jumper came the broken words.

"They—killed—him!"

Glancing over her shoulder, Mark picked up the paper that had fallen on his desk. It was open to the second page. He read:

> *The Great Western Highway was closed westbound for a period of two hours yesterday following an accident in which a motorist drove off the road into a valley near Bullaburra. The car hit a tree and burst into flames. The accident brings the road toll to forty-nine this year. The driver was later identified as a Michael Willis of Penrith. Police are investigating.*

The article included a picture of a burnt-out wreck being winched back onto the road.

Mark felt physically ill. Holding Candi tightly, he kissed her on the head and said quietly. "Candi, we don't know what happened. He may have been drinking. It may have been foggy. We can't assume that GPC had anything to do with it. I'm really sorry this has happened, but we mustn't jump to dreadful conclusions."

"I—can't—breathe." The words were muffled and punctuated with gulping sobs. Little by little, comforted by the arms that held her, she grew calmer and the sobs abated. Mark felt her body slowly becoming softer against his chest.

Slater opened the door. He took one look at Candi in Mark's arms and swore. "This is an engineering works, not a bloody bordello," he said. "Hold it down until you get into the bedroom, or there will be consequences."

Mark felt Candi's body go rigid in his arms and heard her intake of breath. He held onto her tightly. "Perhaps you have not heard of the death of Michael Willis. Dr. Leblanc is distressed. I am comforting her."

"Making out with her, more likely. Get back to your office, Leblanc."

"Dr. Leblanc stays right where she is," Mark said without raising his voice. "You may not give a damn about her feelings, but I do."

Slater sneered at him.

"I'll have your pay reduced for failure to meet your performance goals."

"Do it, then." Still holding Candi tightly in his arms, he looked right into Slater's eyes. "If you haven't anything else to say, get out of my office."

Malice swept over Slater's face. He swore, turned, and slammed the door so hard that a panel of glass fell out of it.

Candi turned her face upward and gazed wordlessly into his. Her eyes brimmed with tears and overflowed with gratitude.

Looking into them, Mark felt a deep stirring in his heart: a desire to take care of her, to protect her against men like Slater.

Her lips turned up into a little smile. "Thank you." The woman snuggled her head onto his shoulder again. "Hold me," she said. "I'm not afraid when I'm here."

Holding her seemed so right. It was as though she truly belonged there, in the arms of someone who really cared for her. He felt the warmth of her body against him, her soft hair against his lips. That felt right, too. He tightened his arms and held her for a long time.

# CHAPTER 22

The transformation from appalling experiment to horrendous power station took the best part of eight months.

At first, very little appeared to be taking place. The project was divided into two parts: one team would install steam turbines and electrical generators in a new building near the old cooling tower, and the other, including Mark and Candi, would remove the glass collision tube and enclose the breach in an evacuated steel sphere of enormous strength.

This was accomplished in several stages. Firstly, a large hemisphere was positioned under the glass tube and its injection port. The hemisphere was roughly three metres in diameter with long antechambers on opposite sides, one to wrap round the old injection port, and the other near the breach end of the tube. Part of the roof above the tube was then removed and a second hemisphere was lowered in through. Then they were bolted and welded together.

Although the process sounded rather straightforward, the anxiety experienced by Mark, Candi, and most of the others who understood the danger, was intense. Only a nail had to fall onto the tube and all would be lost.

The operation was performed slowly and with the utmost care. When the two hemispheres had been joined, special equipment was installed in both antechambers, and the whole lot was evacuated.

On a tense and frightening day in November, the collision tube was severed by laser from the injection port and withdrawn centimetre by centimetre through the antechamber at the opposite end. The condition of the breach was monitored by a sapphire fibre optic let into the wall of the sphere. There were some heart-stopping moments when the breach would flash brilliantly, but at last the collision tube lay on the floor of the laboratory and the breach was finally enclosed in a massively strong evacuated steel sphere.

The antechamber on the right, the former injection end, would become the point at which radioactive waste material would be fed into the breach. The antechamber at the other end was sealed off with a steel plate.

Even Mark felt an enormous relief once the glass tube was finally gone.

With the sphere firmly anchored to temporary steel struts, a section of the floor under that part of the laboratory was removed and excavated to a depth of five metres. The roof above the sphere was removed completely. When the base and sides of this square hole had been concreted, two larger hemispheres were put in, one below and one above the sphere. These were five metres in diameter.

Working a hemisphere at a time, the inner sphere was enclosed by the outer, leaving a gap of about two metres between the two. A large intake pipe was attached to the bottom of the outer sphere, and an output pipe of equal size was attached to the middle of the top one. The two outer hemispheres were bolted and welded together. The whole of the outer sphere was covered with beryllium and lead shielding, and then with thermal insulating material. When all had been done, the roof, which was much higher than it had been before, was replaced along with the walls, which had been removed to make way for the hemispheres to enter the building. Then an expanded steel flooring was secured over the concreted pit.

By then, the original laboratory was almost unrecognisable. In place of the collision tube with its new field magnets was a huge rectangular block that stretched from below ground level to high up into the roof. On one end of the block, the long antechamber with its attachments which led into the inner sphere was visible. On the other end, a similar antechamber, this one with no attachments, protruded from the thermal shielding. One third of the way along from the left, a metre above the expanded steel floor, the sapphire optical port came out, enabling those outside to monitor the condition of the breach in the inner chamber. An insulated pipe led into the bottom of the block and emerged from the top. The pipe was bent at right angles and headed for the steam turbines in the generator building along a gantry supported at regular intervals by metal towers.

On the March 15 at 3:15 p.m., the first radioactive waste was fed into the breach. Coolant water was circulating between the inner and outer sphere. The intake port was connected via a remote flow controller to a heavily lead shielded line that led, via special pumps, into the radioactive waste ponds.

As head of GPC engineering, Peter North had arrived for the privilege of opening the port. It was an honour he would have much rather foregone, but Jenner had insisted on it.

He couldn't understand Jenner. Throughout the construction phase, the only correspondence he had received instructed him to hurry up. Every warning he had sent regarding the necessity of care and safety had fallen on deaf ears. Surely Jenner understood that there were serious risks, and yet he chose to ignore them.

North reflected on his own misgivings, raised by many orders of magnitude in that frightening moment when he had seen the breach for himself. Once he had genuinely believed the discovery would benefit the world, but he wasn't at all sure anymore. Privately wishing himself anywhere else on the planet, he disengaged the safety interlocks and moved the flow control up.

"Flow, one millilitre per second. Report state of ionisation."

Mark was monitoring the breach, and Candi was watching the temperature and pressure of the coolant. There were a couple of engineers watching the flow pumps. All the rest, including Slater, were over in the generator building.

"Fat lot of good that would do them if something went wrong," Mark thought to himself.

"Breach is flaring," said Mark. "Closing down aperture in order to observe spectrum."

"No change in coolant temperature," Candi reported.

"Increasing flow rate to ten millilitres per second." North's voice was far from calm.

"Breach looks like the sun," said Mark, an expression approaching dread on his face.

"Coolant temperature rising—fifty, ninety, one hundred, one hundred and ten degrees celsius … increase circulation pumps to full speed." Candi's voice trembled with anxiety.

"Main pumps now operational," the flow control engineers replied.

They felt the small tremor as the circulating water began to pressurise through the space between the spheres.

"Coolant temperature still rising. It's up to one hundred and fifty degrees celsius. Stop increasing breach flow! Stop!" Candi's voice was almost a scream. "It's still rising. Are the pumps at maximum? Two hundred degrees celsius!"

Water at that temperature will instantly vaporise into superheated steam if the pressure is reduced. In the generator room, the engineers would do that and use the steam to drive the turbines, which in turn would drive the generators. The steam would be sent to the cooling tower, condensed into water again, and returned to the inlet pumps.

"Coolant temperature is now over two hundred degrees," yelled Candi, exercising every ounce of self-control to prevent herself from running out of the building.

North called out. "Mark, status of the breach?"

"It's a thin wedge shape, and huge amounts of energy are coming off. God help us! We're getting X-rays on the shields! Level out in the lab is still within limits."

"Coolant is now two hundred and thirty degrees and rising," Candi called out even louder. "For goodness sake, you imbecile, slow down the flow!"

Through the intercom to the generator building came the sounds of the turbines winding up along with shouts of joy from the power engineers in the control room. A small cloud of steam appeared above the circular opening in the top of the cooling tower.

"Temperature approaching three hundred degrees. Coolant pressure, approaching 200 atmospheres. If that sphere ruptures, we'll all be boiled alive! Reduce the bloody flow rate! Est-ce que vous êtes tous devenus fous? Réduisez le flux! Je vous en supplie!"

"Reduce the flow rate!" Mark yelled to North. "Reduce it until the coolant temperature stabilises, or we'll rupture the sphere!"

North shouted back. "All right! All right!! The feed pump control is sluggish! Reducing now! Candi, what's the coolant temperature? Is it going down?"

"Yes. Two hundred and ninety-five degrees."

"Thank God!" North relinquished the flow lever and wiped the sweat running down his face.

The temperature of the coolant finally stabilised at three hundred and one degrees celsius at a flow rate of eight point one millilitres per second, producing over one hundred megawatts of power from the generators when connected to the grid.

Peter North, sounding a good deal more elated than he felt, called them all into his office and opened several bottles of very expensive champagne.

George Jenner appeared on the video conference phone to hear the news. He congratulated them all.

A short time later, Candi went searching for Mark, who had absented himself from the celebrations. She found him in the car park, shivering despite the warmth of the weather.

She wrapped her arms around one of his. "It is truly terrifying, yes? I wanted to run away and hide somewhere."

"The breach is a hundred times as wide as before. The line has become a wedge shape. Things may be stable now, but what happens when they have to shut it down? What effect does all this waste have on the breach itself? Perhaps it will soon reach a stage when it's completely irreversible, when nothing will shut it down. I feel ill."

Candi's stomach had been threatening to empty its contents for some time. Listening to Mark vent his fears made her feel worse. She swallowed hard. Now was not the time to throw up. She wrapped both arms around one of his and dropped her head onto his shoulder.

"Mark, let's walk. I can't stand still. If I stand here, I'll start to shake all over, and then I'll throw up. Listen to them. I can hear more champagne corks going off. Are they all mad?"

"I don't think North is too happy," Mark said. "I noticed he got in his car and headed off pretty quick."

"He might be worried sick, but that won't stop him," she said. "The company won't be content with this. They'll want more of them. I wonder what the press release will read like. 'Imbecile power company exploits global menace to make money.' I wish I was brave enough to tell them!"

"It wouldn't help, Candi. I think we should tell Daniel what's happened, though. He knows the test was today, and he'll be worried sick."

"You're right, Mark. Doing nothing is unbearable. Let's visit the Back Alley."

They left the plant and headed for the café. Behind them, a cloud of steam rose above the cooling tower. Mark watched it and shuddered.

Fifteen minutes later, they were at their usual place. Two new tails were watching them from a car on the other side of the street. After the essential visit to the bathroom, Mark wrote a distressingly short email to Sun Kyung about a trip to Thredbo in the spring and attached and encoded picture of Mt. Kosciusko.

The message read:

> *Plant operational.*
> *Apparently stable.*
> *Breach a flaring wedge*
> *Plant producing 100 MW*
> *Everyone else ecstatic.*
> *We're terrified sick.*
> *Please report progress.*
> *CM*

Dekker, who had been constantly monitoring the email address in a state of unexpressed anxiety, decoded the picture instantly and ran his hand over his forehead. He encoded a reply.

> *Much relieved.*
> *No progress yet*
> *Do not give up*
> *We are working day and night*
> *D.*

# CHAPTER 23

Dekker was in Zurich. He had spent the day in a closeted meeting with three of the world's leading physicists. Their common alarm had grown throughout the day, their progress toward a solution had not.

"Is that bad news you've received?" Professor Stephen Eagles watched as Dekker typed madly on the keyboard.

"The plant is operational," Dekker said. "The breach is flaring badly, but it hasn't lost containment. I suppose we should be thankful. It's producing over a hundred megawatts of energy. GPC are very happy. My friends are terrified."

Professor Hans Zimmerman shook his head with worry. "And so they should be. I've spoken today to my colleagues at Berkeley. I'll ring them now. They're not going to like this. Some of them thought bombarding the breach with heavy nuclei might cause it to peter out. Now we know. The damn thing is just as dangerous as we thought it was. Perhaps what they're doing will have the opposite effect and make it totally impossible to close. There's a think tank going on at CERN as well. I've made some suggestions as to experiments they could try with their huge accelerator, but they're very nervous about doing them. If one breach can be made, then it's possible to make two."

Zimmerman put his hands over his face. "The trouble is that we have no model for this thing. We have classically assumed that there is nothing beyond the matter we see in the universe, and if there were, it would be inaccessible to us. Now it appears as though we are intimately connected with other dimensions, and that these dimensions and the shadow particles in them influence the moment-by-moment behaviour of the particles that make up our observable universe. When the barrier between these dimensions is fractured ..." His voice trailed off into silence.

Stephen Eagles said, "We must get those two young people to do something or they will fall apart. Make them go through the early data, the measurements you made when the breach was formed. It must exist on the recorders. What were the neutron energies? No one else has managed to make neutrons like that. I am thinking, perhaps they were not neutrons you made? I cannot see neutrons having the ability to puncture the barrier between us and some unknown dimension. I get the feeling there is something staring me in the face, but I can't put my finger on it."

The discussion continued late into the night. By morning, headlines around the world read:

*FREE GREEN ENERGY FOR A STARVING WORLD*

*A new discovery by Australian scientists Drs. Chambers and Leblanc working with world-renowned physicist Dr. Daniel Van Dekker has provided the answer to the world's energy needs through a new process called a quantum bridge. Although not completely understood, the process is capable of converting small samples of matter—including waste materials—into incredibly large amounts of energy. The process not only offers solutions to the world energy crisis, but it also offers a permanent and ecologically ideal solution to the problem of radioactive waste disposal. In the course of the energy conversion, the waste material is completely removed from the environment.*

The article went on to praise the initiative of Global Power Consortium for funding the research. There was a statement from the general manager saying that they intended to licence the technology to other organisations, as well as to proliferate the wonderful new plants throughout the world. More pages followed with suitably vague diagrams showing how the process worked.

Back in Australia, Margaret Marriott was congratulating herself. This was the beginning of a new and wonderful golden age for the University of Southern Sydney. Visions of new buildings, more staff, and more political clout poured into her mind as she power-dressed herself for the business meeting she had scheduled over the phone.

Then there was the press conference to organise. She made another phone call. So the world learned that although GPC had funded the research, it was conducted under the auspices and with the approval of USS.

That morning, Margaret's office was swarming with reporters. She told them all she knew, which didn't amount to very much. The one thing really annoying her was the failure of Chambers and Leblanc to return her emails or phone calls. That was not acceptable. She sent them each an old-fashioned letter, embossed with the university letterhead over which was written in gold "Department of the Chancellor."

It read:

*Dear Dr. Leblanc,*

*The university regrets any misunderstanding that may have caused you to believe that your post-doctoral program had been terminated. Any correspondence you may have received to that effect was sent in error. On the contrary, we are delighted to welcome you and Dr. Chambers to address our next business meeting, which will be held in two weeks from this date on Tuesday in the staff reception hall.*

*Please RSVP to our secretary, Millicent Veronica Smythe-Harris …*

"See if you can get it in the rubbish bin from there," Mark said as he made his third attempt with that very same correspondence wrapped up into a little ball.

Candy balled the sheet of paper and flung it with force towards the bin. "Voilà!" She said. "I am a good shot, yes? I wish I had been throwing the stupid woman herself!"

Several highly idiomatic—and no doubt highly insulting—French phrases followed.

Peter North came into the office. He didn't look pleased. Looking unhappy had become a rather permanent condition for Peter North. "Doctors Leblanc, Chambers," he said. "I pass on sincere congratulations from our general manager, Louis Hakim."

Mark and Candi stared at him without replying.

North waited in case they hadn't heard. Reading their disgusted expressions, he went on. "He has asked me to avail ourselves of your further expertise. Dr. Leblanc, we wish you to reconstruct your microwave energising device, only this time, on a smaller platform. There are some klystrons available that were no doubt beyond your initial budget but are most definitely within ours."

"I beg your pardon?" Candi looked at him with the expression of a feral cat discovering it had just eaten a clockwork mouse by mistake.

North continued. "And Dr. Chambers, we would like you to provide us with a portable form of the accelerator developed from the modified magnetic double layer device. The schedule is tight, but you can have any assistance in terms of staff or resources that you require. Furthermore—"

Mark's mobile phone rang. "Excuse me," he said to North before bringing the phone to his ear. "Hello, this is Mark Chambers here."

"'Wrong number. Very, very sorry." Click.

"Who was that?" North said impolitely. "Not some reporter who got your number, is it?"

"No, just a wrong number. You were saying?"

"We wish to duplicate our success on this site first. A new quantum bridge building is going to be built on the other side of the car park. We want to set up another plant. It will be much easier because we now know what has to be done, and there will be a smooth transition from the breach initiation phase to the power source one. I take it you have no objection? Your salaries, in case you hadn't noticed, have tripled from your last pay period. I think you will also be paid a sizeable bonus direct from the GM."

The gavel had fallen. Both had expected it to come, but not so soon.

"You realise what you are asking?" Candi's voice was the quiet before the storm. "One breach is bad enough, and now you want to make more! Insanity!"

The unhappy expression on North's face turned into a not-so-friendly unhappy expression. "I hope you weren't so naïve as to think that we would stop at one plant when it is working so well. There will be other opportunities for such research. I believe there is already intense interest from physicists around the world already. We have had hundreds of enquiries, and I am sure Dekker is stirring up the pot over there, although he is difficult to pin down. When we have constructed a dozen or so power plants, we will licence the technology to the scientific community. They can study it to their hearts' content then."

A thought suddenly struck him. "You're not in communication with Dekker, are you?"

"We have no idea where he is," snapped Candi. "You're monitoring all our correspondence, and you go through our laptops when we are in bed having the sleep. Ask your spies. Have we contacted Daniel?"

"Those are serious accusations, Dr. Leblanc," North said. "I suppose you have evidence that we interfere with your personal computers?"

"We use a little piece of software produced by Dr. Leblanc," Mark said. "Your IT goons haven't picked up on it yet. As the lady asked, have we contacted Dr. Van Dekker?"

North was somewhat taken aback by Mark's reply. He was not privy to any espionage taking place in the building. Perhaps Slater was organising it. He would ask. Softening his tone a little, he replied, "I believe not. Let me tell you, it would be unwise to do so while the project is so commercially sensitive."

Trying not to explode into a blind rage, Mark felt for the arms of his office chair and gripped them hard. Even so, there was an edge to his voice when he said, "The company must be stark-raving mad. You're exploiting something you do not understand, something that has the capacity to do untold damage. You want to multiply the risk? Why not initiate research into shutting it down? If you can close a breach, then you can open another one, but in the name of God, don't open another you can't close!"

North looked at him intently. He read the expression in Mark's face better than its owner would have wished. Even worse, was the fact that he agreed with him completely.

Jenner was insane and the company was insane, but it was also insanity to oppose them. Ever the self-serving pragmatist, North was not about to sacrifice his career. Someone would find a way to shut the monster down. In the meantime, the profits would be enormous.

Scowling deliberately, North played the company tune. "That's all you want to do, isn't it? Shut it down? Look outside. Do you see any hint of danger? No. Has the temperature risen out of control? No. Has the breach suddenly erupted into some sort of holocaust? No. We have constant, stable energy output. There are few moving parts. On your recommendation, the pumping system has been given five-fold redundancy. If one fails, there are four more of them to ensure the vacuum. We have taken all precautions. I recall you were the one who created this thing in the first place. Before we came here, it was contained in a fragile glass tube, and now it's in the middle of two massive steel spheres. What arrangement strikes you as safer?"

Mark was silent.

North continued. "I like you, both of you. I can appreciate your concern. The breach scares me, too, if you really want to know, but we need courage to press on. You are a believer in God, aren't you, Mark? As I said before, why couldn't this be God's provision for an energy-hungry world? Please take my word for it: any talk of shutting down this power plant after the millions our company has invested in it would not be taken lightly. Do yourself a favour. There is glory and gold just round the corner for both of you. Have the sense to move toward it."

Simmering dangerously close to open rage, Candi picked up her empty coffee cup and hurled it into the metal waste paper basket on the other side of the room. North jumped visibly. "So now you drag God on to your side. How pathetic! Last refuge of a desperate argument! What else?"

"As it happens, Dr. Leblanc, I believe in God."

With that, he turned and went out of the room—leaving two angry people behind him. Mark, furious at North's monumental hypocrisy, and Candi just furious.

"Do you need to go for coffee?" Candi turned to Mark. There was meaning in her face.

"I can step out for a while, I guess."

"You won't mind if I take my laptop?" she asked. "I have to get started on my new project."

"Not at all."

Twenty minutes later in the Back Alley, they decrypted a picture of Trafalgar Square. The message read:

> *Urgent request from think tank*
> *Analyse all early data*
> *Maybe not neutrons*
> *Check energies. Report ASAP*
> *D*

They took turns typing on the keyboard while they debated whether or not the new dress Annette was wearing suited her.

Eyeing it, Mark realised there was a great deal of the woman he had never seen. "It's easy on the eyes."

Candi snorted. "That's all you men ever think about. Boobs."

Leaning over her laptop, she typed: *"Maybe not neutrons?? I thought you were sure."*

Mark grinned at Candi's mock indignation. "It shows off her best features. I think the customers appreciate a little life and colour around here … Not that they don't have it when you come in."

He turned toward Candi while his fingers typed the keys. *"Only neutral particles activate neutron detector. It is a fair assumption–neutrons."*

With half an eye on the screen, Candi replied, "If she spills the coffee, it will really hurt. Look at the guy she's serving. Watch his eyes, see?"

She typed, *"So we analyse all the old data for anything unusual. Want me to help?"*

"I think Annette is enjoying the unspoken compliment," Mark said. "She's smiling. You have to admit, she is."

Mark typed as he spoke. *"Yes. Please buy me some time to work with the data."*

"Some girls are just out for cheap thrills. No class." Candi said, pulling her top down a little so as not to be outdone by the competition.

"I think I'll offer to take her shopping. Something that doesn't look as if it came out of some model's used clothing bin."

She typed, *"I'm not a clever physicist like you."*

"This is a huge project," said Mark out loud. "I can see you're going to need lots of assistance, lots of very expensive gear. Are you going to order any lunch?"

He typed the last line on the screen. *"Make them pay through the nose."*

"I'll do that," she said.

Returning to the power plant, Mark went into the generator building and sought out Tony Slater. Hardly anyone came to the "power source building" as they called it.

In truth, the breach freaked them out more than a little. It was far better to be in the familiar surroundings of a steam-driven power station. There, they never had to think about where the superheated water came from. It arrived in that pipe, the one underneath that gantry from that building over there, where something was going on that they were not required to understand. Such is human nature. See what you want to see when you want to see it.

Peter North was also in the office.

Mark framed his request carefully. "In order to proceed with the construction of more accelerators, I would like access to all the data we have on the original experiment. I believe you have this in your office?"

"Why do you need it?" Slater scowled critically at Mark. "You have the original in the other building. Why don't you go take a ruler and measure it?"

"If you'd been there when the breach was made, you'd know the conditions which created it were unique," Mark explained. "In order to recreate those conditions in a different place, I will need to know a great deal more than I do at present about the condition of the accelerator at that time. We still do not know exactly what caused the breach. Every part of the apparatus may have played a part, including the ion traps. If I do not have this data, I cannot be asked to guarantee further success."

Slater hesitated. He trusted Mark as much as he would trust a cat with his pet hamster. Slater hated cats.

It was Peter North who answered, "You may have access to all the data you wish. I'm pleased to see you're cooperating. I have just had an email from your partner Dr. Leblanc. It seems she has launched into planning and construction with a vengeance. That must have been an excellent lunch you had."

"Thank you, Mr. North," Mark said. "Could you ask Mr. Slater if he could bring the files over, please? In my office in half an hour."

"I will do that."

Half an hour later, the files arrived. Slater dumped the folders and flash cards on his desk in silent fury.

Mark smiled provokingly at him. "Thank you. So kind."

Slater swore and stormed out—slamming the door. This time, the glass did not fall out.

# CHAPTER 24

Over the next two months, the "Quantum Bridge Building" became a hive of activity.

Mark watched Candi manage the small army of engineers placed at her disposal with a mixture of admiration and displeasure. She was a force to be reckoned with—clever, efficient, and ruthlessly demanding. At the same time, it annoyed him that she could be so dedicated to constructing a device that had aided and abetted the initial catastrophe with such enthusiastic zeal. He had often stayed late into the evening, but hitherto Candi rarely had. Now she sometimes remained even when he staggered off home exhausted. He suspected on several occasions that she had slept there as well.

There was no doubt that the project was costing the earth, but why did she have to be so damn eager to do it so quickly? Wasn't she supposed to maximise his time to find a way to shut the whole thing down? The team of construction engineers and machinists had grown to large proportions by the end of the second week, all busy as little beavers in subservience to Candi's commands.

Perhaps that's what it was, Mark thought to himself. She just liked to order people around.

That was unfortunately quite true, but it wasn't the driving force that had plunged Candi into such a spate of frenetic activity. In part, it was the need to atone for destroying her wonderful original creation, but mostly, it was because burying herself in a project she completely under-stood prevented her mind from straying into the unpleasant realities of life, which she didn't understand at all.

While so engaged, she could once again live for the moment and pretend the breach was someone else's problem. There were days when, exhausted beyond measure, she even forgot it was there, and the uncon-scious relief gave her the strength to pursue her goal with renewed vigour and determination.

Roger, who had never encountered a woman who would dare to rank anything else on a par with his superlative ability in the bedroom, was both amazed, angry, and jealous as all hell. He hated anything that deprived him of the pleasure he so richly deserved.

Mark, on the other hand, unable and unwilling to organise his own escape from reality, spent his time in a much less productive manner. He ordered another set of new field magnets and duplicated the double layer apparatus, with a few modifications. Most of his time was spent pouring over data.

He and Candi hardly spoke. She often passed his office on some whirlwind mission and wondered why his head was so often cradled in his hands.

She-who-was-to-be-obeyed drove home that evening at a much earlier hour than she had done for the past weeks. Her project was complete, and she was proud of it. The new microwave energiser was much smaller than the previous one—in fact, it fit onto two very large hydraulic trolleys. And yet, tt output more power. It had cost about ten times more than the previous one did. That also added to Candi's enjoyment. The thought of all the vast amounts of GPC's money she had spent was incredibly satisfying.

She had managed, with almost complete success, not to think about the ends to which her efforts would be employed, consoling herself in the moments when she did by reminding herself she really had no alternative. While she was busy, Mark had more time to come up with a solution to the problem.

The fact that her project had been completed in half the allotted timeframe seemed to conflict somewhat with this noble goal. She excused herself by saying that nobody would expect her to be anything other than naturally efficient. All good things must come to an end, of course, but she was still saturated with the euphoria of success and looking forward to celebrating tonight with a bottle of excellent champagne and a long stay in heaven.

Her anticipation of a long stay in heaven was seriously shaken by the discovery of a strange car parked in front of her garage. Candi parked beside it and let herself quietly in through the front door.

Sounds of laughter were coming from the kitchen. She tiptoed down the hall. Roger and some female stranger were concocting a meal. Candi reflected that in all the time she had known him, Roger had never so much as made her a sandwich.

"Warming up a new dish in the kitchen are we, Roger?" Candi asked.

The object of this verbal fireball turned round so suddenly that he dropped the saucepan he was holding on the floor. The woman with him gave a little yelp.

"Oh, hi, Babe," Roger said, smiling. "Didn't hear you come in and you fair startled me. Good thing I didn't drop this on my foot. You're off early tonight. Oh, by the way, this is Sally. She's a chef at the club. She took pity on me eating by myself night after night and said she'd come and cook me something special. Sally, meet Candi."

Sally placed the frying pan she was holding carefully on the bench and turned round, looking angelically innocent. "Hi, Candi. If I'd known you were coming, I would have made a lot more food. There's really only enough for Roger and me. He's such a big boy, isn't he?"

"You should wear an apron over that cocktail dress," Candi said before turning to Roger. "Don't you think?"

"Err, I hadn't noticed," he said with a stammer. "I suppose so ... I'll get her one."

"You don't know where they are." Candi went over to a drawer and extracted an apron. "Excuse, please."

She advanced on Sally and threw the apron over her head in much the same manner as a hangman would throw the noose over his victim. "Can't have you damaged, can we?"

She dragged the cords together and tied them with several knots behind Sally's back. "Comfortable, yes?"

"You know I'm not." Sally said, trying hard to breathe.

Candi scooped up a generous portion of the contents of the frying pan and deposited it on one of the plates. Grabbing that and a spoon in one hand, and a bottle of wine and a glass in the other, she went toward the door. "I'm having dinner in the bedroom with the television. You can enjoy your dessert in the kitchen. The table is really uncomfortable. I suggest you do it on the floor."

"That's completely offside and you know it!" Roger snapped angrily. "You've no right to speak to Sally that way! She only came over because you seem to have better things to do than come home for dinner."

"But of course she did," Candi replied. "I hope you have enough. I'm sure Sally can make a sandwich for herself if you eat it all because you're such a great big boy." With that, she strode out of the room.

Sally left shortly afterward, after Roger had taken a pair of scissors and cut her apron strings. He came to bed very much later.

Needless to say, there was no excursion to heaven that night.

Totally frustrated by another day of getting nowhere, Mark decided that it was time he spent the evening with Andrew again.

Since they had first met, he had been a regular visitor to the comfortable Tahmoor home, spending most of each Saturday in the garden until it began to look very pleasant indeed. If Andrew was blessed by this careful attention, Mark was blessed even more. Working in the garden, he could forget for a short while about the awful business of the breach hanging over his head. Without that small island of relief, he would have been incapable of a solution, even if it was staring him in the face.

It was dark by the time he walked up the now-familiar path to the back door. Andrew heard him knock and summoned him inside for a glass of wine.

"There's a curry in the slow cooker and some rice on the stove," Andrew said. "If you want to fry some pappadams, I'd appreciate it."

"No problem. I'll go wash up."

An hour later, Mark put down his spoon, crunched his way through the last pappadam, and lay back in his chair. It had been an excellent curry. "When did you learn to cook curries like that?"

"Suzie and I went to a curry course in Camden. Very good it was. Tell me, Mark, how's the project going?"

Mark sighed and picked up his glass of Riesling. "The company is insane. They want to open more breaches they can't close. Sheer bloody madness. North—you remember, their CEO—he thinks it's madness, too, but he's toeing the company line like a good little sycophantic pragmatist. Makes me sick."

"That would be Peter North, head of GPC's engineering division," Andrew said.

"Err, yes," Mark replied. "I didn't think I'd told you the name of the company. Mind must be deteriorating."

"Not at all. You've got a lot to think about," Andrew said. "Tell me, how is Dr. Daniel Van Dekker, the man originally working with you before he was sent overseas?"

"I … suppose he's okay. I've no idea where he is. Supposed to be in Holland working at Utrecht or something."

"Or something. I'm surprised he hasn't been in touch, considering he initiated this whole brouhaha."

Mark sighed. "I'm sure Daniel is working on a solution with the best physicists in the world. Perhaps he doesn't want to be found too easily."

"That I can understand. If I was in his shoes, I wouldn't want to be found too easily, either."

"You really believe GPC would resort to violence?" Mark asked.

"Oh, you may be certain of that," Andrew said. "If you were ever to … ah … get in touch with Dr. Dekker, I wouldn't hesitate to warn him to take great care indeed. I've been doing a little research, shall we say. Your power company has a certain well-guarded reputation for violence. Not to alarm you overly, just take care, will you?"

"We've been taking care. We think we're being shadowed already."

"Tell me."

Mark told him. It was a relief to share his fears with somebody who took them seriously, even if that somebody couldn't do anything to help.

He attributed Andrew's interest purely to their friendship, although he certainly had the knack of asking the right questions.

Ever since that morning on the veranda, he had wondered exactly what Andrew had done for a living for the last ten years of his working life. He assumed he had become a forensic expert of sorts, something vaguely related to his previous occupation as a chemical engineer.

An hour or two more passed, the conversation shifted to lighter matters, and eventually Andrew checked the time on the clock and yawned.

Mark stood up as if to go.

"You should stay the night, Mark, and drive back to the plant from here."

"I'd rather not. Last time ..."

"It's all right, Mark," Andrew said. "I've cleared the room of everything belonging to Anna. Packed up the clothes, and gave them away. Put the picture back in the album where it belonged. I've laid her ghost to rest. I've begun to move on, something I couldn't have done while all her stuff was there. Another blessing from God via Mark Chambers. Even changed the doona to one with ships all over it, not that pink fluffy thing you slept under before. It's your room now—a room for the living, not the dead. Even stuck a picture of Albert Einstein on the wall."

"You didn't," Mark replied.

"Come and see for yourself." Andrew was about to wheel down the corridor, but Mark had gripped him by the arm, with a strange expression on his face.

"Andrew, I ..."

"Don't go mushy on me. It's your room. Okay? I expect you to shove some stuff of yours in the wardrobe so it's here when you're down for the weekend and treat it like your home. I don't want her ghost to return."

Mark tried hard not to express the tide of emotion flooding over him. Even so, his voice was not completely steady when he released his grip on Andrew's arm. "Thanks. It's an honour. I might even come here to work instead of going back to Camden. Give it a week or so and you won't be able to get in the door for all the mess I'll generate."

"Look forward to it. Mess is good. Creative. Been praying you'd find a solution, you know. Any progress?"

Mark ran his hands over his face. "None, but I've decided to run over some early data. Might show us a thing or two."

"I'll pray it will. Topic for another evening. Bed. See you in the morning, Mark."

"'Night, Andrew." Mark went into his room, undressed, and threw himself down between the sheets. He dragged the new doona over him.

In less than five minutes, he was asleep without one thought of Anna.

# CHAPTER 25

The Aubergine Restaurant on Grande Rue at Thonon les Bains on the shore of Lake Geneva was exclusive, expensive, and extremely full of well-heeled patrons enjoying some of the finest cuisine available in all Switzerland.

Louis Hakim dabbed his lips recently moist with duck breast in an exquisite orange and truffle sauce, replaced his napkin on his lap, and turned his attention to the man sitting opposite of him at their table for two. "You say he was actually in Geneva, George? When was this?"

"Two days ago," Jenner replied. There was a meeting between him and Klaus Obermayer, one of the directors of CERN, and some other top physicists. We discovered the location a little late. For some reason, there were a lot of Swiss Strategic Intelligence people around, which is probably routine, so we couldn't interfere. The Large Hadron Collider is pretty high security, and people who work there are protected."

Hakim frowned. "Stern must be slipping. Perhaps he has begun to adopt a pre-retirement stance. Unfortunate for him."

Jenner murmured his dissent. "I don't believe he has. Dekker is incredibly difficult to locate. I told you, it appears that the Kilraen Group is protecting him. Why such a multinational company should take the trouble is not clear to me."

"Competition, perhaps," Hakim said. "I'm coming to the conclusion we are better off without the services of the good Daniel Van Dekker. What think you, George?"

"You may be right," Jenner said. "No doubt these clever physicists are actively thinking of ways to shut down our quantum bridge. Premature, I would say, and until we've got a better idea of how to market the new technology, not in the consortium's best interests."

Hakim nodded agreement. "So I think we'll send Emile to take care of him. An accident, very sad. Now I learn from Peter North that there is possible trouble brewing in Australia. Chambers is apparently as dedicated to shutting down our quantum energy device as Dekker is, even though we've spent millions using it to provide free energy to the world. I trust they're not working together. Quite an unacceptable attitude for an employee, wouldn't you say, George?"

Jenner put down his wine glass. "I would. Ericsson and Hodges are ready to fly to Sydney at a moment's notice. Leblanc has finished her part of the project, and Chambers will complete his soon. I don't believe they're working with Dekker. If we were to discover some sort of conspiracy ..."

"Quite so." A slow smile caressed Hakim's face. "Ericsson should take care of Leblanc. He finds young women a pleasure to work with. Hodges can take care of Chambers, when you give the word, George. In the meantime, I would like to read the sad news of Dekker's departure. Can you organise it with Stern?"

"Not a problem. This is a good wine, Louis. Complements the meal perfectly."

"Loyalty has its rewards, George. Keep me informed, won't you? Shall we order dessert?"

Not five kilometres away from Thonon les Bains, Daniel Van Dekker had dined alone while waiting for the taxi that would take him to the airport. Soon he would be back to the Isle of Skye where Jasmin was anxiously waiting for him.

Both were oblivious to the fate so recently decreed to be their lot.

# CHAPTER 26

Roger had gone when Candi woke up the following morning. She showered, dressed quickly, and left the house in a bad mood that was about to get worse.

"I need a coffee," she said aloud to herself, slamming down the accelerator and passing half a dozen commuters on their way to work at a more sedate pace. Parking in front of the Back Alley café, she slammed the car door and strode inside.

A little deterred by the look on her face, Annette came over. "Hi Candi. How are things this morning?"

"I'll be better after a coffee. Have you got a copy of the *Sydney Morning Herald*? I feel like something to read to take my mind off some things."

"Sure. Won't be a second." Annette placed the newspaper and a flat white on the table in front of her.

Candi took a sip of her coffee and then flipped open the paper. She stopped drinking, coffee cup poised in mid-air, and stared at the headlines. The two other patrons in the shop were treated to some highly idiomatic French phrases spoken very loudly. Annette shrank back behind the counter. Candi got up and strode out of the café without finishing her coffee.

Annette stayed behind the counter. The bill could wait until next time when things were calmer.

The scrunch of tyres in the car park and the slamming of a car door caused Trevor in the gatehouse to look up from his newspaper. He saw Candi sprinting toward the power source building. Someone, it appeared, was going to get blasted this morning. He was glad it wasn't him.

Candi didn't go into her office. She decided instead to visit Mark rather than spending the morning in her own company. She threw open the door to find the gentleman at his desk, his head cradled in his hands.

Candi knew what he was doing— he was praying—and this morning, in keeping with everything else, it really annoyed her. "What are you doing?"

"I'm praying, you know that."

"You should be trying to solve our problem while your mind is still fresh, scribbling big equations on your white board rather than mumbling mantras to the ceiling. What do you expect God to do about it anyway?"

"Show me how I can close the breach, of course."

"Perhaps he doesn't know how," she replied sarcastically.

"Do you really think the God who made the universe would have a problem with this trivial matter?" Mark said wearily.

"But he's not telling you is he? Is he? You still don't know, do you? Perhaps he doesn't want you to close it. Why doesn't he just do it himself anyway, if he's all that powerful and wonderful. Perhaps he's already answered and the breach has gone—poof! You don't believe that, do you?"

Mark wiped his hand across his eyes and looked up at Candi. The expression on her face should have told him to tread with caution. She was angry, and there was something else in her face he couldn't read.

Walking blindly in where angels fear to tread, he continued. "God uses people to carry out his purposes, Candi. I know—"

"Is that because he isn't powerful enough to do the job himself?"

"No! God is totally powerful, totally in control. How could he be God if he wasn't?"

Candi's expression hardened, and her voice became dangerously quiet. "So, you say this God of yours is always in charge, nothing happens that he doesn't want to happen. Is this what you're telling me?"

"Yes."

Candi reached over to the chair where she had thrown the paper, snatched it up, and flung it on the desk in front of Mark's face.

The headline read "STUDENT RUNS AMOK WITH RIFLE—SEVENTEEN DEAD."

Candi went on, her voice gradually becoming louder and louder. "Some young punk takes his father's gun, goes to school, and kills seventeen kids because his girlfriend left him." She stabbed her finger on a picture further down the page. "This is her. He shot her in the stomach. And presiding over all this carnage is your wonderful, great, in-charge God! Les pauvres innocents! They are ripped apart with bullets! Their screams are his morning music. Perhaps he wants to hear more screaming? How can you pray to a sadistic monster like that? You have no answer, do you?"

There were tears in Candi's eyes. She snatched the paper from under Mark's horrified gaze and threw it into the rubbish bin. "Now why don't you get back to work so there won't be more screaming music for your God to enjoy?"

"Candi, God didn't kill those children, some angry, young kid did," Mark said quietly. "We are still responsible for the things we do—God hasn't taken that away from us. He doesn't like the slaughter of innocent lives any more than you do."

"So, let me get this straight. God is in charge of everything, but at the same time we are responsible for what we do?"

"That's it."

Candi snorted. "This is the complete rubbish, yes? You make the contradiction. How can a clever man like you believe such nonsense? Why do you turn off your brain?"

"I can't explain how it works all the time, Candi, but God has given us a really good example of how it did."

"What?" she snapped. "An example of how black equals white? Easy. Turn off the light, and you can't see the difference. Live in the dark. Is that it?"

"Suppose I put some hypnotic drug into your coffee that made you do anything I wanted—"

"I'd die of boredom!"

"Perhaps, but even though you did everything to please me, you wouldn't be in love with me, would you? In order to love me you would also have to be able to hate me. You would have to have the freedom to choose to love, or love ceases to have any meaning."

"I'm still dying of boredom."

"Well, when God made us creatures who could love him, he had to give us the freedom to choose not to love him— and that is just what we did," Mark explained. "The mother and father of the human race chose to turn away from God and do their own thing, and we continue to follow in their footsteps. Our loving relationship towards God was broken, and we became guilty of cosmic treason. But right then and there, God put into place a plan that would bring us back to him."

"Well, so he should. It was his fault."

"No, Candi! There was nothing wrong with the way we were made. God never forced us to disobey him. You can't disobey God without consequences. God is completely fair. He can't pretend we haven't made ourselves his enemies and sweep our rebellion under the carpet."

"Much better if he did," she said. "I've had enough hellfire and damnation preached at me when I was a kid to last me a lifetime."

"Do you really want God to ignore our behaviour?" he asked. "What about the guy who shot all those people? You really want God to pat him on the head and say 'forget it, boys will be boys?'"

"If I had my way, I'd shoot him in the stomach with his own gun and make him suffer the agony he gave others. Then a bullet to the head."

"Exactly. God can't ignore it when people break his laws. You wouldn't want him to. No one will get away with it. One day, the books will be completely balanced. No one will be able to accuse God of injustice. Trouble is, none of us have even lived up to our own moral code, let alone up to God's. We are doomed under God's justice. The only way we can be rescued is if someone steps in and takes the rap that we deserve."

"I don't see anyone doing that for me!"

"But that's just it, Candi! God has done exactly that. Right from that first unloving act of rebellion, God promised to send his one and only Son to die on our behalf. By accepting what Jesus did we could be forgiven and restored to our proper relationship with God. The plan worked out exactly as God said it would, because he is completely in charge. When his own people were nailing Jesus to the cross they were doing their own thing—and they bore the consequences—but all the time they were doing what God had planned thousands of years before."

"How completely barbaric!"

"Is it barbaric to give your life for someone else, Candi?" he asked. "That's love—real, costly love. The Bible says that God loved the world so much—"

"So, God loves the world so much, does he?"

"Yes, he does."

"Does he want this world he loves to end right now?"

"I don't believe so," Mark declared. "No. He doesn't."

"Would you be prepared to wager your faith on that?" Candi's voice was dangerously soft again.

"I don't know what you're getting at."

Candi reached over and picked up a spanner from the toolkit that Mark kept in his room. "Then I fix your problem. I go out there and turn the feed regulator full on. The breach will melt the cauldron and then start eating the world. God looks down from heaven and says 'Oops! That naughty Candice Leblanc is going to end the world and kill all those nice people! I must stop it' and he snuffs out the breach—poof! Problem solved. If he doesn't, then he's going to have a lot more scream-ing music to listen to. Perhaps he just let Candi scream because she has been such a bad girl by forcing him to save his own world."

Mark stared at her, incredulous. He realised that his mouth was open and made a deliberate effort to shut it. He could see the spanner trem-bling in Candi's hand and the fire of anger in her eyes.

"Not so sure of your faith now, are you?" she screamed. "Okay in theory, no good in practice, is it? I dare you, tell me to go ahead!"

It was a long time before Mark replied. At last, he put his head back in his hands and spoke quietly through them. "Go ahead, Candi. Open the regulator. Let the breach out. Try to force God's hand—go on, you're a powerful, clever woman. You've got it all worked out. Just remember God holds you accountable for whatever you do. Go on, what are you waiting for? I'm ready to die."

Her whole body simmering with fury, Candi stood there. She had a good mind to do it, to stomp her way over there and open the regulator and smash it so it couldn't be shut. If people died, it would be God's fault, not hers.

Then she remembered the headline. A young man sacrificed seventeen innocent people because he was angry. And now an angry Candice Leblanc was preparing to sacrifice the world. If he was a monster, what did that make her? The enormity of her intention hit her squarely in the face and left her shaking all over. Was she going mad? It was Mark's fault—all this rubbish talk about religion.

She flung the spanner away from her as if it were a loathsome thing. It ricocheted off Mark's desk and embedded itself in the plaster wall.

"Damn you to hell!" she screamed at him, and ran out of the room.

An hour later, she was back. "I'm sorry," she mumbled. "But you provoke Candi too much."

Mark didn't even look up at her. He tried to keep his feelings out of his voice. "These spectra you took when we first discovered the breach. They're all out of focus. Was there a problem with the slit control?"

"The focus was perfect. Change your glasses." Candi snapped at him and almost ran out of the room.

The morning changed into afternoon, and the afternoon deepened into evening. The altercation with Candi had left him feeling upset and tired. Outside his office, all that could be heard was the deep throb of the coolant pumps.

Their time in heaven that night was not going the way Roger had planned it, which was more or less to get naked and get going. Candi had seemed distracted, and her touch, normally so successful in arousing maximum pleasure in her partner, seemed careless and insensitive, as though her head was in a different place than her heart.

In the end, Roger, unused and unwilling to put up with anything less than total dedication to his physical pleasure, rolled himself to the edge of the bed and sat up with his back to her. "Babe, I can tell when you're not in the bubble. You haven't done it with someone else today, have you? The geek?"

"But yes, of course," she said. "That's what I do all day. Come and have the sex with Candi. I put the ticket machine on the door, with the sign 'please take the number.' Sorry to keep you waiting. Practice makes perfect."

"Sorry, Babe. Shouldn't have said that. What's wrong?"

"What's wrong? I'm worried about things at work."

"Listen, Babe, if it will help you to relax you can tell me what's worrying you. Would you like me to rub your back while you talk?"

Candi turned face down on the bed and cradled her head in her folded arms. "Oui, that would be nice … that's not my back, Roger."

"Sorry, Babe, you were saying?"

"You remember the three of us, Daniel, Mark, and me?" she asked. "Well, we did some experiments with some very high energies, and we created this thing everyone is calling a quantum bridge."

"Yeah, like it said in the paper. I read that, remember, when you brought home the Telegraph one evening."

"What the article didn't mention was that the breach is getting bigger, and we can't shut it down. If it keeps going like this, it'll break loose and destroy everything. That's what—"

"You saying that you've made something you can't control, and it's threatening to destroy the Earth, Babe?"

"Yes, Roger. I'm afraid it's—"

As an answer Roger threw himself down on the bed, roaring with laughter. He rolled over and over until Candi, finding her position of calm relaxation bouncing like a wave on the ocean, stood up and wrapped a sheet around her.

"Just what's so funny?" she asked with annoyance.

"It's the Sorcerer's Apprentice all over again! Can't you see?"

"No," she snapped. "Can you?"

"Babe, nothing happens that way," Roger laughed. "Nature always protects herself, even if we mess stuff up. Nothing gets out of control. It's complete bullshit. Surely you haven't fallen for that end-of-the-word rubbish! You sound just like the geek. Don't let him get to you. It's all hype and Arma-gettin stuff, Babe! Forget it! Come back to bed!"

Nature always protects herself. It was a new thought to Candi, and for a second she conceded that Roger, among all the rest of the nonsense, might just have made a point.

Her mind was suddenly flooded with a mystical sense of peace and assurance, based entirely upon nothing at all. Nature would redress the balance, of course, she always did and always had. Why, the Earth had been there for billions of years, and life had weathered every storm and every disaster. How foolish she had been.

"Are you saying if we lose control of the breach, then nature will restore the balance and choke it off?"

"Ying and yang and all that stuff," Roger said. "Come on, get that sheet off."

The strange, irrational feeling of comfort began to grow. It would be all right. It would always be all right.

She slowly loosened the sheet around her, watching Roger's eyes light up with satisfaction. Her covering removed, she lay herself down and stretched up her arms around his neck. "Take me to heaven. I'm ready."

She closed her eyes as Roger's lips closed over hers and felt her body relax. She was back in the bubble.

The loud, discordant strains of the Marseillaise synthesised in four voices made them both jump. The bubble burst. Roger swore, and Candi picked up her mobile phone.

Mark re-read the figures in front of him—the estimates of the neutron energies.

They must be wrong, he thought. Neutron energies could not be that high. He picked up one of the spectra and studied the out-of-focus lines.

Then he noticed something.

He peered closer. And closer.

He went over to a cupboard and took out a small low-power microscope. With the aid of the instrument, he examined the spectrum again. Each line was split into two: one shifted toward the red end of the spectrum, and one toward the blue.

For the next hour, he measured and calculated until he had examined a good number of the lines. The pattern was always exactly the same. Finally, he removed his glasses and leaned back in the chair.

"The ions are rotating," he said to no one. "They're not just travelling down the tube, they're spiralling down it. But there's no magnetic field. Why are they spiralling?"

Suddenly another thought struck him. He raised the palm of his hand and pressed his forehead. "I'm so stupid!" He replaced his glasses and rummaged through some other papers. "Lord, why didn't I see this before?" He did more rummaging and more calculations. He picked up the pictures they had taken of the breach on that first day and examined them in a new light.

He picked up the phone and called Candi.

After several rings, she answered. She sounded slightly breathless and very annoyed. "What? Ring me tomorrow, Mark."

"Candi, why doesn't the breach suck matter off the other end of the tube?"

"Pardon? What nonsense is this?"

"It's much closer to one end, but it sucks matter off the other end. Why doesn't it take matter off the closer end?"

"It just likes being difficult," she said. "Its lips are pointing the wrong way. It needs another straw, and it's only got one. I don't know. You're the physicist. Ask Daniel in the morning."

"You're almost right, though. It is like a straw in a way. We've always thought of the breach as a point. It's not. It's a tear."

"A what? Not now, Roger." She returned to Mark. "Pardon? A tear? What do you mean?"

"The ions are not just falling into the breach. They're spiralling along a tear, rotating with enormous speed. That's what's producing the energy. They're spiralling just like they were when the new-field magnets were there."

"You are saying we've torn the fabric of space and time, and not just punctured a hole in it?"

"I am not sure even about the hole," he said. "I think we may have discovered a new boson, a carrier type particle or a shadow carrier type particle that changes the nature of mass. We're not converting all the mass we throw into the breach into energy. The energy produced is not large enough. I think mass is mostly being changed into something else. The theory of super symmetry suggests that every particle we observe has a massive super-symmetric shadow particle. Perhaps we've discovered—or created—a boson like the Higgs boson, but it doesn't give mass to particles that spiral through it, it does something else. Whatever it is we've made, it's fixed in space like a field, and when mass enters this field, it gets converted … to another form of matter, perhaps super-symmetric matter."

"In other words, I think everything we've thrown at the breach is still present at the end of it, but in a different form. I think we are turning mass into some sort of dark matter. That's why we can't see it or detect it. The act of doing this creates a lot of energy. Very little, if any, mass is being lost. It's the dark matter that's drawing the matter we can see into itself, via this new boson. The more we throw into it, the more it will attract matter. In order to close the breach we have to change the particle we have created into something else, or remove it, and pray the dark matter we've already created will somehow be rendered inaccessible. I know this is a lot to grasp but what do you think?"

It was some time before Mark realised that he had been talking to himself. Candi had hung up the phone. He took his laptop and walked slowly to the car—rather disappointed with her.

That night he didn't sleep. In the early hours of the morning he dozed off in a chair. He had prayed that somehow he might discover a way of closing the breach.

Before he went to sleep he thought he might have done it.

# CHAPTER 27

Before he went to work the next morning, Mark called in to the Back Alley Café. He wrote a very short letter to Sun Kyung and attached a coded picture of a raging surf breaking on the rocks at Jervis Bay. There was a lot of encoded material, and several other pictures he had tried appeared far too odd when he had encoded the data into them.

Dekker, he prayed, would tell him he was wrong, that the method he had proposed was flawed, or that there was some other way. He dreaded the consequences of being right.

He finished his coffee and headed off to work—a seriously tired man with a heavy burden.

What if they sought to implement his solution, and it was the wrong one? The world would not get another chance, and he would be responsible—responsible for the end of the world. It sounded so melodramatic, so ridiculous. It wasn't.

He parked his car and went into his office. He cleared up a good deal of the paper that littered the place by the simple expedient of stuffing it all into the wastepaper basket, and sat down to write a work order for the construction of the new field supply.

A short time later, Candi strode through his office door in no better a mood than the one he left her in the previous evening. The comforting sense of mystical balance in the universe had evaporated after a certain phone call.

Without introduction, she launched the assault. "What do you mean ringing me up last night? Am I not entitled to the privacy? You rang at a bad time. Roger and I have had a … a bad fight. Do you think you have the right to interfere in my life whenever you want to?"

Mark gazed up at her.

She was shocked to see his face in that condition, but not for one second did she show it.

He replied wearily, "My mistake. I should have realised there's nothing more important in all the world than your personal pleasure."

"It's my life! Keep out of it!"

Mark had had enough. Normally, he would have been able to deflect her wrath by a carefully chosen word. But he saw her eyes blazing, felt her anger directed so selfishly towards him, and replied with far less diplomacy than he was accustomed to using. "It's not your life, Candi. It belongs to the God who holds it in his hand."

Candi picked up a notebook resting on edge of his desk and threw it at him. No doubt it was meant to hit him fair and square in the face, but she was so angry her aim wasn't good and it bounced off his shoulder. "Shut your stupid face!" She turned on her heel. When she reached the door she turned back and shouted. "I'm sick of your religion! Learn that! Sick of it! Keep it to yourself and get out of my life!"

She slammed the door. The pane of glass fell out again.

Tired and upset, Mark turned back to the work order he was writing.

He was fond of Candi and their friendship had been growing, or so he had thought. Well, now he knew better. How could she be so appallingly indifferent to the peril hanging over the world? How could she be so incredibly self-centered? Well, it was better knowing the truth now than later. He could rely on her for nothing—not even for a friendly word. He felt as though one more burden had been laid on his shoulders, one that he could have done without.

The next face through the broken door was Slater's. "Girlfriend not getting enough?" He sneered. "Show you how it's done."

Laughing, he sauntered into Candi's office.

The muted buzz of conversation was interrupted by a loud slapping sound followed by a much louder screaming match of foul language, half of it in French.

Smiling to himself, Mark wondered how Slater had invaded Candi's sacred personal space. Thinking about that piece of mobile slime nursing a bruised cheek was the nicest thought he had had all morning.

Sitting in her office, Candi held one hand to shadow her face so that no one staring through the glass pane in the door could see the tears in her eyes. With the other, she touched her breast where Slater's hand had groped her.

She felt dirty and cheap.

Immediately she had thought of going to Mark—telling him, hearing his wise words and feeling his comforting arms around her.

That course of action was no longer possible. She had cut herself off from him and hurt him deeply. Her pride would not allow her to repair the damage.

She should ring Roger—after all, he was her lover. She lifted the phone and then slowly replaced it in its cradle. It was a pointless exercise. He was mad at her.

Besides, Roger fondled girls all the time. Why, he might have even sided with Slater, and if he didn't it would only be because some other male was trespassing on his claim.

Did Roger care about the way she felt? Only when it affected her performance in the bedroom. Only when it cast a shadow over his own enjoyment, his own pleasure. How selfish! How ... her body flinched.

That was exactly the way she thought.

She had fought with Mark concerning that very right. Her very own worldview had turned round and bitten her.

Paradox.

It was time to buy some new shoes. They did nothing to solve paradoxes, but they made her feel better almost at once. She deserved a day off, and she was going to have it.

Half an hour later, she was browsing around the shoe shops in McArthur Square. The anger had almost gone, although the nagging feelings of guilt and shame had inexplicably chosen to remain.

# CHAPTER 28

Louis Hakim, general manager of GPC, sat on his plush, leather armchair and leaned his elbows against his exquisite, custom-designed mahogany desk.

The lights reflecting in Lake Geneva twinkled though the window. The man sitting on the plain wooden chair opposite him was not somebody you would have expected to find in the opulence of Hakim's office. He was thin and wiry; a small scar marked his otherwise unpleasant looking face. His cold dark eyes seemed to be staring at you no matter if they were or not. He wore an Armani suit and patent leather black shoes. His tie was of the same colour. His hands were thin and moved constantly against his knees to stroke the black material covering them.

Not many people had ever seen Gustav Stern, and those who had wished they hadn't. The head of GPC security was the epitome of the invisible man. He travelled about under a dozen different names and was wanted on three continents in connection with violent crimes of various sorts.

"This you are sure of?" Hakim asked. "I owe these two people a great deal. It is because of them that I have lucrative contracts for quantum energy devices. I rely on their expertise to initiate more of these. I take it you spoke to Jenner before invading my office?"

Stern's voice was soft and chilling, devoid of any emotion. If a corpse could talk, it would have sounded exactly the same. "Of course.

Jenner has informed me the two scientists in Australia are working with Dekker. You have already authorised his removal. Jenner believes Eric and Hodges should be sent. I need your personal authorisation."

"I will authorise after I've spoken to Jenner. Please wait in reception." Hakim dismissed him with a nod. He touched a button on the intercom.

His personal assistant answered. "Sir?"

"Send Jenner in here now."

George Jenner appeared, went towards the mahogany desk, pulled over another leather armchair, and sat down.

"So, we are the victims of conspiracy, George?" Hakim asked. "I take it the evidence is unambiguous."

"Leblanc mentioned talking to Dekker in a conversation with Chambers. We monitor their phones."

"I find it hard to believe," Hakim said. "Leblanc has designed another energiser unit, North tells me, in less than half the time expected. Chambers has manufactured the other components. As far as I can see, we are ready to begin the second stage of the project—the opening of another quantum bridge, which would double our power output."

"Dekker is about to be eliminated. I would not like to remove essential elements from the equation while they are still useful to us. I have also seen correspondence from North that says there are real safety concerns. I take it you have read them?"

"I have," Jenner said. "North is being an old woman. Always overly cautious. I think you chose the wrong man, Louis. This is new technology. Any new technology has its scary moments. You need a man with a few more guts. I've got Slater there for just that purpose. I wager you haven't heard a whisper of danger from him."

"Indeed not," Hakim said, "but then, North has been the faithful and careful executor of many power station projects in the past. I have learned to rely on him. His advice can usually be trusted, yet you are saying his advice is misleading in this case?"

"I am, Louis. As I said, nuclear power is well understood. North is used to it, and he does his job well. This is something different, and he is required to be entrepreneurial, show a little initiative, step out of the square, and take calculated risks. North has never taken risks of any sort, and so he is overly cautious. There are no real safety issues with the plant in Australia. Pretty soon, someone will come up with a theory that will explain the phenomena, and we will be able to shut them down and start them up at will. This is the biggest single advance in the power industry since the advent of nuclear power. In some way I feel responsible for bringing the baby to birth, if you want to know."

"I understand your sentiments, George. There is a great deal at stake here, as you realise. I trust you are not being one-eyed. Tell me you're not being one-eyed."

"I've estimated all the risks most carefully, Louis," Jenner assured him.

"I'm relieved to hear it, because if I find you have not done so it will be very bad for your mental health—in fact, for your health in general. Now I want your carefully-considered opinion on this. Do we need Leblanc and Chambers? Can we run without them? What are your thoughts?"

Jenner said, "Leblanc and Chambers have finished construction of the equipment necessary to open up another quantum bridge. Their equipment has not been tested yet."

"Do you foresee any problems with the equipment?" Hakim asked.

"It worked once, so it can work again."

"Once again, I take it you have assessed the project and deem it of low risk?"

"Negligible risk," Jenner said with a carefree shrug of his shoulders. "I suggest we dispense with their services."

"That's your recommendation? Please think very carefully."

"That would be my recommendation, Louis."

"Very well," Hakim said. "Why don't you go and have dinner now? I've kept you far too long. There's an excellent restaurant down by the lake. Use the company card. Ask my secretary to make a booking for you—and your friend, if you want to take one."

"Thank you, Louis. I appreciate it."

"I trust I'm going to appreciate your advice, George. Good evening."

George Jenner stood up and left the office. The temperature seemed to have gone up a notch or two.

Hakim reached out and touched the complex device on his desk. "Send Stern back in here, would you, Frieda? And book a table for Jenner and his latest courtesan?"

# CHAPTER 29

Since their argument, neither Candi nor Mark had spoken at length to one another. Candi was content to be with Roger, with whom she had apparently made up. Knowing how she felt about his presence, Mark simply kept out of her way. Dekker had contacted him several times since and told him many people were working on his theory and solution, but that no one had come up with anything definite.

The following Monday morning, Candi received the "wrong number" call. She went into Mark's office. "I need to go the café. Are you coming?"

"I have some things to finish," he said. "Slater came in a minute ago and said everyone is having a special lunch over in the control room as guests of the company. Something about months of successful operation. I'm not going. I'll meet you at the café for lunch."

"I'll be gone by then." Candi impatiently flicked her hair over her shoulders.

Mark turned back to the papers on his desk. "Are you taking your laptop?"

"Yes," she said. "That's why I thought you might like to come."

"If you get any inspiration, let me know."

Candi tossed her head and turned towards the door. "Suit yourself."

Ten minutes later, she carried her laptop into the café.

Something was wrong.

For one thing, Annette was not behind the counter. The place seemed empty, which was strange for that time of the morning.

She headed toward the bathroom. A stranger she hadn't noticed before was standing near the doorway. When she passed him, he turned and gripped her around the mouth. A sharp pain sprang from the bottom of her spine. She tried to turn round, but the man pinned her against his body. The pain in her spine became much, much worse.

Quietly, he said, "We can do this easy or hard. I'm going out the front door, and you're going to walk by my side—all friendly like. We're heading for my car. You will get in the passenger side and then move to the driver's seat. If you cry out, I will sever your spinal cord. You'll go through life being unable to feel from the waist down. You wouldn't like that, would you? Move, bitch, or it's the wheelchair."

Candi was terrified. She turned around and headed obediently toward the door with the stranger's hand—and, hidden underneath it, the knife—in her back. The pain as she moved was almost more than she could bear.

No one else was in the café to call on for help. Together, they went out onto the pavement and down the street to a newish Toyota parked a little way along the road.

The stranger took the thin knife out of her back. Candi winced with pain. Blood spread over the top of her dress.

"Get in, don't try to be clever."

She climbed in and clambered over the passenger seat to get to the driver's side. Her hands felt clammy and her heart was beating furiously. She could feel blood dripping down her back where his knife had penetrated her.

The assassin closed the door and took a gun out of the glove box. He pointed it toward her with his left hand, and with his right, handed her the keys. "Drive. I will tell you where. If you do the slightest thing I don't like, I will put a bullet in your stomach and another in your pretty knees. You'll die in agony. Please don't give me the pleasure."

Her hands shaking with terror, she started the engine. The car pulled away from the kerb and headed down the street.

"Where are we going?"

"Toward Picton. A friendly farmer has a property there. He has been using his tractor to dig a hole to bury some of his cows. They're going to have company. You don't mind being buried with a few dead cows, do you? Your boyfriend will be with you. He'll arrive by car in a little while. In the boot, I think. Please keep driving. It'll be much nicer that way. There's no need to worry. We'll have lots of time to get to know one another better when we get there."

He touched her knee—running his fingers upwards along the inside of her leg. His touch made her flesh crawl.

Nothing else could have so summoned the dying embers of her courage and self-control. "Take your filthy hand off my leg."

He dug his fingers into her flesh until she cried out. Removing his hand from her thigh, he murmured in a horrible, leering voice, "That's the last time you're going to order me to take my hand off anything."

Candi feel as though she was going to vomit all over the car. "You're disgusting."

"I hope so. You're going to find out just how disgusting I can be when we get there."

Candi stared at the road.

Soon they would be completely out of town. The last set of traffic lights was ahead. From there, the road widened into two lanes for a while, and then narrowed down for the remainder of the journey to Picton. There would be no hope on that road.

Candi found herself silently praying to a God she didn't believe in. "Please," she said, "help me. Please don't let me be degraded by this animal."

Camden council has a wonderful program for learner drivers. They attach an identifying flag to the back window of their car and travel in convoys along routes specially designed to improve their driving skills. Such a convoy of ten of them was currently travelling the same route as the Toyota, carefully following one another in the left hand lane.

"Pass them, and no tricks." The assassin jabbed the gun into her side. Candi accelerated into the right hand lane.

She was almost in front of the leader when she spotted the parked car. It was now or never. She threw the wheel over to the left.

The car swerved into the left-hand lane in front of the first learner. Candi braked heavily and smashed the Toyota into the back of the parked car. The head learner crashed into her rear. Behind her, seven of the ten learner drivers tail-ended into each other. Both air bags deployed.

Expecting that to happen, Candi dived towards the door while releasing her seat belt with her left hand and opening the driver's door with her right.

Her passenger was struggling to free himself from the air bag. He fired. By then Candi was rolling on the ground outside the car. The bullet passed over her head. People were beginning to get out of cars as she sprinted down the line, keeping her head low.

Another shot rang out, and the windscreen of the car next to her shattered. People screamed.

The assassin could see her clearly. The contract was almost in the bag. He sighted the gun carefully.

Constable Lee Philips had been delighted to accompany his young daughter on her driving lesson. What better way to spend his overdue lunch break? She had met him at the police station in Campbelltown. In an unmarked police car, they had joined the convoy in fourth place and driven along Narellan Road through the bypass and into Camden town. Delighted with her competence, Lee had chatted with her.

The accident had taken him by complete surprise. There was nothing his daughter could have done. She had slammed on the brakes as soon as possible, but not soon enough.

She was crying, something that made Lee angry, but nothing as angry as the bullet that smashed through the windscreen and narrowly missed his daughter's head. She wasn't crying now, she was screaming flat out.

Some hysterical woman had raced past the car with her head down. He wrenched open the door and vaulted out. The man with the gun was clearly visible, firing at someone behind further down the line of cars.

Drawing his revolver, Lee yelled. "Put the gun down!"

The man fired at him and the bullet ricocheted off the roof near Lee's arm. Lee fired.

He had only a small target, but he didn't miss. The gunman slumped onto the roof of his car and slid down to the ground.

Candi knew nothing of those events. She was flying, her heart pounding like never before. Another bullet sang in the air around her. She hardly noticed.

The last car in the pileup had skewed sideways before re-shaping the bumper bar of the vehicle in front. Behind it was a young man in a lowered Ford convertible with flames painted in orange on its black shiny sides. He had managed to bring his car to a standstill without touching the car in front. He could not see the chaos happening at the head of the pile-up, but he could hear the shots and the bullets whining overhead.

Candi threw herself over the door, over his back, and landed in the passenger seat. She screamed at the astonished youth behind the wheel.

"Drive, drive! Madman trying to kill me! Turn! Now!"

Having a pretty girl vault over him into the passenger seat of his car was the stuff of dreams and legend. To save her life only added to the fantasy. "Anything for you, doll!"

The car slewed round and took off in the opposite direction, leaving a trail of rubber behind it.

"Faster!" screamed Candi. "Turn left up ahead!"

They roared along Burragorang Road heading towards the power plant. As they approached the familiar gates, Candi yelled in the driver's ear. "Cut the engine. Drive over there and let me out."

"Fine by me."

They rolled quietly to a stop a short distance from the boom gate. No one was on duty in the guard box.

Candi wrapped her arms round the young man's neck for a second and kissed him on the cheek. She vaulted out of the car. "Hey," he said, "can I see you again?"

"I go to the Back Alley for lunch sometimes." With that she was gone, racing towards the laboratory.

"Dear God," she prayed again, "please let him still be there!"

Her swipe card opened the laboratory door. She ran a few steps down the corridor and then stopped. What if the assassin was in the building? What if he had already carried out his assignment? She took off her shoes. With her heart in her mouth, she crept along the corridor.

She passed one empty office then another until she came to the one with the broken glass door.

Mark was nowhere to be seen.

Mark had left the building not long after Candi. He needed to do some shopping in Narellan, and hadn't seen fit to tell the woman who had so vehemently ordered him to mind his own business. He spent a leisurely time moving from one shop to another, gradually collecting the items he had come for, then got back into the car and drove to the Back Alley Cafe. Several police cars screamed past him. He parked and went up to the familiar door.

An older man with his wife on his arm were coming out. "No use going in there, sonny," he said. "Nobody there to serve you. My wife and I waited for half an hour."

Fear gripped Mark's heart. He sped past the couple and raced inside. The place was empty. He ran to the men's toilet and opened the door. Broken tiles littered the floor. The flash card was gone. He pushed open the door of the ladies. The same sight met his eyes.

His ears were startled by a faint noise. He whipped around, but there was nothing to see. The faint noise continued. He ran across the café, behind the counter, out to the storeroom in the back.

The banging sound became louder. The storeroom was bolted on the outside but not locked. He slid the bolt back.

Annette and Robert were there, gaff tape wrapped round their mouths, hands and feet. Robert had a nasty gash on his head and did not appear conscious. Annette was terrified. Mark removed the tape from her mouth and almost wished he hadn't. The poor hysterical girl made such a noise he could hardly concentrate on freeing her feet and hands.

"Have you seen Candi?" he shouted again and again while freeing her.

All she could do was shake her head and scream, which Mark took to be a "no."

"Call the police," he told her. "I have to go."

He raced back into the café and then out the door. Glancing along the street, he saw her car. Almost not daring to hope, he ran over to it. No Candi.

Another police car roared past.

Beside himself with worry, Mark ran back to his own car. He phoned her home number and got her answering service. He phoned her mobile. A strange voice answered.

"This is Constable Phillips here. To whom am I speaking?"

In the background he could hear a girl's voice sobbing, "I'm never ever ever going to drive again, Daddy," or something like that.

He answered, fearing the worst. "This is Dr. Mark Chambers from the GPC power station. I am looking for Doctor Candice Leblanc. Is she there?"

"This is her phone, apparently. What does she look like?"

Mark described her briefly.

"There is no one of that description here, although there may have been."

"What do you mean?"

"A woman matching that description was seen being driven away from the scene of a serious accident in the company of a young man. We wish to interview them in connection with certain events associated with this incident. Have you any idea where she may be found?"

"What direction were they headed? What was the car like?"

"Back along the road towards Camden and at high speed. The car was a Ford Convertible, black with orange markings on the sides. We do not have the registration number. What is your connection with Dr. Leblanc?"

"We are scientists working on a highly confidential project for Global Power Consortium. I fear someone may be trying to kill her."

"I need you to come to Camden police station to make a statement—"

Mark snapped the phone shut. The man she was with couldn't have been Roger. He drove a top-of-the-range Alfa. "Think!" he told himself. Why would she have been travelling like that? An accident? She was escaping. But where to?

He rang her home again. This time, Roger answered. "Gault here."

"Mark Chambers."

"The geek."

"Have you seen Candi?" Mark asked.

"What business is it of yours?"

"Is she there with you?" There was a tone in Marks' voice that halted Roger's petty jealousy.

"No, I haven't seen her."

"If you do, tell her to stay put and ring the police."

"Why the hell should I?"

Mark snapped the phone shut. There was only one place left to look—back at the lab— but why would she have gone there? Then it hit him. She had gone to warn him. He raced back to the car and headed for the plant. The staff would still be enjoying their party, and the lab would be empty.

Barefoot and bleeding from the wound in her back, Candi traced her path down the entire length of the corridor and out into the lab.

Nothing.

The pumps throbbed quietly, steadily. She had reached the far end and cautiously moved around the back of her own microwave creation, mounted as it was on a large wheeled platform.

Nobody.

Light streamed down from the high windows in that side of the lab. She glanced out of one of them to the pipeline leading toward the generator complex and saw him. He was squatting on the gantry above the high pipeline, rifle in hand with a perfect view of the entire car park.

She peered out a small window on the opposite side of the building.

Mark's car was just coming in through the boom gate. It was heading for the car park.

Candi panicked. She could race out and warn him, but there wasn't time. If she came round the corner into the car park, the sniper would take her out as well. She could hear the car as it ran along the side of the lab. There was no point in calling out. As soon as Mark stepped out of the car, he would be dead.

She searched around her, desperate. Suddenly, she ran to the energiser. Loosening the clamps, she angled the waveguide up until its end was pointing toward the pipeline through the window. Racing to the control panel, she turned on the supply. It would take time to charge the capacitor banks.

It hit ten percent.

The car was turning into the parking area.

Looking through the high window, she could see the sniper stand to his feet and cock the rifle.

Twenty percent.

The car engine died.

The sniper took aim.

Thirty percent.

Candi could wait no longer. She pressed the trigger control.

She instantly felt as though a red hot iron had swept through her body. The microwave pulse spread out from the open end of the wave-guide, spread out through the laboratory.

She choked.

Most of the energy by far travelled straight out the window and ran along the pipeline, treating it as a large antenna. Sparks showered off the gantry. The effect on the sniper was instantaneous. He jerked forward, the rifle discharged.

Mark Chambers, getting out of the car, heard the shot and saw him. The bullet travelled down through the expanded mesh floor of the gantry, missing every strand. However, it didn't miss the pipe. Superheated water burst through the bullet hole and turned instantly into a plume of superheated steam. The enormous pressure widened the hole into a tear.

The plume became a geyser, shooting a thousand metres into the sky, carrying the incinerated body of the sniper high above the gantry before dropping it into the car park below.

The scream of the escaping steam was deafening.

Mark raced around the side of the building, through the door and cannoned into Candi running the other way. The impact knocked them to the ground.

Mark was on his feet first. He ran over to Candi and lifted her up. Her dress was soaked in blood.

Headed by Slater, running figures burst through the doorway. He gazed at Mark and Candi as though he had seen a ghost.

Suddenly, the lab began to shake. The coolant in the cauldron between the spheres was beginning to boil.

Slater screamed. "Shut down the feed! Shut down the feed!"

"What's happening?" one of the other technicians asked nervously.

"The feed pipe to the generators has split," Mark said, "and the pressure is going down. As the pressure drops, the boiling point of water does too."

Slater shut the feed off. He kept the coolant pumps running to drop the temperature of the cauldron.

Mark turned to Candi. "You've been hurt. Let me see."

Candi pushed his hand away. "I'll loosen my own dress. I think it's stopped bleeding. Can you see now?"

Mark pulled the top of her dress gently away from her back. There was an ugly wound about a centimetre long near her spine. "It's still seeping badly. It looks awful. Come outside and I'll take you to Camden Hospital."

They went through the door and turned round the side of the building.

"I saw the man on the gantry," Mark said. "What made him fall over like that?"

"I microwaved him. It was the only thing I could do. He would have killed you."

Mark stopped and turned to gaze into her face. It was white. Her eyes were dull. Shock was beginning to set in.

"Thank you," he said quietly. "Did the swine on the gantry do this to you?"

"No, somebody else." Candi said quietly.

"What happened to him?"

"I left him in a car."

Mark took her hand and together they went towards parking area. The pain in Candi's back was growing, or at least she was becoming aware of it. She gave a small groan. Mark looked anxiously at her face and placed his hand under her shoulder to steady her.

The geyser was only a couple of hundred metres high now, but it still made a deafening noise. There must have been a lot of heat stored in those spheres, Candi thought.

Mark opened the door of the car.

A man came flying around the corner of the building, waving his arms. "Stop! Stop!" he yelled. "They can't shut it down! They can't shut it down!! Slater needs you inside now! It's still boiling like mad!"

Mark and Candi turned to one another, a sense of deep foreboding reflected on their faces.

"You're hurt," Mark said. "Stay here while I see what's going on."

Candi grabbed hold of his arm. "No! I'm coming." She shut the car door.

They followed the man into the building. The cauldron was not boiling as furiously, but it was still boiling.

Slater ran over to them. There was fear in his eyes. "The temperature went down, and now it's going back up again. We've cut the feed. Why is this happening? I need you to shut it down. Pronto!"

Mark and Candi ran toward the optical port and looked in. The breach was a brilliant white line of light.

"Spectrometer!" said Mark. "Candi, what's being ionised in there?"

Candi turned on the instrument and made a few adjustments. "Iron, mostly. It's iron, Mark."

"It's eating the end cap on the injection chamber. How thick is that plate?"

"Three centimetres."

Mark raced up toward Slater and the other technicians gathered up the other end of the lab, as far away as they could get from the boiling cauldron in between the spheres.

"Listen!" Mark shouted. "It's eating the end cap on the injection chamber. You have to feed something else in so it can eat that in preference."

Slater was scared, but his arrogance was not diminished.

"No way, brain boy! There's no way I'm going to let you stick anything else into that chamber!"

Mark turned to the other technicians. "Help me!" he ordered. "Take the radioactive feed line off!"

The technicians stayed rooted to the spot.

Slater sneered. "Find another way. That's what you're paid for."

Mark did a calculation in his head. He screamed for all he was worth at Slater and the others. *"You have five minutes before the end cap fails!"*

Slater smirked at him. The other technicians looked terrified, but they didn't move a muscle.

Mark felt a shove on his shoulder. Candi flew past him, but Candi as he had never seen her before.

There was a light of pure madness in her eyes. She advanced on Slater, dragging a laboratory stool along with her in one hand. Her back had begun to bleed again, and there was a trail of blood on the floor. The sight of a young woman with an insane look in her eyes and blood all over her back made Slater retreat a step.

*"You!"* She grabbed Slater by the arm and dragged him over towards the injection port.

"Stand on this! Go on! *Stand on it!*"

Mesmerised by the sight of her, Slater stood on top of the stool.

*"Face the port!"* Candi screamed at him.

"Four minutes," shouted Mark.

"Why am I doing this?" Slater tried to use his most contemptuous voice but failed.

Candi screamed up at him. "Because when the cap blows in four minutes your tiny penis will be the first thing into the breach! It's symbolic, yes? I hope you feel nice, because the next thing you see is your testicles following, then your intestine will stream out of your gut. You will like that? Then as you sink down you will see your ribs explode and your heart come out through your lungs. There will be blood, see, like this!"

She turned her back to Slater for a second. "Then your head explodes, and your brains come out through your eyes. Are you ready? Is that enough foreplay?"

"*Three minutes,*" Mark yelled.

Sweat and terror broke out on Slater's face. He started to shake uncontrollably. He gave a horrible scream of terror, leapt off the stool, and flew out of the lab wrapping his arms around his head and screaming.

"Disconnect the feed!" ordered Mark. "Bring me the garden hose next to the door outside! *Quickly!!*"

As though some spell had been broken, the technicians sprang to do his bidding. Two of them wearing radiation-proof suiting disconnected the lead shielded pipe from the ponds, and another appeared dragging the hose.

*"Turn it on!"* Mark ran over to the injection port, wrenching the nozzle off the hose as he went. Reaching it, he jammed the end of the hose over the port and held it there as water spurted all over the place. *"Open the injection valve!"*

The boiling sound became worse. Outside the building, the steam geyser rose majestically to a height of fifteen hundred metres.

"Coolant pumps on maximum!" he screamed as loud as his lungs would allow. "Candi, are we still getting iron?"

She ran to the spectrometer. There was a pause. "No!" she shouted back.

"Turn the garden tap off a bit," yelled Mark to the man standing near the door. "Candi, tell me when you see iron."

Eventually, they found the minimum flow of water necessary to stop the breach from eating its way through the steel injection cap. The water was still boiling in the cauldron, and the steam, screaming its warning to the watching world, rose high into the afternoon sky.

Mark returned to his office. He felt as though there were lead weights on his shoulders, his heart, his head.

Candi was sitting in his chair. Her face was ashen grey, her hair matted to her head with dried sweat, and her dress sodden with blood that had somehow got all over her hands and arms.

"It's done." Mark's voice was wooden. "The safety of the world now hangs on a garden hose and a household tap."

Candi paused before answering. "I've rung Roger. He'll be here in a little while to take me home."

The little while turned out to be an hour. Accompanied by a security guard, Roger came in. He looked as happy as a fish in a blizzard. Candi went over to him. She tried to put her arms around him but he saw the blood all over them and stepped back.

"What happened?" Roger said, staring up and down at Candi's bloodstained attire.

"Someone tried to kill her." Mark replied wearily.

Roger wrapped his arms protectively around her. He swore. "I'll kill the bastard!"

"You don't have to," Candi said. "He's dead. Police shot him. It's on the news."

"That was you? The woman they're searching for?"

"Me."

More swearing.

"You need to take her to the hospital, and then, if she's well enough, to Camden Police Station."

"I'm taking her home!" Roger said.

"Take her to the hospital, you bloody fool, she needs urgent medical attention."

Mark almost spat the words at Gaunt. Truth be known, he wished she had turned to him for help. There she was in pain, and all this toad could think of was taking her home. Fat lot of good that would do.

For answer, Roger swore at him, picked Candi up in his huge arms like a baby, and carried her out of the door. It really hurt to be carried like that.

Mark read the pain in Candi's face as she disappeared, and he wanted to smash Gaunt over the head with a blunt object. He groaned loudly, folded his arms on his desk, and lowered his head onto them.

The next visitor, Peter North, arrived an hour later looking very unhappy. "I believe we have a problem," he said when he walked into the room.

Mark lifted his head from the desk. Rubbing his hands over his face with his hand, he motioned North to a chair. The boiling cauldron could be heard rumbling in the background, along with the distant scream of escaping steam.

"I hope you didn't trip over the hose that's running across the floor out there?"

"I saw it," said North. "What's it for?"

"It's all that's stopping this world from being eaten by the breach. Tread carefully when you go out."

North tried to speak. He opened his mouth, but nothing came out.

Mark cradled his head in both hands, not even acknowledging his presence.

After a short while, North found his voice. "I heard something had happened to the plant on the evening news. That stuff about the shooting. I've been trying to contact Slater, but he's not answering. I thought I'd better come down and see what was really going on. Is it that bad?"

Mark dropped his hands and glared at North. "Bad? Bad? The world almost came to an end. You call that bad? The coolant pipe was ruptured by a bullet intended for me. The breach cannot be shut down. I'm feeding it with water from the tap outside the door. Oh, yes, your company has ordered our assassination. It was almost successful. Candi has been badly injured. It was she who saved my life, and the lives of everyone on this planet. You owe her a debt you cannot pay. I've phoned a statement to the police. If you kill me, the world is finished. If you kill her, I'll finish it myself. Now get out and update your superiors. Tell them to call their wolves off."

Mark returned his head to his hands.

North left, his unhappiness had reached truly alarming proportions. Surely, surely it couldn't be true … yet the sound of the rumbling cauldron, the scream of the geyser rising above the building, the garden hose …

North called Jenner.

Earlier that evening, Jenner had taken a call from Louis Hakim, and a most unpleasant call it had been. The information Hakim had received had not been precise, Jenner was told. There would be serious consequences and he was responsible, he was told. Jenner did not like to be told anything.

"We will meet soon to discuss this matter," were Hakim's final words.

They chilled Jenner to the core.

When Peter North rang, Jenner was in no mood to even attempt politeness. "They think we were responsible for two attempted assassinations? Are they out of their minds?"

"There's no doubt they were targets," North said. "Both hit men are dead, and the police are not saying anything. Who do you think was responsible? What do you want me to do?"

"Your job, North," Jenner ordered. "Do it better. If there have been security breaches, you've been derelict in your duty. If anything happens to Chambers or Leblanc, you will be held accountable by this company. Oh, and get the plant back into operation within twenty-four hours."

"There are serious safety issues with the process that need to be addressed. The quantum bridge is in imminent danger of losing containment. If I put more waste into it, we will jeopardise an already dangerous situation. "

"Not you now?" Jenner replied. "If you can't do your job, I'll send someone out there who can. Now fix it, and earn your money for a change. You have twenty-four hours, and you had better find out who is bleating this rubbish about assassinations and tell them to stop. And tighten security before some other competitor takes out our assets." Jenner slammed down the phone.

North replaced the receiver slowly. He stared at the pages of notes he had made for a considerable time. There were serious discrepancies in the information he had been given, serious enough to make Chambers's accusations believable. He picked up the papers on the desk and filed them carefully away in his safe—noticing that his hands were trembling.

Going over to the cocktail cabinet, he opened a bottle of whiskey and attempted to pour himself three fingers in a glass. His hands were shaking so badly more of the liquid ended up on the floor than its proper destination.

# CHAPTER 30

Candi did not return to work the next day. Despite the inconvenience, Roger had taken her to Camden Hospital, where she had been admitted.

The wound required a surgeon's skill to repair. Unfortunately, there would be a scar, albeit a small one, the surgeon reassured her. They would not release her the next day either, because the doctor was not happy with her progress.

They treated her anxious state with sedatives, not knowing she had every right to feel the way she did. The job of medicine was to make the patient stable. Her delusion, repeated often while under light sedation, that the world was in deadly peril from some disastrous scientific experiment, was clearly the result of stress, perhaps with some added psychosis.

There might be legal ramifications if they allowed her to go home before she had been assessed by a competent psychiatrist. The psychiatrist had not been able to shake her delusional state, so he had prescribed some antipsychotic drugs, and Candi had refused to take them. There had been a very unpleasant incident between her and a young nurse who had attempted to administer the medication as a suppository.

The psychiatrist had threatened to schedule her, and Candi had threatened to put his suppositories to a far better use. Around that stage in the proceedings, special security staff had arrived, apparently with permission from the hospital administration board, installed themselves in the corridor outside Candi's room, and insisted on checking the identity of everyone who came within calling distance.

The hospital staff, who objected most of all to having their personal identity queried every time they went from one end of the ward to the other, complained bitterly to management, who concluded the patient had made a satisfactory recovery after all, and sent her home with a bag of pills.

Candi had thrown them down the toilet.

Roger continued to dismiss the incident as the work of some deranged psycho. He had been sympathetic at the beginning of the week, indifferent by the middle of it, and irritated by the end.

Despite her aching back Candi demanded that Roger make love to her again and again over the next few days, as though only his hands on her body could purify her and remove the memory of the assassin's touch, the sound of his words.

Toward the end of the week, even Roger, who regarded his capacity to satisfy women as legendary, was beginning to tire of the exercise. To him, it seemed as though his partner were trying to use their physical relationship to some other end, to convince herself of something, as indeed she was.

In Candi's view of life, the universe, and everything, pleasure was both purpose and answer, but recent events had served to so seriously shake her worldview that pleasure had to be reinstated in its life-defining place. Unfortunately, the more she forced her body to maximise the ecstasy of each encounter, the less it seemed willing or able to do so, and as the week progressed they became less and less effective in alleviating the growing sense of angst and disappointment stealing its way into her heart.

Mark had gone to Andrew's place, given him a brief report of events, gone to bed, and slept solidly for a day and a half—something he had not intended to do.

He found his thoughts so muddled that, when he finally came to consciousness, he decided to go back to bed. He slept badly, plagued by nightmares of the breach losing containment in a hundred different ways.

On Thursday morning, he woke up late and staggered into the kitchen.

Andrew emerged from the study and insisted Mark remain seated while he cooked him bacon and eggs for breakfast. "How do you feel today?"

"Awful. Grateful to be alive," Mark said. "If it hadn't been for Candi, I'd be dead. It's a strange feeling knowing someone else has saved your life."

"You're very fond of her, aren't you?"

"Of course I am. Sometimes I'd like to bash the sense out of the jerk she's living with."

"What's this, jealousy?" Andrew raised his eyebrows. "Don't forget, she chooses to live with him and not with you."

"Yeah, I know," Mark said. "I'm worried sick about the breach. I'm worried about my solution. It's a one off, Andrew. It either works, or it doesn't, and if it doesn't, we won't get another chance. I don't think one human being is meant to have such a weight on his shoulders. I'm certainly not."

"Yet you're the one God has allowed to bear the burden. You think He's made a mistake?"

Mark groaned. "Well, it doesn't look too good from where I'm standing right now. And I'm worried GPC will have another go at killing us. In fact, I'm worried about everything, if you want to know."

"Don't blame you. Better after breakfast. Here." Two eggs, sunny-side up surrounded with nicely cooked bacon arrived on the table.

Mark set to work. Two cups of coffee and three slices of toast and marmalade later, he left, and Andrew went back into his study. There was urgent work to be done. He rang Brian Hill on a secure line.

Mark arrived at the lab to find Peter North in Slater's office.

"What happened to Slater?" Mark asked. "Did they kill him?"

Peter North motioned Mark to a chair. "That's foolish talk. I've contacted George Jenner, the CEO, and he believes some rival energy company is responsible. I've heard nothing from the police. No, Slater has had a nervous breakdown. He was admitted to some psychiatric establishment near Sydney, out at Ryde, I think. I've decided to take charge here for the foreseeable future. I hope you don't mind."

"What's the status of the breach?"

"It's stable," North said, "but we're feeding a bit more water into it to keep it from munching on the antechamber end cap. We've strengthened that, too. There is now half a metre of steel on that end. We had to support it with some struts embedded in the floor."

"What of the pipe?"

"Being repaired as we speak. A team from New Zealand is here. They're used to capping geysers that result from ruptured bores. They're very good. Want to come and see?"

Mark followed North out into the car park.

The New Zealand team was living up to its reputation. They had removed part of the gantry and replaced it with temporary supports. Further along, they had covered the pipe with another length of tubing, originally split lengthwise and since welded together. The cover pipe was just a little larger than the original, creating a small gap between them.

The following day, using remote arms, they slid the outer pipe over the tear in the inner one, plugged the gap on one side with special adhesive, and welded the outer to the inner pipe. They did the same on the other side.

In three days, the pipe was repaired, the cauldron stopped boiling, and the generators were turning out about eight megawatts of power, which wasn't bad considering the energy was coming from the water in a garden hose.

To his credit, and despite several demands from Jenner to do otherwise, North refused to reconnect the radioactive feed to the breach. He told Jenner that a solution had to be found to the problem of shutting the source down, should the situation require it, and asked what Jenner was doing about it.

The answer, delivered along with many expletives, was apparently nothing at all.

# CHAPTER 31

Oblivious to the events that had occurred in Australia, the elusive Dekker sat at the table in a meeting room on the third floor of a building at Berkeley University campus. It was still the early hours of the morning. There were papers strewn on the polished wood and utter silence in the room.

Hans Zimmerman looked up from the paper he had been studying and cleared his throat. "We have too many unknowns. We have to persuade this company, this GPC, to abandon the plant so we can do scientific research. There may be other solutions, rather than this one proposed by Chambers."

Stephen Eagles joined in the conversation. "And besides that, the Chambers solution requires two point five grams of material. There are only three accelerators on Earth that could produce any of it, and even those produce only milligrams, I think. Besides, there's the problem of containment. None of them would be willing to even try."

Dekker scanned from face to face without speaking.

Professor Laurie Hadfield from Berkeley cleared his throat. "I'm deeply troubled by this proposal. It's a once-for-all attempt. If it fails, we will not get another. Surely there must be some other way." He shook his head and lapsed into silence.

Dekker pushed the papers littering the table in front of him away with his hand and leaned back on his chair. "Look around you. Are not the best minds in the world of physics gathered around this table? We have discussed Mark Chambers's model for the phenomenon. Some of you agree with him, some of you disagree, but none of us are sure. How long do you think it will take to reach a unified agreement here?"

There was silence.

Stephen Eagles shrugged his shoulders in a gesture of despair. "Forever—at least without experimentation."

"We do not have that long," Dekker said. "We have incontrovertible evidence the breach is becoming more and more of a threat each second it is allowed to operate. Such evidence fits the Chambers model. Mark has somehow persuaded North to remove the radioactive feed, and now they're trickling water into it. The energy given off is still capable of generating eight megawatts of power. But that was last week. Now the flow of water necessary to contain the breach is greater. It has been generating twelve megawatts since Friday. I have plotted a simple graph."

Dekker switched on an overhead projector. "By the end of next month, if they can supply it with enough water—and that's doubtful—we will be up to twenty megawatts. By the end of next year, one hundred. How long do you think the steel spheres will last at those pressures? My dear colleagues, how long?"

Laurie glanced up from the paper he had been scribbling on. "Less than eighteen months."

"How long would it take our three large accelerators to produce the given amount of material—assuming that they were willing to try?" Dekker asked.

"It might take months, and I say again, if they were willing." Hans Zimmerman sighed.

"So," Dekker said. "What choices do we have? None of us have come up with a solution that is guaranteed to work. The Chambers model and solution may not work, either. What happens if it doesn't? Our Earth will be slowly and terribly destroyed. It would take years, perhaps, before all life ceases to exist, but cease it will, for the Earth will turn to dark matter orbiting the sun. What happens if we sit here and do nothing? Exactly the same result. Be very sure of this one thing, my friends. You are not out of its reach, even in these hallowed halls."

There was silence. The sense of foreboding, already present, seemed to grow into something almost tangible.

Hans Zimmerman asked, "Laurie, would you consider using the accelerator on this campus?"

There was a pause.

Finally, Laurie reluctantly stood to his feet. He looked out the window towards the accelerator buildings. Below him on the paths surrounded by lawn and trees, men and women walked, oblivious to the danger about to be decreed as their lot.

"Yes, I would," Laurie said. "Provided we agree on the design and complete the construction of a suitable bottle. One that has been tested. Not until then would I dare undertake to put the people on this campus at risk. I don't think we'll be able to produce very much of the material at all, even then."

"Thank you, Laurie," said Dekker. " And you, Hans?"

"I will talk—no, we must talk to the director of CERN. Even then, I do not like our chances. Fermi labs may also be able to help." Shaking his head, Hans cupped his hands around it. "I wish I did not live in these times."

Dekker nodded. There was an icy determination in his voice as he spoke. "So do I, but we did not choose them. We have the responsibility to make sure we have a legacy to hand on to our children so their times may be better. Gentlemen, colleagues, friends—we have work to do."

The meeting broke up soon afterwards. Dekker went out the doors of the physics building and followed the tree-lined path whose lights cast bright circles in the early morning darkness. He was moving toward Professor Laurie Hadfield's quarters, where he was going to spend the night.

Taking care to avoid the lighted pools, a shadow followed Dekker. His target was acquired. He checked the small pistol in his hand and released the safety. One small thud, hardly audible, and the lethal dose would penetrate the target's neck. By the time the coroner examined the victim, it would appear to all the world like a heart attack. It was perfect, but only worked at short range.

He quickened his pace because the target would soon reach his destination. He had to risk being seen. Stepping onto the path, he began to run, his rubber-soled shoes silent against the paving. Not far now. He drew the trigger back on the injection device.

"Daniel!" Another man was running up the path toward them.

Emile sprinted back into the shadows and waited some distance away to see if the newcomer had taken any notice of him.

Dekker stopped in his tracks and turned round.

It was Laurie Hadfield himself. "Daniel, I've got some good news," he panted. "Or at least some better news. I've been speaking to our chief engineer in charge of our accelerator—he's often on duty at night—and he's willing to construct the magnetic containment bottle to hold the stuff. When it's ready, I'll give the word to begin accumulating the material. We can transfer it to the bottle in small stages. It's the only way we can do it without the power of the large hadron collider. He wants your input, now if you think you can manage it—tomorrow morning if you're too tired."

Dekker brightened considerably. He gripped Laurie around the shoulders, all thought of sleep evaporating from his mind. "Now!" He said eagerly. "Where is he?"

"Down in the accelerator building. Shall we go?"

They set off running.

Emile released the trigger on the injection device and cursed under his breath. The target would get to live for another day. Still, there was something useful he could do before he returned. He would contact Stern and seek approval.

The pale light of dawn shone through the windows of Sam Treadwell's office in the accelerator building, casting a pinkish glow on the faces of the three tired men working around the paper-strewn table. Screwed up paper littered the floor as well. Laurie was running a program on his laptop, Dekker was punching numbers into a calculator, and Sam was drawing on a sheet of A3 paper.

Dekker scribbled some numbers on a pad and dropped back into his chair. "It will work. We will need to dedicate the entire resources of one on-board computer to maintaining the magnetic potential well in the bottle, which will keep Mark's material from touching the sides. When the bottle is moved, there will be small changes in the Earth's magnetic field that will have to be compensated for, as well as changes in the magnetic environment. "

Pausing, Dekker dropped his pen on the table, and wiped his arm across his tired eyes. "The slightest hiccup in that field will bring disaster. We will install a second computer system to monitor the energy coming from the breach, as well as the vacuum in the sphere around it. When conditions are ideal—or as close to ideal as possible—it will shut off one of the magnetic fields and propel the material through the opening at high speed without touching the sides. This makes the final design—including batteries—fairly large, about the size of an average washing machine."

"We program it to give the operator time to get away." Laurie stifled a yawn.

"Of course," Dekker said. "All Mark has to do is to make sure the bottle is installed on the port opposite the injection end, close the water off, and let the pumps start building the vacuum. He'll be miles away when the actual attempt occurs, but my guess is he'll be close enough to hear the bang."

"Let's hope that's all he hears." Sam shook his head with weariness and reached for his coffee—the third he'd had in the last hour. "It's a one-off attempt. Dear God, I hope his theory's right. If it's not, do we have a plan B?"

"Not yet." Dekker threw down his pen on the table and ran his hands over his eyes. "Furthermore, unless someone has a flash of inspiration—no pun intended—we're unlikely to get one. No doubt by then every scientist on the planet will be working for their lives. Personally, I think if this attempt fails …"

He didn't verbalise his thought, there was little need.

Sam threw the remains of his coffee down his throat, gathered up the finished plans from the table, and headed off to the engineering workshop.

It was only 6:30 a.m., but all the engineers would be there, ready to begin. What to tell them, he thought to himself. Better concoct some good story.

# CHAPTER 32

There was far less camaraderie, but no less foreboding, in the meeting between Jenner and Louis Hakim coincidentally occurring in Geneva.

Jenner could feel the sweat running down his back.

Hakim watched him, his eyes cold and impassive like an eagle watching its prey.

"I tell you," Jenner said, "there's no problem. The tear in the pipe was caused by a bullet fired by the man hired to kill Chambers. Hodges bungled the job."

"As I recall, he was hired on your recommendation," Hakim said. "I'm sure I can find a transcript of such a conversation if your memory is not able to recall it."

Beads of sweat appeared on Jenner's forehead. He wiped them away with a handkerchief before replying. "In any case, the tear has been successfully repaired, the source is stable, and we will proceed as planned."

"Yet according to my information," Hakim said, "the plant has not returned to full operating capacity. We are generating only a few megawatts of power. I believe Peter North has taken charge. I have received quite a number of reports that indicate the quantum bridge is far from stable, and your promised shutdown procedure has not materialised in any form. I am tempted to believe you may have started something that will cost our company as much as you predicted we would profit."

"Louis, the plant is completely under control," Jenner assured him. "The only reason it's not generating its quota of power is simply that North, quite contrary to my specific instructions, has not recommenced using the nuclear waste fuel."

"He is, at present, unwilling to do so." Hakim glanced at the papers on the table.

"I suggest he be replaced by an officer who has more regard for company policy." Jenner tapped the table nervously with his forefinger.

"Perhaps he has more regard for company policy than you give him credit for. It would seem to me that this project of yours, George, is far from the golden rainbow you promised me it would be. Your other most competent officer is, to the best of my knowledge, in an asylum for the insane. You don't seem to be making a lot of useful calls lately, George."

His legs shaking, Jenner clamped his feet even more firmly on the floor. "Allow me to fire North and put another man in charge. I'm sure you'll find everything to your satisfaction in forty-eight hours or less."

"North is a careful man, George," Hakim said. "I ask myself, why is he showing reluctance? I discover that the construction of several other plants is also on hold. I get the feeling you're not in control of this project. I have invested a great deal of money. I am not seeing the expected returns. Buyers do not like uncertainty."

"I will attend to it immediately," Jenner said. "North is being over cautious. He's been listening to Chambers. I'll talk to Stern. They can both be killed in a car accident this time."

"You will do nothing of the kind, George. I am not convinced by your report that their services are no longer needed. There is a police investigation into the assassination attempts and people are attempting to implicate this company. There are loose ends to tie up, people to manage. I trust I have your cooperation in these matters?"

Jenner told him he would have it until all hell froze over.

# CHAPTER 33

Candi came through the door of Mark's office shortly after his inspection of the New Zealand team. He was instantly on his feet. Candi ran to him, wrapped her arms around his shoulders, and pressed her head against his chest. For a long while, they wordlessly held one another while drawing comfort from the silent embrace.

Candi's words were somewhat muffled in his shirt. "Mark, I have been wanting to tell you I'm sorry for the words I said to you before all this happened. I hurt you and I feel terrible. Your friendship means more to Candi than she knows how to tell you."

Mark tightened his arms around her. "You saved my life. You put your own life in jeopardy. You're so precious to me, Candi. Sounds so inadequate. Thank you for loving me so much as a friend." He kissed her hair. "Thank you."

Feeling her arms tighten around his shoulders, he kissed her hair again.

She raised her head, touched her warm lips against his cheek, and snuggled her head back down on to his chest. "Hold me. I feel so ... right ... when I'm here."

No doubt they would have said a lot more to one another, but at that second North came through the door. Mark and Candi detached themselves and turned to face him.

"Good to see you both. Candi, how is your back?" The apprehension in North's voice betrayed the friendly welcome in his eyes.

"What are you doing here?" Candi snapped at him.

"I am replacing Mr. Slater for a while."

"The pissy little lecher," she said. "That will be a change. Have they killed him yet?"

North repeated the advice he had given Mark, following it with a brief summary of the state of the breach. A grunt was all he received for his trouble.

The telephone rang. Mark answered it. A short conversation followed.

"It's Camden police. They want us both down at the station this morning," Mark said. Then he turned to North, "I hope that's okay with you?"

"Of course. I recommend caution if they ask about the operation here. It will do no good to panic the general public, would it?"

Rolling her eyes to the top of her head, Candi snorted. "No good for your precious profits, you mean."

"No, I don't," North said. "It would only make a dangerous situation ten times worse."

"So you think there might be something a tiny bit dangerous here? Is this what you think? How very unexpected and surprising." Candi's voice dripped with sarcasm.

"I forgive your cynicism," North said, "but if you want to know the truth, yes, we are dealing with a situation that has the potential to become very dangerous indeed. Why do you think we're still feeding water into the breach when I have been ordered—several times with threats—to resume normal operations?"

The admission took them both by surprise.

"We appreciate that," said Mark. "No, we won't say anything, but I don't think that's what the police have in mind. Something about property that might belong to us." Mark saw Candi's eyes flicker a little. "Shall we go?"

They went towards the car park.

"I can't see your car." Mark scanned the area. "Did you park outside, or did Roger give you a lift?"

"I bought another one," she said. "It's the BMW Cabriolet over there. Nice, isn't it? Retail therapy. Actually, the thought of getting into a car with a roof over my head makes me go funny."

While they drove to Camden, Candi continued to recount in endless detail how she had come to see the car advertised, how she had beaten the seller down, and how she liked the colour, the leather, the sound of the engine, and the way the car handled. Mark felt that she would have said even more if the journey had been longer.

Having listened to her in silence until they turned the corner into the main street, he decided an interruption was definitely called for. "Would you like a coffee before we go in?"

"I would."

They headed over to the familiar café.

Things had changed. There was a wire security door in place of the old glass one on to the street and a security system pulsed its little red light on the wall. Annette, who was behind the coffee machine, looked up without welcome and went straight back to the kitchen.

Mark and Candi sat down.

Eventually, Robert, wearing a bandage round his head, came out and approached their table. "I want to thank you for saving my life," he said. "At the hospital they told me if I hadn't gotten there when I did, I would have been dead."

He seemed a bit uncomfortable. "They wrecked my bathrooms. You put something in there, didn't you? All this violence, it's because of you, because you used my café for some secret business. We thought you were our friends, but you were using us. I want you to go and not come back here. If something else was to happen, I would not be able to get insurance. This has already cost me a lot of money. And my head still aches."

Without a word they stood up and left with Candi mumbling a lot in French under her breath. When they reached the street, she exploded. "What about our lives? Does the cretin think we enjoyed what happened to us? Was he shot at? Did anyone try to...to ...?" She burst into tears.

Mark put his arm round her shoulder. Candi responded by turning against him and burying her face in his chest. Once again, Mark held her tightly while rubbing his lips through her hair.

"I'm all right now," she said after she had regained control, "I don't like losing friends. They were nice, they were friends. Now they're frightened of us. I hate that. I really hate that."

The went round the corner to the police station. The sergeant on duty motioned them into a room in the back. They were joined by Constable Lee Philips who, for some reason, had been reallocated there.

The constable placed two small items on the table. "Are these yours?"

They were the two flash cards from the Back Alley Café. One had a "C" written on it in black text, the other an "M."

"Yes, they are," Mark said, "where did you get them?"

"They were in the pockets of the deceased gunman," Philips said. "He's been identified as a high-profile underworld assassin. You were very fortunate to survive. He has a history of abusing women before he kills them. In this case, I think it kept you alive. The other assassin who attempted to kill you, Dr. Chambers, has a similar hit profile. Whoever wanted you dead was prepared to pay top dollar for it. These two came through Sydney airport over a week ago from Munich. I ask myself, why would international assassins be hired to kill you both? It's because of what you're doing at the power plant, isn't it?"

Mark and Candi looked from one to the other.

Finally, Mark answered. "That's very likely. There's a problem at the power plant that we've been working on. I believe our employer may not like my solution to that problem. How he found out what I was proposing, I have no idea."

Candi's lip began to tremble a little.

"Mark, it was me, I told them. I didn't mean to! This is so bad! You rang me the other night, remember, at a most inconvenient time, and you were telling me about what you thought was happening at the power station. Do you remember?"

"You hung up in the middle of it as I recall."

"It was really bad moment, and I was so annoyed. I told you to contact Daniel in the morning. Never thought about it! Mon Dieu, they're tapping my phone! Or my house is bugged! There's someone listening every time we … I am feeling so … humiliated." Candi covered her face with her hands and shook her head. "I've really had enough! My life has become the nightmare. I think I'm losing my mind …"

Lee Philips had taken some notes while Candi had been speaking. He closed his pad and spoke. "I have your address in Mt. Annan, don't I, Dr. Leblanc? Yes, I do, thank you." He pushed the two flash cards across the table toward them. "It may be none of my business, but couldn't you find a better way to organise communications with Dr. Dekker?"

Mark and Candi stared at him.

"I don't believe I mentioned that name." Candi said warily.

"You didn't," Constable Philips said, "but I read the papers. I recall a Daniel Van Dekker was also working on the project at the power station. There was some political scandal before that. Now I believe you're persona non gratia at the Back Alley Café down the main street? Don't take it too personally. The owner is frightened, and I can't say I blame him. If you look across the street, you'll see another café—Café L'Amoré. For some reason, the new owner came into the station the other day with a free coffee for all of us—just to drum up customers, I guess. Anyway, the coffee's not bad, and quite a few of the boys go there now. It's also a WiFi hot spot, so you can use your laptops if you go there. Might be a good place to try. I suggest you find some other way of storing your information or doing whatever it was you were doing in the other place."

"Thank you," Mark said. "We'll give it a go."

Lee continued. "I don't know what's going on at this power station, but I don't like it. Free energy from waste? There's no such thing. I've got three daughters. We live at Narellan. I don't want anything unpleasant to happen to them or the people who live around here. Are my fears justified?"

"Yes, they are." Candi blurted out the words without thinking.

Mark gave her a meaningful glance and put his hand over hers. "It would be very unwise of us to say more at this stage, you understand?"

"No, I don't," Philips said. "However, I believe you're trying to help."

They left the station with the flash cards in their pockets. They bought some goodies at the bakery for a picnic lunch and drove the short distance to Camden Park. No one followed them.

After finding a shady tree, they sat down and munched on sandwiches made with freshly baked bread. The sun was warm for that time of the year, and although the poplars were bare, there were signs that spring was not too far away. Small green buds were already forming, and in the patches of bush growing around the river bank, some early wildflowers were beginning to appear.

Candi brushed the crumbs off her cardigan. She studied the ground near her feet. "He told me he was going to kill me—worse. He said you would be killed, too. We were going to be buried together under some cows. I could feel death coming and I am terrified, Mark. Then I did something that has worried me ever since. I prayed to a God I didn't believe in. Still don't, really. But I meant my prayer. Not like in the church back home. I was always cynical then. I knew my words were just bouncing off the ceiling, that there was really no one there. People who pray are self deluded, I've always believed that. But I pray! Why? And I think God might have heard me," she added in a small voice.

"I am sure God did hear you, Candi," Mark said. "Look at what happened. The learner drivers, Lee Philips being there. The guy with the car. The assassin missed—an experienced assassin! Then you saw the guy who would have killed me, and you stopped him. Think what had to be in place for that to happen. Seconds later, and I would have been shot. I am too much a scientist to believe in chance coincidences."

"But bad things happen to other people," she argued. "If there was a God, wouldn't he stop all the bad things happening? Or can't he?"

"God doesn't do the bad things, Candi, we do. Why He allows some things to happen and not others—I don't know."

"You don't know—that's just it," she said. "What amazes me is that you—and inside the lab you are so, so brilliant—when it comes to faith you hold on to all this for no reason at all."

"You think I don't have a reason?" he asked. "That I have to turn off my clever little mind so that I can actually be a Christian?"

"You must have to. I can't—"

"Well, I don't," he said. "I look at the physical world around me and I see design everywhere. I don't have enough faith to believe all this complexity came about by pure chance plus time. I look back into reliably-documented history and I find an account of a man who was put to death on a Roman cross and on the third day after rose from the dead. He went around talking to people—on one occasion to over five hundred of them. I read the eyewitness accounts of people who saw what happened and wrote it down. Wouldn't you listen to a man who claimed he would come back from the dead and then did just that? Would you write him off as a lunatic?"

"And just why would this God-man ... thing ... go to all that trouble?"

"God sent Jesus into the world to pay the price for our indifference," Mark said. "Our attitude separates us from God. I believed you when you said you couldn't find him. That's just what Jesus came to do—to pay for God's judgement on us so we could be forgiven and have our relationship with God restored."

"Are you saying I'm a bad person?" she asked. "That I need forgiveness?"

"We all need God's forgiveness, Candi. We're all guilty of ignoring God to some extent. Even if God were to judge us with the same moral code we apply to others or to ourselves, we would still not measure up."

Candi snorted angrily. "I've heard it all before. Hell fire and judgement! Pay up or be damned!"

"No, Candi! It's not like that."

"But according to you, I am a bad person, and the only way I can get this forgiveness I desperately need, but have managed to do without all my life, is to say 'Dear Jesus, forgive me!' Well, I won't do it! If God wants to forgive me, then He can do it Himself."

"We are all guilty of living in ways that God does not approve of ..."

"So we're back to Roger and me, is that it?" The fire was beginning to kindle in Candi's eyes.

"No, that's not it," he said. "I'm talking about your relationship with God—not Roger."

"The trouble with you, Mark, is you are so narrow-minded. You have made yourself a lot of rules to live by because you are frightened of the freedom of life."

Mark sighed, a long, rather sad sigh. In a quiet voice, he said, "The important thing is truth, Candi. If Jesus died on a cross about two thousand years ago and rose from the dead, then you have to take what He said about you and your need for Him seriously. If He didn't do that, then I'm a fool."

"I don't believe that nonsense!"

Mark smiled at her, finding it impossible to be annoyed with the passionate expression on her face. "But a couple of weeks ago you didn't believe in God, either. Now you are open to the possibility."

"Perhaps I am, perhaps I'm not. Coincidences happen." Returning his smile, she squeezed his arm. "But I'm glad I saved you, Mark, really glad. One day I might understand this Jesus stuff you go on about. I can't right now. I lost two friends today. I couldn't bear to lose your friendship."

Her eyes were saying so much more than her words, and her hand felt warm and alive upon his arm. He turned and looked at her, his beautiful, living deliverer. His eyes strayed from her face to the curve of her breasts nestling in her cardigan, softly rounded in the sunlight. They travelled slowly down her legs, long and shapely, her pretty toes unconsciously intertwining the stems of small flowers growing in the grass. She was so beautiful, so desirable.

Suddenly he found himself wanting to kiss her, lay her down beside him, make love to her, feel her lips against his, her body moving passionately against.. ...

"What am I doing?" he thought to himself. He shut his eyes and mechanically, deliberately turned away, surprised and alarmed at his own desire. She belonged to Roger, and there he was, looking her up and down just like the other men she despised.

What a pathetic way to treat the woman who had risked her very life to save him.

It was only a split second, but Candi had noticed it—seen the way he had shut his eyes and turned away. Shock registered on her face and instantly she wondered why it had. She knew that look, knew what usually followed it, but Mark had exercised his incredible self-control and the moment had passed—leaving her feelings in unexpected disarray.

He turned and smiled back at her. "You know," he said softly, "there's every chance I might fall in love with you. After all, you're the beautiful woman who saved my life."

Candi's gentle reply was slow in coming. Her eyes, wide and pleading, never left his face. "Please don't do that, Mark. I don't want you to say you love me."

Seeing the surprise, disappointment, and confusion register in his face, she went on, her voice gentle and a little sad. "I've heard so many men say those words, and they always mean only one thing. When they get what they want they go away and say those words to someone else. Love is the angel dust, Mark, a moment of pleasure, sometimes not even that. I have had many lovers, Mark, but only one friend. If you say those words, I will think you want only one thing, and then you'll go away, too. I don't want you to go away, Mark." She shuddered involuntarily. "You have the special place in Candi's heart that no one else has. I want you to know that."

Mark stared at her lovely face, her eyes large and looking almost fearfully into his own, and a new understanding began to dawn in him. He smiled at her. "All right, I'll just keep reminding myself you have an awful temper and you don't like talking about God."

Candi laughed, leaned over, threw her arms around his neck, and kissed him on the cheek. "Well, you make Candi cross. But she will always be your special friend."

They stood and went to the car. Somehow their hands had brushed, lingered, and joined together.

Rather than going straight back to the lab, they called in at Café L'Amoré.

Alan Todd was a jolly, rotund man of medium height. He wore a white apron with coffee stains all over it strapped around his abundant waist with what could have been a piece of black string. He regarded the newcomers over the top of a pair of half-frame glasses and ushered them to a corner table at the rear of the restaurant.

"This is a nice table," he said, "because you can see everyone in the room as well as out into the street. There is no one behind you. Some customers do not like having people behind them. Now you order your coffee. We have a tradition here. We always bring you out a little tray of biscuits, specially chosen to go with the blend of coffee we're serving." He sighed. "And most people don't even notice. Sometimes my patrons leave little things on there they forget to take with them. I just keep them safe until they come back. All part of the service."

He went back to the coffee machine behind the counter, leaving a rather puzzled couple behind him.

"What do you suppose all that was about?" Candi said, screwing her face into a confused expression.

Mark shrugged his shoulders. "I'm not sure, but at a guess I would say Alan Todd has been talking to Lee Philips, or, rather, Lee Philips has been talking to him. I wonder if it was sheer coincidence we were directed here?"

"Mark, do we trust him? Candi is not very trusting of strange men."

"I guess we have to trust someone. Let's give him a little test. I have a blank flash card in my pocket. How about we add it to the biscuit tray when it comes and see if it returns the next time we have coffee here. If all is well next time, we leave the real things."

"Good idea, Mark. Here comes the coffee."

The coffee was good and the hazelnut biscuits were a well-chosen complement. They left a tip: an empty flash card tucked in the folds of the napkin under an uneaten biscuit.

# Chapter 34

Margaret Marriott walked briskly from her BMW parked in its allocated place at the University of Southern Sydney. It was a glorious day. She was early for her first business meeting, scheduled at 9:47a.m. Margaret liked to schedule meetings at odd times. It gave the impression that her life was organised to the second.

There was a young man seated in the waiting room when she passed into her spacious office.

Shortly after Margaret's arrival, Millicent Veronica Smythe-Harris strutted into the room bearing coffee, a small portfolio of papers to sign, and the news that a Mr. Robert Foster from the *Sydney Morning Herald* was asking for an interview.

"Send him in, Millie," Margaret ordered. "I can spare about thirteen minutes."

Robert Foster entered. He produced a business card, handed it to Margaret, sat down on the proffered chair, and withdrew a small recording device from his pocket. Placing it on the table, he began. "I'm working on a story concerned with the experimental energy plant at Camden. If I may, I would like to ask you some questions about your involvement with the project."

"Certainly," Margaret said. "The university welcomes public understanding of the proactive roles we engage in on behalf of the environment."

"Thank you." He started the recorder. "Am I correct in saying that you were the one who personally endorsed the research undertaken by Doctors Van Dekker, Chambers, and Leblanc in high-energy collisions?"

"The university assessed the project thoroughly worthy of our support."

"Yet here," he produced a folded paper from his coat pocket, "I have a letter signed by the head of your academic committee saying funding for the project could not be approved because certain quality assurance matters were not adequately dealt with."

'Where did you get that?"

"Is it true the funding was never approved?"

"No! The funding was approved—there would be no equipment and no experiments if it hadn't been." Margaret was beginning to wish that she had gone straight to her meeting.

"Then if the academic committee did not approve the funds, where did they come from?"

"I don't have the figures in front of me right now. I'm telling you that the funds were—"

"Is it true the funding for this project, as well as the funding for the construction of the new building to house the faculty of nursing and business, came from General Power Consortium?"

"The university has many sponsors," Margaret said. "I believe that GPC is among them."

Foster plunged on. "And the university has always supported the actions of the three scientists associated with the project?"

"Yes, we have. Their research is, of course, assessed by our academic committee."

"That would be the same committee who wrote them each a letter of dismissal signed by yourself."

"I have no idea what you're talking about."

"How unusual," he responded. "You apparently sign things without reading them. I take it, then, that the university is completely happy to endorse the experimental work going on at the plant right now?"

"Yes, it is," she said. "I can't see where this is driving."

He asked, "Are you aware that the plant is no longer producing very much electrical power, and that it has stopped using the radioactive waste material on site as it was contracted to do?"

"I am not aware of that. There was a minor incident some time ago, a burst pipeline, I believe. The plant is obviously still repairing any damage caused by the incident if they are not back to full operational strength."

"Thank you for your time, Chancellor Marriott."

Robert clicked off the recording device and stood to leave. He did not show her the other crumpled letter he was carrying. There was a story here, all right. His source had been correct. He left the office and reported in to his boss, dialling an international number, which, for a reporter associated with a Sydney newspaper, was an unusual thing to do.

Robert Foster was not the only one on the scent.

Joseph McTierney was, at that very moment, reading the email he had received from Peter North. So it was true—his information had been correct. The plant was not using up the radioactive waste as they had promised the good people of his electorate to do. The reply from North was most unsatisfactory. Yes, there had been a problem. Yes, it had been repaired. Yes, they were still operating at very reduced output. No, they were not considering the use of radioactive waste in the immediate future. He lit another cigar and pushed the button on his intercom.

"Get Ms. Carson-Jones to ring me now."

"The Greens senator?"

"No, the Madam for Bedlam." He clicked off the intercom. Secretaries were so stupid and unreliable. He had gone through five of the bimbos in the last twelve months.

The call came through twenty minutes later. "This is Julie Carson-Jones. You wished to speak to me?"

"I do," McTierney snapped. "Are you aware that the experimental power plant in the Camden valley is reneging on its promise to remove all the radioactive waste material from the environment as it promised to do?"

"I heard a rumour, probably from the same place as you did. It would be untrue to say we're happy about operations at that establishment."

"In what way?"

"I take it you read the press release when the plant became operational," she said. "Lot of gobbledegook. Where is the waste going? Off the planet? If they're using radioactive material to produce power, they're using a nuclear reactor. You're such an idiot, McTierney. You closed a nuclear reactor down on that site and let someone else build a bigger one right in the same place. Now it's got problems. Think of it, McTierney. A nuclear reactor accident right in your own backyard! Didn't even notice, did you, McTierney? The power company fed you bullshit and you took it all in! Little present for the wife, was it? Or maybe not for the wife. Doesn't look very good, does it, you being minister for the environment and all! There are going to be some questions asked in the next session of parliament, I can tell you. I'm going to be asking them."

She rang off before McTierney could vent down the phone line the torrent of foul language which followed.

Hearing the explosion of profanity delivered at full volume, his secretary trembled at her desk while waiting for the inevitable demands that would be bellowed at her in the next few minutes.

Surprisingly, nothing came.

In the office next door to her, rage had given place to apprehension.

McTierney was worried. He dragged out the paper clippings Carson-Jones had referred to and reread them. Gobbledegook. She was right. He had read them too quickly the first time, assuming his complete ignorance of atomic physics had made unintelligible what was straightforward and reasonable to those who did not have his handicap.

Now he saw things in a different light. He had been conned. Damn it! He had been conned! "Nobody cons McTierney," he muttered. The problem was how to proceed without making himself seem like an ignorant fool.

McTierney dialled a number.

Peter North picked up the phone. "North here—"

"I know what you're up to, North. You've got a nuclear reactor down there, a reactor with problems. By the time I finish with your company you'll be looking for a job sweeping toilets."

North recoiled from this verbal barrage, unassigned as it was to any name. "Who is this?"

"Joseph McTierney, minister for the environment. Your lot tricked me into thinking you had done something clever. Now I know better. What's gone wrong with your reactor, North? Come on, tell me! If you don't tell me there will be an anonymous tip leaked to the six o'clock news. You will be arse-deep in reporters by tomorrow morning. Time to 'fess up."

Peter North was no fool, but the attack had caught him unprepared. "We're not running any sort of nuclear reactor down here. Your source is misinformed."

"Oh yeah? Then tell me, Mr. Smart Engineer, where was the radioactive material from the ponds going? Into thin air? Dematerialising? Leaving the planet? Being pumped into groundwater? Come on, North, don't take me for a complete fool."

North said, "The material was being converted into other non radioactive matter by a new and confidential process—"

"Bullshit it was," McTierney said. "Looks like it's time for the reporters."

"McTierney, such action would be irresponsible in the extreme. We do have a problem down here, but it is not a problem with the nuclear waste material. We are working toward re-using the remaining material, but we cannot do that just yet."

"Because there's a danger of the reactor becoming unstable? Come on, level with me North. Next phone call is to channel nine."

Sweat broke out on Peter North's forehead. His mind was racing. He felt that the fuse of the time bomb he was sitting on had just become shorter. How right he was.

"All right," North said. "We are using nuclear processes here, but not in a conventional reactor. There was a problem with containment, but that has been stabilised. We are searching for a permanent solution. If you come barging in here, trying to make political mileage out of a potential disaster, then I guarantee you it will make the situation worse."

"Not good enough. Your company has misled the public. I intend to set an enquiry in motion at the ministerial level. You'll be out of business within twenty-four hours. I shut down one nuclear reactor on that site, and I can shut down another. You're finished, North."

"So are you, McTierney."

"What do you mean?" McTierney exploded.

"You were quite in favour of the project when Global Power Consortium discussed the matter with you. We have recordings of that conversation. Should reporters arrive here, we would be obligated to release them to the media."

"Your company lied to me. That will come out. You can't stop this at the ministerial level. The Greens have got hold of it. They're going all the way. Better start looking for another job, North!"

McTierney hung up without waiting for a reply. Peter North thought for a long time and then went into Mark's office. Candi was there as well.

"We have a problem," North said, "and I'd like your advice on how to proceed."

The discussion continued for a long time.

Candi's suggestion that they feed McTierney into the breach so he could understand how it worked was not taken seriously, but at the end of three hours nothing productive had emerged.

"McTierney is a fool, but a fool to be reckoned with," Mark said. "He's entirely dedicated to self-aggrandisement and the preservation of his political career. If it were only him, I think there might be a way forward, but if others have got wind of things—if the Greens have gotten hold of it—we are in serious trouble. Perhaps your CEO could speak to him."

"Or you could assassinate him," said Candi, not very helpfully. "Bury him under some cows and say he ran off with a bimbo he was having an affair with. He's been married so often everyone will believe it."

The suggestion was met with silence.

Peter North looked extremely uncomfortable. "I don't think GPC was involved in that dreadful business," he said. "The company has enemies, some of whom are very serious. If they thought we were on to a new method of power generation worth billions of dollars on the open market, they might want to remove the people who drove the technology. That's you two. I prefer to think that's the truth. I really hope that's the truth."

Candi snapped back at him. "That makes so much more sense. Some rival company learns we're redundant and tries to kill us, but now they know we're not so they leave us alone."

"Yes," Mark said, with much the same voice. "That makes perfect sense – the more indispensable we become the safer we are. So very understanding of your unprincipled competitors."

North looked even more uncomfortable.

"I will have to contact Jenner regarding this development," North said. "And I really don't know how GPC will react to the news. I'm very apprehensive. Shall we go for a stroll among the gum trees? It's very hot in here."

It wasn't.

They left the office and went down to the border of the property. A slight breeze rippled through the leaves above their heads. It was chillingly cold, but none of them noticed it.

North turned to Mark. "If we wanted to shut it down, could it be done?"

"I may have some ideas on the subject," Mark said, "but no means of implementing them."

"What do you need to shut down the breach?"

"Are you serious? You want to shut it down?" Candi's voice was edged with anger. "You are full of the bullshit. We say one word about closing the breach, and tomorrow another bullet comes and some more cows get buried." She picked up a stone and hurled it towards a fence post. It was a good shot.

Anxiety written all over his face, North turned to her. "I beg you to believe that I had nothing whatsoever to do with the people who tried to kill you. I want to believe the company had nothing to do with it either, but regardless, I have doubled the security around here to protect you. I need you to believe something. The breach frightens the life out of me. It frightened the life out of me the first second I saw it. I was a fool not to have written to the directors immediately, but let me tell you, I have done so many times since. I've told them how dangerous it is and begged them to let me investigate safety measures. They're taking no notice at all. This whole thing is Jenner's pet project, and he's determined not to have egg on his face. Now I don't know what to do.

The company is putting pressure on me to recommence operations. I can only hold out for a short time. Soon they will order me to use the radioactive waste and produce real power. If I don't comply, they will send someone else who will."

"How nice," Candi said, picking up another stone. "Things just keep on getting better, don't they?"

"Let me ask you again, Mark," North said, "If you had the appropriate resources, do you think you could shut it down?"

Mark thought for a long while before answering. He was in a dilemma. Should he speak to North about Dekker? But then, Dekker had offered no help so far. Then there was the solution he had proposed. North might want to shut down the breach, but he might not go along with the consequences of using the Mark Chambers shutdown method. There were personal reasons why he did not want to open his mind to anyone except Dekker. His suggestion was so tenuous, so much a clutching at straws.

There was another reason, too. He was afraid. There had to be another answer, he told himself. But what if there wasn't? What if his theory was adopted and it turned out he was wrong? The world wouldn't get another chance. The possibility scared him silly. He couldn't tell Candi. Besides, his one and only straw was so far incapable of being obtained.

He spoke deliberately and carefully. "Let me say that there are people working on a possible solution, but they have not come up with anything practical yet. I don't think the company would approve of the discussions taking place. The most helpful thing we could do would be to keep your management in the dark as to their existence and stall for as long as possible."

"I understand what you're saying," North said. "I'll do my best."

Mark continued. "There's another problem I think you should know about. The breach is demanding more water to stop it from eating the injection end cap. In a month, the garden tap will be fully on. This makes the situation worse, of course. I'm afraid there's more. I've drawn a graph of the power output versus injection demand. You needn't worry about producing power again. In two months, we'll be back to around one hundred megawatts. In six months, we will be producing twice that amount of power just to keep the breach contained.

"Perhaps that will suffice to quieten McTierney," said North.

"I don't think so. By then, the matter will be public knowledge."

"Why?" Candi and North spoke together.

"Because by then the pressure on the cauldron will have ruptured the outer sphere. So you see, Candi is right. Things just keep getting better. If you feed radioactive material into the breach, this period will get shorter. It's a matter of closing the breach or close the Earth. Sorry to be a party pooper."

They walked back to the lab in complete silence.

Feeling ill, Candi found Mark's arm and hung onto it for support.

North was a hairbreadth away from total panic.

# CHAPTER 35

**M**cTierney had not been idle. He believed that when you are threatened, you should attack. That simple rule of life had always stood him in good stead. He believed in coming out of your corner with guns blazing.

The Greens weren't going to deprive him of the glory of kicking the stuffing out of this Global Power Consortium. Perhaps GPC could be encouraged to contribute to his favourite charity if he turned the heat up sufficiently.

Chuckling at his own joke, he phoned Peter North. "I'm coming on an inspection tour of your nuclear facility. Don't try to stuff me around with bullshit when I come. When would be a particularly inconvenient time?"

"Why not next week—Monday would be good?"

"I'll be there tomorrow. Early. Don't stop looking for another job." He hung up the phone in North's ear.

At that very instant, Candi and Mark were passing his office door while heading down the corridor on their way to lunch at Café L'Amoré. North called them in. "McTierney is coming tomorrow," he said. "He's hell-bent on proving that we're running a nuclear power plant. I don't know what's worse, making him think we are, or letting him find out the truth. Got any ideas?"

"Leave him to moi," Candi said. "Don't give it another thought. By tomorrow afternoon, you will be able to relax."

"You're not going to feed him into the breach, are you?" asked Mark. "I know you wanted to."

"Of course not, silly. I would never do anything like that. I'm going to throw him into one of the holding ponds." She looked from one astounded face to the other and laughed. "A joke, yes?"

North relaxed. In his short experience with Candi, he had learned that she was capable of pretty well anything that took her fancy. Throwing McTierney into a thirty-metre-deep pool of radioactive waste seemed to fit perfectly with what she thought of the man.

He smiled at her—mostly out of relief. "Well, that's good to hear. Just what awful fate did you have in mind for him?"

"Patience. Tomorrow you will see how I manage Mr. Slime McTierney."

"He's a fairly nasty customer," said Mark.

"Oui, but he is also a man. I know men."

Twenty minutes later, Mark and Candi were at their usual table in Café L'Amoré. The coffee arrived with the complimentary tray of biscuits, chocolate coated with a chocolate and hazelnut filling. Between the folds of the napkin on the tray they found the compact flash cards they had left after the previous visit.

Candi discreetly and carefully palmed them with her left hand. "You or me this time?"

"I'll do it," Mark said. "Still think we should keep Daniel in the dark about what happened to us?"

"Oui, this news will worry him enough."

Mark took the card from Candi, inserted it into his laptop, and encoded a picture. It contained a simple message:

> *running on water*
> *only two months left b4 containment lost*
> *advice v urgent*
> *repeat v urgent*
> *M*

A short time later, Lee Philips came through the door and went over to Alan Todd, who was serving behind the counter. He waved at Mark and Candi before the two men disappeared out the back toward the store room. They left the coffee making to Abby and a server they had not seen before.

Alan typed a few numbers on a small keypad and opened the door. Bulk supplies of coffee, tea, and the like were piled high on shelves next to a large refrigerator. Further in, there was a long desk that functioned as Todd's office. Two large computer monitors dominated the loose array of papers and invoices. A couple of computer towers rested on the floor underneath the table, along with quite a lot of other gear connected by a web of cables. A casual visitor might have wondered why such a lot of computing power was necessary to run the business end of a small café.

Lee was not a casual visitor. "You want to see me?"

"There have been developments. Our two young scientists are talking to Dekker again. He has just replied. I believe there is cause for serious concern."

Todd sat at the keyboard. The printer chattered. He tore the sheet off and presented it to Lee.

It read:

> Berkeley out of running
> Fermi not enough grunt
> CERN only hope
> Pray
> D

"How do you get this stuff?" Lee asked. "Are they sending this in plain language? Is all the world listening?"

"Trust," Todd said. "It's so beautiful. They trust me with their compact flash cards. On the cards is a program that encrypts and decrypts the pictures containing these messages. I've had a little play with it. Whenever they load and run that program, they load something else as well—a little routine that grabs hold of their wireless hardware and logs it on to our secure network. The wonderful world outside doesn't even know they're logged on."

"Is there anyone listening in this wonderful world outside?"

"Oh, yeah, oh yeah. Two of them. They must be somewhere close. They take turns wandering around my system and poking their noses into certain files."

"Isn't that rather a risk?" Lee asked.

"Think about it," Todd replied. "They need to see something, or they become suspicious. If they become suspicious, they may take it into their heads to do something stupid. So we give our interested friends things to see, to ponder over. They look, they find what I want them to find. I've created files that look like images of Chambers's and Leblanc's laptops. They're always sniffing though them. Sometimes they find spreadsheets and letters that look interesting. It keeps them amused and occupied. I keep them happy. A happy agent is a careless agent."

"What happens if they try to pull off another Back Alley stunt?"

"I don't think they'll do that, but just in case you haven't noticed," Todd chuckled, "I have a new girl, Claire. She's very good at taking care of unwanted guests."

"What do you want me to do with this?" Lee waved the paper in his hand.

"I think you should pass it on to your boss. He has been talking to mine, apparently. Some sort of combined effort may be needed if we're going to handle this properly. I have no idea what this message means, but it has an unpleasant ring to it, doesn't it?"

"Indeed it does," Lee said. "I'll pass it on straight away. Better get back to the station. Don't want anyone getting suspicious, do we?"

They returned to the café, Todd carefully shutting the door of the storeroom behind him. He went over to the new girl and supervised her sad attempts at being a barista. "You brew about thirty mills, not half a cup. If you do that, the coffee will be very acidic and unpleasant. You're not very good at this, are you?"

For an answer, Claire lifted up her apron. Underneath, nestled away in a holster, was a Beretta. "I'm extra good with this. How about you make the coffee and I collect the special biscuits on the tray after they've finished with them?"

At their table, Mark had already decoded the message. He looked grey with worry.

"What does that mean?" Candi asked him. "What are they trying to do?"

Mark answered, "They're trying to construct some material that will remove every last trace of matter travelling through the boson we have created. I think this will close the breach. The physics is complicated."

"Don't patronise me!" Candi said loudly. "What are they trying to make? What do Berkeley, Fermi Labs, and CERN have in common— wait a minute! They all have accelerators! That's it, isn't it?"

"That's it," he said. "You need a powerful accelerator to make what we need."

"And what do we need? You tell Candi, yes?"

"Better not. It's not safe if too many people know."

Candi's eyes flared at him. "You don't trust me, do you? I thought we were friends."

"This has nothing to do with trust and everything to do with safety," he explained as calmly as possible. "Candi, I believe this is the only solution. Daniel and company must think it is, too, or they wouldn't be risking such expensive gear to put it into practice. If this fails, we're really done for. Please believe that!"

"You could at least tell me," she said. "You think I don't understand, or that I'm a security risk. That's so unfair!" She turned away from the laptop screen and studied the menu, muttering something that could have been in French, but might not have been.

Abby, seeing Candi staring intently at the menu, came over to their table. "Are you ready to order now? Was the coffee good?"

"Coffee was like drinking acid. Who's the new girl? Does she enjoy poisoning the patrons?" Candi snapped at the poor girl.

"That's Claire," Abby replied, and then added in a confidential tone, "She's one of those girls out on parole, you know, doing useful community service. We try to give her a break. Alan's doing his best. The béchamel lasagne is excellent. I made it. There's a bottle of wine under the counter with your name on it if you don't make it too obvious. I can bring it in coffee mugs. No one will ever know. It will take away the taste of the dreadful coffee."

Mark laughed. "We'd love to try your lasagne, Abby, but I'm not sure about the wine at this time of day. I would just go to sleep. Candi can have some if she wants."

"Oui, cherie," Candi replied. "Bring me two big mugs so I go to sleep and don't have to listen to this physicist telling me I'm stupid."

Unsure of how to respond to that remark, Abby retreated.. The lasagne turned up a short time later with two mugs of liquid that was dark in colour and did not smell like coffee at all. The meal was excellent.

Mellowed by a second mug of liquid, Candi turned to Mark and gave him one of her most beguiling smiles. "You forgive Candi? I say things I don't mean when I get cross. It's better you don't tell me. If something happened, I'd be a big coward. I would tell, I know I would."

Mark reached out toward her, and in his usual way, gave her hand a squeeze. "Thanks. I'm very anxious, Candi. The odds just got much worse. I fear we might not make it in time. I've no idea how Dekker is going to get the stuff out to us, even if he manages to make it."

He glanced around the cafe. "Look. It's so normal, isn't it? People going about their business, doing their shopping, enjoying the sun, making love, and the world hangs on a knife's edge. Even my dreams are haunted by it. I don't know what I would do if the breach got loose."

Candi thought for a little while in silence. "I know what I would do. Shall I tell you? I would drive down the highway to Nowra and then out to Point Perpendicular. I would wait until evening, and hope there was a moon. I would take off all my clothes and stand on the edge of the precipice above the sea, and feel the wind over my face and my breasts and my back and in my hair. I look down and see the moonlight shining off the silver surf, and I say 'This is beautiful. I am content.' Then I tip myself gently forward and glide down into the sea. I sense just the wind over my body, the joy of being weightless. I put my head down, and then I am no more. It is so quick, this end, so painless. That is what I do. Oblivion swallows Candi forever. I go back to the Earth I come from, then the breach takes my elements into another world, but I do not feel and I do not fear anymore."

There were tears in her eyes. Mark longed to hold her and tell her it would never happen, but he knew his words were empty. Instead, he reached out for her hand. Candi took it in her own and pressed it against her tears. "Come with me, Mark, dying together is better than dying alone. I don't want to die alone!" She held his hand against her face for a long time.

# CHAPTER 36

Four hours beforehand, Dekker; Sam Treadwell, chief engineer of the high energy accelerator; and Laurie Hadfield were standing amidst the ruins of the Berkeley instrument. One of the feeds off the main accelerator line was only half as long as it should have been. The superconducting magnet assembly and cryogenically cooled feed tube ended abruptly in a ring of jagged metal. Holes were blasted in the walls and the floor of the containment tunnel. In other places, molten metal had solidified onto the concrete. The place reeked of burning plastic.

Dekker, the last person to arrive on the scene, shook his head. "Laurie, I'm so sorry. What happened?"

Sam replied angrily. "Bloody sabotage! A small explosive device detonated against the accelerator feed. Disaster! Magnetic field collapsed, and about ten milligrams of product went straight through the wall. You can see the result. Spiked the high voltage supply, took out the generator, and damaged most of the control electronics. Bloody disaster!"

Dekker looked aghast. "What? Are you sure?"

"No doubt about it." Laurie's voice reflected the anxiety he was feeling. "Millions of dollars down the toilet, and one of our security guards is in hospital with serious head injuries! Our security was slack as all hell. Why didn't you warn us, Daniel?"

"Warn you? How the hell was I to know they'd stoop to this madness? Damn GPC! Madness!" Dekker almost spat the words. His fists were clenched, and he felt himself shaking with rage. "There's a damn mole in the system. How else could they have found out? Not even Mark or Candi knew we were doing this. The mole must be here, someone close to one of us. Damn GPC to hell!"

Laurie shook his head with worry. "You've no idea how difficult this is going to be to explain!"

"Tell them it was terrorists," Dekker snapped. "That's what they are, bloody terrorists! Tell the university it won't cost them a cent. The Kilraen Group has agreed to underwrite all losses. I have an arrangement with Andrew Kilraen."

"That will help a lot," Laurie muttered. "Money's all the administration cares about these days."

"This will take a year to repair. We're out of the running!" Sam groaned and ran his hand through his hair. "We had at least two hundred milligrams of the stuff. Now look at it! Insanity. Raving insanity!"

"Was the bottle damaged?" There was an edge to Dekker's voice.

Laurie turned away from Dekker and stared at the floor. "I … I'm afraid it's bad news. It appears the voltage spike has done considerable damage."

"Meaning?" Dekker was close to screaming.

"One of the on-board computers has been destroyed along with its monitoring hardware. The other one which handles the magnetic potential well may be damaged as well, we don't know at this stage."

"Replace them! How long will it take?"

"Several days, I think, and that's if the interface is still intact. I'm sorry, Daniel. I've already placed the calls. We have to check the remaining computer too. One small hiccup and the bottle turns into a small atomic bomb. We're doing all we can. It's up to CERN now, or Fermi Labs, but I don't think they'll come at it after what's happened here." Sam sounded as desperate as he felt.

Laurie turned to Dekker, his brow wrinkled with consternation. "We've tripled security on the accelerator building. Small point now. Oh, and I've ordered personal security for you. When I ran up to you the other evening there was someone else directly behind you. When he saw me, he ran off. Thought it was a student then, but now I'm not at all sure. You're a key player in all this, Daniel. GPC must know that."

"We must reconvene with the others. I'm so dog tired." Dekker rubbed his eyes with his hands and continued. "Here isn't safe any longer. I'll spirit myself away to the Hague, and we'll meet there. We'll contact every member of the think tank personally. No emails or phone calls. We don't know who to trust anymore."

"You'll let our friends in Australia know?" Sam flicked a piece of metal out of the wall with his fingers.

"Not on your life!" Dekker shook his head. "They've got enough to put up with without being worried about what's happened here! I'll just say Berkeley is out of the running. "

"Besides," Laurie said, "our communication method might have been compromised."

"No," said Dekker, "Neither of them knew where I was or what we were doing. As I said, we have a mole close to the think tank. From now on, we have to be far more careful. The odds just got much longer, gentlemen. May God help us!"

"Amen to that," Laurie said with fervour.

# CHAPTER 37

Early the next morning, Candi arrived at the office wearing a black designer dress instead of her usual casual outfits. It was obvious, Mark thought as he looked her up and down, that the poor man who made it must have had very little material to work with.

McTierney arrived half an hour later.

Candi went out to meet him, carrying two drinking glasses in her hand. She approached him slowly, moving her hips slightly from side to side, an angelically innocent smile on her attractive face. "Good morning, Senator McTierney."

McTierney's attention was captured immediately. "Skip the pleasantries. Show me the reactor."

"But of course," she purred. "You're a clever man. You work out we're using nuclear processes here, even though others tell you different things."

"Of course I bloody well know what you're doing here."

"But the nuclear process we're running here is not the fission process you may think it is. May I demonstrate?"

"And who are you?" he snapped out his question.

"Dr. Leblanc at your service." She smiled another angelic smile, her eyes open wide with innocence. "Please, would you call me Candice?"

"Okay, Candice. Where do we begin?"

"Outside this door, Monsieur, if you will follow me, please?"

McTierney followed. He was enjoying the scenery, if not the tour. Candi took him to the place just outside the front door where the hose feeding the breach was attached to its tap.

She turned her back on him, and, bending down low, filled one of the glasses from the other tap on the stem. "Senator, please hold this glass?"

McTierney took the glass. What was coming next? Candi turned her back on him again and bent down to fill the second glass, giving McTierney another opportunity to exercise his private fantasies.

She stood up and stretched out her arm, a full glass in her hand. "Voilà! Senator, we have a glass each, yes? Now we drink!"

"Just what makes you think I appreciate tap water? You might have at least tried champagne."

"But that will be later. I must convince you that this is water, clean and fresh. That is why you drink, yes?"

"If you insist." McTierney swallowed half a glass. He threw the rest on the grass. "Okay, it's water. So?"

"Follow the hose with me, please."

Candi led him along the hose, inside the lab, and up to the injection port where the hose joined the metal pipe that led, via the regulator valve, into the inner sphere and the breach.

"You can see the water pours into this chamber. We are using this water to make the energy that drives the power station. Inside this chamber is a quantum nuclear particle bridge. The physics is very complicated—we do not understand it perfectly ourselves, but the water injected through this pipe is broken down into atoms, and these atoms are accelerated to high speeds. They give off energy. The energy is collected in this chamber and transferred to water circulating around it. The water is heated up. It travels in that pipe," she pointed upwards, "to the generator building over there."

McTierney was not convinced. "Are you telling me you're generating all that energy from tap water? No, I don't believe it!"

"We can use anything—water, nuclear waste, sewage—anything nobody wants. It doesn't matter. The heavier the nuclei in the waste, the more energy will be generated. The material that goes in travels through the bridge and ends up in super symmetrical particles we cannot detect. For all practical purposes, it vanishes. It is good, no?"

"Is rubbish, yes," McTierney declared. "This tap, it cuts off the water, does it?"

"It regulates the water going into the converter." She gave a little uncertain smile as though she was hiding something and stepped away slightly. "It's so very important that we do not to shut off the flow—"

McTierney reached in front of her and shut the inlet port off. "Like the flow is shut off now."

Before Candi could answer, the breakers in the switching yard opened with a loud crack. Warning lights flashed and bells sounded.

McTierney looked alarmed. "What's going on?"

"You've just shut down the feed, so the converter has stopped producing heat. The turbines have slowed down and the generators have gone off line. That was the sound of the breakers jumping open."

An engineer from the generator building came flying in through the door. "What the blazes is going on? We've lost pressure! The turbines are running down! You know how difficult it is to regulate them up to speed again!"

So sorry," Candi replied. "I closed the port by mistake. Here," She opened the valve fully. "We have flow again. The turbines should come up to speed now. Sorry again for the trouble."

McTierney looked dumbfounded. "So it's true! This is fantastic! You've cracked onto a gold mine! But the information you sent out in your press release read like gobbledygook!"

"But not to clever people like you, I'm sure. The process is very new, and as you can see, it's the answer to the world's energy needs. We have to be very careful that our competitors don't steal our ideas before we can patent them. You understand?"

She looped her arm around his and guided him towards her office. "Now we have the champagne. We will enjoy together!"

McTierney, believing totally in his superior ability to read the simple minds of women perfectly, was eager to further the direction this one appeared to be taking him in. "That would be very nice. Where's North lurking? And that mate of yours, what's his name?"

"Dr. Chambers. He is around somewhere. Mr. North is in the generator room. Are you convinced this is not a nuclear fission plant?"

"Yeah, I guess so," McTierney said. "But you're reneging on your agreement to use up the radioactive waste. You'd better connect that pipe to the holding ponds pretty quick if you want the Greens off your back. They can do a lot of damage to a company that's trying to keep a new process quiet while they get the paperwork right."

Candi hugged his arm. She turned and ushered him to her office while making sure that McTierney could appreciate the attributes her designer dress allowed her to share so generously with the world. When they arrived, she pushed him into a chair, opened the bottle of champagne sitting in a tub of ice, and poured them each a generous glass. They drank.

McTierney leaned back in his chair.

Candi sat on the table next to him with her crossed legs dangling deliciously in front of his face. "Is good, yes?"

"Yeah, it's real nice. Say, I'm staying at the Camden Motor Inn tonight. How about we have dinner and then you come to my room. We could watch a movie together or something. I think we have chemistry."

"But yes," she replied. "Of course, we have the chemistry! But I ring Roger first."

"Who's Roger?"

"My lover. See, I have his picture in my purse." She extracted her purse from a drawer in the desk and opened it. There was a picture of Roger with one of his tree-trunk arms around Candi's waist.

McTierney stared at it. "Is that Roger Gaunt, the guy who plays for Wests?"

"Oui. He is handsome, yes? A lovely man, but such a dreadful temper. It's not good to be so jealous. It gets him into so many unnecessary fights."

"Why don't we just not tell him?"

The excited expression on her face changed to a worried one. "But Roger is expecting me home. It is no problem. I will phone him and tell him I have been invited to have dinner with Senator McTierney and watch a movie in his motel room. It will be all right. Roger is very understanding."

"I'm sure he is." McTierney's mind recalled the picture of Roger Gaunt. He could imagine one of those massive fists heading in his direction powered by one of those tree-trunk arms and thought it best to avoid the experience. Besides, football players were close to God when it came to the public. A one-night stand with his obviously willing girlfriend might lead to lots of bad publicity.

His third marriage was already heading for the rocks. Something like this might make the bitch want to pull the plug, and then there would be all that nasty business with dividing property and alimony for their daughter, Patience.

McTierney decided that in this case, the pleasure wasn't worth the possible pain and inconvenience. "Look, perhaps you'd better not. Second thoughts, I have some business in Sydney I have to take care of this afternoon. Sorry about the offer."

Candi put on her sorrowful angel face. "We will never know if we had chemistry now, will we? Have you had a good visit? Would you like some more champagne?"

"I've had a good visit, but you better tell North that the waste goes into the converter or there will be trouble. Okay?"

"But of course. Do you wish to go now?"

Holding him by the arm, Candi escorted him out to his BMW and waved "goodbye" as he drove out towards the boom gate.

Mark and Peter had watched him go. They were waiting impatiently in her office when she returned.

"Yetch! I have to have the shower," Candi said. "The creature was smearing his eyes all over my body! Do you know he even gives me the proposition! 'Come to my room' he says! We have chemistry, he says. We have chemistry all right. He is the rat and I am the strychnine. Next time I put it in his champagne!"

"Err, Candi, how did it go?" Mark thought it wise to interrupt the flow of Candi's thoughts.

She smiled triumphantly at them both. "Perfectly! Of course it went perfectly! What did I tell you? Men like him are so easy."

Only later would she tell them about the business of reconnecting the waste feed. She bounced out of the room to the sound of male praise.

McTierney phoned Ms. Carson-Jones as he drove along the Hume Highway towards Sydney. He couldn't wait until he arrived in the office. "McTierney here. I just thought I should let you know I've been out to the power plant in Camden. They're going to reconnect the feed tomorrow. The waste is going to disappear as planned."

"But they're running a nuclear reactor in your electorate!"

"Yeah, why don't you go into print about that?" McTierney suggested. "Take the lead. Make a fuss. Raise questions in parliament like you wanted to. I think you should. This is the Green's big moment. Far from me to steal your thunder."

"You want the Greens to raise the issue?"

"Yeah. Get right on it. Ring the papers."

"Aren't you going to support our case?"

"Clever, powerful people like you don't need my support." He rang off.

Ms. Carson-Jones turned to Sandy, her personal assistant. "It's not a nuclear power plant," she said. "Cancel the press release. Cancel all action. We don't want to make fools of ourselves."

Later on that day, Peter received a phone call from Jenner. He called Candi and Mark into his office. "The gavel has fallen, I'm afraid. Either we reconnect the waste line, or I'm out of a job. They'll send someone else. I don't want to sound indispensable, but you could get someone much worse than me running this place."

"There's not a chance we can hold out a bit longer? Any length of time would help." The expression on Mark's face said it all.

"I will reconnect on Monday. We will try to keep the flow as small as possible. I can't do anything else. If they send someone else, he'll insist the flow go right up to maximum, and remember, he won't have seen the breach, so he won't worry about it in the least."

They went into Camden for lunch and Mark sent another message to Dekker.

*RA Feed reconnect Monday*
*Best estimate three weeks*
*God help us*
*M*

# Chapter 38

The atmosphere inside the Colloquium Room was tense indeed. The hour was late. Seldom would you find a gathering of such eminent physicists at any university, and such a gathering had never before taken place at the Radboud University of Nijmegen in the Netherlands.

Hearing a small beep from his laptop on the table, Dekker put down the sheet of paper he had been reading, decoded the picture, and read the message Mark and Candi had sent. Fear and apprehension gripped him round the heart. He looked across the table at Hans Zimmerman. The other physicists from CERN were silent.

"We have three weeks, gentlemen," Dekker announced. "If we cannot produce the material in that time, catastrophe will ensue. What chance have we got?"

Klaus Obermayer answered, "If we began tonight, it would take most of that time. We would pump the material continuously into the bottle and allow it to accumulate there, relying on the bottle's own magnetic potential well to store the material safely. The energy demands are going to be quite enormous. I'm uncertain if the Swiss grid will be able to sustain them. A power failure at the wrong time—" He shook his head.

"We have no choice, learned colleagues." Zimmerman continued. "We are the last hope. We have the biggest accelerator. If we do not attempt this, then no one will. We know what that will lead to."

Laurie Hadfield removed his glasses and rubbed the bridge of his nose. "I'm afraid there remains a problem with the bottle itself. The damage was extensive. The superconductors generating the magnetic potential well are not functioning properly. Sam and his team have been working around the clock, but ..." His voice trailed off into silence.

"But what, Laurie?" Dekker shut the lid of his laptop with a snap. "What's the delay? Sam said twenty-four hours!"

"We tested the bottle on the large hadron collider yesterday. We sent a small amount of material into it. The well didn't hold. I'm afraid we did more damage." Laurie shook his head wearily. "Sam thinks we might have to rebuild the whole thing."

"How long will that take?"

"A week." Laurie's voice was far from steady. "I'm sorry."

"A week!" Dekker exploded. "We don't have a week! Get some more people working on the damn thing!"

"We've got everyone we can working twenty-four seven. Repairing the bottle is still the best alternative. Sam thinks he can replace some of the damaged superconductors."

Dekker groaned. "Klaus, how long can we delay connection?"

Klaus Obermayer replaced his glasses, plucked a pen out of his pocket, and began scribbling on the pad in front of him, occasionally punching numbers into his calculator. After a short time, he threw his glasses on the table and lay back in his chair. The apprehension in the room was almost tangible. He gave a sigh.

"Twenty-four hours. Not one minute more. If we cannot begin then, we do not begin at all. I remind you, if the Chambers's solution is correct, providing less than the minimum quantity will be tantamount to initiating the destruction of the world ourselves."

"God help us!" Dekker's voice was thick with emotion. The fear on every face was palpable.

Hans broke the long silence. "God help us all," he said quietly.

# CHAPTER 39

On Monday, they reconnected the nuclear waste feed. Power production rose to one hundred twenty megawatts.

After supervising the changeover, Mark disappeared. Lunchtime arrived, and still there was no sign of him.

Candi became anxious. After a long search, she found him under a gum tree near the border, his head cradled in his hands. "Do you know how worried I was?" She scolded. "What are you doing here?"

"I'm praying," he said. "When they reconnected, I had to get away from the place. Candi, we're caught in some inexorable spiral towards annihilation. We know the consequences of our actions, but we still do them. We carry on as though we were in control of our lives. We kowtow to political power, play games, seduce fools, and live for pleasure today without thought of tomorrow. We shuffle deck chairs on the *Titanic* and pretend we're masters of our own destiny. Yet all the while, the clock ticks on toward the end prepared for us."

"The glass is really half-empty today isn't it?"

"The glass has been drained of almost all hope."

"How can you say that?" Candi asked. "You tell me your God does not end the world this way. Have you made the mistake? Perhaps He is fading, becoming a little less omnipotent? Fading into the mist? You are a brilliant physicist, Mark. I trust your brain much more than I trust your God!"

"My God is still God, Candi," he said, "even if the world ends. I haven't lost hope in God, rather I've lost hope for something else. The time is coming when my faith will be put to the test. It's me who is fading, Candi. I had hoped it would not be this way, that some other solution would be found. Now I have no way out. If Daniel succeeds, then I must follow through. If I'm wrong, the world ends. Now that I have to act on my faith, I find I have no courage. Dear God, help me!"

"What is this you are talking about?" she asked. "What is this following through? It's nonsense you talk. I believe in your solution. Daniel will come through, you will close the breach, and it will be as you say—the world will not end. You mustn't give up, Mark. I am relying on you—we are all relying on you."

She knelt down beside him and put her arms around his shoulders and her cheek against his head, rocking him a little side to side. "You are a brave man, Mark. I believe in you. I admire your faith. Sometimes I wish it was mine."

She kissed him on the cheek. "It's lunchtime. You need some food. Come on, my turn to buy. How about some Indian today?"

She stood up beside him, took his arm, and pulled him to his feet, smiling encouragingly into his upturned face.

For just a second their eyes met.

Candi felt her own being held, drawn through those blue portals into the depths of his heart. In an instant she was overwhelmed by the extraordinary and irrational certainty that he loved her—loved her so deeply that it caused her own heart to falter then thump hard in her chest.

So many times she had heard those words. So many men had said they loved her, yet this silence was more captivating of certainty. Here was love of a different kind, a different quality, for which she had no name.

The moment passed.

"Nonsense," Candi said to herself, shaking her head as if to banish the idea. She was not in love with him. That was certain. She didn't want him to be in love with her. Besides, love was not declared by a pair of blue eyes.

I must get a grip, she thought. It was the tension, that was all.

A soft breeze ruffled the gum leaves above her head, and there was Mark standing by her side looking out over the fields, not even holding her hand.

How could she think he was in love with her? Love was expressed in other ways, in the heat of passion, in whispered promises, even though they turned out to be empty.

They set off towards the car park. Candi suddenly felt Mark's hand take possession of her own. A fleeting anxiety, sponsored by her recent thoughts gripped her, yet rather than pull her hand away she felt her fingers involuntarily curl around his and hold them tightly against her palm.

She turned around to face him—unsure of her own heart.

His eyes were looking at her the same way, and once again she felt the same thumping in her chest. "He needs me," she thought to herself, and almost simultaneously, "and I need him."

She stopped walking, turned round and stood directly in his path.

The next second, she felt his arms around her, holding her close, and Candi, still controlled by some force she could not explain, wrapped her arms around his shoulders.

For a long time they clung silently to one another, content for their embrace to express the feelings their words would not allow.

Candi reached up and kissed him softly on the cheek. And so their embrace ended, but in the years to come those feelings would return, and her heart would falter in exactly the same way.

# CHAPTER 40

Sam Treadwell and Hans Zimmerman stood one hundred seventy-five metres beneath the Franco-Switzerland boarder in the twenty-seven-kilometre-long circular tunnel containing the large hadron collider.

Not far away from port three rested the bottle, from which a number of cables protruded. Klaus Obermayer and Daniel Van Dekker, who had just descended from the surface, ran along the service pathway to join them.

"You've finished it?" Dekker sounded breathless.

"The magnetic potential well is operational," Sam replied, his voice lacking the expected enthusiasm.

"Magnificent job! And only twenty-two hours!" Dekker laughed, "We have time on our hands!"

"Not exactly." The tone in Zimmerman's voice extinguished the smile on Dekker's face.

"What ... what do you mean?"

Zimmerman reached out and gripped Dekker's arm. "Daniel, I'm sorry. Sam has almost worked a miracle, but it's not finished. That's what we need to talk to you about."

"Not finished?!"

"The computer system controlling the magnetic potential well in which we store the material is working perfectly. The other computer, the one that handles the breach monitor and delayed triggering—cannot be repaired in time."

Dekker's face turned grey. He clutched at the service railing to prevent himself from falling. After regaining his composure, he spoke. "But surely, you must be able to jerry-rig something! You know what you're asking me to do? What you're asking Mark Chambers to do?"

"We can continue working on the triggering computer if you wish, but it will take time." Sam ran his hand through his hair. "At least another twenty-four hours, possibly more. The motherboard has been replaced, but there are still problems with the hardware interface, and the power supply. When we start up the second computer, the magnetic potential well becomes unstable. We're not sure why."

Dekker turned to Klaus. "Can we afford to delay another twenty-four hours?"

Klaus Obermayer said nothing. He didn't have to. The look on his face was enough.

"It's your call, Daniel," Zimmerman said, removing his glasses and wiping his forehead. "We can delay, but the chances of accumulating the minimum quantity are not good. We have calculated on a maximum rate of production in any case, and we may not even be able to achieve that."

"Could we work on the bottle when it's connected to the port? While it's accumulating the material?" Dekker knew he was clutching at straws.

"It would be madness to try." Sam's face reflected the fear in his voice. "If the well collapsed, it would destroy the collider, as well as the bottle. Our last and only attempt—gone. Good-bye world."

Cradling his head in his hands, Dekker groaned loudly and bent over the railing. No man should have to make this sort of decision, he thought to himself. He did not have the right—no man had the right.

Suddenly he stood upright with fierce determination on his face. "I'll do it myself. When the bottle goes to Australia, I'll be the one who goes with it." He looked desperately towards the other men. "I beg you not to tell Jasmin until it's all over. I charge you to take care of her, to—"

"No, Daniel." Obermayer spoke softly but firmly. "We have talked at length. If this attempt fails, if the Chambers solution is incorrect—then while we live, we must seek another. We cannot leave billions of people to perish without trying again."

"Of course you'll try again! I would expect, demand, you try again!" Dekker thrust his arms out towards them. "You're the best the world has!"

"No, Daniel. We are all agreed. Without you, the chances of finding an alternative diminish substantially. You may be prepared to risk those odds, but we are not." Zimmerman gripped Dekker's arm again. "Besides, if the Chambers solution works, there will be much to do. The men who perpetrated this heinous disaster must be brought to book. You are the one to prosecute that goal, Daniel. You have already begun. You must continue."

Dekker once again buried his head in his hands and groaned loudly. "No! How can I ask another man—a friend—to surrender his life?" That's what you're asking me to do, isn't it? Mark would have to monitor the breach and the vacuum pumps and decide when to trigger the release!"

"Yes," Obermayer said softly. "This decision was not taken lightly."

Dekker scanned the haggard, sorrowful faces of the three men. Sam had tears in his eyes. He knew they had spoken the truth.

Finally, Obermayer broke the long silence with his quiet voice. "Daniel, we need a decision. The final call must be up to you. Sam is willing to bring his team back. They would work without ceasing to bring the trigger computer back on line. Every hour they spent would take us closer to the end of the world."

A full minute ticked by. Dekker cradled his head in his hands. "Connect the bottle," he said, and burst into tears.

# CHAPTER 41

Louis Hakim leaned forward on his plush, leather armchair. On the other side of his mahogany desk sat George Jenner, bearer of bad tidings. His agents had reported in. It was a disturbing report.

"Leblanc and Chambers are still not communicating with Dekker. We knew he was working independently on something. We've found out what."

"So, what is he working on?" Hakim raised his eyebrows and replaced the note he had been reading on his desk.

"He has built a bottle of some sort to contain material only an accelerator can produce. Emile sabotaged their first attempt at Berkeley after he failed to remove Dekker. The material blew half the accelerator to smithereens."

Hakim's face registered surprise. "The material itself, or the detonator Emile planted?"

"The material itself," Jenner said. "This was unclear at first, and we have since confirmed it. Emile's small explosive charge was simply meant to disable the accelerator, not destroy it. It was the material, and at the time of the detonation they hadn't manufactured very much, apparently."

"Disturbing, George. So this material is extremely dangerous. Now I hear they are attempting to make more."

Jenner's forehead beaded sweat again. How Hakim had obtained the information he thought he alone possessed was worrying indeed. He twisted the end of his tie around his fingers and replied, "They are trying again at CERN, not far from here. I believe the experiment has been running for a couple of weeks or more. Dekker has moved to a hotel in Rue du Lac at Geneva. Half an hour ago he was eating in a pizza shop—on the same street. He no doubt intends to send the finished product to our plant in Australia."

"To what end?"

"Why, I would have thought it was obvious," Jenner said. "He plans to employ the material to completely destroy the plant. From what happened at Berkeley, we must assume the material capable of achieving this goal."

"I take it you have organised a similar accident on the collider?"

Jenner slid his fingers around his collar, which suddenly seemed to have become tighter all by itself. "No. Security around the collider has been beefed up enormously. I've heard reports that SND and maybe even others are involved. It's impossible to penetrate, even for the likes of Stern and his team."

"Even more disturbing, George," Hakim said. "Opposition to your pet project has increased dramatically. Perhaps you have grossly underestimated the dangers in the process. I am beginning to believe you have. And what do you recommend in the light of these new developments? Think very carefully. Last time you told me Leblanc and Chambers were surplus to requirements. That proved incorrect."

Jenner removed his tie and opened his collar. "We must eliminate Dekker immediately. Without him, whatever they're making is useless. No doubt he's worked out some method of transporting the material and himself to Australia so he could put it to use. Chambers and Leblanc won't know what to do with it. "

"You're sure we shouldn't let him go ahead and close the quantum bridge?" Hakim asked.

"And destroy everything we've worked for? No way!"

"Everything *you've* worked for, George," Hakim noted. "Once again, you are confident Dekker wants to destroy the plant, as well as close our quantum bridge? I would frame your words carefully."

"Louis, think! How could you close the thing down by blowing it up? Dekker's contemplating an act of terrorism! You have to stop him!" There was a desperate tone in Jenner's voice.

"Very well, George. I suggest you go and have lunch in a public place, and dinner, too, for that matter. I'm sure you're capable of finding company for the rest of the day and evening? That will be all." The tone in Hakim's voice left no room for further discussion.

Jenner left the room feeling ill.

Hakim summoned his secretary. "There are arrangements I want you to make. Get Gustav Stern to ring me immediately."

The bedside phone rang and woke Dekker. He rolled over and looked at his watch. It was 1:00 a.m.

"Dekker here. Who is this?"

"It's Hans. I'll pick you up in ten minutes." He rang off.

Jasmin, woken by the sound, sat up and looked at her husband. "What's happened? What's gone wrong?"

"I don't know. Hans says he wants to see me. I'll have to go, sorry. Don't answer the door for anyone."

"Daniel, you're frightening me again."

"I'm so sorry, my love," Dekker said. "I'm simply taking precautions. Pray that it's good news and nothing has gone wrong with the accelerator. If it has, we're really finished."

"I will, darling. God take care of you."

They kissed. Jasmin followed him to the door and locked it. Returning to her bedside, she knelt down to pray.

Hans drove him in silence to one of the entrances leading down to the large hadron collider. He swiped his security card, and the two of them caught the lift down into the tunnel.

In front of them, Dekker saw his bottle, coupled as it was to port three. It reminded him of a rather oversized washing machine with a short pipe and flange sticking out of one of its sides about two-thirds up from bottom. Wires and hoses came out from under it. There were a lot of people around for that time of the morning. Coolant pumps hummed constantly and control panels displayed a changing array of different coloured lights and illuminated gauges.

"We've done all we can do," Hans said. "We've accumulated two point five grams of material in the bottle. I dare accumulate no more. So far, it's gone well, but if an accident were to happen now—" His voice trailed off into silence.

He continued. "The material is suspended in a magnetic potential well at one point two Kelvin inside the bottle as you know. This will be maintained by the bottle's own internal power supply when we disconnect it. You have no idea how much power has been used from the Swiss grid to do this."

Tears in his eyes, Dekker embraced him. "I cannot begin to thank you, my friend. You have given the world hope, although slim hope it may prove."

However, Hans was not finished. "Daniel, there's another problem you must be aware of. When we disconnect the bottle from the supplies, it must continue to be maintained by its own power source—lithium ion batteries."

"In heaven's name, why?" Dekker asked. "Can't we connect it to another source of power while it's in transit as you did while you were filling it? We planned to do that."

"Unfortunately, not with any safety. The power supply must have been damaged at Berkeley. In the early stages of filling, there was a minor hiccup in the Swiss power grid—and the bottle almost lost containment. Disconnecting and reconnecting an external supply would cause a spike. If there was as much as a murmur in the supply, the computer would hiccup and disrupt the correction field. I don't need to tell you what would happen then. No, right now the batteries are fully charged and the external supply is connected. When you're ready, we will slowly remove the supply and finally the cable, and then the bottle has to stand on its own."

Daniel stared at Hans as if he hadn't heard. The nightmare continued to worsen. "How long with the batteries hold up?"

"We have done many calculations." Hans produced a small piece of paper from his pocket. "They cannot maintain the cryogenic pumps and the computer for more than twenty hours. Even the last few hours will be uncertain."

Dekker smashed his fist into the walkway railing. "It's impossible! There isn't enough time!"

"A commercial jet could reach Australia within that limit."

"A commercial jet, yes. Where's that coming from?! Can you see them agreeing to take this in the hold? I was never going to use a commercial jet. I was going to use the Kilraen Group's aircraft. They don't have the range. There would be fuel stops, and we would have to go carefully. There are only certain airports were we could land without arousing the attention of customs. It would be pushing it to get to Camden in under thirty hours. We'll have to take the risk of connecting an external supply while on board."

"That would almost certainly be disastrous," Hans said, seriously alarmed. "Remember, this bottle is all you have. If it blows, more than one aeroplane will disappear. We've taken huge risks to bring you this stuff. Don't waste our efforts. How long do we have before it's endgame at the plant?"

"Barely three days."

"My God! What are you going to do?"

Dekker shook his head slowly. He had never felt such a deep sense of despair. Against all odds, they had obtained the material Mark requested. But he couldn't deliver it.

His newly found faith in God—the God who cared for the world He had made—was taking a serious battering. "I have absolutely no idea," he said sadly.

Earlier that evening, Emile had strolled along the Rue du Lac watching the twinkling lights reflected in the dark waters of Lake Geneva.

Life was good, he thought, good, but fragile. His profession often brought him face to face with the impermanence of life. All that was needed for life to end was a small bullet hole in the chest or a small knife wound in the neck.

It was late. There were few people about.

He strolled along the lakeside and sat down on one of the pavement seats, apparently at random. Reaching under the seat, he retrieved the package and opened it. He smiled. There was not enough light to see what he held in his hand, but the thickness of the wad told him it probably contained the agreed sum of ten thousand Swiss Francs.

There was no mistaking the Glock pistol and its silencer, presently unattached to the weapon. His employer had thought of everything. Items like this were getting hard to obtain in Switzerland. After pocketing the cash, he attached the silencer and stowed the finished instrument in a holster under his coat.

Keeping in the shadows, he strolled down the Rue du Lac until he was opposite Dekker's hotel. He had memorised his room number. His wife was staying with him, apparently. Unfortunate for her, but he would still stick to the agreed price. Another bullet would not add to the fee.

A car drew up blocking his view of the entrance. Dekker hurried out of the door and into the car before Emile could take a clean shot. He had a revolver, not a rifle. He could miss. In his profession, you did not miss.

He stood still in the doorway opposite. His quarry would return to his wife, Emile felt sure.

Two hours passed before the same car drew up outside the hotel entrance.

# Chapter 42

I t must have happened in the early hours of the morning. At first, the engineers in charge of the generators were delighted, but as the pressure continued to rise, their delight changed gradually to concern.

At one hundred-forty megawatts, close to the capacity of the turbines, they began to route the excess energy directly into the cooling tower. With the evaporator pumps flat out, a plume of steam slowly grew above it, reaching high into the cool early morning air.

They rang Peter North.

The phone call at 5:20 a.m. from North did not find Mark asleep. He stood up from the chair in which he had been dozing for the last three hours and picked up the phone.

"It's Peter. Could you come down to the lab as soon as possible? We have a situation brewing that doesn't look too good."

Mark was glad that the roads were fairly empty at that time of the morning.

In less than ten minutes, he and North were staring at the same pressure gauge

"They're diverting some of the energy directly to the tower," North said, "but it doesn't alter the fact that the pressure in the sphere is way too high."

"What's the waste material feed rate?" Mark asked.

"That's the funny thing—it's gone up too, but we haven't altered the pumps."

Mark went over to the panel monitoring the rate of flow from the radioactive holding ponds. It had increased by twenty percent.

"The breach is sucking the solution in. It's sucking it through the pumps. Check for iron in the breach spectrum."

North ran to the spectrometer attached to the visual port. "There is some, but not a lot. It's difficult to tell because there's so much other muck coming in from the ponds. There might even be some iron in the feedwater. In any case, it's low."

Mark ran into his office and added some numbers to the program he had written. It drew a graph on the screen. The graph showed a line climbing upwards at an ever increasing angle. Some of the line was in red.

"We have eighteen hours, maximum," he said in a solemn tone. "Then the sphere ruptures."

Peter North could feel his throat tightening. He couldn't swallow. Never in his life had he felt so paralysed by fear.

Mark continued. "If you don't disconnect the radioactive waste feed, we're all finished. At least that will buy us some time, but I suspect you will have to find a stronger hose. The breach is likely to try and pump more water in than the tap could normally supply."

Without waiting for North's reaction, he put his hands over his face and prayed out loud.

"Heavenly Father, have mercy on us. We're in desperate need. Send us the solution—I beg you!"

His was not the only "amen" that followed.

Finding the strength to stand and then to run, North tore out of the room bellowing orders. Within the next half hour, clean water was rushing into the breach. Power production resumed at one hundred twenty megawatts. They monitored the flow rate for an hour.

Mark went into his office and did some calculations. Around lunchtime, he visited Peter in his office. "That has bought us more time. Now we have about thirty-six hours."

"Dear God," said North, "help us! Help us or we're finished!"

"What god is that you're praying to?" Mark demanded to know. "The same one who allows you to work for a collection of criminals and enjoy taking home your pay?"

Mark was emotionally exhausted and worried sick. It was around lunchtime, he still hadn't had breakfast, and right now, North's religious pragmatism stuck in his nose like a rusty fork.

North turned toward him. Rage spread over his worried face. It disappeared as suddenly as it had come.

He uttered a great sigh. "You're right. Damn it all, you're right. I've compromised my belief to the point where I've become a practical atheist. I've purged my conscience so many times that it's practically dead. I'm bloody terrified. I've been a bloody fool. You were right. You've always been right. I've tried to make amends—but it's too late. Mark, if there's anything I can do ... I'm not playing the company tune any more. I ..."

Right then, Candi's casually dressed figure framed itself in the doorway. She took one look at Peter and caught her breath. "Mon Dieu, what's happened? Has someone died?"

"Not yet," said Peter, "but don't hold your breath."

"Is that meant to be funny?" Candi snapped back at him.

"We have had a situation," Mark explained briefly.

Candi shuddered. "This tests your faith in that God of yours, yes? If this is one of the last meals I will have, I am going to make it a good one."

Grabbing Mark by the arm, she led him out to the car. On the way, she chatted about nothing in particular, as if all were good and right with the world.

"If only I could lapse into denial so easily," Mark thought to himself. The burden of reality was a truly dreadful one sometimes.

"We have to go to the café first. There might be news from Daniel. Dear God, I hope it's good," he said.

It wasn't.

# CHAPTER 43

Dekker got out of the car, and it pulled away. He noticed the man coming toward him. "Perhaps this is the miracle I've been waiting for," he thought.

"Professor Van Dekker?" Emile strode toward the man, his right hand extended.

"Yes."

Emile's hand whipped into his coat. Now it held a silenced Glock pistol.

Dekker stared uncomprehendingly at his assassin. "No," he thought, this could not be happening, not now, not to him, the singularly and tragically most important person in the human race. If anyone was to survive, it had to be him, or the entire world would follow him into the grave. There was some ghastly mistake. He had to explain.

Yet even as his tongue began to form the words, the gun flashed in the darkness.

Dekker threw himself sideways in a hopeless attempt to dodge the bullet that must already have entered his body, yet so great was his anguish he didn't even feel it.

The gun flashed again, his assassin's face calm and unperturbed, the unfeeling face of a man whose business was death. The pavement was rushing up toward his face far too quickly. His head crashed against it and his sight went out.

His last despairing thought before the blackness took his mind away altogether was that God had chosen to abandon the human race after all—and Dekker didn't even blame Him.

Emile stared at the body on the ground. Something was wrong: the victim was lying face down, but there was no blood oozing out onto the pavement. He released the Glock's magazine to check the rounds.

Then there was movement among the shadows on the other side of the entrance. What next? The dead man was beginning to stir slightly.

Everything was going wrong.

There was a soft noise from the shadow.

Emile staggered back. He felt one bullet enter his own chest, and then another. A man stepped out of the darkness and moved toward them.

Emile collapsed onto the pavement. The impermanence of life had finally caught up with him. It was much more painful than he had expected it to be.

The man continued to advance.

Stunned by the fall and shock, Dekker was still lying on the pavement, wondering why he was alive and whether he would be for long.

The stranger came closer and lifted him onto his feet.

"Is there any other service I can render you, Dr. Van Dekker?" He retrieved Emile's weapon. The magazine was loaded with blanks. He also collected a wad of notes from his pocket.

Dekker stared down at his assassin lying prostrate on the pavement—the red flower of death opening on his chest. His head felt dreadful. The world had suddenly taken on a surreal appearance. He turned groggily round to the stranger who was tucking his own weapon back into its holster after removing the silencer.

"Wer zum Teufel sind Sie?" Dekker asked. *(Who the hell are you?)*

The stranger replied in English. "Johann Kreutzer, Swiss Security Intelligence Service, Professor. A car will arrive shortly. Ah, there it is now. If you would be good enough to accompany me?"

"My wife ... is she ..?"

"Safely in our care. Now, if you would be so good ... here, let me help you."

Steadying Dekker by the arm, Johann opened the door of the car, which had just come into the kerb, and helped him inside. Dekker took out his handkerchief and wiped the blood away from his forehead.

The world still lacked its usual solidity, but from somewhere in his heart sprung a small shimmer of hope. Perhaps God did care for the human race after all.

Ten minutes later, the car turned off the road into an underground car park. It drew to a halt in front of a doorway guarded by several Swiss army officers carrying submachine guns. Dekker was hurried out of the car, down a corridor, and into a lift that descended a good distance and then stopped. The doors opened.

Dekker stared stupefied at the sight that met his eyes. The world had become surreal with a vengeance.

"Good evening, Daniel." Standing in front of a number of people was Professor Sarah Cole.

She stepped forward and grabbed hold of Dekker to prevent him from falling. Together, with the two other men, they almost carried him to a chair next to the table. Someone was holding a glass of water to his lips and someone else was bandaging the wound on his head. Slowly the world began to settle into its usual solid form.

He lay back in the chair and turned his head toward Sarah Cole. "What in heaven's name are you doing here? Just what is going on?"

"These people are doing their best to help you fix the mess you've made. Ross Baker—" she indicated a man to her right, "is head of MI6, the others are from SND and ASIO. We've been working very hard to keep the predators off your back. Not hard enough. We have had a couple of close calls, unfortunately."

"Mark and Candi! Are they …"

"Safe. Tales can wait. The Chamber's solution is complete? I've heard nothing from Klaus."

"Yes, but there are problems …"

Ross Baker took over the conversation. "What do you need?"

"Transportation. The bottle must arrive at the plant in Australia in eighteen hours or less. Mark will need assistance to connect the thing. Can you …"

"Done. Tomorrow a long-range Boeing will take it from Genève Aéroport to Richmond Air Force Base Australia. From there, a Chinook will carry it straight to the lab. Are you well enough to supervise its removal from the accelerator? Tomorrow morning?"

"Yes, I will." Dekker put his head in his hands and wept.

# CHAPTER 44

There was no message for them at Café L'Amoré.

They had the obligatory coffee that neither of them felt like and then moved down the main street to another restaurant that had taken up residence in one of the original Camden buildings formerly occupied by a bank. The sweet duck with plums and star anise was magnificent, but only Candi's taste buds appreciated them. They finished off the excellent meal with Hazelnut Mt. Blanc and then Irish Coffee, which was such a relief from the brew they had been forced to endure in the other place.

For all its excellence, the food had little effect on Mark. Throughout the meal he had seemed far away and sad, and nothing Candi did made any difference.

By the end of it, her irrational optimism had taken a severe beating, not from anything Mark had said, but from his silence. He needed her comfort, she knew, but to provide it in any meaningful manner would mean she had to face reality, which was the last thing she needed.

No, it was better to simply live in the present and try to envelop Mark in her existential enjoyment, rather than whatever doom and gloom awaited around the next bend in the road.

They arrived back at the lab much later in the afternoon than was customary.

Peter North met them when they came in. "I've had a phone call from Café L'Amoré. It sounds strange, but an Alan Todd has found some property he thinks is yours and wonders if you would be so kind as to call around there this afternoon. He said something about free Abby coffee, whatever that is. There's nothing much you can do here, so why don't you see what this is all about?"

Candi was not particularly happy about returning to the café. It was a trap of some kind. They had not left anything there, she was certain.

Despite their fears, twenty minutes later, they were sitting at their usual table in a state of unusual apprehension. Abby brought them coffee and the usual tray of biscuits. After she had left, Alan Todd came over with a handbag that Candi had never seen.

"I do apologise, but is this yours? We found it on the floor near your table. It contains quite a bit of money. I'm sorry to trouble you."

"It's not mine," Candi said, "and Mark never goes for handbags with pink flowers on them."

"Once again, my apologies. I see you haven't made use of the biscuits on your tray."

"We haven't," Mark said, "But perhaps we should. Candi, is your laptop in the car?"

"Yes, but we tried this morning," Candi said rather foolishly. "All right, it's worth another go, just in case I suppose."

The laptop was fetched, and Candi inserted the compact flash card into it and logged on. There was a message with a picture of the Eiffel Tower. Candi decoded it, and they gasped.

*Solution finished*
*Transport tomorrow*
*Enemies close*
*Take great care*
*D*

Mark only read the words "solution finished."

He felt a chill settle in his heart. Had he got it right? What if he was wrong? The rest of the room disappeared into his own thoughts.

Candi only read the words "enemies close." She was terrified. Suddenly, the horrors of the last attempt on her life surfaced with renewed clarity before her mind. She tried to fight them off, but failed.

"I have to go home," she said. "Roger will protect me."

With that, she almost pulled Mark out of his chair in her eagerness to leave. Alan watched them go and signalled to Claire. The new girl walked away from the mug of coffee she was murdering and followed them out the door at a discreet distance.

Candi dropped Mark at the lab, and without waiting, drove home to Mt. Annan. Roger was there in his usual position, watching replays from the bed.

"They're trying to kill me!" Candi burst into the room.

"Steady on!" Roger stopped the tape. "Who's trying to kill you?"

"People from GPC."

"You're crazy," Roger said with a scoff. "This is Australia. I know some perverted weirdo tried it on a while ago, but now you're saying there's some kind of conspiracy. It just doesn't happen. You had a really bad experience. Don't let it make you neurotic."

"Roger, I'm serious. They're trying to kill me. You stay at home for the next couple of days with me, yes? You protect your Candi, yes?"

Roger looked annoyed. Coping with neurotic females had never been his strong point. "Look, Babe, I have to go to training tomorrow. The team is expecting me. I think there may be selectors watching. I can't afford to miss this opportunity."

"Roger, I'm frightened," she begged. "Please stay. I haven't asked you for anything before, but I'm asking now. I … I need you."

"You'll be all right," he said. "Lock the doors. If anything happens, ring the neighbours."

"They go to work. There's no one around during the day. Don't go to training. Stay. I'll make it worth your while." She tried to move seductively towards him. It didn't work.

"Listen, Babe. There's no danger. It's in your head. Are you having PMS or something?"

Candi exploded. "You think this is because I'm having my period? Is that what you think? I'm telling you my life is in danger. You're telling me I'm stupid, even though I have the PhD and you are the football player!"

"How many people are on a football team, Miss Smartarse?"

"How the hell should I know?"

"You're not so smart then, are you?"

Candi took a deep breath. Roger had to stay. Her life was in danger, and he didn't seem to care. "Roger, I'm sorry I don't know how many people are on your team, but you think microwaves are a brand of oven. We're different, that's all, but we belong together, yes?"

"If you say so, Babe."

"But we do," pleaded Candi. "Surely I mean more to you than the woman you make love to? Don't we have something else?"

"That's just it," he said. "There is nothing else, Babe. We take each other to heaven, isn't that enough? I don't make demands on your life, and you don't make any on mine. We have really great sex. What more could you want?"

"So if you found another woman who could do it better, you would do it with her and not me?"

"No one could be better, Candi. You were born to do it. I'm not complaining. I don't know what all this nonsense is leading to. We've always got along really well. Why are you so upset?"

*"Because someone is trying to kill me!"*

"It's bullshit," he said. "You're just exhausted, it's been building up. Last couple of nights you had a bit of trouble getting there, remember? Take a couple of sleeping pills. You'll feel better in the morning. Tomorrow night we can go to that restaurant in Camden, you know, the fancy one in the old bank building. A few glasses of wine, and you'll be feeling yourself again."

"You mean, I'll be back on form to give you the wonderful sex, yes?"

"I wouldn't put it that way," he said.

"How would you put it?" she asked.

"Simple, Babe. Life is what life is. Don't fight it."

"And what is life according to Mr. Roger Gaunt, big-time football player and mighty guru?"

"Life is doing what you want and enjoying it. I play footy, I enjoy it. I come home, make love with you, and I enjoy it. That's what life is, Candi. Enjoyment. Mad if you go for anything else."

"That's all life is?" she asked. "Nothing about having a purpose or using your life for someone else?"

"You told me yourself that to live is to have fun remember? I asked you why you came here one day and you said 'to have fun.' You went with me because making it with me was fun. I went with you because you didn't have any of those bloody mad do-gooder hang-ups. Now you want to change your mind? Why? All that geek talk must be getting to you. Are you having it off with him, too?"

The last remark reduced Candi to tears. She stood there and sobbed until Roger, with great reluctance, climbed off the bed and put his great arms around her. At least it would stop all that racket. He hated it when a girl cried. It made him feel bad, and he didn't like feeling bad.

After a little while, Candi stopped. She snuggled her head into his chest and murmured, "So you stay with Candi, yes?"

"No, Babe. If you knew how important it was for me to play in front of the selectors, you wouldn't ask."

"Then that's how it is."

He felt her body relax in his arms. All the tension seemed to go out of it, and Roger, thinking he had finally made her see sense, went back to the bed and turned on the tape again.

In actual fact, Candi had given up.

All the fight drained out of her even as she had prepared to use it to bend his will to her wishes.

Her own worldview, shaken as it had been of late, had turned round and delivered her the final crushing blow.

Roger, she reflected, was no different from her. Theirs was a relationship of mutual self-gratification, ecstasy, and nothing. Even in asking for his protection, she was only thinking of herself. Not for a second had she considered the consequences of putting his life in danger, neither did her own fears count for anything to him. She was afraid, yes, terribly afraid. Yet, something worse than the fear was enveloping her—a creeping sense of emptiness, of purposeless.

If she died, who would care?

Roger would have another woman in his bed within twenty-four hours.

She had reached the likely end of her life, and what had she accomplished that was worthwhile? Nothing. On the contrary, she had used her skill to imperil the whole human race. She had taken the life that God had given her and poured it down a rat hole.

She paused in her thought. The life that God had given her? Yet perhaps He had, perhaps He had. What a waste of the divine gift she had been!

In this frame of mind, she went to the kitchen and poured herself a long drink from a bottle of Shiraz. Another followed until the bottle was empty.

Then she felt better because now she felt nothing.

The shadows of evening deepened. Mark Chambers sat on a kitchen chair, his elbows on the bench and his hands propping up his cheeks. His eyes were vacant, and his thoughts were far from his simple domestic surroundings.

The constant buzzing of the doorbell slowly broke through into his consciousness. He stood, walked along the hall into the lounge room, and peeked carefully through the curtain at the man standing outside his front door. To his utter surprise, he saw Alan Todd, one hand on the bell, the other holding a box wrapped in gift paper.

Mark opened the door.

"I am sorry to disturb you, but I have a gift. May I come in?"

Mark opened the door warily. It was too bizarre. Alan Todd handed him the package and went into the lounge room

"Who is this from?" Mark asked. "It's not my birthday."

"It's from me. Open it, please."

With the utmost reluctance, Mark slowly slit the paper covering the cardboard box—keeping his eyes on Todd all the time. Surely it wasn't a bomb. He lifted the cardboard lid. It wasn't a bomb. It was a mobile phone, one that was much larger than a normal one with a larger aerial.

Mark lifted it out of the box. "What's this for?"

"A friend of yours wishes to call you. May I?"

Mark handed him the instrument. Alan pressed a few numbers and then handed it back.

It was ringing someone. A voice answered. "Mark, is that you?"

"Daniel! What's going on?"

Alan interrupted him. "I'm going now. I can see myself out."

Mark continued speaking into the phone. "Daniel, what's happening? I've been handed this phone by the man who runs the café we eat in. Why?"

"The man is Alan Todd, I think. He's also been responsible for making sure nobody else could intercept the messages we were sending to each other. Not everyone thought your original warnings were crazy, Mark. We have a few friends we didn't count on."

"Who are they?"

"Alan is from ASIO, and so is your friend, Andrew," Dekker said. "It doesn't matter. That's not why I'm ringing you on this secure phone. The package is ready to go, Mark. It will arrive tomorrow evening."

"Where?"

"Right at the lab," Dekker said. "It contains just two and a half grams of material. I hope that's enough. In any case, we can't make more. This is the best we can do for you, I fear."

"It is more than I could have hoped for."

"Mark, there's something else you have to know." Dekker's voice cracked with emotion. "The bottle was damaged by sabotage at Berkeley campus. There's … there's no breach monitoring. There's no remote trigger … oh God! … Mark … I'm so sorry, dear God, I'm so sorry! I've no right to ask … you have to go ahead by your own choice, no one can demand, especially me. "

There was silence.

"Mark, are you still there?"

"Yes, I'm here."

Dekker was almost weeping. "They won't let me come, Mark. I wanted to do it myself. They won't let me. They say if… if the attempt fails I'll be needed here to discover some other way. I told them you could do that. They're not listening to me. They said if you succeeded, then I'd be needed here for the next phase. Dear God, I'm so, so sorry."

"Was there no other solution offered?" Mark asked. "Must it be this way?"

"There was no other solution. The best minds in the world agree with you. Believe me, there is no other way." Dekker's voice cracked. "Mark, you must believe me, there is no other way. We did our best …"

"It's all right, I didn't think there was." Mark's voice was soft and sad. "Daniel, it's not your fault …"

"It will haunt me all my life that I could have prevented this. If only I had not proposed the accursed experiment in the first place."

"You mustn't think like that. You knew of no ill outcome when you thought of it. I'm just as guilty as you, if anyone is to blame. Daniel, I don't know if I have the courage. Pray for me, Daniel, please."

Mark couldn't go on for a long while. Finally, he put the phone back to his ear. "When will the package arrive?"

"In the evening around six o'clock," Dekker said. "Some men will help you attach it. The superconductors holding the material in a magnetic potential well have been fitted with a small explosive device. When it detonates, the field will propel the material through the opening at very high speed. You'll have to monitor the breach and the vacuum to decide when to initiate. There's a keypad on the bottle. The key word is 'close.' Easy to remember, and dear God, I pray it does. Where's Candi?"

"She's gone home to be with Roger. Best thing, actually. She's gone back to living in denial. You can ring her around seven-thirty tomorrow evening to see what's happening. I guess the need for secrecy will be over then, one way or the other." He paused to regain his composure. "I'm going to go now. I want to be alone with God, Daniel. Can you understand?"

"I understand. My dearest, bravest friend, I understand. I …" The rest of Daniel's words were muffled with weeping.

Mark put down the phone, crossed the room to a comfortable chair, and sat down. As he did so, a most unexpected sense of peace enveloped him. Somehow, he knew his answer would work and the breach would close. Perhaps the hand of God had indeed touched him then, because in less than five minutes he was fast asleep.

# CHAPTER 45

Candi did not go into work the next morning. She woke up in the kitchen with a dreadful headache and a pain in her neck from going to sleep with her face on the kitchen table. A quick and hopeful visit to the bedroom revealed that Roger had gone to his training day as he had said he would.

She checked that all the windows and doors were locked and bolted and drew the curtains. As she was pulling the heavy drapes in the living room together, she noticed the car across the street. There was a woman in it just sitting there.

Candi stared. Her heart hammered in her chest.

It was the new girl from the café. She was drinking coffee from a paper cup, the Café L'Amore logo clearly visible on the side.

What had Abby said about her? A criminal on parole. That was it—a willing tool in any dirty business. Now she was staring straight at the window, putting down her coffee, and making a phone call.

Candi flipped the curtains shut.

The woman couldn't see her—but perhaps she was getting out of the car or aiming a high-powered rifle at the window. With a sudden movement, Candi flung the curtain wide, thinking that it was better to know what her enemy was doing. This time, there was no doubt that she had seen her. For a long time, they stared at one another. Neither gave the slightest sign of recognition. The woman in the car sipped her coffee from time to time while never taking her eyes off Candi.

"Hope it poisons you!" Candi said loudly. Without taking her eyes off the car, she reached into her pocket, drew out her phone, dialled triple zero. There was no response simply because she hadn't charged the thing the night before.

"I'm trapped," she said to herself. "They're closing in on me!" She felt physically sick with fear.

The woman in the car was on the phone again. Then she started the engine and moved off.

Candi ran to the window and watched while the vehicle rounded the corner at the end of the street. She stood there watching for a long while, but the car did not return. Finally she went into the kitchen, put the phone on charge, and sat down at the table.

The trapped feeling did not diminish. She took another trip into the living room and a furtive glance through the window, but the car had not come back.

There was another one now—a Ford utility parked on the opposite side of the street. A young man was wheeling a motor mower out of the back.

"Enemies close," Dekker had said.

Her whole world seemed to be imploding around her, disintegrating even before the breach sucked the life out of the planet.

Several return trips to the living room confirmed that the car had not returned. The young man across the street was taking forever to mow the grass verge. Keep watch, she thought, drawing the curtains almost closed.

She needed a shower, but it was out of the question. She had seen movies where awful things happened to girls while they were in the shower.

Mark arrived at work that morning looking surprisingly fresh. He went into Peter's office, and, after a brief word, the two of them went outside the building to the gum trees on the perimeter.

Mark continued the conversation that had begun in the room. "Remember what you said about not playing the company tune, Peter? The time has come to put your promise into practice."

North nodded. "What do you want me to do?"

"The material we need to close the breach will arrive this evening. I want you to go round the plant and tell everyone about a compulsory meeting in Camden Town Hall tonight. Don't worry, I've already booked it. Tell them you are going to reveal secrets. I've also contacted the local paper, so there will be others present. When they get there, tell them the story of this place, the whole lot. Tell them about the breach. Tell them how we couldn't stop it. Tell them about the way the company and the university conspired to ignore the warnings."

"But won't that incite mass panic?" North asked.

"By then, it won't matter. I want you to keep them going until around eight o'clock. Don't let them leave for any reason. I'm relying on you to spin the tale out. Answer questions, do whatever. If the breach closes, then all will be well, and if it doesn't, then panic cannot be avoided. Either way, I want them to know who is to blame for this disaster. Keep them busy until my attempt to close the thing is over."

"How will I know it's over?"

"Trust me, you'll know. Promise you will do this for me."

Peter North looked at him. Never before had he seen such calmness and command in a young man. Right in front of him was a living demonstration of the power of the God he had chosen to ignore for most of his life.

Such ignorance was no longer possible. North nodded his head slowly. "I give you my word it will be done."

"I want no one on the site," Mark said. "I want the alarms on the generators and the switching yard disabled. I want the phone system and the ethernet routers to the computers shut down. Will you do that for me?"

"The order will be given. Luke, the head security guard, will take responsibility for getting all staff off the premises. All except you, I suppose."

"Yes. It would be a very bad idea for anyone else to be hanging around. You understand?"

"No, but I'll do exactly as you ask."

Candi had spent a completely miserable day huddled in one room or another in her house. She had found that creeping from window to window and peeking through a slit in the curtains was an excellent way to scare herself out of her wits.

A growing sense of helplessness and finality settled upon her. She felt like she was being propelled by powerful unseen forces toward a place she didn't want to go.

Once again, she saw herself standing naked on the cliff top, leaning outward into oblivion, but now the vision filled her with an unexpected dread. Did death bring the empty nothingness of non-existence, or did it bring you unprepared face to face with the God you had spent your whole life ignoring and denying? Did all paths lead inexorably to this terrible end? As fast or as far as you ran, He had only to recall your breath to issue that last unrefusable summons.

> Golden lads and girls all must
> Like Chimney sweepers, come to dust.

From somewhere in her memory, the words of Shakespeare's sonnet echoed in her ears.

Candi shuddered.

"Why are you hounding me?" she called into the silence. "What have I done to deserve this? So I don't love Roger, and he doesn't love me—but what is love anyway? Sex is real, hate is real. Love? Love is the empty promise, the angel dust. Love is not real." Then, shouting, she added, "I dare you to show me it is! The world is dying, and you don't lift the little finger to save it. This is love? No! See? Even you don't believe in it!"

It was hardly a prayer, and yet Candi sat rigid—expectant of an answer, even a whisper—anything to make her believe she had not emptied her passion into an empty, unfeeling room.

The silence mocked her desire and drowned her hope.

Candi balled her fists in fury and smashed them down on the table again and again until they hurt. Never had she felt so abandoned and alone.

Love was an illusion, yes, but then why did she crave it like the air she breathed?

A God who was apparently indifferent to the peril of his creatures angered her, but the thought of a universe without one at all stole over her in that moment and froze her heart.

If blind chance was the father of all living, then screaming was the sound of mankind worshipping its maker. Whether the breach closed or ate the universe mattered not at all. She was no more than a chance collection of atoms, with no more significance than a blade of grass. Yet, even the grass was better off than she, for deep in her being rose impossible notions of grandeur, a fear of non-being, a need to be loved and to have purpose, whereas the grass was completely fulfilled in being just what it was—grass.

> *All the world is grass,*
> *And yet, and yet.*

She needed Mark—that was it.

It wasn't right for him to be alone at a time like this. They had begun the breach together, and they had to stand together at the end. Right then and there, she made up her mind. If these were the last remaining hours of her life, she would dedicate them to him, to the man who was, in truth, the closest friend she had ever had.

Did she love him?

She no longer had words to describe the way she felt about Mark. There was something solid and real about him. She loved the way he treated her, always with gentleness, always with respect, always protective of her dignity without even realising he was doing it.

His faith in God was so strong, so very strong, and for all her passion, Candi had never managed to shake it. He would face the end like that, too, however horrible it was, with strength and courage.

Yes, this would be her purpose. She would go to him, dedicate her every living, breathing minute to his pleasure, his desire, his comfort. She would make her body his willing servant to do whatever he wanted, and her own desire would be simply to make him happy, to ease the final sorrow. All her powers of distraction and delight she would employ to that goal.

Perhaps before the world ended they would make love. Yes, she would like that. So what would she wear? What would Mark like? On the other hand, if she were to go out of the house, her enemies might find her. Perhaps she would stay put for a while.

The phone rang loudly next to her ear.

Candi shrieked and jumped up from the table. The chair tumbled backwards on the floor. With a trembling hand, she answered the phone.

"This is Peter here, Candi. We're going to have a public meeting at Camden Town Hall tonight starting a seven o'clock. I'm telling the truth about the breach to the world. It's time everyone knew. I hope you're not too sick to come."

"Why have you decided to do this?"

"You know the state of the breach," he said. "If it's going to blow, then the world deserves to know who killed it."

"I suppose so," she replied.

"Are you coming into work today?"

"No, I'm still not feeling well."

"Forget it. Try and come to the meeting. God knows what will happen afterwards."

"I might do that."

Candi closed the phone, but the call had troubled her even more. Where was Mark in all this? Where was Dekker?

By mid-afternoon, the continued absence of anything amiss had given her sufficient illusion of courage to put her plan into effect.

Creeping into the garage, she took a jemmy bar off the tool shelf and had a shower with it. If someone interrupted her toilet, they were going to get a lot more than they bargained for. No one did. The comfort of water trickling over her hair and face and down her naked body made her fear subside even further.

She would wear her black dress, Mark liked that one. All she had to do was to find out where he was. Wrapping herself in a towel, she rang the lab, but nobody answered.

"Must have gone home early," she thought to herself. "I'll go round to his place. We could go out to dinner to begin with, yes, that would be nice."

Three dresses and two sets of shoes later, Candi rang the familiar doorbell. No one answered. She tried again and again with no response.

Fear gripped her. Perhaps they had killed him! Perhaps he was in the house lying wounded!

She hurried round to the back door. It was locked. She ran round the other side of the house. The bedroom window was open. Gripping the edge of the flyscreen, she ripped it out, pushed open the window a little more, and squeezed her lithe body inside.

Her heart was thumping in her chest while she ran from room to room, but Mark was not there. She reached the lounge room. On the table was a rather unusual looking mobile phone. She picked it up.

It was six thirty.

# CHAPTER 46

The thudding of the Chinook's twin rotors sounded loud through the walls of the breach building.

Mark checked the time on his watch. It was six o'clock exactly.

The huge machine landed in the car park. The side hatch opened. Eight men jumped out. With military precision, six of them carried what appeared to be a washing machine with a flanged pipe attached about two-thirds up one side. The other two carried an oversized hydraulic scissor lift.

Mark met them at the door.

The leader spoke. "My men are at your disposal, awaiting instruction."

Mark led them inside the lab.

They positioned the bottle on top of the scissor lift opposite the left-hand antechamber. Mark went over to the right-hand one and shut off the water injection pumps. He heard the crack of the breakers in the switching yard jump out, taking the generators offline when they slowed. Lights on the generator complex and the cooling tower went out. No alarm sounded.

Using a wrench, Mark disconnected the water feed from the inlet port and pulled off the hose. He opened the port valve wide. There was a sound of air rushing in through the opening, air sucked in by the breach.

"We have to equalise the pressure or we won't be able to get the other end plate off," he said. "It will be pretty hot anyway."

The team moved down to the other antechamber.

Mark pointed at the end cap. "We remove that and then connect the bottle in its place. Spanners are over there. The cap will be hot. Don't look into the chamber, because the breach is still giving off a lot of energy."

It was not the easiest of operations, but in no more than twenty minutes the washing machine-like device, raised by the scissor lift, was attached to the flange where the end cap had once been.

Mark closed the port on the other antechamber and started the pumps. "I'm going to evacuate the inner sphere. It will take some time, but there must be hardly any matter going into the breach when I open the bottle. The more there is, the less likely this attempt will be to succeed."

The man who had led the team came over to him.

"There's something you should know." He led Mark to the bottle.

On the side was a small keypad and an illuminated screen. The display read "1:32:19." It was counting backwards.

"This is the time left on the batteries," he said. "I have been advised to tell you that the sooner you can open the bottle, the better. When this display gets to zero, containment fails and, well, you know the rest. "

"I know the rest."

Ready to depart, the men had assembled near the door. In unison, they turned toward him and saluted.

The leader moved forward, took Mark's hand, and shook it. "Dr. Chambers, it has been a privilege, sir."

Again in unison, they turned and went through the door—leaving him alone.

A short time later, he heard the rotors thudding loudly and then slowly begin to fade. As they did, so, too, did the bubble of serenity that had kept him moving throughout the day without panic.

He was alone.

He tried to watch the pressure gauges while they slowly headed toward zero.

He sank to his knees.

"Dear God," he said, "if it is somehow possible, even now, show me a way out so I don't have to do this."

Sweat broke out on his forehead. Minutes before he could perhaps have walked over and keyed the word into the pad, but with every passing second his resolve seemed to be slipping further away. He did not have the strength, he did not have the courage.

He prayed.

"I can't do it. I'm not strong enough. The world is going to die because I don't have the courage. Help me! Help me! Damn it, HELP ME!"

He banged his fists on the vacuum line and sank further to the floor.

Candi examined the phone. She had never seen anything like it in her life.

"What's Mark doing with this?" She asked herself. "Who's he been calling?"

There was a "redial" button on the keypad. Candi pressed it.

After a few rings, a voice answered. "Mark, what are you doing here? Has anything gone wrong?"

*"Dekker!"*

"Candi, is that you? What are you doing with Mark's phone? Has it happened already?"

"What's going on, Daniel? Where is Mark? How did he get this phone?"

"It's a long story, Candi— "

"When does the material Mark wanted arrive?" she asked. "There isn't much time. We have less than a day left … "

"The material is there already, Candi. It should have arrived at the lab about six o'clock."

"And that's where Mark is, yes? Tell me!"

"Yes, Candi. He should be there for sure, connecting things up."

"What exactly is this material, Daniel?"

"Mark didn't tell you?" Dekker asked.

"No, why do you think I ask?"

"Perhaps it's better you don't know. I believe there is a meeting—"

"Tell me!" she demanded.

"As I said, I think it's—"

Candi felt her whole body going rigid. She screamed into the phone, barely in control of the words that came out of her mouth. "Dekker, if you don't tell me I swear by all that's holy, I'll search the earth for you and when I find you, I'll kill you!"

She could hardly believe her own words, and neither could Dekker.

There was a pause. "The material is two-point-five grams of anti-hydrogen. Antimatter. It's the only—"

Candi was already at the front door. She didn't need to be told what antimatter was or what it did when it came in contact with ordinary matter. Antimatter and matter annihilated one another, leaving nothing but an enormous release of energy.

Mark had ordered a small, highly specialised atomic bomb.

She drove toward the lab like a woman possessed.

Mark stood up from the floor where he had been sitting and looked at the pressure gauges. They were almost on zero. Then the oil diffusion pumps would take over and remove what little was left inside the sphere. Of course they would not prevent the breach from eating iron atoms off the antechamber end cap. But that was over a metre thick. He had time.

Time! He ran to the bottle. The display read "1:01:08."

He only had an hour!

He groaned. He would ring Andrew and beg him to pray for courage.

He stepped a few paces toward his office before remembering that the phones had been disconnected. He tried to picture his face, but it was fading.

He thought of Candi, of how very much he cared for her, of the enjoyment of holding her in his arms, of how very much he had wanted Roger to vanish down a black hole; yet, irony of ironies, he was about to save him so he could continue to misuse her for his own self-centered pleasure. He shuddered at the thought.

He tried to picture her as he loved to see her—laughing, her eyes shining with life—but each memory was more blurred than the last, and eventually, try as he might, he could not see her at all. Once again, he looked over toward the vacuum gauges.

The time he dreaded was rushing upon him too quickly.

Again, he told himself that this was his gift to Candi, to Andrew, and to everyone he loved and cared about, but they had diminished into a shimmer, unreal and insubstantial.

"I can't!" he said out loud.

He could run away, the bottle would explode and the breach would eat the world. Nobody would blame him.

For a brief second, he saw a vision of Candi standing naked on the precipice above the sea, throwing her life away and entering an eternity of darkness.

"No!" He buried his head in his hands. "I know what I have to do. I know what You want me to do. I feel so alone and helpless! God, help me!"

He wiped the sweat off his forehead.

In his office, there was a water cooler. He went inside and took a long drink, turned round, and there was Candi, alive and real.

She sprinted over to him. With a great cry, she wrapped her arms around him in a fierce embrace. Then she was kissing him, his cheeks, his eyes, his mouth, soaking his face with her tears. Mark held her against him. She was shaking like a leaf.

Abruptly, she pushed herself away. Tears streamed down her cheeks. "Why you not tell Candi? I know what's in the bottle. The explosion will destroy everything. If it doesn't work, we're finished. Now I know why you suffer! Oh, Mark! Why didn't you tell me?"

She was searching his face with huge, frightened eyes.

Before he could answer, she took a deep breath and went on. "I ... I want to be with you, Mark. If the breach doesn't close, I want to be with you. Candi belongs to you, Mark. I want to end my life beside you." She hesitated, her pleading eyes still staring up into his face and her arms by her sides. "And if the breach closes ... I still want to end my life beside you, Mark."

He looked into her lovely face, rendered all the more beautiful by the tear streaks down her cheeks. In that instant, he knew that God had answered his prayer. He could not live knowing he had done nothing to save her. If she died, she would be lost forever. In that instant he saw in her face a vision of all the things she could be if he would only grant her life. The laughter would come again, the joy. Perhaps God would open her eyes to other truths as well. The world could be a better place because Candi loved and lived free in it. Only by saving her did he earn the right to say he loved her.

His mind formed a plan. Yes, it would work.

The silence was too long for Candi. "Mark, please say something! Candi has never made this confession to another man, not Roger, not anyone!"

She was suddenly struck by a new and frightening thought. Why would Mark want to walk with her to the end of his life anyway? She closed her eyes. The whole of her self-centered existence seemed to flash before her mind, and she shuddered. A companion less worthy than she would be impossible to find.

She hung her head, longing to hear the words she had once begged him not to say.

Suddenly she felt Mark's arms around her, drawing her against him and lifting her head, his eyes shut. His lips explored her face until they found her own and covered them with a soft, long kiss. She felt her heart race. Drawing a long breath, she wrapped her arms around his neck, the fervour of her embrace eloquent in its silence.

Holding her, he felt the warmth of her body and the softness of her lips still pressed against his own, a final, beautiful experience.

It was enough.

Candi lifted her face and kissed him again softly and tenderly, her eyes still shut, her arms still round his neck.

She let go and stood beside him. "What do you have to do now? Is there some sort of timer to set? How far do we have to drive away? I'd like a quiet place where I can just be alone with you ... Mark, what's the matter?"

"I've forgotten my laptop. I need to plug it into the ethernet port on the bottle to set the timer up. Could you go and get it from my car? I'll take the covers off the diffusion pump control panels while you do. Here's the keys."

Without a word, Candi took the keys and bounded out into the car park. There were only two cars. Clicking the remote, she raced towards his Toyota and flung open the back door. The laptop wasn't there. She opened the passenger door. Not there either. Then the boot, empty.

With a howl of frustration, she tore back to the lab. The door was shut. On its white paint some words had been hastily written.

*THERE'S NO TIMER*
*I LOVE U CANDI*
*RUN!*

She stood there, paralysed with horror and rooted to the spot in fear, her hand poised on the handle. The door was locked, but Candi never tried to open it.

"I have to be with him!" she said to herself. "I said I would be!"

From inside the building she heard the diffusion pumps beep zero pressure. Terror overmastered her and she ran. Her feet seemed not to touch the ground when she flew toward the car. With one bound, she was in the driver's seat, the engine started, and the tyres screaming as the car slewed round. She accelerated towards the gate.

Reaching the entrance, she spun the car to the left and roared up the road to climb away from the menace in the valley.

Mark checked the vacuum gauges. The diffusion pumps had done their job. He walked slowly over to the bottle. The display read "00:40:05."

He touched the pad.

He pressed "C."

"Dear God, I thank you for the privilege of laying down my life for Andrew and Candi and the others."

Then "L"

"For taking away my fear at this last."

Then "O."

"Please close the breach."

Then "S."

"Into your hands I commit my spirit."

And finally, "E."

The car roared up the incline. Glancing left, Candi could see the dreaded power plant with its few remaining lights glimmering in the valley. She felt a soft rain on her face.

An embankment rose to her left, cutting off her sight. Suddenly, the clouds above dissolved into blinding white, brighter than sunlight.

Candi screamed and threw her arms around her head. The engine cut out, the car rolled a short distance up the embankment and stopped.

Then came the shock wave, louder than a hundred thunders, shaking the very bones of her body. She felt it smack into the metal, felt the car lift under her and then settle down.

Hundreds of small stones that had been dislodged from the top of the embankment rained down on her.

Then there was darkness. Candi kept screaming, threw herself down on the passenger seat, and covered her head with her hands.

The thunder echoed and re-echoed among the hills, growing fainter and fainter until there was nothing.

She had to know.

Trembling like a leaf, she opened the door and struggled up the embankment. From the top, she could see right into the valley. A ring of fire burned brightly where the lab had been. In its flickering light, she saw the cooling tower, its surface scarred with jagged black breaches where debris had smashed through it.

But the centre of the fiery circle was dark. No brilliant blue-white line of discharge and no ball of incandescent plasma.

Darkness. Blessed, beautiful darkness.

"You did it," she stammered out loud. "You closed it. We're safe! The world is safe! I'm safe! Safe!" She repeated the word.

The terrifying threat of future annihilation that had hovered over her in judgement was gone, and as the magnitude of her salvation began to dawn on her so, too, did its purchase price.

As one grew, so did the other. This was love, pure, unselfish, giving love.

She trembled at the thought of it. Her legs unable to support her any longer, she sat down hard on the damp ground, buried her face in her hands, and sobbed.

"Mark, oh Mark," she kept repeating. "I couldn't. I couldn't. You had to do it. No one else had the courage, the … love. You … loved … me … you … really … loved me … oh, Mark!"

In anguish, she threw herself from side to side on the ground while crying out his name. Her whole frame shook with grief.

A gentle rain fell.

Behind her on the road came the mournful wail of sirens. She did not hear them. She turned her face to the earth and cried into it, cried until there were no more tears. Even then, she didn't get up but instead lay there, shaking, a small, wet bundle of sorrow.

Finally, when body and mind could take no more, she rose, stood to her feet, and looked into the valley. There were people moving about like ants, fire trucks spewing their water on the flames, and searchlights penetrating the darkness.

One of the lights was shining on the cooling tower. It captured in its beam what must have been a piece of jagged wire. On that ruined surface, it cast a great shadow in the form of a jagged Roman cross.

Candi saw it. She drew a great intake of breath and screamed into the darkness.

"ÇA SUFFIT!"

In her mind, she saw the shadow of the Christ hanging there, his arms spread by the nails, his mind piercing her heart. In fury she stooped and clawed her hands into the wet earth, picking up handfuls of stones and hurling them towards the distant image.

"ÇA SUFFIT!"

She screamed over and over again until her rage had spent its fury into the unresponsive silence.

For a long while, she stared out into the valley at the tear-blurred image of the cross on the ruined tower. It burned into her heart, the love, the necessary, gracious sacrifice. The image began to soften in an unfelt rain, heavier now.

Mud and water streaked down her face. Her clothes were barely recognisable, her hair matted and filthy. Finally and deliberately, she turned away.

Stumbling carelessly down the slope, she got back into the car and drove home. Roger was there as usual. She went into the bedroom.

The sight of her made him turn off the player immediately. "What happened to you? Get caught in the storm?"

"What storm?"

"I heard thunder a while ago, and all the power went off. Thought there had to be a storm somewhere. Lucky it wasn't off for long."

"That wasn't a storm. Mark closed the breach."

"No shit?" he replied.

"It cost him his life." Her voice was soft and unemotional.

Roger paused while taking in the bedraggled mess standing in the doorway.

"So one man saves the world. That's a first."

"No."

"Whatever," he said with a shrug of his shoulders. "Don't feel too bad, Babe. I guess he's shaking hands with Saint Peter right now. He was always one of those religious types. Good for him. Say," he added, "why don't you get cleaned up and come back? We can go to heaven ourselves for a long time tonight."

"Hold that thought."

She went out of the room, past the bathroom, and into her study. She reached for a green shopping bag lying on the floor, opened a desk drawer, and tipped its contents into it. She moved to close the bag and then hesitated.

Rummaging in the next drawer, she pulled out a small green Bible that someone had handed her as she had gone through the university gates a long time ago. She had never opened it, never thrown it away. She turned the front cover. Someone had written a verse of Scripture on the first page.

> *"For God so loved the world that He gave his one and only Son, that whoever believes in him shall not perish but have eternal life."*

For a long time Candi stared at the words. Then, in silence she closed the book and added it to the other items. With the bag in her hand she went quietly down the hall. Sounds of yet another replay came loudly from the bedroom.

She opened the front door and walked through, closing it quietly on the other side.

She paused, lifted up her face into the rain, and spoke quietly into the night.

"Bien Dieu, if you want what's left of this French trash, you're welcome to it."

Without looking back, she walked on down the pathway, away from the house, and into a brand new life.

# CHAPTER 47

On hearing the news, Dekker served up the meal he had long prepared for the executives of Global Power Consortium. Headlines throughout Europe, the States, and Australia ran various versions of the phrase, "Power Company Holds the Human Race to Ransom," in huge letters.

Detailed accounts followed, as did transcripts of interviews, memos, and letters demonstrating unequivocally the complicity of Hakim, Jenner, and the executives of GPC in the most terrible act of ecological vandalism the world had ever known. The report made mention of the irresponsible roles played by fools, citing McTierney and the management of the University of Southern Sydney.

Within twenty-four hours, Hakim was behind bars, and Interpol also added charges of murder and attempted murder to his lot.

All in all, nine people were tried before the world court that convened in Geneva that year. Hakim and Jenner received the death sentence for "crimes of treason against the Human Race." Two days before it was due to be carried out, both men disappeared. They were never to be found.

North was sentenced to ten years imprisonment, but it was reduced to three because of his service to the prosecuting council, as well as his support in bringing about the closure of the breach.

GPC was placed in the hands of an administrator with a brief to dismantle the company.

McTierney was demoted to the back benches, but he succumbed one month later to public pressure calling on him to resign.

Margaret Marriott was dismissed as Chancellor from the University of Southern Sydney, her erstwhile friends in high places doing all they could to distance themselves from the scandal. The entire academic committee disappeared with her.

Mark Chambers was posthumously awarded both the Nobel Prize of Physics for the discovery of the Chambers Boson, as well as the Nobel Peace Prize for that year. Heads of the all the great nations conferred countless other honours upon him.

For his tireless efforts, Dr. Daniel Dekker was awarded Knight Commander De Orde van de Nederlandse Leeuw, Knight Commander of the Netherlands Lion, the highest order the land of his birth could bestow. France followed suit.

Dr. Candice Leblanc was honoured with the Chevalier de la Légion d'Honneur, the only woman to receive such an accolade in silence and tears.

A new building was erected on the campus of the University of Southern Sydney. It housed the Chambers Institute of Atomic Physics, erected just two years after the closure of the breach. The faculty quickly established a reputation for excellence under the direction of the world-famous Professor Daniel Van Dekker.

# EPILOGUE

On the plains to the west of Camden, along the Burragorang Road, one will find the Mark Chambers Memorial Gardens, perhaps the most beautiful parkland in Australia.

Within its walls, gardens from all over the world thrive in magnificence—gardens that many nations eagerly donated as expressions of gratitude towards the young man who saved their world from extinction. In the very centre of the parkland there is a large pool contained within a circular black granite wall that is polished like glass.

Words are engraved on its circumference, embossed in pure gold.

*"He saved others, but he would not save himself."*

In the centre of the pool, his feet washed by gentle fountains, is the statue of a young man in a laboratory coat kneeling in prayer.

Not far from the pool is a slightly circular concrete bench, its top scalloped into a seat with a low back. In stark contrast to the beauty all around, its sides are rudely pock-marked with many scars. The plaque on the end explains that it was part of the concrete shell of the cooling tower, which once stood on that spot.

He is always there on a Friday—the man with the greying hair. He walks slowly and sits down with both hands clasped in front of his knees. He sits alone, staring at the statue. Sometimes he bows his head as if in prayer.

But today he will not be alone, for a young family are coming to join him all the way from Paris. The mother is an attractive woman with long, brown hair who walks arm in arm with a man wheeling their baby son in a stroller. Their daughter, whose face is rather like her mother's, skips along holding her hand.

They recognise each other from afar.

The older man stands, and the others run to him. They embrace, laughing and hugging one another. Tears are shed.

Together they return to the bench. The young girl sits on one side of the older man, and the woman on the other with her husband.

Out of her purse she takes a small, well-worn, green Bible, and together they read the passage from Matthew's gospel that inspired the writing on the wall.

Then, holding one another by the hand, they bow in thankful prayer.

# ABOUT THE AUTHOR

Mac Cusiter was born in Lewisham, a suburb of Sydney, Australia. His boyhood fascination with science culminated in his graduating from Sydney University with a doctorate in physical organic chemistry. He began his professional life as a chemistry teacher at Sydney Institute, and retired as head of the science department. He has been a church youth leader for much of his life, and in this capacity scripted and produced several feature length amateur movies in which young people were involved as actors and technicians. He lives with his wife Val in Sydney's northern suburbs.

MAC CUSITER